AN IRRESISTIBLE DESIRE

In the dim candlelight Fiona studied Gideon's expression, trying to discover him anew. The lines in his face did not measure the passage of years but only the memory of pain.

She laid a hand on his arm—a gesture of friendship, no more. He seized it and brought her palm to his lips. The shock of the contact ran the whole length of her body. His eyes, those luminous dark eyes, sought and held her own and she was trapped, caught in the web of her own desire.

A current of physical longing swept through her, too intense to be denied. She struggled to remember who Gideon was and what he had done to her, what she had been and what she had become, but it was futile. She could no longer separate herself from him, or his passion from her own . . .

A Touch of Scandal

Anthea Malcolm

ZEBRA BOOKS
KENSINGTON PUBLISHING CORP.

For Carin Cohen Ritter

ZEBRA BOOKS

are published by

Kensington Publishing Corp.
475 Park Avenue South
New York, NY 10016

First printing: December, 1991

Printed in the United States of America

I have . . . killed a love, for whose each drop of blood
I would have pawned my heart.

John Ford
'Tis Pity She's a Whore

Prologue

October, 1812

"Alastair?" Lady Prebble turned to the footman standing in the doorway, a frown of annoyance marring the smooth skin of her forehead. "I don't know a Miss Alastair. Who is she?"

The footman had seen only three months' service in the Prebble household, but he knew how things ranked in the scale of importance and he had no difficulty understanding the question. The problem was how to answer it. He hesitated. "Not one of your ladyship's friends. A lady, but not a lady, if you understand. I put her in the parlor behind the dining room," he added, as though this would more precisely define Miss Alastair's claims on the Prebble hospitality.

Lady Prebble's frown deepened. "Get rid of her." She made a gesture of dismissal and turned her attention to the papers littering her writing desk. Could the woman have been sent by her dressmaker? No, Madame Fouquet would have come herself, and in any case, she would not risk offending a valuable client who was only seven months in arrears. Lady Prebble sorted through the papers, the invitations she would answer and those she would ignore, the bills she would give to Hugo and those it would be better to hold back for a time. Not that Hugo objected to the expenditures. He liked fine things as much as she, and when it came to his coats and boots and horses he would have only the best. But with the endless years of the war, things had grown dreadfully expensive, and Hugo was inclined to be fretful when she wasn't able to manage as he thought she ought.

Lady Prebble smiled wryly. She knew who Miss Alastair would be . . . one of the army of dark-gowned, respectable women who preyed on their betters in the name of some obscure charity or other. In heaven's name, what did these women expect? Didn't they understand the responsibilities that came with wealth and position? Didn't they know of the endless claims made on one's income? Lady Prebble considered the outrageous bill presented by the man who had replastered the drawing room, an absolutely necessary refurbishment if they were to entertain properly, and put it under a stack of writing paper in her desk drawer.

She was interrupted once more by the footman who returned to say that Miss Alastair would not be got rid of. "She was very pleasant about it, ma'am, but she said it was important that she speak to Lady Prebble, and that no one else would do. She wouldn't state her business. It was personal, she said, something about a message she had to deliver in person."

Hugo? Lady Prebble stifled a laugh. Was it possible that her husband had found himself saddled with an inconvenient mistress? Hugo was hardly a passionate man. His liaisons were infrequent, discreet, and of short duration, but he could be trapped by his vanity. She supposed she would have to see the woman. It might even afford her some amusement. "Tell her I am presently occupied. I'll be with her when I am able."

Lady Prebble allowed her visitor to wait for a full half-hour. Whether Miss Alastair's message was a request for charity or a demand for justice, it was only prudent to render her anxious and uncertain of her reception.

When the allotted time had passed, Lady Prebble rose

from her desk, smoothed the Polish twill of her morning gown, and walked to the door, pausing only to glance in a pier glass and make certain that her heavy dark hair was as carefully arranged as her maid had left it two hours before. She smiled at her reflection. Though she was no longer in her first youth — she had passed her twenty-seventh birthday — not even two children had left their mark on her face and figure. She was at the height of her beauty, and she had a marquis as her lover. Lady Prebble's face softened momentarily at the thought of Adrian. It did not matter that he had once been the lover of Hugo's sister. Aline was dead. Adrian was hers now, the joy of her life.

Her thoughts on Adrian, she had reached the foot of the stairs before she recalled the importunate Miss Alastair. She turned toward the small parlor at the back of the house in which the Prebble housekeeper received her instructions every morning. The footman — she could never remember his name, Daniel or Donald or something of the sort — had chosen well.

She pushed open the door. The room was dark, for it stood on the north side of the house, with windows partially blocked by the box hedge that was in want of cutting, and ill furnished, containing discarded bits of furniture that were thought too good to be relegated to the servants. Miss Alastair was standing, but her back was to the door and she did not immediately turn round. In that brief moment, between the opening and closing of the door, Lady Prebble studied her visitor. She was wearing a slate-colored pelisse, well cut but of a plain material, and a straw bonnet ornamented with black ribbons. Not, then, one of Hugo's little friends. This would not be at all amusing. Lady Prebble pursed her lips in distaste and prepared to be severe. She did not relish calls upon her charity.

She pushed the door shut behind her and the soft click of the latch sounded unnaturally loud in the quiet room. Miss Alastair turned around, not quickly, as though she

9

had been found in an unbecoming position, but slowly and gracefully, as though she recognized an undisputed right to be there. There was something in that movement that stirred a faint warning chord of memory, but before Lady Prebble could identify it, Miss Alastair spoke and the memory exploded in a nightmare of anger and resentment and envy.

"Hullo, Clare."

The voice was as she remembered it, low and unusually clear, with a flexibility and cadence that made other women's speech sound expressionless and flat. The visitor was standing now with her back to the window, the brim of her bonnet shadowing her face so that it could not be clearly seen, but Lady Prebble knew the exact shape and color of the long gray eyes that were watching her, appraising her. She knew their expression, too, that look that had always made her feel she was being judged. What rot! She wasn't a child any more. She had nothing to fear from Fiona.

Lady Prebble took a deep breath. "Where the devil have you been?"

The other woman hesitated, as though debating how to frame her reply. "I've been in Sardinia," she said at last.

"Sardinia?" Lady Prebble was not surprised to find Fiona in the garb of a servant, but she had hoped for a more complete degradation. Sardinia seemed too exotic a punishment for her behavior.

"Yes, I went out as governess to the Tassio family, and I've come back to England with them. The boy has been entered at Eton and I'm to companion the daughter. My name is Fiona Alastair, Clare, and I want nothing from you save your silence."

The Tassios. But of course, Fiona said she had gone to Sardinia. How had she managed a post of that sort, a post with one of the great families of the Court of Savoy? Clare had intrigued fruitlessly for an invitation to the ball that introduced the widowed Princess di Tassio and her children to the ton. "You'd better sit down," she said abruptly, indicating a chair that faced the window. "Take off your hat. I want to see your face."

Fiona moved to the chair, undid the ribbons of her bonnet, and placed it in her lap. Clare watched her carefully, then moved to a chair a few feet away. Fiona Martin, her father's ward and bastard and firstborn child. Her sister, but not her sister—Clare had been twelve before she'd learned of the relationship—and a constant, unwelcome presence in her life. She looked older now, Clare noted with satisfaction, remembering the glimpse of her own ripe beauty as she'd left her sitting room upstairs, and the past five years had drained Fiona of life and color. Or perhaps it was the effect of the clothes, somber to the point of mourning, and the way her fair hair was pulled back, exposing the fine bones of her face. Even so, Fiona still had pretensions to beauty, and despite the change in her circumstances, she had lost none of the elegance nor the authority that had driven her sister to despair. Clare felt a flash of the familiar envy. "You didn't write."

"Should I have?" Fiona's voice held a touch of weariness. "We saw the English papers. I read of Uncle James's death," she added, using the name by which she had addressed their father.

"He left you nothing, you know."

Fiona looked steadily at her sister. "I didn't expect him to."

"No. There was no will," Clare added, driven by some compulsion to make the point clear. "He tore it up when Jamie died. It was a nuisance, his not making another, but in the end it all came to me."

"I don't want money, Clare. I want it forgotten, all of it."

"Then why did you come back?"

"There was no help for it. The Tassios expected it, and now it looks as though I'll have to stay." She hesitated. "I didn't want you to be surprised. I try to live quietly, but there are times when I go into company with Lady Alessandra and it's not impossible that you might see me. If

11

you do, remember that I am Miss Alastair and that we have never met."

Why, she was frightened. Clare felt an unexpected surge of pleasure. She had never been able to touch Fiona, to reach that private core that protected her against the slights and insults that followed from her uncertain position in James Woodbourn's household. But now Fiona had something to fear and she, Clare, held the reins. "You'll never get away with it," she said.

"Why not? It's been five years, and I was rarely in London in any case. Who is to know me here, save you and Hugo? And Lady Carne."

Clare would not give her the satisfaction of knowing that Aline was dead. "You're forgetting George." She let the name hang deliberately between them.

"Yes, and George," Fiona returned calmly. "But none of you has reason to revive an old scandal. George least of all."

Clare knew this was true, and in her annoyance she tried to wound her sister. "He didn't break his heart over you. He married scarcely a year after you left. Quite a splendid match, a sister of the Marquis of Parminter. They have a child."

"Then I hope that he is happy."

At these words, spoken with insufferable restraint, Clare felt a sudden blinding rage. "You sanctimonious bitch! How dare you come here and fling your whoring past in my face! Wasn't it enough to expose my children to your fornication? Wasn't it enough to kill Jamie? Wasn't it enough to drive Papa to his death?"

Clare's color had risen to an alarming hue. Fiona had gone quite white, a sign, had Clare been able to heed it, of danger. They were both on their feet, Clare swaying uncontrollably, Fiona standing rigid, her bonnet clutched in her hands. Then Clare made a sudden movement to the wall behind her and tugged viciously at the bell-rope. "I'll keep your foul secret. I don't want to think or speak of you again. Stay away from me, Fiona. Stay away from everything that bears the name of Woodbourn, or I swear I'll see you in hell."

Clare's rages, to which she had been much subject as a child, did not last long, and by the time the footman appeared she was able to tell him with tolerable composure that Miss Alastair was leaving. When the door had closed behind her sister, Clare allowed herself the luxury of a few angry tears. She sat quietly for a while, to let the ravages of passion dissipate, then went upstairs to write a letter to George Barrington-Forbes.

Fiona walked quickly down the steps of the Prebble house and turned down Davies Street, heedless of her direction. A low blanket of clouds overhung the city and her throat ached, unaccustomed to the soot-filled air. Or perhaps from her unspoken fury. She had mourned Jamie bitterly, but his death did not lie wholly at her door, as Clare knew very well. Nor did her father's, for he might still be alive had he not lost his son.

A carriage had pulled up ahead, and she was forced to stop to allow two well-gowned women to alight and pass into a nearby house. The younger woman glanced at her, then looked away as though she were a creature not worth regarding. Fiona waited patiently, her eyes discreetly fixed on the street beyond. It was prudent to pass unnoticed.

Yet what a fragile web of safety she had spun for herself. Everything hung on the goodwill of the Princess di Tassio, and if she forfeited that, her services of the past five years would count for nothing. She had worked so hard to conceal her past. If she had had her way, she would never have returned to England, but now that she was here she must do whatever she could to avert danger. That was why she had called on Clare, though she had known the visit would bring her nothing but distress. It had been easier than she'd expected, but it had also been far worse. Their childhood hung over them, a bitter miasma that clouded judgment and vision and simple self-interest. She had forgotten how much Clare hated her.

She should not have been surprised. Even Simon and Alessa, her Tassio charges, had their moments of jealousy, though they were six years apart and insulated by wealth from the more obvious causes of discord. Fiona was not immune to the baser feelings herself. Clare had roused demons she had thought long since vanquished. Thank heaven she would not have to see her sister again.

Fiona arrived at an intersection and realized that she'd lost her direction. London was still an unfamiliar place. She had visited the city seldom in the years before her exile and had been here scarcely three weeks now. Hesitating, she struck out at random and soon found herself in a small, quiet square with a high-fenced garden at its center. The sound of high-pitched voices reminded her that she had forgotten to ask Clare about the children. Sallie had been four and Hugh a year younger when Clare had brought her sister to Digby Hall to help in the nursery, and in the year that followed, Fiona had grown quite fond of them. The memory brought her a small pang of regret and drew her to the gate of the garden. A half dozen children were playing inside, watched over by a pair of bored nursemaids and a black-gowned woman with a pinched and humorless face. The latter turned a disapproving eye on the intruder, and Fiona, searching for the spark that must once have animated that bleak shell, returned her gaze with an intensity that caused the other woman to look away.

Fiona shut her eyes. Dear God, have mercy, she breathed, the words a bare whisper in the air. Was this to be her future? She had thought only to preserve her position with the Tassios, but that position would soon be lost in any case. Simon was in school, and Alessa, if she had her way, would be married within the year and Miss Alastair would have to seek another post. She would find one, of course, granted the princess's favor, and when the new position came to an end there would be another and then another . . .

14

It was not the future she wished for herself. It was not the future she intended to have, though at the moment she saw no alternative. Fiona had always regretted the loss of her father's affection. Now she regretted the loss of the competence that would have given her some measure of independence.

But Fiona had not survived the past five years by giving way to self-pity. Seeking direction from one of the nurse-maids, she dismissed the black-gowned woman from her thoughts and made her way out of the square. By the time she approached the house the princess had taken in Bolton Street, the pain of the morning's encounter had receded. Clare could rage as much as she liked, but she was a careful woman who never did anything to disturb her own comfort. Hugo would do whatever Clare asked, Aline would follow Hugo, and George, of all people, would say nothing. He was a vain man, and the story only made him ridiculous.

There was, of course, another person. As she mounted the steps and rang for admittance, Fiona realized that the most significant thing about the whole interview was that neither she nor Clare had dared to mention Gideon.

Chapter One

June, 1813

Gideon Carne stepped out of the cool evening air into the musty confines of the Bow Street Public Office and was immediately shown into a small, rather dingy reception room. Though he was still laboring under the shock of the message he had received not half an hour since, he automatically appraised the other two occupants of the chamber, a police officer and a lady. The officer was young—almost as young as the fresh-faced recruits Gideon had seen cut to pieces on the Peninsula with wearying regularity—and struggling to conceal his anxiety. The age, state of mind, or any other particulars about the lady were impossible to discern, for she did not move forward when the officer came to greet him, and Gideon could see nothing other than the back of a dark print dress and a deep-brimmed, unadorned bonnet.

The young man, who introduced himself as Officer Wilson, greeted Gideon with evident relief. "Thank you for coming, my lord. As I've been explaining to Miss Alastair—you *are* acquainted with Miss Alastair, aren't you?"

At that moment the woman turned round and Gideon felt a jolt of emotion that he could not have defined save that it was stronger than anything he'd thought he was still capable of feeling. It was probably not her, of course. His

17

wits were dulled by worry, and though there was something familiar about the long, elegant neck and the proud tilt of the head, the woman's bonnet shadowed her face so that he could not make out her hair or eye color, and even her features were difficult to distinguish. But then she spoke, and he knew beyond a doubt that this was no trick of his imagination.

"As it happens, Lord Carne and I have never met." The voice was exactly as he remembered, warm and clear, with a rich, vibrant overlay. She moved toward the two men, and he saw that her carriage was as graceful as ever, though more controlled, as if she'd learned to hold herself in check. "Officer Wilson has been telling me that your son Peter and my charge Simon have become the greatest of friends this past term, but he has no idea what brought them to London. I collect you thought Peter was safely at Eton, as I was sure Simon must be."

Gideon inclined his head, both in agreement and in acknowledgment of what was supposedly their first meeting. Fiona—for so Gideon would always think of her, no matter what she called herself now—did not offer her hand, which was probably just as well. Alastair. It was understandable that she had changed her name, and it would be understandable if she wished him at the devil for threatening the new life she'd built for herself, but there was no hint of that in the cool, direct gray gaze which appraised him as if he were truly a stranger. As often in time of crisis, Gideon felt a twinge in his bad leg.

Fiona turned to Officer Wilson with quiet authority. "If you could take us to the boys."

"Oh, of course, ma'am." Wilson seemed grateful to have been given some direction. "Right away. My lord," he added, apparently feeling Gideon should be acknowledged as well. He led them out of the room and did not speak again until he stopped to knock at a door. A few moments later a soberly dressed middle-aged gentleman emerged. There was a moment of silence, the gentleman frowned, and Wilson, realizing that introductions fell to him, stam-

18

mered, "Mr. Read, Chief Magistrate." He turned to Mr. Read. "Miss Alastair, the Prince di Tassio's governess. And Lord Carne, Master Peter Carne's father." He drew a breath, pleased at having got through it without mishap.

Read's appearance did nothing to allay Gideon's fears. The Chief Magistrate of Bow Street was a man with easy access to the Home Office, a man whose attention was more likely to be devoted to ferreting out French spies than coping with the peccadillos of two schoolboys. The matter must be even more serious than he'd first supposed. He glanced at Fiona. There was a line of worry between her brows and there were faint but unmistakable signs of strain about the set of her mouth. Gideon was aware of a quite impossible desire to comfort her.

Read motioned Wilson to withdraw, then thanked Lord Carne and Miss Alastair with the careful courtesy of a man used to handling inquiries of a sensitive nature. The boys were inside — he indicated the door behind him. If they would be so good as to confirm the young gentlemen's identity and then, if the boys were who they claimed to be, he would be very much obliged if Lord Carne and Miss Alastair would answer a few questions.

Gideon followed Fiona into a chamber which appeared to be the Chief Magistrate's private study and saw the boys seated side by side on a dark leather sofa against the back wall. Their clothes and faces were grubby, their hair was disordered, and Peter's jacket had a nasty-looking tear in one sleeve, but on the whole they appeared to be in good spirits. Gideon felt a wave of relief which was irrationally strong, considering that the note which summoned him to Bow Street had assured him that Peter was unhurt. Both boys were grinning when the adults entered the room, but as they scrambled to their feet, Peter's smile vanished. He stared at Gideon with eyes that were at once frightened and hostile, but he did not speak.

His companion, a slender boy with dark hair and a fine-boned, un-English face, gave a contrite smile. "I'm sorry, Fiona, I'm afraid I've rather landed in the briars."

"Yes," she agreed, without apparent alarm or censure, "you have rather. I'm pleased to see you at least had the wit not to get hurt." She turned to the magistrate. "This is undoubtedly the Prince di Tassio, Mr. Read."

"Thank you, Miss Alastair."

There was another pause, but it did not occur to Gideon that they were waiting for him to speak until Mr. Read said, "Lord Carne? May I take it that this is your son?"

Gideon nearly laughed. The answer to Mr. Read's question had plagued him for the past five years, but he could scarcely say so. "Yes," he said, with a hint of harshness he had not intended. "This is Peter Carne."

"Well." Mr. Read appeared relieved. "Glad that's settled. I apologize for my caution, but under the circumstances—"

"We gave you our word." The faintly impudent contrition which Simon di Tassio had displayed a few moments before had given way to a dignity beyond his years. "I thought Englishmen always accepted the word of a gentleman."

"Ah—of course." Clearly surprised at being spoken to thus by a twelve-year-old boy, even if that boy did happen to be a prince, Read indicated that they should all be seated and then addressed the boys. "I think you had best tell your story again. From the beginning."

Peter and Simon exchanged glances. Gideon sank down into a straight-backed chair and crossed his legs, carefully paying Fiona no more heed than he would give to the governess of one of his son's school friends. He'd been afraid that Peter would recognize her and blurt out something damaging, but the boy did not seem to connect Miss Alastair with the Fiona Martin whom he'd last seen five years before.

"Peter and I left Eton this morning. The reasons are complicated and have nothing to do with what happened later," Simon added with complete self-assurance. "We hid in a farm cart that was going to Brentford. Then we asked about at one of the inns and found a man who was delivering hops to a brewery in London and he agreed to give us a ride. But by the time he let us off, it was getting dark."

"And you weren't sure of your reception at home?" Fiona inquired.

"Well, I know you wouldn't have kicked up a fuss, Fiona, but I wasn't so sure about *Maman*. We'd left rather suddenly, you see, and we wanted to go somewhere where we could"—the prince hesitated—"think about it."

Peter said nothing. Something had happened that was bad enough to cause him to run away from school and yet he had hesitated to go to his father. Gideon could scarcely blame the boy. Peter was not responsible for their estrangement.

"Then Peter remembered that the company you and his uncle own has a warehouse," Simon continued, addressing his friend's father.

"You're telling me you found Woodbourn-Prebble a safer haven than either of your homes?" Gideon demanded.

"Only for the night," Simon assured him. "We wanted a bit of time to think things over and talk about what to do next. It was past seven, so we thought the clerk would have gone home and the warehouse would be empty. Peter knew it was in Rosemary Lane, but we weren't sure where that was, so we had to stop and ask questions, which took a bit of time. I must say, everyone in that part of town seems in a fearful hurry. Peter had been to the warehouse once with his uncle, so he recognized the building, which was a good thing, because from the outside it looks just like an ordinary house. We were going to see if there was a window open or something, but as it turned out, the door was unlocked."

"Unlocked?" Gideon's eyes narrowed.

"Yes, sir." It was clear that the significance of the unlocked door had not been lost on Simon. "There weren't any lamps or candles lit in the hall, of course, and we couldn't see very much, so we went into the nearest room.

21

It seemed to be an office, but it was even harder to see there, because so much smoke was coming from the next room."

"Smoke?" Fiona asked.

Simon frowned and looked from Fiona to Gideon in sudden concern. "Didn't anyone tell you? There was a fire in the warehouse."

"What?" Gideon swung round to stare at the silent Chief Magistrate. "Why wasn't I informed of this earlier?"

"I thought it best for you to hear the story from the boys," Read returned, not in the least unsettled.

"You thought it best—" Gideon could feel the pulse beating in his temple.

"There is little you could do at present," Read pointed out. "The firefighters have been summoned, and the fire has been brought under control."

"And the damage?" Gideon demanded.

Read's face was impassive. "At last report it was impossible to determine, but I believe the building is still standing."

"I can't tell you how much you relieve my mind. The other partners should be notified."

"They have been. Sir Hugo Prebble is already on his way to the site. I expect you will wish to join him when you are finished here." Read paused. "I believe Sir Hugo is your brother-in-law, Lord Carne?"

"He is my wife's brother, yes."

The children were watching the scene in wide-eyed silence. As befitted a governess, Fiona pretended to be invisible.

"Quite so." Read smiled. "Nice to keep these things in the family."

Gideon was not deceived by the magistrate's mild tone. He could think of only one reason why Read would have wanted him to hear the news of the fire from Peter and Simon: in order to observe his reaction. And that meant the magistrate suspected the fire at Woodbourn-Prebble might be more than an unfortunate accident.

Fiona had turned back to the boys. "What did you do then?"

"Tried to put out the fire, of course," Simon said. "Don't look like that, Fiona, I know you say I shouldn't run unnecessary risks, but this was a necessary one."

Fiona held any alarm she might feel at bay. "You went into the adjoining room? Is that where the fire had started?"

"I think so. It was hard to move around there because the room was full of boxes and chests and things—I suppose it's used for storage—but the flames seemed to be near the back wall. It was worse than we thought at first. When some timbers fell down from the ceiling we decided to leave."

"There were ledgers on one of the desks in the front office so I grabbed them on the way out," Peter added. "Then one of the parish watchmen saw us."

"Slipping out of the burning building?" Fiona inquired.

Simon nodded. "When I told him I was the Prince di Tassio he laughed and said that was one he hadn't heard before. But he did send someone for the firefighters right away, Lord Carne. He sent someone to the nearest Public Office, too, and a police officer came."

"He took the ledgers away," Peter said, his face darkening. "He said they were evidence."

"Then," Simon continued, in precise tones, "he said he was damned if he knew how to deal with a couple of young swells, so he put us in a hackney and brought us to Bow Street." Simon brightened, as if visiting Bow Street had been worth it whatever the circumstances.

"When we got here, he brought us to Mr. Read," Peter concluded.

"The officer-in-waiting thought it best to summon me," Read explained. "Bit of a nuisance as I was to dine out, but these things can't be helped."

Gideon nodded. Two boys caught sneaking out of a burning building, one claiming to be the Prince di Tassio and the other the son of a viscount, obviously posed a ticklish problem, which would explain why Read had been called in. How bad had the fire been? Even assuming it had not been set deliberately, what would it mean for his own already precarious finances? He would have to visit the warehouse and see for himself, and that meant he would have to deal with Hugo. What of the other partners? Would they converge on the warehouse as well? Or would Read summon them to Bow Street? Gideon grimaced. The last thing he wanted was for Hugo and the others to arrive at Bow Street while Fiona was still there.

"Excuse me, sir." A man several years older and several degrees more sure of himself than Officer Wilson poked his head around the door. "Could I have a word with you?"

"That was Officer Hopkins," Simon confided when Read had excused himself and stepped into the corridor. "He was at Bow Street when we got here, but then he went to investigate the fire. I wonder if this means they've put it out."

As no one was in a position to answer the question, silence descended over the room. Peter lowered his eyes to the scuffed and muddied toes of his boots. Simon regarded Fiona. "Does *Maman* know?"

"No, she and your sister had already left for the Windhams' when I received word that you were here, and after dinner they're to go on to the Cowpers' rout. Your stepfather was called to Whitehall unexpectedly, so we won't need to trouble anyone with the details for a time." Fiona gave him a smile at once reassuring and faintly conspiratorial.

She had always been good with children. Watching the way the smile lit her face and was echoed on Simon's own, Gideon realized that behind the anger and bitterness and guilt and betrayal some happy memories of their time together remained. As she leaned toward Simon the lamplight picked out a few strands of gold beneath her bonnet, and the sight stirred other memories, memories to which he had no right. Fiona might not have been wholly blame-

24

less, but she did not deserve what had happened to her, and the responsibility lay at his door. Gideon looked away and resolutely turned his mind to the problem of the fire until Read rejoined them.

"Could I have a word with you in private, Lord Carne?" His tone was as polite as ever, but there was a faint furrow between his brows, as if the news Hopkins brought had further complicated an already complex situation.

Gideon followed Read back into the hall without comment. When the door closed behind them, the boys relaxed visibly. "They must have learned something more," Simon said, leaning toward Fiona. "Do you suppose the fire was set deliberately? Oh, I say, Peter, I'm sorry, it's beastly for your father."

"That's all right." Peter waved Simon's qualms aside. "Anyway, Woodbourn-Prebble doesn't really belong to my father, he only owns a little bit of it. It belongs to my Uncle Hugo," he explained to Fiona, "though he's taken on partners and my father is one of them."

Fiona nodded. Surely a disinterested observer would have long since dissolved in helpless laughter at the absurdity of the situation. That Simon had become friends with Gideon's son and unwittingly brought about this unexpected meeting—just when she'd thought the war would keep Gideon safely out of the country until at least the end of the year—was bad enough. That the meeting occurred because the boys had stumbled upon a fire in the warehouse of the company which had once belonged to Fiona's father and which now belonged to Clare and Hugo and apparently Gideon as well was an irony worthy of the keenest satirist.

Had she not alienated her father so completely by her own folly, she too might have had a share in Woodbourn-Prebble. As it was, she could not acknowledge any connection to it. Mercifully Peter did not seem to have recognized her. Fiona smiled wryly. Had she changed so much in five years? Gideon had obviously recognized her at once, just as she'd recognized him. She'd had a few minutes' warning, of course, thanks to her talk with Officer Wilson, but even so, she'd have known him the moment she looked into the haunted dark eyes which never seemed free from the memory of pain, or the moment she heard the deceptively quiet voice with its rough but oddly musical timbre.

Not that the intervening years hadn't left their mark on Gideon. The dark hair which always looked in want of brushing was untouched by gray, but the lines in his face had deepened and he walked with a limp, no doubt a legacy of his years on the Peninsula. Strangely, when she first noticed the limp she'd felt a genuine stab of compassion. And that, more than anything, told her how great a threat Gideon posed.

Fiona, who had resolutely subjugated everything to the task at hand for the past half hour, was forced to face what her meeting with Gideon might mean. She drew a steadying breath and told herself that the sudden chill she felt must be due to a draft. Gideon had played along with her charade thus far, and there was no reason he should not continue to do so. Whatever else he might be, he was neither malicious nor vindictive.

"If the fire's out, I suppose Hopkins can start looking for clues," Peter said. "Do you think he'll want us to go back to the warehouse and explain what we saw?"

He looked so hopeful that Fiona nearly smiled, then hastily schooled her features. The worst mistake one could make with a twelve-year-old boy was to wound his dignity. "I don't know," she said truthfully.

Peter nodded with the air of a man inured to disappointment. Taller and sturdier than Simon, he was a good-looking boy, as might be expected of a child with two such handsome parents, though he took after Lady Carne more than Gideon. He had her clear dark blue eyes and thick glossy hair in the ash-brown shade she had turned into a fashion. But in the five years since Fiona had last seen him, his face had acquired a pinched look, as if he did not smile very often. It occurred to her that

Gideon's extended absence had probably made things worse for his children. In some ways he had been the most positive influence on their lives.

"If Mr. Read and Officer Hopkins want us to answer a lot of questions," Simon said thoughtfully, "I suppose sooner or later *Maman* will have to know. I'll take full responsibility, Fiona."

When Gideon stepped into the corridor, he found Hopkins standing at attention, but it was Read who spoke first. "I'm afraid I'm going to have to ask you to accompany us to Rosemary Lane, Lord Carne."

"Of course. I intended to go there in any event."

"Yes." Mr. Read coughed, the first sign he'd given of real unease. "I assumed you'd want to inspect the damage. Hopkins tells me the fire has been put out and that much of the building has been saved. However, I'm afraid there's been a slight complication."

"What sort of complication?" Gideon inquired evenly.

"Once the fire was extinguished, Hopkins was able to search the premises," Read explained. "As the boys said, there was a great deal of damage in the back office. Papers everywhere, furniture pushed about—"

He paused, as if expecting some reaction. If so, he was disappointed. "It's obvious someone broke into the building," Gideon said. "Are you telling me something was stolen?"

"That," said the magistrate, "is one of the reasons we would like you and Sir Hugo to inspect the building. Hopkins wasn't able to determine whether there'd been a theft." He coughed again. "As I was saying, the room was in considerable disarray, and he was lying behind a desk, which probably explains why the boys didn't see him."

"He?" Gideon asked in the same even tone.

"A man. Mid-forties, Hopkins says, thin, shabbily dressed, graying hair. Sound familiar? One of your clerks, perhaps?"

27

Gideon shook his head. "We have but one clerk and it doesn't sound like him, though it's scarcely the most detailed of descriptions. I have little to do with the management of the company. I've been back in England less than two months. What does the man have to say for himself?"

"Nothing, I'm afraid." Read looked squarely at Gideon. "By the time Hopkins found him he was beyond the questions of any mortal man."

Chapter Two

While Peter stared moodily at the floor, Simon fell to contemplating a stain on his red superfine jacket. Fiona could have sworn he was wondering how to explain its condition to his mother, but suddenly he looked up at her with the air of one who's decided to offer a confidence. "Fiona," he began and got no farther, for at that moment the door opened and Gideon and Mr. Read reentered the room.

Gideon's expression was unreadable. Mr. Read was no longer frowning, but Fiona suspected this meant his concern had been masked rather than allayed. "Thank you for your patience, Miss Alastair." The magistrate's courtesy had become even more elaborate, which told Fiona that the situation had become correspondingly more complicated. "I have just a few more questions for the young gentlemen." He surveyed the boys, who regarded him with renewed interest. "You're quite certain you've told us everything you saw in the warehouse?"

Peter frowned in genuine puzzlement. Fiona thought she saw an odd glimmer in Simon's eyes, but she decided to ignore it. For the moment. "Are you accusing us of lying?" Simon inquired, at his most princely.

"Certainly not, my lor—your excellency." Mr. Read coughed.

"Then," Simon continued, "you're saying that Hopkins

found something strange in the warehouse and you wonder why we didn't see it."

Mr. Read's gaze was steady. "Do you think it's possible that there was anyone else in the back office while you were there?"

"*In* the office?" This time Simon was as startled as Peter.

"I say," Peter exclaimed at the same time, "do you mean the fire was set? Do you know who did it? Has Hopkins caught him?"

"I think," Gideon said quietly, "that you had better answer Mr. Read's question, Peter."

Peter frowned again. "I didn't see anyone," he said cautiously.

"Nor did I," said Simon. "But it was dark, and there was a lot of smoke." He looked at Mr. Read, curious but too well bred to ask further questions.

Mr. Read planted his feet firmly and clasped his hands behind his back. "There were a great many boxes piled up in the back of the room. Did either of you look behind them? Think carefully," he continued, as both boys shook their heads.

"We didn't go into the back of the room," Peter insisted. "That's where the fire was worst." His eyes widened. "You don't think someone could have been hiding there, do you, sir?"

"Of course not," said Simon, "no one could have breathed with all that smoke." He broke off and looked from Mr. Read to Gideon, his eyes suddenly hard. "Is that it?" he demanded. "Hopkins found a corpse?"

From Mr. Read's expression, it was clear that he had underestimated Simon. Fiona sympathized. Adults were always underestimating the prince. Gideon, on the other hand, regarded Simon with appreciation. The war might have damaged his leg, but it had done nothing to dull his wits. "Better tell them the truth, Read," he advised. "It's safer than letting their imaginations run riot."

Mr. Read cleared his throat. "As it happens, you've hit

upon the truth, your excellency. When Hopkins searched the premises, he discovered the body of a man behind the boxes. At this point we know little more, and I'm sure I don't have to tell boys of your understanding that no one is to speak of the matter to anyone outside this room." He turned to Fiona with an air of finality. "I am sure you are eager to take your young charge home, Miss Alastair. There will be no further questions for the present."

Gideon addressed Peter. "I'm going to the warehouse with Mr. Read, but I'll drop you in Dover Street on the way."

Peter's disappointment at this abrupt banishment from the adventure was patently obvious, but he got to his feet without protest. It was Simon who spoke. "Couldn't Peter have supper with me, Lord Carne? You can collect him on your way back from the warehouse. It won't be any trouble."

"I rather think Miss Alastair should have something to say about that." Gideon turned to Fiona, and though his look was appropriately impersonal, she realized that he was offering her a way to avoid further time in his company. Further time in Gideon Carne's company was the last thing Fiona wanted, but Simon's appeal and the look of guarded hope on Peter's face could not be ignored.

"Simon's right, it won't be any trouble at all," she said. "The rest of the family is out for the evening, and Simon and I will be glad of the company." She smiled at Peter, relieved at the excuse to look away from his father.

If Gideon was surprised by her acquiescence, he gave no sign of it. He ascertained the direction of Simon's home in Bolton Street, and then he and Mr. Read escorted Fiona and the boys out to the pale green landaulet in which Fiona had been driven to the Public Office.

Though its magistrates were on good terms with Whitehall, the Bow Street Public Office was not situated in a very savory part of town. As they left the building, Simon and Peter looked with unabashed curiosity at the public houses and rum mills that lined the street and were already doing a brisk business, though the evening was young. When the landaulet, its top raised to shield the occupants from the night air and the unappetizing sights, pulled away from the Public Office, the boys pressed their faces to the glass.

"There's the Brown Bear." Simon looked round at Fiona. "It's a public house," he explained, "but the Bow Street officers use one of the rooms for prisoners who are waiting to be questioned by the magistrates."

As they moved into the more sedate streets of Mayfair, the boys turned back to the brightly illuminated, silk-lined interior of the carriage. Fiona looked from one young face to the other and saw that the reality of their last exchange with Mr. Read was beginning to sink in.

"I say," Peter ventured in a small voice, "you don't suppose that man was still alive when we left, do you? If we'd looked more carefully—"

"You might have suffered the same fate," Fiona told him. "Though I question the prudence of going into a burning building, once you had done so you acted with great presence of mind."

Peter seemed cheered, but not wholly convinced. "Could the man have still been alive?" he insisted.

"It's possible," Fiona acknowledged, "though if the fire was as bad as you say, I should think it most unlikely."

Peter nodded, as though he found this more comforting than a blanket reassurance which he'd have known to be false. Simon was mulling over another problem. "Mr. Read probably won't tell us anything. But he might talk to you, Fiona. Will you promise to tell us whatever you learn about the fire?"

His eyes couldn't have been more guileless. "You know I can't possibly promise anything of the sort," Fiona said amiably as the carriage pulled up in Bolton Street.

The house which had been taken last year by Simon's mother, the Princess Sofia—she'd remarried in November, and had reverted to the title which she'd held as the daughter of a Russian nobleman—was an imposing three-story structure of Bath stone with a graceful Corinthian portico. In response to Fiona's ring, the front door was opened by Christopher, the second footman, who'd brought Fiona word of the message from Bow Street some two hours earlier.

Christopher was a friendly young man with attractive dark eyes which tended to stray to Fiona in a manner she found most heartening, especially as she'd attained the exalted age of nine-and-twenty on her last birthday. His face plainly showed relief at their return, not to mention curiosity, but Fiona knew he could be relied upon to hold his tongue.

"This is Master Peter Carne," she told him. "His father will call for him later in the evening, but in the meantime we're all shockingly hungry. Could you convey my apologies to the kitchen and see if they can send sandwiches or something up to my sitting room? Thank you a thousand times."

Fiona gave Christopher one of her warmest smiles and led the boys between a pair of white marble columns to the staircase. Unlike the Tassio homes in Sardinia, this house had no apartments designated as schoolroom quarters, for Simon now went away to school and Alessa had left tutelage behind completely. Fiona had a pretty bedchamber on the second floor with an adjoining sitting room which connected to the room Simon occupied when he was at home. In theory, the sitting room could be used for lessons during the holidays. In practice, it had not yet been used for anything more serious than a game of chess.

Fiona sent the boys to Simon's room to put themselves to rights, then retired to her own chamber, taking Peter's jacket to mend. For the first time since her meeting with Gideon she was quite alone. She stripped off her gloves, untied the ribbons on her bonnet, removed her shawl, and placed it in the mahogany chest of drawers. Then she moved to her dressing table and lit the bronzed lamp which stood beside the glass.

Her face looked thin and pale above the starched white

habit shirt with its prim, narrow band of lace. She had always counted herself fortunate that she could scrape her hair back in the sober manner required of a governess and still appear more than passable, but suddenly she hated the severity of the style and the confining feel of the pins. Without thinking, she began to pull them free. It was only as she felt the heavy locks fall over her neck and shoulders that she recalled a similar moment five years before. But then it had been Gideon who'd loosened the pins, run his fingers through her hair, and pressed his lips against her neck, finally pulling her into his arms. It had been their first and most memorable kiss, though hardly the most passionate of those they'd exchanged.

Fiona clenched a hairpin, snapping the delicate metal. Not for one moment had she doubted he loved her as deeply and irrevocably as she loved him. Now she knew she'd been foolish and naive beyond permission, but at the time nothing—not Aline, not George, not the censure of society—had seemed of any importance beside the fact that they obviously belonged together. She did not blame Gideon for her seduction—if the word could be applied to an act in which she had been such a willing and eager participant—but even were it not for Jamie's death, she would never be able to forgive Gideon for holding her love so cheaply.

Suddenly brisk, Fiona rose, shook out her dark chintz skirts, picked up Peter's jacket, and opened her workbox. A few minutes later, Simon and Peter stepped into the room, faces freshly scrubbed, hair carefully combed. Fiona smiled at them. "That's better. Here," she added, smoothing the jacket and holding it out to Peter, "not quite as good as new, but it should do."

Peter took the jacket with a shy smile. Simon remained by the door, regarding Fiona in surprise. "Your hair's different."

Fiona had forgotten her impulsive gesture. "I took the pins out," she told him. "I was getting a headache." It was a half-truth. She was indeed developing a headache, but

34

she doubted that it had anything to do with her hair.

"I like it," Simon said. "Do you think supper is ready yet?"

They adjourned to the sitting room and were soon supplied with asparagus soup, cold boiled capon, summer cabbage, a small meat pie, cauliflower with cream sauce, baked ratafia pudding, and gooseberry tartlets. The day's adventures had increased the boys' already vigorous appetites, but the food proved ample even for them. Subduing her curiosity, Fiona refrained from questioning them about their reasons for leaving school. Simon, she knew, would never take such a course of action lightly, so whatever had happened must be serious; and it would best be discussed when the two of them were alone.

As she poured herself a cup of tea from the enameled china pot which had accompanied the supper tray, Fiona realized that Lady Carne must be in London as well. She had seen and heard nothing of Gideon's wife since her return to England—Fiona's excursions into society were still relatively infrequent—but Lady Carne was not one to immure herself in the country. Gideon had said nothing about letting her know of Peter's whereabouts, and though Lady Carne was not the most devoted of mothers, she could not be wholly lost to maternal feeling. Fiona carefully returned the teapot to the coromandel Pembroke table and smiled at Peter. "In all the confusion, your father may not have had a chance to send word to your mother. Perhaps we should send one of the footmen round."

Peter had begun to relax, but at this his face shuttered. "My mother's dead," he told her in a cold, flat voice.

Hot drops of tea spattered into Fiona's lap. Lady Carne was dead? It certainly explained Gideon's sudden return, but it was shocking nonetheless. Fiona righted her teacup and gathered her scattered wits. "I'm sorry, I didn't know," she said gently.

Peter hunched one shoulder. "It was almost a year ago. Last August."

In August Fiona had been preoccupied with the removal from Sardinia, and then they had spent some weeks in Ireland before coming to England. She had seen little of the English papers. Clare had said nothing of Lady Carne, but that was hardly surprising.

"Peter's father just came back from the Peninsula," Simon put in. "His uncle and aunt were looking after him before that. The uncle and aunt who own Woodbourn-Prebble."

Fiona nodded, wondering why the devil it had taken Gideon so many months to return home. Surely he had enough wit not to leave his children to Clare and Hugo's ministrations.

"I must say," Simon continued, helping himself to more of the pudding, "your father seems quite a decent sort, Peter. He didn't ring a peal over you, which is more than my mother would have done."

Peter's silence was more eloquent than any reply he might have made. After Fiona's mention of his mother, he had stopped eating. Simon finished his second helping of pudding in silence, then pushed back his chair and calmly proceeded to unbutton his jacket and waistcoat. From beneath the waistcoat he extracted a handful of papers. "I found them," he announced. "In the back office where the fire started."

Peter's moody reflectiveness vanished. "When? I didn't see you."

"When you ran into the front office to get the ledgers. There were a lot of papers on the floor, so I picked them up. I thought they might be important."

"Why didn't you tell me?"

"I was going to, but when the police officer took the ledgers I decided it would be best to wait until we were alone." Simon laid the papers on the table. "You can give them to your father when he comes to collect you."

"No!" For the first time Fiona saw a hint of Gideon in Peter, not so much in his features as in the sudden anger which blazed from his eyes.

"Honestly, Peter." From Simon's expression, Fiona suspected this was not the first time the two boys had discussed Peter's father. "What else are you going to do with them?"

"Give them to my uncle." Peter drew the papers over to his side of the table.

"Your Uncle Hugo?" Simon's dubious tone told Fiona that Hugo had come under discussion as well. "You don't like him either."

"Woodbourn-Prebble belongs to him."

"Not anymore. It belongs to all the partners, and your father is one of them. Besides, from what you've said, your Uncle Hugo sounds a prize ass."

It was so accurate a description of Clare's husband that Fiona choked and quickly raised her napkin to her lips. Peter did not argue the description, but neither did he concede defeat. In frustration, Simon turned to Fiona. "It's the only sensible thing to do. Tell him, Fiona."

"I can't tell Peter how to handle a family matter. But if you keep the papers from your father and go to your uncle behind his back, you will only create problems for everyone, Peter."

Peter scowled. "I'll think about it," was all he said, and Simon had the sense to let the matter rest. Fiona rang for a footman to clear away the supper things, and the boys fell to discussing the fire and the dead man and the possible connections between the two until Christopher announced the arrival of Lord Carne.

Gideon hesitated a moment on the threshold to collect himself. The sitting room, warm with lamplight and bright with children's voices, secured against the outside by soft dove-colored walls and cheerful yellow curtains, seemed a wholly alien environment. This was the fortress Fiona had built for herself, and he had no right to invade it. It was only when he felt he had more or less regained his self-possession that he looked at Fiona and, with a shock of recognition and a quickening of his pulse, saw that her hair was tumbling about her shoulders. So. She too had been remembering the past. Subduing an unworthy sense of triumph, Gideon murmured a greeting and asked Peter if he was ready to leave.

Peter got slowly to his feet, reached out a hand, hesitated, then with sudden decision picked up some papers from the table and stepped forward. "Simon found these in the back office," he said, holding them out to Gideon. "On the floor. He kept them hidden because the police officer took the ledgers away."

Peter's face was a study in conflict, but the fact that he offered the papers at all was a sign of progress. Gideon smiled, though he knew that to make too much of the incident would be to risk what slender gains he had made. "Thank you." He nodded at Simon as well, then scanned the papers quickly until he came to the last, which he stared at for a long moment.

"Are they important?" Peter asked.

"Not especially, but I'm grateful that you recovered them. They're some old documents which belonged to Mr. Woodbourn, your Aunt Clare's father. I'll give them to your uncle next time I see him." Gideon folded the papers and stowed them in a coat pocket. "Could I have a word with you in private before I leave, Miss Alastair?"

Fiona, who'd been wondering what on earth her late father's papers were doing scattered on the office floor, was caught off guard. "Of course," she said in her crispest voice. "Simon—"

"We'll be in my room." The two boys started for the door to the adjoining chamber, but Simon paused, his hand on the doorknob. "Sir, you don't have to tell us, but did the dead man in the warehouse start the fire?"

"We don't know," Gideon said. "But it appears that his death was accidental. Neither Sir Hugo nor I was able to identify him."

Simon nodded, and even Peter seemed pleased that they were allowed to share in the information, however meager it might be. Without further protest, the two boys left the room.

The door closed with a quiet click, and Fiona was alone with Gideon for the first time since that evening five years before, when he'd told her he had no desire to set her up as his mistress and if she was sensible she'd marry George and take her pleasure where she could. Fiona straightened her back and moved to one of the cane chairs grouped about the Pembroke table, wondering why the devil she hadn't thought to put her hair up again before he arrived. There had been no mistaking the sudden light in Gideon's eyes when he entered the room and turned his gaze on her. "Please be seated, my lord."

"When did you learn that young Tassio is acquainted with my son?" Gideon inquired, moving to a chair across from her.

"This evening, about five minutes before you walked into the Bow Street Office. I haven't seen Simon since he was home at Easter, and it was only this term that the boys became close friends."

Fiona had the familiar sensation that Gideon was able to see past all her defenses while giving away nothing of his own thoughts. Though she had known this would be difficult, she hadn't fully appreciated that, for all her anger and disillusionment, the current of desire between them was as strong as ever. "You wished to ask me something, Lord Carne?" she inquired, clasping her hands in her lap.

Gideon did not speak at once, and when he did, it was not at all what she expected to hear. "Camford found you the position."

"Did he tell you so?" Fiona had specifically asked Gideon's solicitor to do nothing of the kind.

"On the contrary. He told me only that he'd been able to be of some assistance to you and that you never wished to see or hear from me again. But as I know you categorically refused my money, I can only assume Camford's assistance involved obtaining your position with the Tassios."

Infuriatingly, she felt obliged to justify her actions. "By

the time Mr. Camford found me, I'd faced the fact that without references the only employment I was likely to find was on the street or in a brothel. I knew I could not afford to be proud."

"You were proud enough to refuse money," Gideon said with an air of detached interest.

"There were still some things to which I would not stoop."

Gideon inclined his head, as if in acknowledgment of a hit, though he felt his carefully constructed detachment begin to crumble. Fiona's words were spoken lightly but they were as effective as a rapier thrust. Or a well-aimed bullet. "Then I'm sure you will be pleased to know that the gesture did not go unappreciated. Whose idea was Sardinia?"

"A friend of Mr. Camford's, a fellow solicitor, had been engaged to hire an English governess for the Tassio children. They wanted someone with a good knowledge of Latin and Greek and some Italian. The solicitor was a bit desperate trying to find a candidate who'd fit the qualifications and would also be willing to venture so far from home."

"References?" Gideon inquired.

Fiona lifted her chin. "Forged."

"Naturally." Gideon smiled. "Well forged, I trust."

Fiona had forgotten how unexpectedly and dangerously sweet a smile it was, and she felt a rush of tenderness which had no place between them. "Well enough." She fixed him with a direct gaze. "I went to see Clare shortly after I returned to England. I told her that my name was now Alastair and I wished to have no further contact with any of you."

"An understandable sentiment. But I'm afraid the matter is more complicated. I believe," he said, reaching inside his coat and drawing out one of the papers Peter had given him, "that I have you to thank for this."

"On the contrary. It was the boys who found the papers."

"Yes, and very enterprising of them, though I was less surprised by the discovery than by the fact that Peter presented the papers to me." He hesitated, for personal waters were dangerous, but in the end he spoke anyway. "If you convinced Peter that I might possibly be something less than an ogre, you have my thanks."

"Oh, I did nothing. Peter wanted to give the papers to Hugo, to the outrage of Simon, who said Peter's Uncle Hugo sounded a prize ass—"

Gideon threw back his head and gave a shout of laughter. "Young Tassio is obviously a shrewd judge of character."

"Undoubtedly, which makes it excessively odd that he has taken a liking to you. I suppose even the most perceptive among us can sometimes be mistaken."

"Undoubtedly," Gideon agreed gravely. "If it was Tassio who persuaded Peter to give up the papers, we both have cause to be grateful to him," he continued, holding the page out to her. "I think you'd best read this."

At once reluctant and curious, Fiona took the paper, careful not to let her hand brush against his. Though the paper was faded and yellowed with time, the writing on it was unmistakably her father's, the hand as erratic as the attention he'd bestowed on his children. Fiona's throat tightened, but she had long since learned to ward off incipient tears.

"Read it." Gideon's voice was soft but compelling.

The page was dated September, 1808. Just two months after she'd left England. Fiona could not imagine how anything from that time could bring her comfort, but she forced her eyes to focus on the page.

My dear Bridges,

I am writing to ask that you wait upon me at Barstead at your earliest possible convenience. I have something which I wish to entrust to you in person, and unfortunately my health does not permit me to travel to London. My son-in-law, Sir Hugo Prebble, has been assisting me with the business since my illness, but I prefer to keep this between the two of us.

Yours in haste,
Woodbourn

For a moment Fiona could only stare at the paper she held in her hand. "Mr. Bridges was my father's solicitor," she said at last, looking up at Gideon.

"So I suspected. When an ailing man wishes to entrust something to his solicitor in private, it's a fair guess that we're talking about a will."

A will. A new will, in which her father might conceivably have made some provision for his errant daughter. Afraid to let herself believe that this brief note could represent the financial independence which would free her from a lifetime of insecurity, Fiona folded the paper, her hands shaking. "Uncle James died in September." She could still remember the evening she'd read about it, sitting in the grand salon of the Tassio house in Cagliari. "He must have written this just before he died. That would explain why it was never posted."

Gideon nodded. "The other papers Simon found are inventories from the same time. I suspect Woodbourn wrote the letter, perhaps late at night, and left it with the inventories he'd been reviewing, but he died before he was able to send it off. After his death, Hugo must have given the papers to Woodbourn's clerk. The note to Bridges looked like business correspondence, so it was boxed up and left forgotten in the back office."

"But even the clerk would have been sure to draw attention to a will." Fiona wondered how she could have been so foolish as to imagine there could be anything to this fantasy. "If my father ever got around to writing it, which isn't at all clear from this note, Clare must have destroyed it."

"Assuming she found it. But your father wasn't planning to post the will along with the letter. And he went out of his way to tell Bridges he didn't want Hugo to know about it." Gideon crossed his legs, warming to the puzzle, as he had once to a particularly complicated deployment of troops. "Hugo and Clare were with him during the last weeks of his illness. Clare made a point of telling me what a great sacrifice it had been."

Fiona smiled bitterly. "All the more reason for her to have destroyed the will."

"I'm not sure she had any idea your father had written one." Gideon leaned toward her, completely focused on the problem, so that it was no longer difficult to look into her eyes. "Think, Fiona. Your father decides to make a new will, leaving some of the property to you. He knows Clare will kick up a tremendous fuss. Mightn't he have decided not to tell her, at least until he'd handed the will over to his solicitor?"

"It's possible," Fiona admitted. "Uncle James always tried to avoid any unpleasantness. But Clare could have found the will after he died."

"She could have," Gideon conceded. "But even assuming it was destroyed, you might be able to track down the witnesses. You could make things difficult for her."

Already wondering whom her ailing father might have prevailed upon to witness the document and how she could set about finding them, Fiona tucked the paper into the sleeve of her gown. "Thank you," she said, making it clear that the matter should end there. "There was no reason you were obliged to show it to me."

"Good God, Fiona, I thought we'd agreed I'm not an ogre." Gideon could not have said whether it was her assumption that he might not have given her the paper or her dispassionate tone which made his temper rise. "You will need help, you know," he told her in a more moderate voice. "Unless you think you can run about London asking questions with young Simon in tow, you are going to find yourself at a disadvantage."

He was annoyingly correct. Fiona bit back a protest. "I, on the other hand," Gideon continued, "am quite at liberty. What's more, Clare and Hugo are still obliged to receive me."

Fiona stared at him. "Why this sudden attack of nobility? Are you trying to buy absolution?"

"Something like that." Gideon settled back in his chair. "Besides, it will be very much to my advantage if it turns out that part of Woodbourn-Prebble belongs to you. Hugo, I need hardly tell you, has not husbanded the company well in the years since your father's death. With the capital from the new investors, he has hopes of doing great things, especially if the East India Company's new charter opens up the India trade, but I'm not nearly so sanguine. And I don't have much faith in the other partners."

Fiona was intrigued in spite of herself. She had not thought Hugo would take to trade, but she should have realized her brother-in-law would find the lure of money stronger than the risk of commercial taint. "How many partners are there?" she asked.

"Three, in addition to Hugo and me. The soundest is Magnus Melchett of Melchett's Bank. He's reputed to be very clever, though I don't entirely trust him. The second is the Marquis of Parminter, a reckless young man with a taste for gambling. He and Melchett are distant cousins."

"I've met Lord Parminter. He's been paying rather a lot of attention to Simon's sister, Lady Alessandra." Fiona hesitated, then added, "Clare told me George married Parminter's sister."

"He did," Gideon said blandly. "The third partner is George. Exactly," he continued, reading her reaction in her face. "I have little faith in Hugo or Parminter and I know Barrington-Forbes would quite cheerfully break my neck. I have considerable doubts about the present state of Woodbourn-Prebble, especially in the wake of the fire, but with only a twenty-percent share in the partnership, I have very little influence. However, if we were able to prove that part of the company rightfully belongs to you . . ."

"You might find me useful."

"If you like." Gideon grimaced at the choice of words. "Take your pick, Fiona—guilt or self-interest. You're too sensible a woman to refuse help, however dubious the source."

Fiona gave a small, dry smile. "I always tell Simon not to let personal prejudice keep him from making the right decision."

"Then you agree?"

She hesitated, looked away, felt the folded paper beneath the fabric of her sleeve. "Fiona," Gideon said softly. She looked up, about to correct his use of her given name, but something in his expression forestalled her. "Whatever you decide," Gideon said after a moment, "watch out for Barrington-Forbes. He could prove dangerous."

Once again he had surprised her. "I can take care of myself," she told him. "But I'm not above accepting help when it is needed."

"Does that mean we have an agreement?"

Fiona drew a breath. "Yes, Lord Carne, we have an agreement."

Chapter Three

It was not yet midnight when the sound of voices in the corridor outside signaled the return of the Princess Sofia. Fiona put down the book she'd been pretending to read and glanced at Simon, who was curled up in an upholstered armchair which stood between the tall, narrow windows that faced the garden at the rear of the house. His dark hair was tousled, his face was drawn with fatigue, and he looked, for once, no more than his scant twelve years.

They had long since run out of conversation, but Simon had refused to go to bed. His mother must be told of his return to London, and he would not sleep until he had faced her and learned his fate. Now that the moment was upon him, Fiona saw that he shrank from the encounter.

"I'm glad she's early," Fiona said, rising and brushing out the wrinkles in her skirt. "I didn't expect her till well past one. No, stay here, Simon. I rather think I should prepare her first."

Simon sank back against the cushions with evident relief. "You're a trump, Fiona."

The expression accorded oddly with his faintly accented English, and Fiona suppressed a smile. "Reflect on your sins, young man. You're still in the suds." He did not of course take her seriously, which was just the response she'd intended. Simon had more than his share of imagi-

nation and he took his responsibilities with the gravity be-
fitting a grown man. It made him vulnerable, and Fiona
had learned to treat him carefully.

She closed the door on his now cheerful face and made
her way rapidly down the corridor, wondering how she
would explain to the princess that her son had been
grossly insubordinate to the scholars entrusted with his education, that he'd run away from school in the middle of
term and made his way to London in a brewer's cart, that
he'd then committed felonious entry into a private place
of business and narrowly escaped stumbling onto a
corpse, and that he'd finished the evening by being hauled
before a Bow Street magistrate like a common criminal.
She decided that she wouldn't bring up the trifling matter
of the theft of private papers. There was quite enough to
say about the rest, including Simon's presence of mind in
the matter of the fire and the perils he'd faced inside the
burning building. Not to mention the perils he faced every
day at school. Fiona's brother had known the rigors of
public school, but even Jamie's stories had not prepared
her for Simon's matter-of-fact account of the brutality of
life at Eton.

At the door of the princess's dressing room, Fiona
paused to take a breath and remind herself that, temper or
no, the Princess Sofia was essentially a fair woman and
very fond of her son.

She was also, Fiona saw with relief when she entered
the room, in a benign mood. The princess was standing by
her dressing table, stripping off a quantity of bracelets
and rings and listening to her daughter Alessa, who was
perched on the bed, her vivid face intent on making some
obviously important declaration. Her maid, Lupino, a
tiny, dark-haired woman with a thin, pointed face, stood
nearby, ready to unfasten the princess's gown.

At Fiona's entrance Alessa broke off, looking cross at
the interruption. Lupino frowned, her usual response to
any intrusion on her domain. The princess turned round
and her finely arched brows rose in surprise. The Tassio

governess did not normally disturb her at this hour.

"If I might speak to you privately," Fiona said. "I don't think it should wait until morning."

The princess gave her an appraising look. "This will take some time?"

"I think so, yes."

"Then you had best sit down, Miss Alastair, I will not be long." The princess turned to Lupino and indicated that she was ready to be relieved of her gown and helped into a dressing robe, but she refused any further ministrations and dismissed her maid for the night. Lupino protested with the familiarity of long acquaintance, but the princess was not to be bullied and Lupino was forced to retire with a glance of malevolence at Fiona, bearing the gown of sea-green gauze and silver net in her arms.

"You must be tired, Alessa," the princess said when Lupino had left the room.

"I am not at all fatigued, *Maman,*" Alessa said in a sweet, determined voice. "Besides, it's about Simon, isn't it? If it's about Simon, I have a right to hear it."

Alessa's affection for her brother was genuine, but it was tinged with envy which was evident in the note of annoyance in her voice. There was no need to fan her jealousy by making a secret of what she would know in the end. The princess knew this as well as Fiona, but she left the decision to her. "If Miss Alastair wishes to be private . . ."

"There is no reason Alessa should not know," Fiona said. "It is about Simon."

"I knew it." Alessa tossed her head with an air of satisfaction. "He has been—what is it they say here?—sent down."

"No," Fiona said quickly. "He left of his own accord, for what he saw as sufficient cause, and came to London with one of his friends. He's here, in my sitting room, and in quite good health, though he'd be rather better for some sleep. He didn't want to go to bed until he'd seen you."

The princess frowned. "This friend, he has much influence over my son?"

"No, not in that way," Fiona hastened to assure her. "He seems a dependable boy. He's the eldest son of Viscount Carne." Fiona felt her face grow warm as she said the name, and she continued rapidly. "The boys came across a fire in a warehouse belonging to Peter's uncle and were taken to Bow Street—"

Alessa made a small sound of disbelief, but her mother's frown deepened. "Let me tell you what I have learned," Fiona went on, "and then perhaps you will see him." Taking the princess's silence for assent, she quickly sketched the events of the day as she'd heard them from Simon, glossing over the matter of their entry into the warehouse and the man who'd died there and the readiness of the police to believe they'd committed a criminal act.

The princess, who was not a fool, understood what had been left unsaid. "I see. You will send Simon to me. I will not keep him long. And then, if you please, you will put him to bed." She turned to her daughter. "Alessa, go to your room. I will send Lupino to you."

"Maman!" Alessa had found the story enthralling, and she did not intend to miss the fuller account that Simon would be required to give.

Fiona left the room and did not hear the princess's reply, but as she reached the door of her sitting room she heard Alessa running toward her. "Fiona," she called, her breath coming in quick gasps, "I want to see him."

Fiona had always ruled with a light hand. "A moment only. I can't answer for Lupino."

Alessa smiled in triumph, then threw open the door and ran to her brother's side. "Simon, you are to go to *Maman* and tell her everything, but she does not want me there, so you must tell it all to me tomorrow. You are not to worry. She is in a good mood tonight, and it will be all right. I know her."

Simon's face, which had grown tense at their entrance,

49

relaxed into a smile. He stood up, brushed back his hair, and straightened his coat. "Fiona?"

"I told her what happened, though not in much detail. She's in her dressing room. Don't keep her waiting. I'll be here when you're through."

Fiona watched the dark-haired pair as they moved down the hall, the grave, slim boy with the erect carriage and the graceful, unreflecting girl. They had little in common save a casual affection and a strong sense of their own worth. The Tassio name had given Alessa a touch of arrogance, rendered harmless by her youth, but it had given Simon a burden he was too young to carry. She closed the door and occupied herself in straightening pillows and rearranging objects on the mantel. It was pointless occupation, but it held her worry about Simon at bay.

And it kept her from thinking too much about Gideon. The image of his face came to her suddenly and she halted, a pillow clutched in her arms, trembling with anger and despair and the remembrance of desire. It was unfair, it was grossly, abysmally unfair that Gideon should have returned to her life, bringing back the sting of his rejection and her guilt over Jamie's death. She had carefully constructed a new life, a life that left no room for passion or caprice, and now, after an hour in Gideon's company, she saw her hard-won peace crumbling to bits. She threw the pillow down. It was not going to happen. She would not let Gideon destroy her.

By the time Simon returned, the moment of fervor was gone and Fiona was able to greet him with her usual composure. She searched his face as he came into the room and saw that the interview had gone well. His eyes were glazed with strain and fatigue, but his relief was palpable. "It's all right," he said, "she's not angry. At least not with me. She doesn't want me to go back, not until she talks to Michael. She says she doesn't understand English ways."

Fiona smiled. Born in Russia, married at an early age to the Prince di Tassio, who'd taken her from Savoy to Sardinia, the widowed princess had not set foot in England until she'd decided that Simon, like his father before him, should have a proper English education. But shortly after she took her children to England, the princess unexpectedly married Michael Langley, an English diplomat she'd known briefly in her youth. Fiona was relieved that the princess would turn to her new husband for guidance in the matter. Langley was sure to be sensible about Simon's escapade.

"She's going to write to Lord Carne," Simon added, "and when she understands it properly she'll write to the school. I told her I didn't want special treatment, and whatever I did, I was ready to pay for it. I'd do it again, no matter what the consequences. It wasn't fair, what they did to Peter."

"No, it wasn't fair, and you were right to stand by him. But there's a lot of unfairness in the world, Simon, and sometimes—"

He shook his head. "I know what you're going to say. There are some things you can't change right away and there are some you can't change at all and sometimes you have to be devious and sometimes you have to compromise. But I can't do that, Fiona. I'm a Tassio."

It was pride, but more than that, it was a statement of obligation to his name. Fiona had come up against it frequently of late and knew she could not alter it. Nor would she want to, though it robbed Simon of some of the spontaneity of youth. "There is that," she agreed, making a show of consulting her watch. "But now it's well past one and you should be in bed. I'll leave word that you're not to be disturbed."

Simon grinned. "At school we aren't allowed to lie abed." He moved toward the door which led to his room, then stopped as though struck by a worrisome thought. "I say, Fiona, what do you suppose Lord Carne will do about Peter?"

The question was much on Gideon's mind when he left

Bolton Street well after ten that same evening. He'd seen nothing of Peter since his return to England save for a brief and strained visit to Eton, where he'd learned only that Peter did not like his father and would prefer to have as little to do with him as possible.

As he gave the grays their office, Gideon looked at the boy who'd once seemed the only unsullied thing to come out of his marriage. Peter was sitting as far away from his father as possible, his hands between his knees, his eyes on the carriage floor. They'd once been very good friends. God, how many years ago had that been? When had he last looked at his son in joy and thankfulness, with no trace of the doubt Aline had sown to poison his life?

He closed his eyes in pain, seeing again his wife's lovely face suffused with mockery and anger. Yes, she had lovers. She had always had lovers. She had lain with another man not a week before their marriage, but what did it matter where she took her pleasure? She'd never denied her husband, had she? She had given him whatever he wanted. She had given him a son.

Gideon remembered the horror of that declaration. Peter, his son. His son? The question rose from his bowels in a despairing cry, but he had uttered only a whisper of sound. Whose son? Aline had laughed in his face. She didn't know, and she didn't care.

It had not been Peter's fault. Gideon knew that, but he had not been able to put the knowledge of his wife's betrayal behind him. Peter had sensed his withdrawal and, confused and hurt, had withdrawn in his turn. There had been no way to mend things between them. What the devil could one say to a seven-year-old boy?

For that matter, what could one say to a boy of twelve whose father had left him without a word of farewell more than five years before, and who'd been told God knew what lies by his mother? They might have mended matters had it not been for the duel which had taken Jamie Woodbourn's life. Afterward, Aline sent the children away, leaving her husband, wounded and feverish, to recover as he might and plan his escape to the Peninsula.

Gideon had returned to find all his children strangers. Teddy had been barely two when he'd left and Beth had not yet been born. His sons were now openly hostile, while Beth, the only one of the three children he was certain could not be his, maintained a grave distance.

Gideon glanced again at Peter. He'd been so preoccupied with what had occurred at the warehouse he'd asked no questions about what had brought Peter and young Tassio to London. What random bit of cruelty had induced the boys to run away? The consequences of that act must seem of far more moment to them than the unreality of a trip to Bow Street. He would have to talk to Peter tonight, if only for the boy's peace of mind.

He pulled up in Dover Street before an austere porch flanked by Doric columns. The house was dark save for a dim glow coming through the fanlight above the front door. Aline for a mercy had not mortgaged the London house, but there was little money to keep it up. He could have let it and taken rooms instead, but Gideon had determined, against all prudence, to give his children a home. He would not leave Teddy and Beth to the mercies of the Prebble nurse in Hertfordshire.

The door was opened by a lean, dark-haired man with an expressive face and an air of unquenchable good humor. "Time you were back, Major. The joint's burned, but if you can't come home when you're promised, you'll have to make do with a cold supper. The tots are asleep—here, who's this?"

"My son, Peter. He's to be with us for a while and you're to treat him with respect. Peter, this irreverent monkey is called Adam. He was with me on the Peninsula and he thinks it gives him liberties. Adam, light some candles, for God's sake, we're not in dun territory yet. We'll be in the library. Send Barbara in when she's free, find me something to drink, and make a posset for the boy." He turned to Peter. "All right?"

Peter nodded, then added a distinctly servile, "Sir."

Adam raised his crooked brows, then hastened to open the library door and light an indecent number of candles. "I suppose you'll be wanting a fire as well," he said in an aggrieved tone. Gideon raised his arm and Adam, an impudent smile on his face, scuttled out of the room.

"He was my batman," Gideon said. "I owe him my life." Then, with a calculating glance at his son, he flung himself into an armchair and extended his legs. "You could give me a hand with my boots."

Peter, who'd been standing uneasily in the middle of the room, hastened to comply, and for a moment, intent on the simple task, his face lost its strained look. When the second boot was off, he looked up at Gideon with something approaching a smile, but the brief moment of engagement did not last, and he scrambled to his feet and retreated to a chair across the room.

Still, it was a beginning. Gideon thanked Peter gravely and closed his eyes, pretending to an exhaustion that was not far from real. "I rather think you should stay here for a while, till we sort things out," he said. "I imagine you had good reason to leave school"—his eyes flickered open and he saw Peter tense—"but that can wait till you're rested. We live quietly here. Most of the house hasn't been opened. There's just Barbara, who dusts the rooms and looks after the children, and Adam, who keeps us fed and does everything else."

"Sir?" Peter had moved to the edge of his chair. "Beth and Teddy, are they—I mean, can I see them?"

"They're in health, if that's what you want to know. Whether they like it here or miss Hertfordshire I don't know, you'll have to ask them. They're asleep, or I'd take you up, but you'll be nearby. You can look in on them if you like. Ah, Adam."

Adam had returned bearing whiskey, hot water, a loaf, and a plate of sliced meat, as well as a steaming mug for Peter. Gideon, who had not eaten since morning, fell to hungrily. Adam stood nearby, providing a running commentary on the events of the day, most of them, he pointed out, requiring an immediate expenditure of money if the house was not to fall down about their ears. "Improvise," Gideon growled, filling his glass for the second time. "Forage and improvise." He winked at Peter, who looked shocked at this unexpected levity. But from that moment the boy relaxed, and though he had previously refused food and would barely touch his posset, he began to eat and drink with all the avidity of youth, quite as if he had not already had supper with the Tassio boy a few hours since.

Ten minutes later Barbara, a small, plump young woman with straight light brown hair and an unremarkable but kindly face, entered the room. "So this is Master Peter," she said. "The children will be that glad to see you. I opened up the room next to the one your brother and sister have"—she glanced at Gideon, who nodded his approval—"and the sheets are warming. Adam will loan you one of his night shirts, he's more your size than Lord Carne, and I'll brush out your things while you're asleep."

Peter frowned. "I've seen you before."

Barbara smiled warmly at the boy. "I didn't think you'd remember. I'm from the Runford farm, near the village beyond Hartwood. I worked for the Prebbles up at Digby Hall the last few months, helping in the nursery, and when your father came for your brother and sister, they had to let me go. I was right happy to come here, for I'd grown fond of them, and I'd never seen London." She turned to Gideon. "I'm sorry, sir, I didn't mean to go on so. I'll wait for the boy upstairs."

"Peter? You can go up now if you like. You must be tired."

"If you please, sir." He followed Barbara out of the room with evident relief, leaving Gideon to face his former batman, who had no intention of following their example.

"All right," Adam said. "Something uncommon has been going on tonight. What kind of pickle are you in now? Tell me the whole, or I'll never be able to get you out of it."

"Go to the devil," Gideon said amiably.

"Come, man, I've given up a nightshirt."

"Damn your soul, I'm tired. Oh, very well." Gideon had every intention of telling Adam, but he wanted to think about Peter and he wanted, even more urgently, to think about Fiona. He put these thoughts aside and went through the whole of the story, omitting only his prior acquaintance with the Tassio governess and the discovery of the letter addressed to her father. "So there are many unanswered questions," he concluded. "The fire was no accident. I want to know about the man who died. Who he was, who sent him there, and why. I'll need to be here in the morning. Get out early and see what you can learn."

Adam shook his head in mock despair. "Like Spain, isn't it? Find the enemy's bivouac, pinch a blanket or two, locate a spare wagon, and bring a stray chicken back for supper. Need anything? No? I'll be off to bed then. Don't drink any more, you'll have the devil of a head. Goodnight."

Gideon scowled and put down the bottle. Until those last months in Spain, when his wounds made travel impossible and his leg was a daily torment, he had had no urgent need for drink. But drinking, he found, eased the pain. And now that he was back in England, facing the shattered remnants of his life, there was a new kind of pain, and it was all too easy to seek that remedy again. Gideon pushed the bottle away and forced himself to think of the golden-haired woman who called herself Miss Alastair and who wanted no more to do with him than did his son. They had been a doomed pair from the start. The affair had had a grievous ending, but if the fault was enough for both, she had had the harder road to follow. He would make amends to her, if she would only let him.

His thoughts were no more coherent than this, but his senses were alive with memory: the warmth of her skin, the brilliance of her eyes, the grace of her movement. It

56

took him a moment to hear the tentative knock on the door and to focus on the small figure in the voluminous nightshirt. "Peter?"

"May I talk to you, sir?" Gideon nodded and Peter slipped into the room and stood in front of his father. "It's about school. I know you said it could wait, but I'd like to tell you what happened."

Gideon gestured to a nearby chair and Peter sat down gingerly. "It's not that I mean to complain, because I know it's important to be at school, but there are some beastly things that happen."

Gideon grunted assent, afraid to say anything that would stop the flow of confidences.

"It's not being flogged, for I'm not flogged more than anyone else, and maybe less, and when I am I daresay I deserve it. It's the other boys." He stopped.

"The older ones," Gideon prompted.

"Yes, that's it. There's no one in Long Chamber at night, and they do just as they please and sometimes it's hard on the others."

"I put you in a lodging house," Gideon said, remembering with anger that Hugo, to save a few pounds, had seen fit to enter Peter as a scholar, with residence in the college, rather than paying for his lodging in one of the nearby houses.

"I know, sir, but I still have friends among the Collegers, and I go there sometimes. The boys do. At night, I mean. They climb out of their houses and into the College and join in whatever is going on. You know, gambling and drinking and ragging the younger boys. I can take care of myself, so it wasn't too bad when I was living there." He leaned forward, and there were tears in his eyes. "But some of the boys can't. It's cruel. It's not just being made to feel small and stupid, it's being hurt, really hurt. A boy was scalped last year, before I came. It was a game. They were tossing him in a blanket and they threw him up too high and he hit his head on the corner of a bedstead and it took his scalp right off. It was an accident and they sewed it on again and he was all right, but when I think of Teddy coming into that—"

This was followed by a long silence. Gideon schooled his voice. He was growing angry, but anger would not help Peter now. "There was something more, wasn't there? Something that was bad enough to make you want to leave?"

Peter took a deep breath. "It was Norton. He's nearly eleven, but he's small and, well, easily frightened, and I used to look after him. But after I left Long Chamber I couldn't do that and it worried me. So two nights ago I climbed in with some of the other boys to see how he was. There was a fight going on. They were making Norton stand up against one of the bigger boys and he was getting the worst of it, but every time he went down they'd make him stand up again, and when he wouldn't they'd pour brandy down his throat until he got on his feet, and—It was so bad I couldn't stand it and I yelled at them to stop, and then I ran in and started hitting the other boy so he'd leave Norton alone. I'm not sure what happened, but I saw more candles than ever burned in church, and the next thing I remember I was lying in a corner feeling sick and Norton—he was curled up with his arm over his face and I thought he was dead. Everyone else had gone away as though it didn't have anything to do with them. I couldn't understand it. I crawled over to him and he was breathing, so I did what I could for him and then I had to go back to my house. The next day I heard that his mother had been sent for and she'd taken him away." He shook his head in disbelief. "It wasn't right, sir, it wasn't right at all."

The pointless carnage of the battlefield was bad enough. It was the willful cruelty after battle that sickened Gideon. "So you decided to leave."

"Not then," Peter hastened to explain. "I went to the Lower Master the next morning and told him about it. If it had happened to Norton, it could happen to another boy, and something had to be done. He told me to stop sniveling and start behaving like a man. So I went to the Head Master, but he didn't want to hear anything about it either. Norton brought it on himself, he said, and anyway, it was an accident. Don't be a troublemaker or you'll be flogged for your pains. I was so angry it was all I could do not to go at him with my fists. When I got out of there I knew I couldn't stay, not in a place that let things like that happen, so I went to find Simon. He's my best friend, and I wanted him to know why I was leaving. I didn't mean for him to get into trouble too, but I'm glad he came away with me."

Gideon was silent, wondering what he could tell the boy to reconcile him to a brutish world. His own experiences of school could not match the harshness of what Peter had just told him, but Gideon could still remember the loneliness and fear and the arrogant contempt of those in authority. His parents had treated him with casual indifference at best, and there had been no one else to turn to. Was that how it had seemed to Peter? "You were right," Gideon said at last. "You did the right thing."

"Thank you, sir." Peter stood up, relief quickly replaced by a new worry. "If it's all right with you, I'd rather not go back. I don't mind working. I know there's not much money, and I'm willing to go out as an apprentice—"

Gideon bounded out of his chair. "An apprentice? Good God, that's unthinkable. You don't have to go back. I don't know what I'll do with you, but not that. Go. Go now. Get some sleep."

Cowed by this unexpected outpouring of anger, Peter quickly left the room, forgetting the other reason he had come downstairs. He had wanted to ask his father to put in a word for Simon.

The next morning Gideon left the house to pay a call on his brother-in-law. As he had hoped, Hugo was not at home, and Clare was not yet receiving visitors. He left a brief message to the effect that he would find Sir Hugo in Rosemary Lane and returned to his curricle. He had already accomplished the object of his visit. Rakes, the Prebble coachman, had previously worked for Fiona's father, and Gideon, who wished to trace the Woodbourn servants—the most probable witnesses of a will, had one been written—had obtained what little information Rakes had to give.

It was meager enough in truth. Bridges, Mr. Woodbourn's solicitor, had offices somewhere in Chancery Lane. As far as Rakes knew, he had never visited Mr. Woodbourn at Barstead. The housekeeper was dead. The valet, whose name was Maddox, had retired somewhere in Kent, and Rakes knew nothing of the whereabouts of the other servants. No, wait a bit . . . Margaret, one of the parlormaids, had gone off to London after Mr. Woodbourn's death. Pleasant woman. She had a brother somewhere in Clerkenwell, a baker or pastrycook or something of the sort, he'd lost his wife and Margaret went to keep house for him. What was her surname now? Slattery, that was it, her brother would be named Slattery. Or maybe it was Slater.

It was some hours before Gideon could put this information to use. He had several other errands, the first of which was to locate Hugo and find out how much damage had been done by the fire. It had been impossible to determine last night, though Gideon had learned to his disgust that Hugo did not employ a private watchman. The expense, Hugo had muttered, and Gideon had been hard pressed to hold his tongue. The matter would better be raised at the next partners' meeting.

Gideon found Hugo outside with one of the guards he had posted the night before. The wooden storage shed behind the house was completely destroyed, but the building itself, which was made of brick, showed little sign of damage. Inside the story was different. The room in which the unknown man had died was nearly gutted. Part of the ceiling had collapsed, exposing burned timbers in the rooms above. The front office was badly damaged as well, and the other rooms were filled with soggy, charred bales of goods awaiting shipment abroad. From the stench Gideon deduced that these included the cargo load of wool Woodbourn-Prebble had bought to ship to the Baltic ports.

Hugo accepted the papers Simon had retrieved from the fire with scant gratitude and kept repeating, "A disaster, it's a disaster." It was, of course, though not one beyond remedy. The building could be repaired. As for the damaged goods, their loss would be covered by insurance, though the delay in obtaining another cargo would put the company under some financial strain. "What am I to do?" Hugo cried to the empty space, as though an answer might be found in the blackened beams above his head. Gideon told him and only then learned the reason for his despair: Hugo had let the insurance lapse. "It was damnably expensive," he said in an aggrieved tone. "How was I to know some prig would take it into his head to force the door? Curse the bratchets!" This last was directed to a group of small boys who had eluded the guard and were now trying to explore the ruined building.

Gideon threw up his hands and went outside. The sky was gray, but after the darkness of the warehouse the day seemed unusually bright. The smell of the river came sharp to his nostrils. The boys, who had been ejected from the warehouse, ran off with jeering cries. Gideon remembered that there were other problems besides his own. A man had lost his life, and he needed to know why.

He sought out the guard, who was trying to keep onlookers at bay, but learned little more than that the police surmises of the fire's origin were probably correct. A thief had broken into the office, then stumbled and hit his head for his pains, oversetting his torch, which took a wicked vengeance for his act. Nothing was known of the man's identity. Gideon hoped that Adam's inquiries would fare better.

He drove to Bolton Street to offer his apologies to the Princess Sofia for the escapade in which Peter had involved her son, but she was not at home. He left his card and a hastily scrawled message, then drove to Chancery Lane to find Woodbourn's solicitor. Bridges proved to be an elderly man with failing eyesight, but his memory was quite clear. James Woodbourn had destroyed his will shortly after his son's death and had written no other, nor had he communicated with his solicitor in any way in the remaining months of his life. What, might he ask, was Lord Carne's interest in the business?

Gideon made an evasive answer and quickly concluded the interview, then turned his horses north to Clerkenwell and began the tedious business of tracking down a baker named Slattery or Slater. It proved to be Slater, and it was nearly three when Gideon found him in a small shop in Aylesbury Street. Slater was a thin, harassed-looking man who wore a deep frown, but he acknowledged cheerfully enough that he had a sister called Margaret; she might be found upstairs in the parlor, where she was entertaining a lady.

The word should have warned Gideon. As it was, he felt a shock of mingled pleasure and dismay when he was shown into the parlor and found himself looking into Fiona's clear gray eyes.

She had brought the Tassio boy with her. Simon jumped up at Gideon's entrance and asked eagerly after Peter, then, remembering his manners, apologized for his forwardness. Margaret, a pleasant, unassuming woman, murmured something about refreshments and left the room, taking Simon with her. The move showed considerable tact and allowed Gideon to explain his intrusion. "I confess I thought myself clever," he said with a rueful smile. "I spoke to your sister's coachman this morning and learned Mistress Slater's name and her brother's occupation. I have been half the day tracing him, and now I find you are before me."

"I have known Margaret all my life. I'm sorry, I should have told you, but—"

"You don't like to depend on anyone, and you wanted to do this yourself."

Fiona gave him a reluctant smile. "Precisely. But I'm afraid Margaret knows nothing of the will."

"Neither did Rakes. Your father's housekeeper is dead, but his valet is somewhere in Kent."

"Yes, Margaret told me he married a widow with a bit of property and is living near Greenhithe."

"Then bless Margaret for that bit of news. It should not be difficult to find him."

Fiona nodded, determined not to let him see that she had qualms about their partnership. It was galling to be in the position of accepting help from this man, the more so as there was nothing to take exception to in his present manner. He was much as he had seemed in the first days of their acquaintance, kind and gentle, with a trace of self-mockery to lend him sharpness. If she was not careful, she would find herself liking him once more, in danger of forgetting the things he had done.

She pushed these thoughts aside and asked about Peter. Gideon told her the substance of his son's late-night confession. "It's appalling," Fiona said. "I heard much the same story from Simon, though not in such harrowing detail. I'm glad you're not sending him back. I was afraid—"

"That I would insist he be a man? I'm not such a brute."

He was seated now a safe distance across the room and she was able to look at him without distress. "I didn't suppose you were, but I know men view these things differently."

"Not I. I've had my fill of terror." His voice held an unexpected note of passion. Fiona would have liked to ask him more—what had happened to him in the past five years, and how he had come by the disfiguring limp—but at this point Margaret and Simon reentered the room and the moment for asking was gone.

For the next few minutes they drank tea and devoured a seedcake that Simon pronounced wizard and that brought Fiona memories of her childhood. Gideon directed his attention to Margaret, drawing from her an account of the vicissitudes of her brother's business, the prospects of his son, who was learning the trade, and the character of the young woman who helped in the shop and would soon become the son's wife.

Margaret, Fiona saw, approved of Lord Carne, and so did Simon, who turned an eager face to his governess when Gideon offered to drive them home. Fiona had brought Simon to Clerkenwell in a hackney, not wanting to have her visit talked of among the Langley servants, and she could give no reason for refusing. "Thank you," she said. "If you will drive us as far as Oxford Street. I have a small commission to undertake for Simon's sister." She rose to take farewell of Margaret, promising that she would not let five years elapse before her next visit.

"I hope not," Margaret said. "At my age you get to thinking that time is short, and there's so much to be talked of. I hope you come again soon."

Surprised at the unspoken message behind these words, Fiona studied the other woman's face. "If there's something I should know, Margaret, you can tell me now."

Margaret glanced at Gideon with a worried frown, then turned to Fiona with a look of inquiry.

"It's all right," Fiona said firmly. "Lord Carne and Simon may hear anything you have to tell me. But perhaps we should sit down and be comfortable while you do it."

"It's about when you were brought to Barstead," Margaret said when they were settled. She looked suddenly doubtful. "Are you sure?"

"Quite sure."

"Very well." Margaret's hesitancy was gone. "I was there, you know. Mrs. Woodbourn had hired me just the week before. She said you were Mr. Woodbourn's ward, and that he'd gone to London to fetch you because your mother was dead and there was no one else to look after you."

"That's right." The story was vivid in Fiona's mind. Her mother had worked for a hatmaker, she had lost her position when her pregnancy became known, she had turned to the man who'd got her with child, and she'd not survived the birth.

"I don't think so," Margaret countered. "I had the story from Maddox, who went with your father to fetch you, and it wasn't to London they went, it was to France."

France? Fiona looked at her blankly. "My mother was a Frenchwoman?"

"As to that I couldn't say. Maddox, if you'll forgive me, was inclined to be above himself, and he wasn't about to waste his breath on a young girl hired for the nursery. But France was what he said when he came back, and I had no reason to doubt him, for Mr. Woodbourn was gone for several days, longer than it would have taken him to reach London and back. And London or France, Mrs. Woodbourn was so insistent that it never be talked of that I thought there was more there than they wanted to let on. I suppose they had their reasons, but it's always bothered me and I thought you ought to know."

"Oh, Margaret, I do thank you." Fiona's thoughts were in confusion. If her mother was French, why would her father have said she was English? And if she was English, why would he have sent her to France to have her baby? A hatmaker's assistant, without friends or family. The story was common enough and no disgrace at that, and her father had never been a wealthy man.

There were obviously secrets to be learned, and for the moment they drove out all questions about the will her father might or might not have made. Fiona took her leave of Margaret, followed Gideon down the narrow stairs to the ground floor which housed the bakeshop, and mounted the curricle which had been left in the care of a half-grown boy. She wanted no reminders of Gideon's physical presence, and Simon provided a welcome buffer between them on the narrow seat. To their credit, neither he nor Gideon referred in any way to the information Margaret had given her.

To whom could she turn for help? Certainly not Gideon. It was difficult enough to maintain an impersonal facade when they discussed the will. It would be quite impossible with a matter as personal as the question of her parentage. She searched her memory for clues that would tell her how to proceed. To whom would her father have confided nearly thirty years ago? And then, as Gideon turned the curricle into Oxford Street, the answer came to her: she would have to swallow her pride and call on Tom Constable.

Chapter Four

"You must advise me, Fiona, I am in the most terrible quandary." Alessa stood in the doorway of her governess's sitting room, her pale lavender skirt billowing slightly in the breeze from the open window.

Simon, who was curled up on the windowseat, looked up from his book long enough to cast a brief glance in his sister's direction. "Torn another flounce?"

Alessa pulled a face at him. "If you aren't going back to school—where you most certainly belong—I should think at least you ought to be conjugating Latin verbs or doing sums or something. Do come quickly, Fiona, Lord Parminter and Lady Lydia will be here at any moment."

Simon gave a derisive snort. Fiona set aside her own book, cast a brief glance at Simon—whose only response was a cheeky grin—and followed Alessa into the corridor. Alessa was very much on her dignity as they exited the room, but once the door was safely closed she tugged at Fiona's hand and fairly dragged her into her own chamber, a charming pink-and-white apartment which, despite all her maid's best exertions, rarely remained in an orderly state for more than an hour at a time.

"The quilted satin bonnet matches my spenceret, but I have the most lowering feeling that it makes me look like a round-faced little schoolgirl," Alessa said, flitting over to the cheval glass and staring critically at her reflection. Though she'd inherited her mother's high, wide cheekbones and large almond-shaped eyes, she was very conscious that her youthful features had not yet acquired that fine-boned elegance which characterized the princess. "The straw is much more dashing, but the plumes do not quite match my gown. As for the highland helmet—" She wrinkled her nose and turned back to her governess with a faintly rueful smile. "It may seem silly, Fiona, but there's no denying people notice such things. Besides, Lord Parminter—" Alessa colored and broke off, an action far more illuminating than anything she might have said.

Moving to the bed, Fiona surveyed the half-dozen headdresses strewn haphazardly on the silk counterpane, then crossed to the wardrobe and selected a hat from the near empty shelf. "Wear this."

Alessa stared doubtfully at the simple plaited straw. "It's dreadfully plain. I'm not a child any more, Fiona, whatever you and *Maman* think."

"I hardly consider you a child," Fiona assured her. "Ribbons and ruffles are for little girls. Nothing can be more elegant than simplicity."

Frowning, Alessa took the hat and settled it experimentally atop her dark ringlets. Fiona watched with well-masked amusement. Despite her words, she found it difficult to see Alessa as a grown-up young lady, but the simple lines of the hat did emphasize the maturity in her charge's features. Though Alessa's chin might still be rounded, it had the imperious tilt of a young woman who never quite forgot that her father had been close to the House of Savoy and that her mother's cousin was the Emperor of all Russia. This assurance, combined with a substantial dowry, connections to two royal houses, and an exotic beauty which set her apart from even the prettiest English girls, had made Alessa easily the most sought-after young woman of the Season.

Alessa surveyed the effect of the hat and gave a smile of unaffected girlish delight. "How very clever of you, Fiona. You always know what will look right. It's a pity governesses must wear such dreary clothes."

Giving Fiona an impulsive hug, she missed her rueful expression. Alessa broke away, carefully smoothed the lace on her spenceret, and was just drawing on her gloves when Christopher tapped at the door to say that Lord Parminter and Lady Lydia were awaiting her in the green parlor. After checking her reflection one last time, Alessa snatched up a parasol of pale blue shot silk, composed her features into an expression of suitably adult gravity, and swept from the room.

Fiona hesitated, then crossed to the window and glanced down into the street below. The straw-colored barouche and cream-colored pair drawn up before the house belonged to Lydia Barrington-Forbes, whose husband had once been Fiona's betrothed. Though Fiona had never pretended to love George, it was impossible not to feel some curiosity about the woman he had married. Fiona had met Lady Lydia briefly, as well her brother, the Marquis of Parminter, who had begun to figure so prominently in Alessa's conversation.

The two women were the first to come into view, descending the shallow stone steps side by side. As usual, Lady Lydia, a beautiful woman some seven years Fiona's junior, was dressed in the first stare of fashion, though Fiona noted with satisfaction that her poke bonnet trimmed with moss roses looked fussy beside Alessa's unadorned straw. Lord Parminter followed, his beaver hat held negligently in one hand so that Fiona had a good view of his burnished gold hair and broad shoulders. While the liveried footman handed Lady Lydia into the carriage, Parminter bent slightly forward to say something to Alessa, who looked up at him with all the radiant devotion of a girl in the throes of first love.

Fiona's throat constricted with remembered hurt. She knew that look, she'd worn it herself once at the mere mention of Gideon's name. Alessa was protected by every advantage of fortune and family, and there was no reason to think Lord Parminter's intentions were anything but honorable, yet Fiona could not like the marquis, who seemed to think far too much of himself and not nearly enough of Alessa. Then too, Fiona acknowledged as she moved from the window, she had a perfectly selfish reason to dislike the attachment, for it would be awkward if her charge married into the Parminter family. Still, she had known from the moment she'd arrived in London that she might have to face George. It was nothing on which to waste her energies at present.

The past five years had taught Fiona to make good use of her rare moments of free time. Ten minutes later she had spoken with Simon, donned a bonnet and shawl, and settled herself in a hackney which she directed to Upper Seymour Street. Fiona paid off the driver and rang the bell of a neat brick house, aware that there was a very good chance she'd be denied admittance. When she gave her name as Fiona Martin and asked to see Mr. Constable, the young manservant regarded her with such evident curiosity that for a moment Fiona was certain the scandal had preceded her. Then she realized that his interest was aroused not by her name but by the fact that a young unmarried woman was calling on his master. As he showed her into the parlor, Fiona was hard put to keep her countenance. She would have to apologize to Mr. Constable for the impression she'd left on his servants. Assuming, that is, that he consented to see her.

Fiona glanced around the parlor, a close room filled with the scent of an overly sweet potpourri. The fussy dark trellis wallpaper was new but looked precisely the sort of thing Mary Constable might have chosen. With any luck, Mrs. Constable and the children—who must be nearly grown by now—would be in the country, where they usually spent their summers. Mrs. Constable had been a friend of Charlotte, Fiona's stepmother, and was even less likely than her husband to receive Fiona.

Minutes later the door opened to admit the short, precise man who in so many ways was her father's exact opposite and yet had been his closest friend for more than thirty years. Tom Constable's sparse brown hair had more touches of gray than Fiona remembered, and his carefully pressed coat looked a bit strained about the middle. Otherwise he was unchanged, save that she'd never seen his features drawn into such a disapproving expression. He regarded her in silence for so long that at last Fiona spoke. "Thank you for agreeing to see me."

"This isn't meant to be taken as any sort of condonation," Constable cautioned, motioning her to a chair, "but I'm willing to spend a quarter-hour hearing whatever it is you've come to say."

If it was not as much as she'd hoped for, it was less than she'd feared. Mr. Constable had never been one to give his approval lightly, but he was a fair man. "I didn't come to make excuses or ask for sympathy," Fiona said as she seated herself. "I've learned that Uncle James may have lied to me, and I think I have a right to the truth."

"You think *James* lied to *you?*" For a moment Fiona thought he was going to berate her for her own deceit, but true to his word he waited for her to continue.

As usual, when she had something difficult to say, Fiona went right to the point. "What do you know about my mother?"

It was clearly not what Constable had expected to hear, and his surprise momentarily overcame his disapproval. "I thought James had talked to you about her years ago. I'm sure he told you more than I ever knew."

"He said she was a hatmaker's assistant in London who died giving birth to me. As far as he knew, she'd no living relatives."

Constable nodded. "So he told me as well. I've never had any reason to doubt him."

His look suggested that Fiona also had no business doing so, but she was far from convinced that Mr. Constable knew nothing more of her mother. It was one thing for her father to have kept her mother's identity secret from her. It was another for an impulsive young man of twenty-three to have concealed the truth from his best friend. "When did you first learn about me?" she asked.

71

Constable's expression hardened. "I said I'd listen to you, Fiona. I did not agree to answer a lot of impertinent questions which are not suitable—"

"For the ears of an innocent young girl," Fiona concluded. "But I am neither innocent nor young, and if nothing else, I think I deserve the truth."

"You were always too curious for your own good." Fiona thought she detected a faint trace of approval in Constable's voice, though perhaps she'd only imagined it. "To the best of my knowledge, James did tell you the truth."

"He didn't even tell me my mother's name," Fiona said softly.

"He didn't tell me either."

"But he did talk about her?" Fiona found she was nervous and began to draw off her gloves.

"Not until—" For a moment Constable had spoken almost freely, but now he checked himself, frowning. "I'm sure James told you whatever he thought suitable."

"Uncle James, as you know perfectly well, always avoided talking about anything in the least unpleasant," Fiona retorted, giving the second glove a rather vicious tug. "What he thought suitable may have had nothing to do with the truth."

"And you think that should influence me? Why?"

"Because you're an honest man."

Constable regarded her in silence for a long moment, then gave a slight shrug of resignation or acknowledgment and settled back in his chair. "The first time I heard of your mother was the night before James's wedding. We'd both drunk a bit too much. Much too much. I made some rather coarse remarks about setting up his nursery before the year was out, and James said he meant to start even sooner. There was a child—or there soon would be—and Charlotte had agreed to bring the baby into their household as soon as it was born."

"But—" Feeling rather stupid, Fiona stared at the stone-colored gloves in her lap. She'd always assumed her father had taken her because her mother had died. "Had my mother agreed to give me up to Uncle James?"

"So it would seem." There was a gruff note of sympathy in Constable's voice.

Fiona recognized the sympathy and the honesty behind it. Dispassionately and without prevarication, she told him what Margaret had revealed about her father's journey to fetch her from France. "You knew nothing of this?" she asked.

Constable shook his head. "I assumed the lying-in took place in London."

"So did I." Fiona leaned forward, the gloves now twisted in her hands. "Uncle James was hardly a secretive man and you were his best friend, yet he didn't tell you about my mother until he was too well disguised to know what he was doing. He didn't tell you that I was born in France, let alone explain why it was necessary for a shop-girl with no living relatives to go abroad in such secrecy for her lying-in." She drew a breath. "I'm quite sure my mother wasn't a shopgirl, and I'm no longer certain she died when she bore me."

Constable made no effort to deny her words, but neither did he speak. "I was born in June," Fiona continued, making an effort to recover at least a semblance of detachment. "Where was Uncle James in September of 1783?"

"Oh no, Fiona, now you really *do* begin to ask the impossible. I'll grant you there may be some mystery about your mother, though if you ask me, it's best to leave well enough alone. I've certainly told you all I know. To remember where a friend was one summer thirty years ago—"

"You'd both have been twenty-four. Not long down from Oxford. Didn't you often visit each other in the summer?"

"Not at that time. I was slaving away at the Admiralty, hoping for preferment. James was still a man of leisure and in my view woefully failed to appreciate his good fortune. He used to complain that it was deadly dull to be marooned in the country, especially on his meager income. Of course he was off on visits whenever possible—" Constable broke off, his brow creasing in sudden recollection.

"You think he was on a visit in the summer of '83?"

"I'm not sure if it was that summer—yes, it must have been, he came up to London not long after and we joked about having lived almost a quarter-century. Then the next spring he married Charlotte."

"Where was he that summer?" Fiona could hear the edge in her voice.

"Visiting Jack Bowder. I don't think you ever met Jack. He was at Winchester with us, more James's friend than mine, but I think James lost touch with him after he married. He was from Scotland, just over the border—near Castleton, I believe."

"Did he have any sisters? I'm sorry, Mr. Constable, but delicacy is a luxury I cannot afford."

"As I recall, Bowder came from a large family, but as to who was in residence that summer, I know no more than you. I'll say it again, Fiona. For your own good, I don't think you should pursue this."

"Could you ignore it?"

"I don't know," he said, with characteristic honesty. "But I wouldn't like to see you—disappointed."

"Thank you." Genuinely touched, Fiona sought refuge in drawing on her gloves before her feelings could overmaster her.

"I said I didn't condone your behavior," Constable told her, his voice gruff once more. "That doesn't mean I haven't worried about you these past years. I'm glad to see you're all right, and I know James would be too."

Fiona smiled bitterly. "You needn't pretend for my benefit. The last time I saw Uncle James, he refused to speak to me."

"Oh, I don't deny he was angry. But the last time *I* saw him it would have been difficult to say which was uppermost, his anger or his worry about what had become of you."

Fiona was surprised at how much this improved her spirits. She gave Constable a brief explanation of her whereabouts in the past five years, omitting Mr. Camford and the forged references, stressing the advantages of her situation, and avoiding her fears for the future. None of this prevented Constable from offering her his assistance, which Fiona firmly declined. His salary as a clerk at the Admiralty was not large, and he had four children to provide for, three of them daughters. She asked no further questions about her mother, though she did inquire about the will. Constable knew nothing, though he admitted he would not be surprised to learn that his friend had made another one. When Fiona finally rose to go, he said simply, "Be careful."

Fiona smiled and pressed his hand. "Dear Mr. Constable. If nothing else, the past five years have certainly taught me that."

Warned by the flint and chalk quarries that he was nearing Greenhithe, Gideon turned his curricle into the yard of the Red Lion, a half-timbered inn on the outskirts of the town. Experience told him that he would learn far more about the local residents here than at a larger establishment in Greenhithe proper.

He was greeted by the pungent smells of ale, roast meat, tobacco, and wine. One glance about the taproom, with its dark-paneled walls, smoke-stained brick fireplace, and customers who all appeared to regard the Red Lion as a second home, told Gideon that he had chosen well. The cheerful, balding man behind the bar, who seemed to be the innkeeper, greeted him with alacrity. Gideon introduced himself as Charles Glenden, solicitor with Glenden, Glenden & Markby, seeking Mr. Maddox about a matter of business. Adam had helped him devise the identity, saying that it was just like old times and in the same breath lamenting that a disguise which didn't require an accent, let alone a foreign language, and which necessitated clothes only slightly more sober than those Gideon customarily wore was a woeful waste of their talents. Still, even Adam admitted that the neatly printed card was a nice touch. People always had more faith when they saw things in print.

The innkeeper was quite taken in, though judging by his open face he was not much of a test. Mr. Maddox, he said, lived little more than a mile away, but he always stopped by at three o'clock, and as it lacked but half an hour of that time perhaps Mr. Glenden would prefer to wait for him here. Gideon agreed—the interview might be easier here than at the Maddox home, where he would also have to contend with Mrs. Maddox—and ordered a pint of ale. He put the half-hour wait to good use, learning that Mr. Maddox was very affable if (in the words of a thin man who appeared to be some sort of shopkeeper) a bit inclined to put on airs, considering he'd once been in service. Still, he made Mrs. Maddox very happy and they were all pleased because her first husband had been inclined to drink which, the innkeeper said, he could not like, no matter how good it had been for business.

When Maddox made his appearance, not a minute after the clock struck three, the innkeeper introduced Gideon like an old friend. This was all to the good, for Maddox was plainly not the trusting sort. Gideon appraised him as they shook hands: the well-cut coat of light green cloth which suggested that he wished to see himself as a man of leisure, the comfortable girth and well-tended hands which indicated that he was able to indulge that wish, the shrewd eyes which hinted that he had not entirely forgot his origins and was determined to guard his hard-won place in the world.

Gideon bought a round of ale and they carried it to a scarred but well-scrubbed deal table by one of the mullioned windows. He would have preferred to wait until Maddox had drunk the pint before launching into his story, but Maddox did not take so much as a sip before saying, "Can't imagine what business you have with me, Mr. Glenden. It's years since I've been to London."

"You're a fortunate man," Gideon returned with a smile. "This corner of the world is infinitely more tranquil. I should explain that I have recently been employed by Sir Hugo Prebble in regard to matters pertaining to Woodbourn-Prebble, formerly Woodbourn & Woodbourn. I understand you were once valet to Sir Hugo's father-in-law."

Maddox's manner went from shrewd to actively wary. "I never had anything to do with the business."

"Quite so." Gideon downed a long draught of ale. Maddox had still not touched his tankard and showed no inclination to do so. "This has to do with Mr. Woodbourn's personal affairs. As I'm sure you know, Mr. Woodbourn destroyed his will when his son died," Gideon explained, subduing the impulse to reach for the ale again. It was difficult to speak with equanimity about someone for whose death you were responsible.

"So I heard," said Maddox, his face wooden, "though naturally it wasn't any of my business."

"Naturally." Gideon had regained his composure. "But as a member of the household you must have been aware that no other will was found after Mr. Woodbourn's death. Recently I chanced to be going through some of his old papers and I came across a note which suggests he may have made a second will after all."

Maddox's shoulders tensed, as if he was preparing to defend himself, with his fists, if necessary. "I wouldn't know anything about that, Mr. Glenden."

"It's a ticklish business," Gideon acknowledged, with the smile that had disarmed cautious Spanish peasants, suspicious French officers, and occasionally even Tory politicians. "I should perhaps say that no second will could change any bequests which Lady Prebble made out of her father's estate." Gideon was not entirely sure on this point, but he quieted his conscience with the thought that Fiona would not let her father's valet suffer.

Maddox's shoulders visibly relaxed. He took a sip of ale and stared thoughtfully into his tankard. "See here, Mr. Glenden, you wouldn't happen to know what became of Miss Martin, would you? Mr. Woodbourn's ward she was, but she—ah—she left home not long before he died."

There was genuine concern in his voice. Unsure of how the valet felt about Fiona, Gideon had hesitated to mention her, but now he saw how that concern could be used to his advantage. "I am endeavouring to locate her. I understand she received nothing on her father's death, but if I am right about the second will, Mr. Woodbourn may have made some provision for her."

"And you say Sir Hugo engaged you to do this?" Maddox asked, plainly dubious.

"Not exactly." Gideon smiled again. "I said Sir Hugo had employed me in matters regarding Woodbourn-Prebble. In the course of my work, I became aware of the possibility of a second will. Sir Hugo could hardly forbid me to look for it. It isn't often one gets a chance to right an old wrong, Mr. Maddox. I'd like to see justice done." Gideon was surprised at the genuine conviction in his voice. Though he was a good dissembler, normally he could not fool himself, yet he sounded quite as he might have ten years ago, when he still believed it was possible to make some difference in the world.

Maddox nodded slowly, took another sip of ale, swirled the contents of his tankard, and finally spoke. "Always thought it was odd that it didn't come to light. Still, as I said, it wasn't my place to ask questions."

"Do I take it you have reason to believe there could be a second will?"

"Well, yes and no . . . it was a funny business. Mr. Woodbourn had us into his room the night before he died, me and the housekeeper. Wanted us to witness something. Can't say for certain that it was a will, but that's what I suspected."

"Did you mention it to Lady Prebble?"

"Oh yes, right after the funeral. In a rare taking, she was. Afraid he'd left some of the money away from her, if you ask me." Maddox paused, as if suddenly remembering that Gideon was employed by Lady Prebble's husband.

"Yes," Gideon murmured, "I've had some dealings with Lady Prebble and I'd say she's not—not an easy woman."

"That she isn't," Maddox agreed fervently. "Still, she did look for the will. Fair took the house apart. But nothing came to light and finally she said we'd best forget about it." He shifted on the oak settle. "It was her father, mind, Mr. Glenden, and if she was satisfied, who was I to make trouble? I was already promised to Mrs. Maddox then. I had to think of my future."

"To be sure," Gideon agreed affably.

Maddox seemed relieved to be over the worst of it. "We had some anxious moments when we learned there wasn't a will, I can tell you," he said, taking another swig of ale. "Mr. Woodbourn could have been trusted to provide for us, but Miss Clare—well, as it turned out she was more than generous, which was quite a surprise to us as knew her when she was a girl. Regular little termagant, she was. Mother spoiled her, of course. She wasn't a bad mistress, Mrs. Woodbourn, but she'd a blind spot where Miss Clare was concerned."

The ale was making Maddox expansive and the conversation was headed exactly in the direction Gideon wished. "And Mr. Woodbourn?" Gideon inquired, leaning back against the settle in a comfortable manner to indicate that the business portion of the talk was at an end. "He favored the boy, I suppose."

"Yes, well, poor Master Jamie was his heir, of course. Mr. Woodbourn hadn't much time for the girls, but if you ask me, it was Miss Fiona who was his favorite. Fair drove Miss Clare wild."

"Ah." Gideon coughed. "Both Sir Hugo and Lady Prebble have been somewhat vague as to Miss Martin's exact connection to the family. Naturally when a gentleman makes himself guardian of a child one is inclined to think—"

"This is more than assumption, Mr. Glenden. Why—here, your tankard's empty. No protests now," he said, signaling for the innkeeper, "I insist on buying the next round."

The taproom was not busy, but the landlord was a talkative man, so Gideon was forced to wait some ten minutes before the pewter tankards were refilled and Maddox took up the story. "As I was saying, it's no mere speculation about Miss Fiona. I was there when Mr. Woodbourn fetched her." He paused, then added with a good sense of drama, "From France."

"France?" Gideon affected a very creditable look of surprise. "The mother was a French girl, then? She went home to have the child?"

"No, I fancy it was more to get away from her people." Maddox was warming to the story. "Mr. Woodbourn never talked about it, of course. We took a wet nurse along with us, Ellen, her name was, pretty thing, younger than they usually are, which made the journey a mite more enjoyable, if you get my meaning. Died having a child of her own not five years later, more's the pity." He paused for a moment, as if to honor Ellen's memory, then shrugged off this burst of melancholy. "I waited in Boulogne, see, while Mr. Woodbourn and Ellen went to fetch the child from a small village nearby. They found Miss Fiona with another wet nurse, a French woman, who told Ellen she'd collected the child from a house off in the country somewhere—and not a simple cottage, mind you."

"A rented house?" Gideon inquired with casual interest.

"I suppose it would have to be, for this French woman told Ellen the mother was an English lady who called herself Mrs. Smith. I ask you! You'd think the quality would have more imagination. Well, apparently this Mrs. Smith was young and very beautiful. She'd been staying in France for some months with her own mother, but they both planned to return to England."

"Quite a romantic story," Gideon murmured. "Did you ever hear anything of Mrs. Smith again?"

"Not a word. I doubt she ever saw Miss Fiona, for Miss Fiona scarcely ever went farther than Dartford." Maddox shook his head at this lack of maternal feeling. "I'll say this for Mr. Woodbourn, he had the decency to provide for her. Leastways, he did until—I hope you find her, Mr. Glenden. She got herself in a bit of trouble, but she didn't deserve to be cut off without a shilling."

Gideon bought a third round of ale and lingered at the Red Lion for another half-hour but learned nothing more that might help locate the will or identify "Mrs. Smith." It was nearly seven before he returned to Dover Street, to be greeted by an excessively cheerful Adam. "Teddy skinned his knee, but Bab says it's nothing to worry about. Peter's been giving us a hand with the cleaning. He's a well-mannered lad, I must say, never would have guessed he's your son. Oh, and Beth's been asking when you were going to get home since four o'clock. It's the most I've ever heard her say at one time. Was it a successful trip?"

"I think so." Gideon relinquished his hat, knowing he should go up to the nursery, not sure he was ready to face it.

"They've just finished supper," Adam informed him, "but as it happens I've something to tell you, so perhaps you'd care to step into the library for a few minutes first."

"I knew there must be something to account for so much nauseating good humor," Gideon said, moving to the library door. Adam had already learned that the victim of the fire was a petty thief named Jimson, but Gideon was sure there was more than theft behind Jimson's visit to the warehouse. "Is it about the fire?" he asked, dropping into his favorite armchair.

"Can't be sure, but I'd lay you odds it is. Turns out our friend Jimson had a visitor just three days before he died. A stranger to that part of London. Quite a few people remembered him. He said his name was Brown, but of course I discounted that—I say, have I said something funny?"

"It's a long story," Gideon told him. "Go on. Were you able to trace Brown?"

Adam looked affronted. "It was child's play. Several people remembered that he left a hackney waiting during his interview with Jimson. A couple of boys were admiring the horses, which got the driver upset, so their older sister had to come and smooth things over and the driver got quite chatty. He told the girl he'd come from Bloomsbury Square. Once I knew that it was simple enough to go to the square and make inquiries."

"And?" Gideon inquired.

Adam leaned back in his chair, arms folded in front of him, a look of great satisfaction on his face. "Brown's real name is Potter, Arnold Potter. When he isn't holding furtive meetings in questionable parts of town, he's employed as a groom.

"And his employer's name?" Gideon inquired, though at the mention of Bloomsbury Square his suspicions had taken root.

Adam's air of satisfaction deepened. "George Barrington-Forbes."

Chapter Five

Gideon swore softly.

"Another stir in the pot. They're a havey-cavey lot, ain't they."

They? Gideon passed a hand over his face. Yes, of course. George, Hugo, and the golden Parminter boy. In Adam's eyes, George's foray into theft and destruction was one more bit of evidence, if evidence was wanting, of the parlous state of affairs at Woodbourn-Prebble.

"You'll have to take a hand, you know," Adam went on. "You can't go on sitting on your bum pretending it doesn't have anything to do with you."

Adam, damn his soul, was right. Gideon pushed himself out of his chair and made for the door. His leg was throbbing and his limp grew more pronounced.

"Here," Adam said, a note of concern in his voice, "leg giving you trouble again?"

Gideon grinned. "No, just a shameless bid for your sympathy."

"Now that's what I call base, appealing to a man's lower nature. When do you want dinner?"

"When I ask for it. I'm off."

"Where to?"

"To follow your advice. I'm calling on my wife's brother."

"Oh, well then." Adam seemed cheerful. "If you can't

hold your temper, I'll bail you out." He followed Gideon into the hall. "What about the young ones? Will you see them first?"

Gideon glanced up the stairs, then shook his head. "They'll keep. Tell them a story or something. I'll look in when I'm back."

Adam remained in the hall, staring thoughtfully at the closed door. He was brought out of his abstraction by the sound of light footsteps descending the stairs. "He's not coming up, then," Barbara said, pausing on the last stair but one.

"A bit of business came up."

She snorted. "Coward, that's what he is. Peter's glum and frightened and the small ones are confused. They need him."

"He has a lot on his mind right now." Adam's voice was defensive, and he realized that he very much wanted her to like Gideon. The knowledge surprised him. Adam was not used to courting women's favor, not unless he had an immediate end in mind, and that was hardly the case here. Barbara was a pleasant enough young woman, but her figure was plumper than he liked, and her face had little to recommend it save the dark eyes that had grown bright with annoyance and concern.

"More than his children? Doesn't he know what they've been through? What could be more important than that?"

Her voice had risen, and Adam's eyes went to the landing above. There were no small faces looking down at them, but he took her arm anyway and drew her into the library. He had to make her understand.

"It's money, mostly," he said when the door was closed behind them.

"Him? He's a viscount, isn't he? He's got this big house and a bigger one in Hertfordshire and Lord knows how much land. And he sends his son to Eton. You can't tell me he's out of blunt."

Adam threw up his hands in exasperation. "Why do you think we're camping here in half a dozen rooms with little meat and not enough candles? He goes off to war and leaves it all in his wife's hands and she turns off the estate agent and takes to the cards and runs through the money like water. And then she dies, and by the time he learns of it we're retreating from Burgos and there's a pointless little skirmish that leaves him stranded in an out-of-the-way village and for months it's a cast of the dice whether he lives or dies. Then, when he does come home, he finds Sir Hugo has closed everything up and turned off all the servants without even paying them what they've earned, and the estate has been neglected, and there's money owing everywhere."

Barbara was stubborn. "Still and all—"

"So what's Carne to do? He pays off the creditors, those he can find, though new ones seem to come after him every day. And he pays off Sir Hugo for Peter's school fees and other monies he lent his sister, and he tracks down the servants to see they get what they're owed, and then he finds his wife was in the hands of the moneylenders and that takes just about every groat he's got, and then he wants to do something about the estate, but that's been mortgaged, see, and the rents barely cover the interest." He paused for breath. "He's been back in the country not much over six weeks and he's done all that. He wants to do what's right for the children, but he doesn't know them. He's not seen them in five years and he's scared silly."

Barbara was fair, he'd give her that. She didn't credit everything he said, but she didn't cluck or give false sympathy either. "That's as may be," she said, her mild tone indicating that she did not intend to argue the matter further. "But you'll not make me believe a man like Lord Carne is afraid of anything."

Adam held his tongue. He'd given Barbara more information than he'd intended. He was not about to tell her that Carne was afraid of more than his children, or that he still woke at night from sweat-drenched dreams shouting sometimes the name of his wife but more often that of a woman called Fiona.

Gideon was relieved to be away from his children. Teddy and Beth treated him warily, like the stranger he in fact was, and Peter had exchanged barely a dozen words with him since their conversation the night of the fire. His uncertain eyes told Gideon that the boy regretted the burgeoning of intimacy between them.

It was not yet seven and still light, an unaccustomedly warm evening with an unpleasant hint of dampness in the air. Gideon turned into Berkley Square, making for the Prebbles' house on foot. He had driven the grays hard today and he kept no others. Besides, the walk would give him time to think about what Adam had told him and time to let his anger cool.

It was hard to think rationally about George Barrington-Forbes. They had known each other at university, but there had been no liking between them. In those days Gideon believed passionately in a great many things, while George, whose arrogant mockery found Gideon a ready target, affected to believe in nothing at all. And now Fiona stood between them.

He might have put it behind him, if Hugo had not persuaded Aline to stake everything her husband owned on the fortunes of Woodbourn-Prebble, if Hugo had not brought George and young Parminter into the partnership. Gideon struck the railing that fronted the house he was passing. Damn, damn, and damn! He wanted nothing to do with any of them, not George, not the blessed Adrian nor his canny cousin Melchett, not the slippery, would-be-clever Hugo. He should have stayed in Spain, pretending to the death that had eluded him for five endless years.

The action calmed him and he slowed his pace. He was in England now and had his children to see to. Think, Carne. Why would George pay a man to break into the Woodbourn warehouse? To steal, to learn something, or to destroy? None of these alternatives made any sense. The warehouse contained nothing but business papers to which George as partner would have access, and goods waiting shipment in which he had a financial stake. If the goods had been insured, Gideon would have suspected a swindle, but as it was there was no gain to be realized by their loss. George had no reason to bring about Hugo's ruin; they were close friends. George was far more likely to be seeking Gideon's downfall. Or George and Hugo between them. If so, it was a subtle game, and George's was the hand that guided it.

But it was Hugo who was going to give him answers. With this determination Gideon turned into Davies Street and climbed the stairs to the Prebbles' house, where he was told that Sir Hugo was at home but was preparing for an evening engagement. "If you would care to wait, my lord. . . ."

"I would not." Gideon brushed by the footman and climbed the stairs two at a time. He knew the house well, from the years when he and Aline had been frequent visitors and from the calls he had made since his return, but as he turned down the corridor leading to his brother-in-law's dressing room it occurred to him that the house was finer than he remembered, more polished, like a sleek cat that has spent long hours grooming itself. Strange that he had not noticed it before, but then tonight his thoughts had turned to money. The house bespoke a well-lined purse.

At the door of the dressing room he lifted his hand in a peremptory knock. The valet who answered his summons stared at him in astonishment, echoing the expression on his master's face. Hugo was in the process of tying his cravat, but at this intrusion he stripped off his neckcloth, now marred with creases where he had clutched it, and threw it to the floor. "Carne? What the devil—"

"We need to talk, Hugo. Now." Gideon glanced at the valet. "Alone."

Hugo measured the message behind the words, then turned to the valet. "Leave us, Baines. Tell Lady Prebble I'll be detained. Not that she'll be ready in any case," he added as Baines left the room. "Women never are, deuce take them. Sit down. It's not a convenient time, but I don't suppose that counts or you wouldn't be here."

Gideon ignored the invitation to sit. He had not seen his brother-in-law since yesterday morning at the warehouse when Hugo had been beside himself with anger and apprehension. He was angry and uncertain now, though he was covering it well, his handsome, somewhat florid face bent over a pile of neckcloths while he made a great show of choosing one that was suitably pristine. Gideon, his own anger rising, did not allow him time to retreat. "All right, Hugo. What damnable game are you playing?"

Hugo's head lifted sharply. He seemed disconcerted, but his voice was cool enough as he replied. "I don't have a glimmer of an idea what you're talking about."

"The fire, Hugo. Have you forgotten already? The fire that nearly took your nephew's life, to say nothing of young Tassio's. The fire that killed your creature Jimson. Though I suppose that doesn't bother you, does it; he wasn't of much account, and it was no more than he deserved."

Hugo's face was blank. Then his color rose. "By God, Carne, are you accusing me—don't you know what I lost? What *we* lost? Five thousand pounds at the least, or is that too paltry a sum to matter?"

"I wouldn't know. I couldn't put my hand on five hundred to save my soul."

"You have no soul, Gideon, don't make bargains with the devil." The door had opened during this last exchange, but neither man had noticed that Clare Prebble had come into the room. She was dressed for the evening in a gown of a shimmering blue that reminded Gideon of a peacock's breast, she wore a sapphire necklace he could swear had once belonged to Aline, and over her creamy shoulders she'd draped a scarf of silver mesh. "What's going on? What do you want?"

Hugo seemed calmed by his wife's presence. "A misunderstanding, I presume," he said with heavy irony. "Gideon seems to believe I had a hand in the fire."

"You? Monstrous." Clare turned to Gideon, challenge in her voice. "Why would he?"

In that moment Gideon was reminded that Clare was Fiona's sister. It was not just the fineness of her features but the proud set of her head and the controlled passion in her voice. Fiona had them too, pride and passion, though her surfaces were all cool. "I was hoping," Gideon said, "that Hugo would tell me."

"I have nothing to tell you." Hugo picked up a neckcloth at random and turned to the mirror, tying intricate folds with practiced fingers. Then he turned back to Gideon, spoiling his pose of unconcern. "Good God, do you think I wanted this?"

"I rather think you did. Though perhaps not the fire. Perhaps the appearance of theft is all you were after. The question is, why?"

Hugo had abandoned his neckcloth, which now hung in dispirited folds around his fleshy neck. "By God, Carne, do I have to call you out?"

"Stop it, both of you," Clare snapped. "Gideon, you're not a fool. What is it you suspect? What is it you know?"

He debated asking her to leave, to let it be between Hugo and himself, but he realized Clare might not be in her husband's confidence. And if not, she might be an ally. "A man named Jimson," he said evenly. "They found his body after the fire was out, in the back office of the warehouse. There wasn't much left of it, but enough to identify him by."

She made a gesture of distaste.

"The man died, Clare. His life may not have been worth much, but it was all he had. He was a prig, not a very clever one; he'd seen the inside of Newgate more than once. He wasn't a man given to association with his betters, but three days before he died, a man called Brown came looking for him."

"So?" Clare was growing impatient with the story.

"So of all the unpromising spots in this benighted metropolis, why did Jimson pick on Woodbourn-Prebble? You kept no money there, did you, Hugo?"

"Little enough," Hugo admitted.

"He wouldn't have done it if money weren't involved. I think the money came from Brown."

"You're saying Brown hired him to torch the warehouse? It makes no sense."

"A competitor?" Clare suggested.

Hugo considered it. "No, that's ridiculous." He looked at Gideon. "You know more, don't you? You know who Brown is."

"I do," Gideon said, watching them closely. "Brown's name is Arnold Potter. He's one of the Parminter grooms."

Clare's hand went to her throat. "Parminter?"

"Not the marquis. Potter works for Barrington-Forbes."

It was a moment before Hugo could take it in. "You're telling me that George—no, he wouldn't. By all that's holy, I won't believe it."

George and Hugo had been friends for years in one of those unlikely pairings that defy expectation. George was by far the cleverer of the two, but Hugo had a shrewdness that served him almost as well. It was this friendship that had taken George to the Prebble estate in Hertfordshire and led to his meeting with Fiona and everything that had followed. It was this friendship that had induced George to put money into Woodbourn-Prebble.

Gideon listened carefully to Hugo's protests. His brother-in-law might be shrewd, but he was a poor dissembler. Gideon would swear he knew nothing of Jimson. He glanced at Clare but saw only shock. Then her face closed and she drew a little apart from her husband.

"All right, Hugo," Gideon said when the other man grew silent. "You have my apologies."

"I would think so," Clare said in a cold voice. "I think you'd better leave, Gideon. You've done enough damage tonight."

"I had no intention of doing damage, madam. I sought only the truth."

"You brought nothing but lies."

"Lies? Why not? What else have I ever heard in this sorry business? Forgive me, I should not be speaking to you, this is between your husband and me." He turned back to Hugo. "I want out, Hugo. I've asked you before, I'm asking you again. I don't care what you're up to. I don't even care what George is up to. I want nothing more to do with it. Buy me out and let's have quit."

"I can't." A muscle twitched in Hugo's cheek.

Gideon looked at him steadily. "Parminter can."

"No!" The exclamation came from Clare. She brought her voice under control. "Why should he?"

"Because I might be tempted to tell this nasty little story at the inquest. Because his sister's husband is involved. Because it would be unpleasant for all of you." Even as he made the threat, Gideon knew it was useless. Hugo had borrowed to the hilt, Parminter's estates were vast but his debts outran his income, and though George's wife had money, her marriage settlement gave

91

him no access to the principal. Only Magnus Melchett had ready gilt, and he was unlikely to put more of it into what was proving a dubious enterprise. Still Gideon waited, hoping Hugo would see a way out.

There was none. Hugo had regained command of himself and he told Gideon this bluntly. He told him several other things. The story of George's involvement was no more than supposition. There was no real proof, was there? No, he'd thought as much. Why blame Aline's brother when he had only been trying to help a sister deserted by her husband? They were in this together now. Gideon's only hope of saving his fortune lay with Woodbourn-Prebble.

"And if you persist with this absurd fabrication," Clare added, "no one will believe you. You aren't exactly in good odor, Gideon, or have you forgotten?"

The veiled threat to Fiona undid Gideon. He couldn't fight them like this, not now. But they must be made to do his work. He ran his hands through his hair and sighed deeply, giving a passable imitation of a man preparing to be reasonable. "All right, Hugo, we're in it together. But if my future is at stake, so is yours. The man calling himself Brown was attached to a house in Bloomsbury Square, and he looked like Potter. That's too much coincidence for me to swallow."

A shadow of uncertainty passed across Hugo's face. "There's an explanation, there's bound to be," he said as though he would convince himself. "I'll talk to George."

The seed was sown. It was as much as Gideon could hope for. "Then I'll take my leave. Forgive my rudeness, Clare. I've been a soldier too long." He took her hand and raised it briefly to his lips, then quickly left the room.

His departure left silence in its wake. Clare was unsettled by Gideon's accusations and by his last unaccustomed bit of gallantry. Hugo returned to the problem of his neckcloth.

"Can you be sure of him?" Clare asked.

"He'll be all right." Hugo's hands fumbled and he stripped off the cloth and took another. "By God, I wish we were rid of him. I wish we'd never brought Aline into it."

"We had to," Clare reminded him. We needed the money."

Adam was waiting for Gideon when he entered the house, a folded piece of paper in his hand. "This arrived earlier. Barbara took it, but with the fuss about Teddy she forgot to give it to you.

Gideon held out his hand for the message and slit the unfamiliar seal. "It needs an answer," he said. "You'll have to go round at once."

"Here, I've not had my dinner."

"Privation's good for the soul." Gideon went to his desk and penned a note to Sofia Langley, the Princess Sofia, to the effect that he and Peter would be happy to call on her the next morning before the inquest. "To the Langley house in Bolton Street," he said to Adam who was hovering over him. "No answer required. Don't dawdle."

"You want dinner?"

Gideon grinned. "I'll wait for you." He followed Adam out of the room and made for the stairs, taking them two at a time. His reluctance to confront his children was, he knew, a form of cowardice, but it was more than that. He didn't know what to say to them and they gave him no opening. Well, tonight was different. He would diligently inquire into Teddy's injuries, he would tell Peter they would attend tomorrow's inquest in company with young Tassio and his mother, and as for Beth—well, two out of three was a start.

It was nine when Gideon and Peter arrived at the Langley house the following morning, a ridiculous hour for anyone as fashionable as the princess, though it was the hour she had named. The inquest was set for eleven and, the princess had indicated in her note, they would need time to talk about the evidence the boys were to give. What she meant, of course, was that they should make sure their stories tallied. The princess, Gideon suspected, was a careful mother and she wanted no unpleasant surprises.

They were shown immediately into a small parlor hung with sea-green silk, where they found not the princess but the Tassio boy and the man who was now his stepfather. Michael Langley was a diplomat who had spent most of his adult life abroad, but Gideon had met him in the past and Langley, a clever, urbane man with an uncanny memory for names and faces, remembered the occasion at once. "It must be nearly fifteen years," he said, offering Gideon his hand. "You were Robert Melchett's secretary then, and he said you had great promise. You've been away, haven't you? I have myself, though with Bonaparte's stranglehold on the Continent I don't travel as much as I used to. This is Peter, isn't it? I'm sorry not to have been here when it happened. Distressing matter all around. I'd like to hear Peter's story."

They spent the next hour going over it. Langley proved adept at extracting information, and under his gentle but persistent questioning, Peter found he recalled more of that evening than he'd told his father—the position of the furniture, and the location of the ledgers, and the route the fire was taking. Peter's recollection did not quite tally with Simon's, but Langley told them to stay with what they remembered. "If you didn't view things differently, it would look like collusion. It's up to the coroner to use what you have to report as he sees fit."

At ten o'clock Simon's mother made an appearance. It was the first time Gideon had seen her and he silently congratulated Langley on his good fortune. The princess was a beautiful woman, slightly built, with delicate, proud features and a mass of golden hair. Langley was very careful of his wife, and Gideon realized with a start that her gently swelling belly, not quite concealed by the folds of her amber silk dress, indicated she was with child.

Both she and Langley accompanied Simon to the inquest, which was held at the Swan, a small public house some two hundred yards from the Woodbourn-Prebble warehouse. The matter was dispatched in less time than Gideon had expected. It was not a case that aroused much interest, save for the presence of a lady of quality in the tavern, and Jimson had no one to mourn for him. The coroner and the jury inspected the ruined building, then heard the testimony of the surgeon who had examined the body, the watchman who had apprehended the two boys, and Simon and Peter. Hugo was present, but none of the other partners, and neither Hugo nor Gideon was called. The fire itself was of little interest save as it related to Jimson's death. The surgeon was quite clear on this point. Jimson had died from a blow to the head, occasioned by a fall against the iron grating of a stove. In his opinion, the man had stumbled and overturned his lantern as he fell. He was dead before the fire reached him.

There was nothing for the jury to do but return a verdict, strongly suggested by the coroner, of death by misadventure. Hugo withdrew a handkerchief and wiped his forehead, then stopped to say a few words to Gideon and Peter. He was obviously angling for an introduction to the princess, but Langley was eager to take his wife out of the fetid air of the tavern and would not remain for an exchange of courtesies. The boys were beside themselves. They had not received so much as the hint of a reprimand for their entry into the warehouse, and they had been warmly commended by the coroner for their presence of mind and their invaluable accounts of what they had seen.

When they returned to Bolton Street, Langley left for a meeting, the boys disappeared, and Gideon and the princess retired to the green parlor to discuss the matter of Peter and Simon's schooling. The princess was not inclined to send her son back to Eton. If this was how English gentlemen were made, she would much prefer that Simon remain a Savoyard. He had been doing very well under Miss Alastair's tutelage, and for the time, at least, that was where he would remain. She was glad that Lord Carne concurred in her sentiments. Her husband did as well. He was the wisest of men, so she knew that her decision was right. Her only concern was that Simon would be deprived of the companionship of boys his own age. If Lord Carne's son, who seemed a charming boy, was to remain at home, perhaps he would like to take his lessons with Simon.

Gideon could not do other than accept her offer. Fiona might not care for the arrangement, but it would be a blessing for Peter and, Gideon suspected, for Simon as well. The boys accepted the news with ill-concealed elation, and Fiona, who'd been summoned to the parlor by the princess, expressed her pleasure as well. Gideon did not dare meet her eyes, but before he took Peter away he found a pretext to take her aside and arrange a meeting for the following day. He'd seen her father's valet, he said, and they would have to talk.

The next morning Gideon proposed to the children that they walk to the Serpentine in Hyde Park. Barbara, who was to accompany them, appeared to be delighted with this arrangement, but the children were subdued as they set out, as if feeling as awkward at this public declaration that they belonged to Gideon as he did himself.

They looked, he thought, abysmally thin, as though they had lost spirit as well as flesh. Teddy, small for his seven years, held himself resolutely aloof. Beth, three years younger, was nearly as tall as he. They were both outgrowing their clothes. Aline's fine features could be traced in Beth's face, though her straight, fair hair and gray eyes did not come from her mother. She walked a little apart from the others, talking softly to herself, and now and again Gideon caught her eyes upon him. Peter, as quiet as the others, stayed close beside his father. Gideon had assured him that he would not be going back to Eton, but he had not yet told him he might not be going back to school at all. An evening with his accounts had convinced Gideon that even this might be beyond him, a realization that contributed to his feeling of helplessness. If he could not provide for his children, what else did he have to give them?

When they reached the park, Beth gave a shout and ran on ahead, and Teddy, after a moment's hesitation, joined her. Peter looked after them with such longing that Gideon told him to run after and keep an eye on them. "They'll be all right, won't they?" he said to Barbara.

"They'll be right enough, sir. I fancy they're used to being on their own, and it's good for them to use their legs. Shall I go with them?"

"Yes . . . no, wait a moment." He'd caught sight of Fiona and Simon a short distance away. "That's Peter's friend, the Tassio boy. Take him to find the others."

Barbara had been feeling more charitable toward Lord Carne since her talk with Adam two nights before, but she was hard put to conceal her disappointment. Lord Carne was not interested in the children after all. The outing was nothing but a contrivance to allow him to meet—well, she carried herself like a lady and she was accompanying the young prince, so she must be the Miss Alastair whom Peter had talked about. Strange that Lord Carne would be interested in a governess, though from what she'd seen of the household since she joined it three weeks ago, differences in station didn't count with him. It was just as well. Lord Carne needed a wife, and if what Adam said was true, he could not afford to be particular. It was some minutes later—she'd met Simon and was walking with him to the water, where the other children were playing—that it occurred to her that the contrived meeting might be related to Peter's lessons and have nothing to do with Lord Carne's private life.

Gideon's private life was far from his mind, though he could not deny the rush of pleasure he felt when he saw Fiona. "Thank you for coming," he said. "I had hoped to see you at the inquest—"

"I was with Lady Alessandra. The princess wanted her occupied. Alessa has shown far too much interest in Simon's escapade for her mother's peace of mind."

"A difficult young woman?"

"Eager for experiences, even vicarious ones. And quite determined to have them. It's a failing of the young." Fiona felt suddenly awkward and turned her head away. She had not been young, but her eagerness and determination had quite matched Alessa's and had undone her. She walked slowly down the path, forcing him to fall in beside her. She had not meant to be easy with him. That road led to danger, as she knew to her cost. Even now his nearness disconcerted her. She found herself aware of his scent and the way that sun and wind had roughened the texture of his skin. He offered her his arm, but she affected not to see it and moved slightly away.

"I saw Maddox," he said, clasping his hands behind his back to signal that he would respect her wishes. "He asked after you."

Fiona permitted herself a slight smile. "I knew him all my life, but he always kept to himself. How is he?"

"He's done well for himself and is anxious to keep it that way." Gideon paused, wondering which piece of information to bring up first. "As you suspected, your mother wasn't a French girl. She was English, and she'd gone to France with her own mother. A small village in Picardy. They'd taken a house there and were living comfortably."

Fiona drew in her breath sharply but said nothing.

"They called themselves Smith. Maddox was left at Boulogne to await your father's return and didn't actually see them. He had the story from the wet nurse your father took to France with them. Unfortunately the woman is dead and we can't question her directly. She got the story from the French nurse, who said your mother was young and uncommonly handsome and planned to return to England shortly. That's all Maddox knew of the matter."

It was more than enough. It confirmed everything Fiona had suspected. Her father had lied to her, but why? Her mother had not been a penniless nobody; she had been a woman of some consequence. She had not died in childbirth. She had given her daughter away and had never, to Fiona's knowledge, sought to learn what had become of her.

It was not a story she wanted to share with Gideon. It was not a story she wanted him to know. He had no right to intrude into her life in this way, not into something so private and so important. Fiona schooled her features into some semblance of composure and pretended he had not spoken of her parentage. "When you went to Greenhithe you hoped to learn something about my father's will."

"Yes, and I did." Gideon ignored the implied rebuke. "There was almost certainly a second one. Maddox witnessed a document the night before your father died, though he didn't know its contents. He told Clare about it after the funeral, and she took the house apart looking for it. Maddox was as upset as she. He'd expected to be pensioned off, and without a will he knew he'd have to rely on Clare's benevolence."

She stopped and looked at him. "And?"

"Your sister surprised him. She was generous. It doesn't sound like Clare, does it?"

"No. Almost as if—"

"As if she didn't want any further search to be made. What would he have done with it, Fiona? I saw Bridges and he knew nothing of a second will."

"He didn't send it to—I spoke to a close friend of my father's, and he denied any knowledge of it. It must be at Barstead then. If it exists at all."

"It exists." He gave her a reassuring smile. "Sheer justice demands it."

Fiona laughed. "If justice does, no one will listen. I wonder what happened to Barstead," she went on in a thoughtful voice. "Clare and Hugo might have sold it, and the furniture as well."

"Or let it. I doubt they'd leave it to lie fallow without turning a penny. I'll find out."

"And then we'll have to devise a way to get into the house. It will be rather like a hunt for treasure." A shout from the riverbank turned her attention to the children who were clustered about some newly found prize.

"I hope," Gideon said, "that having Peter come to Bolton Street will not be a great trial."

"Peter? Not at all. Simon needs a friend, and I daresay Peter does as well."

"That's not what I meant."

"I know what you meant, Lord Carne." Fiona was determined to draw a clear line between them, and she did not intend to let him cross it. "I enjoy teaching children. I get along tolerably well with the Princess Sofia, and I suspect I shall even get along tolerably well with you."

Gideon smiled, but he knew he would have to be careful in Fiona's company. She could rouse him still, and for his own sanity, if not for hers, they would have to be no more than friendly strangers. "I go to Davies Street tomorrow," he said. "Hugo has asked for a meeting of the partners to review our losses in the fire. I'll find out what's become of Barstead."

Chapter Six

"Oh, it's you." Clare did not try to conceal her disappointment as she closed the library door and advanced into the room. She'd hoped to have a few words with Adrian before the partners' meeting began, but only Gideon was there. She had not seen him since the night he'd stormed into Hugo's dressing room and accused George of complicity in the fire, and she was still angry. "Hugo will be here shortly," she said. "He's with his purchasing agent, Morris, I think, I can never remember his name. Shall I order coffee?"

"Thank you, not for me."

"Or something stronger? No? Oh, very well, Hugo can deal with it. I don't know what the others will want."

She would have left then but for the chance that Adrian might still appear before Hugo joined them. Clare knew she was a fool. Adrian was chronically late, driving her to agonies of impatience, but she could not do without him. It had been three, no, four days since they'd been together, and she was determined to arrange an assignation.

Clare was in no mood to deal with Gideon. There had been a time when she'd liked him, for Gideon was a well-favored man with quite splendid shoulders and a good leg and dark, brooding eyes. She had tried to attach him once, with a humiliating lack of success —

which was just as well, for he was not a man one could be quite comfortable with.

Gideon's years on the Peninsula had changed him. He was leaner, there were deeper furrows in his face, and the inward look was more pronounced. But there was something more, a kind of quiet that gave him an inexplicable air of danger. That was nonsense, of course. War did strange things to men, and Gideon's last few weeks in England would put a strain on any man.

He seemed to be studying her, and she returned his look, sensing his challenge. A faint smile crossed his face. "You're looking very handsome this morning, Clare."

It was unexpected, and she could not help being pleased. She was going shopping and had dressed with care in a new carriage dress of lemon-colored sarcenet that fitted her admirably and a new tippet cloak made of bands of white lace and satin ribbons in different shades of yellow. Her hat, a straw with an upturned brim lined in white satin and trimmed with a small ostrich feather that curved down to meet her dark hair, might almost be called daring. But Clare had dressed for Adrian, not for Gideon Carne, so she ignored the compliment and brought up the matter that stood between them. "I hope you've given up that ridiculous accusation against George."

Gideon lifted his shoulders a fraction of an inch. "Hugo assures me there's no truth in it."

"Of course there's no truth in it. The groom, whatever his name is, was pursuing affairs of his own. A woman, you know the sort of thing. He doesn't remember speaking to that creature who broke into the warehouse, but whether he did or not, it's absurd to suppose it means anything at all. You have a suspicious mind, Gideon."

103

"It was a suspicious fire."

"It was a disaster. Do you have any idea how much money we've lost? The goods alone cost near five thousand pounds and would have brought us far more in return. Not one of the partners would have reason to destroy what could bring nothing but profit." She was angry now. "Unless you did it yourself, Gideon," she added deliberately. "Were you so ready to put aside your self-interest? Do you bear us so much ill will?"

He looked startled but made no defense, which was just what she'd intended. "You see, Gideon, where suspicions can lead."

He conceded defeat. "I am satisfied, Clare. The fire was an accident. And I bear you no ill will. On the contrary. I'm grateful for what you did for the children."

"We did what had to be done." Hugo had insisted, though it meant uncomfortable crowding in the nursery at Digby Hall and a most unwelcome expense, even without Peter's school fees. Those had come out of Aline's money, or at least Clare thought they had. Hugo had administered Aline's estate after her death, and what belonged to Aline and what to Hugo was no longer very clear. "How are you managing?"

"Well enough. I brought down the young woman you'd hired to help in the nursery. Barbara Runford. Didn't Hugo tell you?"

Clare shrugged. "I understand you're not sending Peter back to school."

"Not till I've sorted out my debts. You see, Clare, I do have a stake in the prosperity of Woodbourn-Prebble. In the meantime, he's doing lessons with the Tassio boy."

Fiona. Was that starting up again? Clare had never understood how her colorless sister had managed to attach two such devastatingly attractive men in the space

104

of a few short months: first George, who against all probability offered her marriage, and then Gideon, who did not make a habit of dallying with virgins. It would be monstrous if they were to resume that affair.

Gideon must have read her mind, for his next words were a denial. "It was not my doing. The princess requested it. You have to agree it's a connection to be encouraged."

Clare suspected he was mocking her. No, that was not like Gideon. Perhaps his years away had made him sensible, to say nothing of his current privations. It was, of course, a useful connection for Peter, and perhaps she could turn it to her own account. She'd yet to meet the exotic princess who had set London on its ear these past months, and Adrian had been no help at all. "And Fiona?" It was the first time her name had been mentioned between them. "Does she encourage the connection?"

Gideon hesitated. "I believe she would prefer that it had never been formed."

So they had not resumed their relationship. Had Fiona told the princess the truth about her past? No, she would never have been employed had she done so, and she must know that any sign of intimacy with Gideon would endanger her position. Fiona had been mad to throw away a future as George's wife, knowing such a chance would never come again. She was being more cautious now. Perhaps she'd the grace to feel guilt for what she'd done.

In the next moment Adrian and George were shown into the room and Fiona and her dirty little history seemed supremely unimportant. They exchanged the necessary commonplaces and then George, who must have known what she wanted, took Gideon aside. This left Clare free to say, with a modest show of surprise, that she'd had no idea it was so late, she would positively not wait any longer for Hugo, and would Lord Parminter be kind enough to escort her to her carriage. She took his proffered arm and left the room, concealing her triumph. She'd seen the admiration in Adrian's eyes and knew she would get exactly what she wanted.

The others watched them leave. "Women," George said. "Adorable creatures, but it doesn't do to put one's faith in them, does it?" Then without a break, "You've been asking questions about me, Carne."

Gideon ignored the jibe. "It seemed prudent to do so."

"But I rather take offense at the answers you found."

"You were free to offer others."

"The truth . . . such a rare commodity. I wonder, would you recognize it?"

"That comes dangerously near a challenge, George. Take care, I'm not yet fit for the ways of the ton. If I've offended you, I'm sorry. I'm quite prepared to accept your version of events. The fire was an unfortunate accident." But not the attempted theft. It was beyond all reason that a man like Jimson would have chosen the Woodbourn-Prebble offices for plunder, and Gideon had no intention of letting the matter drop.

"You've offended me indeed, but I'm a forgiving man." George moved to a mirror which hung between two windows at the end of the room and made a minute adjustment to his carefully tied cravat. "We were never really friends, were we? How could we be, you were always so intense about everything. It's a pity we seem fated to work together. Not the fate you would have chosen, nor I either, but dear Aline was so impulsive. She could never resist the lure of money."

Gideon felt the rage building behind his eyes. It had been like that at Albuera. Not during the battle—fighting left him cold as ice—but afterward, when the fortress was given up to rape and pillage and the mindless torment of the weak. His leg was throbbing and he took refuge in a chair. There was no point in getting angry. George took a wanton delight in probing the soft belly of the soul and could be deterred only by indifference. "We are all in this for money, George. I intend to protect what is my own."

"And I mine, though my share is small enough. I find it amusing. Adrian, dear boy, is far more serious about the matter. Aline persuaded Hugo to bring him in—or was it the other way around, I never can remember—and he has quite taken to it. His grandmother, I hardly need add, is appalled. The taint of commerce, you know, she is hopelessly behind the times and believes only in the sanctity of land. Ah, Hugo. Are we ready to begin?"

"Not yet, we're waiting for Melchett." Hugo had come into the room, followed closely by Adrian. Hugo was frowning. His face was showing signs of strain and Gideon concluded that the Woodbourn-Prebble agent had not brought good news.

They were a strange group to have come together in this enterprise. It had begun with Silas Woodbourn, an uncle of Clare's father, who throughout the middle decades of the last century had traded successfully with the Baltic countries and the German states. His nephew James had steadfastly refused Silas's offers of employment as a clerk—her father, Clare insisted, was a gentleman by birth—even though his own father had not been prudent and left him ill provided for. It was only when an unexpected legacy enabled James to join his uncle as a full partner that he had considered the possibilities of commerce. The buying and selling of goods on a large scale was an occupation to which a gentleman might aspire. Why, half the directors of the East India Company sat in Parliament, or so Clare had argued in the days when Gideon had first made her acquaintance.

On Silas's death, James inherited the older man's share and carried on the business alone. It had, Gideon gathered, been feast or famine with the Woodbourns. They lived well when they could and put up a defiant show when they could not, but of the three children in the household only Clare grew up with a genuinely acquisitive streak. She had already received her marriage portion, but when her father died she took everything else as well, what would have gone to Jamie and what had once been set aside for Fiona.

Gideon looked at the other three men in the room and tried to swallow his self-disgust. None of them would be here but for his own irresponsible acts. If Jamie had lived, Woodbourn & Woodbourn would belong to him, not to Hugo and his friends. It was only fitting that Gideon was tied to them now. Perhaps he could even undo some of the damage he'd caused.

Gideon knew nothing of what had happened to the Woodbourn company in the years he'd been away, save what Hugo had told him on his return. With Napoleon's efforts to blockade British shipping, trade had become precarious and was even more so since the war with America. But trade had to go on—no country could survive without it—and there were still ways to buy and sell. There had been losses, Hugo said: privateers, venal merchants, ships that were not as seaworthy as they were claimed to be. But he insisted that the company was sound and Aline's—Gideon's—investment secure.

Gideon doubted it. He did not think Hugo actively dishonest, but he did not trust his stewardship. How else could one account for the search for new capital?

"He said he'd be late," Hugo was saying. "He asked us to wait for him."

"What does he know?" This was from George.

Hugo looked worried. "I saw him the day after the fire and again after the inquest. He wanted an accounting of our losses."

"All neatly docketed, from one to infinity." George made a show of stifling a yawn. "Quite dreary. I hope he can cover them."

Hugo grunted and flung himself into a chair. George, who was already seated, stretched out his long legs and examined his well-polished boots. Adrian walked to the window and stared at a display of delphiniums in the garden. He seemed to be hugging a secret to himself. Gideon, who had not missed Clare's contrivances, assumed it had to do with Hugo's wife.

Magnus Melchett was the only one of the five partners who might be expected to find a way out of their problems. A distant cousin of the Parminters, he belonged to a minor and little regarded branch of the Melchett family, known chiefly for the imprudent marriages of its sons and the consequent small dowries of its daughters. Gideon had met him years ago and had thought him then a man of great force, but what he remembered chiefly was that Magnus did not like being cast in the role of poor relation.

Unlike his forbears, Magnus had done something about it. With an enviable singlemindedness of purpose, he set about making money. Reports on his activities differed, but everyone agreed that he was clever, not overly scrupulous, and very rich.

The Parminters thought him a traitor to their ranks, but it is hard to quarrel with success. When Magnus founded Melchett's Bank, he became almost respectable. So it was not surprising that, when Hugo pleaded for more capital, Adrian had gone to his cousin Magnus and offered him the opportunity to buy into

Woodbourn-Prebble. The question was, why had Magnus accepted?

A half-hour later, Gideon was no closer to an answer. Despite the passage of years, Magnus Melchett was much as he remembered him: a heavy face with a wide, thin-lipped mouth; a decided nose, not quite straight; heavy brows shading narrow gray-green eyes. The force that had marked the younger man was still there, but it was no longer a weapon to demolish opposition but a tool to be used, with precision, where it would be most effective. There was no touch of arrogance in his bearing and none of apology.

"The *Apollo* is sailing next week," Hugo said after reviewing their losses. "It's a full month before we expected, but they have to join the convoy or they daren't sail at all. How can we replace the goods in this time? It's insane. Morris has been to our usual suppliers and he's seen every other merchant in London, but it can't be done, there are no woolens to be had. Even if they could assure delivery," he went on, contradicting himself, "they insist on cash." His voice rose in outrage. "Cash! How can you run a business that way? It's these damnable rumors about the fire. Our credit's ruined, and we have no hope in hell of making good on what we've lost."

"Why not?" Gideon's voice was sharp with worry. "What are you trying to tell us, Hugo? There's a shipment of iron due from Riga, isn't that what you told me? And linens and other goods from Hamburg. You said they'd be profitable. Won't they?"

Hugo ran his hand through his hair. "How do I know? Things happen . . . accidents, pilfering, privateers . . . we might not be able to get our price. You can't count on anything in this world."

"And precious little in the next. I know. You've had bad luck, you were in debt. But you said that was all

110

in the past. Why shouldn't our credit be good? You've brought in Parminter and Barrington-Forbes, and now you've brought in Melchett and the slate's been wiped clean. Or has it?"

There was a moment of hesitation. "Near enough." Hugo glanced at Magnus, who was watching him without any sign of disquiet, save for his hands, which played with the chain of his watch. "There've been expenses," Hugo went on, "things we didn't expect. The partners were owed money."

Gideon raised his brows.

"Aline had drawn more than her share, it wasn't fair to ask the others to wait."

"You have a problem, Carne?" This was from George.

Magnus broke his silence. "We all have a problem. It's not insoluble. Though perhaps we need a more precise statement of our affairs."

"I'll do what I can, of course," Hugo said. Now that Magnus had indicated a willingness to help, he had regained some of his customary swagger. "Though you understand that it will be difficult. We lost some of the ledgers in the fire."

"Inconvenient. Very well," Magnus said, "bring me what you can. I need hardly say that in the circumstances we need some better system of accounting for our profits and losses. What has done for one will hardly do for five." He cut off Hugo's protest with a wave of his hand. "You're the senior partner, Prebble, but you no longer have a controlling interest. If you and the others object, tell me now. I'm willing to gamble, but I'm not a fool. If I'm to stay, I shall insist on some safeguards for my investment."

It was perilously close to an accusation, but it was George, not Hugo, who answered it. "We all want safeguards, Melchett. If you can find a way

111

to make us wealthy without risk, we'll applaud you."

Magnus raised his brows. "There's no wealth without risk. Birth confers obligations; marriage confers penalties. For those of us who choose other paths, the reward may be greater, but only if we risk more. We have to be ready to seize new opportunities."

"India." It was Adrian's first contribution to the discussion.

Magnus gave him a sharp look. "India, yes. The East India Company is as good as finished. They'll govern, but they won't trade."

"They're losing money in India," Hugo said. "Their only profit is in the China trade, but that will never be opened to outsiders, no matter what form the new charter takes. We can't bring in silk and there's no market for cotton." He frowned. "Indigo?"

"A possibility, but that's been in private hands for the past twenty years. Listen." Magnus leaned forward, his eyes and voice commanding their attention. "We have to think ahead. One day India will be one of the finest markets in the world for English goods, and when that day comes the profits will go to those who had the foresight to establish themselves there. Forget cotton. Forget indigo. India has iron, the purest in the world. And coal. Think of it, iron and coal together. Fuel's needed to work the ore. We'll need to deal with the question of transport, but labor's no problem, it's cheap. We'll need money for exploration. Once the business of the charter is settled, we can approach the Government. If the matter is put properly, we should be able to arouse some interest."

The proposal was met with silence. Gideon watched the others, waiting for them to voice the obvious objection. It was Hugo who did so. "You're talking years."

"Perhaps." Magnus sat back in his chair. "We can afford to wait."

I can't, Gideon thought. Hugo won't. Nor will Adrian, from the look of him. Adrian was on his feet, impatience written in every line of his well-made body. "Why should we go to India for coal? We have coal in England," he said. "Iron, too, and what we don't have we get from Sweden and Russia. No one's going to put up money to look for more. But here's something we don't have." He held out a closely written sheet of paper. "Gold. There's gold in India, and it's there for the taking. By God, *this* will arouse some interest."

The paper was a letter from his younger brother William, who had been with the army in India for the past two years. Adrian smoothed the sheet and read the letter aloud. It was vague and incoherent, but on two points William was clear. There was a fortune to be made by anyone who would organize the natives properly and turn their attention from making useless trinkets to adorn their wives. And he had established relations of trust with the Hindu ruler of Mysore who was properly grateful to the British for deposing the Muhammadan Tipu Sultan.

The letter was passed among them. George examined it with a speculative eye, then passed it on to Hugo, who devoured it hastily and with growing enthusiasm. Magnus read it through without comment. Gideon stared at the unfamiliar scrawl. He did not know William well and had never seen his hand, but the message was couched in language that accorded well with what he remembered of Robert Melchett's second son, an impetuous, inarticulate boy who had a way with horses and excelled in all manner of sports.

The discussion that followed showed scant regard for the realities of finding and removing unknown quantities of metal from a state that had only recently come under British protection. Magnus's interest was piqued, and without giving up his preference for more prosaic minerals, he allowed that the scheme might have some merit. Gideon's questions went unanswered, and when the meeting came to an end he was both worried and dissatisfied.

He strode rapidly down Davies Street, reviewing what he'd learned in the past two hours. Clare had what was almost certainly an illicit relationship with Adrian and Hugo did not suspect it. Hugo, George, and Adrian between them had a majority share in the company and would stand together. The introduction of William's letter had deflected Magnus's attention from the partners' immediate problems and might have been expressly designed to do so. Magnus was a gambler, but a patient one. Compared to the others, he was a voice of reason and restraint, and his wealth, experience, and knowledge of the City gave him more influence on the other partners than would have been expected from the share of the company he held. And there was little hope of the quick profit that would allow Gideon to buy his way out of his debts.

He had also learned, from a conversation with Hugo at the end of the meeting, that Barstead had been let, but the family was moving north and Hugo would be put to all the trouble of finding other tenants. Hugo was annoyed, but it was just the intelligence Gideon had hoped for. Within two or three weeks it would be possible to search the house where James Woodbourn had died.

Gideon returned home to find a letter, written in a fine and formal hand, from Adrian's grandmother, Hermione Melchett, Marchioness of Parminter, inviting him to dine a week hence. Gideon's first impulse was to refuse the invitation. He knew Parminter House well. He'd lived there for three years when he'd been secretary to Adrian's father, Robert Melchett, but Lady Parminter, who disapproved of politics as a serious

114

occupation for a gentleman, had always resented Gideon's influence on her son-in-law. Then he realized that Lady Parminter was not a woman to do anything without cause; it would be wise to learn what reason she had to desire his company. Adrian would be there, as would George, who'd taken rooms in Parminter House when he'd married Adrian's sister. William, of course, was in India, but the youngest boy, who was called Robin to distinguish him from the father for whom he was named, would be there as well. He would rather like to see Robin who, of all the children, most resembled Robert Melchett. Gideon penned a formal acceptance and rang for Adam to deliver it at once.

The following day he called at Melchett's Bank to lay before the man who was now the dominant force in the partnership his concerns about Woodbourn-Prebble. He debated telling Magnus about Jimson and George's groom but decided against it. He had no proof, and worse, no idea why George was involved. Nothing would be served by sharing his suspicions.

Magnus assured him that the current status of the company was not a matter he intended to put aside. The remaining ledgers had been delivered to him that morning, following a pointed message to Sir Hugo, and they were currently being reviewed by one of his sharper-eyed clerks. Magnus would cover the losses that had resulted from the fire, but only with the understanding that accounts in future should come through his hands. The partners, Gideon included, should not expect much in the way of profits in the next few months, but he was confident that, given time, there was money to be made in India. He was inclined to take the question of gold deposits seriously, though not at the expense of exploring other investments. Diversification, he said, was the key to success. The new charter would give them new opportunities, but political

115

influence would still be important in obtaining trading concessions. Parminter's name would count for something in the circles where decisions were made.

Gideon now understood why a man like Magnus Melchett had bothered to associate himself with a modest company like Woodbourn-Prebble, why he put up with Hugo's obvious incompetence and probable venality. If India were to be plucked, there were many ways to do it. Woodbourn-Prebble should have been beneath Magnus's notice, but Adrian had chosen to associate himself with the company and the Parminter name and wealth promised access to the favors of government. Magnus's influence in the company was helped by the fact that Adrian owed him a considerable amount of money, though Magnus did not say so directly. Nor was he so crass as to mention Gideon's debts. Magnus held the mortgage on Hartwood, Gideon's estate in Hertfordshire, as well as a note for some monies he had advanced Aline two years before.

Gideon left the interview in no sanguine frame of mind. He did not know how he was going to recoup his fortune. He debated letting the London house and taking the children to a small cottage he owned in Dorset, but leaving London meant relinquishing his interests in the company to the judgment of his partners, which would not be wise, and abandoning his efforts to do something for Fiona, which he could not bring himself to do.

So he would stay in London. There was no reason now not to resume his seat in the House. None, save the sense that it was an utterly futile endeavor. For twelve years politics had been his life, first in his role as Robert Melchett's secretary, and then, after his father's death made him Viscount Carne, as a member of the Upper Chamber.

He had been on the losing side of almost every question—the war, the rebellions in Ireland, the Catholic question, the attempts to reform an unfair and corrupt electoral process. In those days he had been perpetually angry. Now he could not remember when his anger had turned to despair. Perhaps it was the death of Fox, a man who could never be replaced. Or the idiocy of the investigation into the behavior of the Princess of Wales. Or the King's refusal to allow Catholics to serve as officers in the army and navy, which brought down the closest thing to a Whig administration in nearly a quarter of a century. By the time Gideon left for the Peninsula, his disillusion with both his marriage and his career was complete.

Gideon put these reflections aside and turned his curricle in the direction of Westminster. It was something to do, and it would postpone the hour of returning home and facing his children. And there were other reasons for him to be present at what proved to be a sparsely attended debate. If his future was to depend on India, he needed to learn all he could about the bill to renew the East India Company's charter.

Gideon's return to the Lords caused a small stir among the men who remembered Lord Carne's passionate oratory which had enlivened even the dullest of debates and regularly disturbed the slumbers of the members who saw the Upper Chamber as a place of rest. It also raised speculation about what his presence might mean for the fortunes of the Opposition.

"Little or nothing," said the Earl of Berresford to a group of men who were gathered in the entrance hall of Brooks's. "I saw him in the House yesterday. He didn't say a word."

"Don't underestimate Carne." Nicholas Warwick, who sat in the Lower Chamber, was angered by Berresford's assessment of a man he respected. "His quietness is deceptive."

"It's the war," Lord John Russell explained. Russell, a younger son of the Duke of Bedford, had been elected to the Commons the previous year at the age of twenty. Carne had been his idol since he was fourteen. "I understand he had a bad time, and he lost his wife. Oh, I say, I'm sorry," he added, for Warwick's wife had died that spring.

Warwick made a gesture to show that he was not offended. "Carne will come through it. Things have changed in five years. He needs time to find his feet."

"Did you say Carne?" A tall, rangy young man with a shock of unruly brown hair stopped by the group on his way toward the staircase.

"Do you know him, Hawksley?" Warwick asked. "I would have thought he was before your time."

"I knew a Major Carne in Portugal," Frank Hawksley said. "It might be the same."

"What was he like?" Berresford asked.

"Quiet, clever, and dangerous."

Warwick grinned. "That's the one. Viscount Carne. He's back in London. Suffered a bit of damage, he's got a game leg."

Hawksley, who had been invalided home two years before, made a sympathetic sound.

"After five years, I would have expected this paragon to be at least a colonel," Berresford remarked.

Hawksley knew Berresford slightly and did not like him. "This paragon," he said levelly, "couldn't be bothered."

"Too busy killing the French?"

Hawksley turned somber. Carne had fought as well and recklessly as any of the men under his command, but he had no stomach for killing. "We were together at Torres Vedras, and he killed his share. But most of

118

the time he was on his own. He knew Portuguese and Spanish and could pass for a conde or peasant or priest. Or a French officer, for that matter. He tried them all, and more. He had a genius for disguise."

"So he played at spy." Berresford's voice held a touch of distaste. "A thrilling life."

"A useful one," Hawksley retorted.

"Good God, it's Hawksley." Gideon, who had just entered the building, strode over to the group and offered his hand to his former comrade. "It must be all of three years. What happened to you? No, don't tell me here, come dine with me." He made his excuses to the others and took Hawksley away, making it clear that they desired no other company. Gideon was not yet ready for an evening of political talk.

But politics could not be banished. After the first exchange of reminiscences, Gideon learned that Hawksley, returning to England with a fierce desire to do something with his life, had found both a patron and a seat in the Commons. Hawksley was impatient, headstrong, and confident of his ability to persuade others to his way of thinking—a reflection, Gideon thought wryly, of his younger self. Torn between amusement and despair, Gideon let him talk.

Hawksley covered it all, the American War, the East India Company, the fate of India, the treaty with Sweden. It was the last which roused his special ire. "If I were still in Durham raising sheep," he said, his voice rising in indignation, "and someone in Northumberland proposed to help my neighbor rob me of half of what I owned on the grounds that I was dangerous because I didn't choose to give it up, would that be an honorable position for Northumberland to take? Would it even be a reasonable one?"

Gideon laughed. "Hardly. But if Russia takes Finland from Sweden, and we choose to help Sweden take Norway from Denmark because Russia and Sweden are now allies, that's a matter of political convenience."

"Denmark is no threat to the allies."

"They must be considered hostile. We destroyed their fleet, remember?"

Hawksley nodded. "A despicable act. I read your speech about it. Will you speak up now, Carne?"

Gideon shrugged and poured some more wine. "Drops of water, grains of sand. It will make little difference if I do. In an eternity of time, it will make no difference at all."

Hawksley looked shocked. "Everything makes a difference. If I didn't believe that, I couldn't go on."

"If I believed it, I wouldn't dare."

They argued in this vein for some time and then moved on to more personal matters. Hawksley was fretted about a woman. Gideon listened, but declined to give him any advice. By the time they rose from the table, Gideon found he was in a surprisingly good mood. He liked the younger man, and their conversation had roused a sudden flow of ideas, none of them having anything to do with his children, his estates, or the fortunes of Woodbourn-Prebble.

As they left the dining room, they were approached by the Earl of Berresford. When Gideon left for the Peninsula, Berresford had been the Viscount Bewdley, a shallow, self-indulgent young man who played at politics. Since that time, he'd come into the earldom, but otherwise he seemed little changed. He had held himself aloof when they met in the hall below, but now he approached them with an affable smile. "I say, Carne, what's this I hear about Parminter's discovery of gold in Mysore?"

Gideon stifled an oath.

"Everyone's talking about it," Berresford went on.

"Parminter says his brother has some influence with the Hindus there."

Within a matter of minutes, a half dozen people had gathered around and the inquiries multiplied. Gideon fended them off, cursing Robert Melchett's eldest son. Adrian—for it seemed that it was Adrian who had put the story about—should have known that the mention of gold makes men greedy. By the time Gideon was able to escape his questioners and take leave of Hawksley, who was bound for the Commons, his good humor had quite vanished. He was about to leave the club himself when the irresponsible young Marquis of Parminter entered it with a boisterous group of friends.

"Adrian," Gideon said, drawing the other man aside, "there's talk going round about William's letter. You'd best hold hard. It's likely to get us into trouble."

"No harm meant," Adrian said coolly, drawing off his gloves, "and no harm taken. You can't stop gossip in any case. Oh, by the way," he added, "I understand you're to dine with us next week. Grandmama wants to meet Lady Alessandra. The Langleys have another engagement, but they're sending her with her companion. Alessa's an enchanting girl. You're sure to like her."

With these words Adrian rejoined his friends and disappeared up the staircase. Gideon left the club and walked rapidly to his carriage. He had not looked forward to going to Parminter House, but if Fiona was to be there it would not be a spiritless evening. Gideon stopped abruptly. No, it would be far from spiritless. For if Fiona would be there, so would George.

Chapter Seven

Reaching over her shoulders, Fiona fastened the last button on her frock and told herself there was no reason to be nervous. It was not as if this was the first time she'd gone into company. In the three months since Alessa's coming-out ball, Fiona had grown accustomed to taking her young charge shopping, driving with her in the park, and accompanying her on calls and even to an occasional ball or rout. But at such functions Fiona always remained discreetly in the background. Tonight would be different. Tonight she would sit down to dinner with a select company, including George Barrington-Forbes, the man she'd jilted five years before.

Fiona turned to the cheval glass, smoothing the skirt of the dark blue silk dress the princess had given her for the ball that had welcomed the Tassios to England. A week ago Sunday, when Fiona was meeting Gideon in Hyde Park and Alessa was shopping with the Davenport sisters, the Marchioness of Parminter had called on the princess with an invitation to dinner. The Langleys were already promised to a reception at the Russian Embassy, but the princess and the marchioness agreed that Alessa would attend with Fiona as chaperon. Alessa had been able to talk of little else since, but Fiona, knowing George was bound to be present, had listened to her charge's transports with a growing sense of unease.

It had not helped that after the chaos of the fire and

its aftermath, the past ten days had been strangely quiet. Peter came every day to do lessons with Simon, but though Gideon occasionally brought his son to Bolton Street or called to take him home, he rarely stayed to talk with Fiona, and then only when the boys were present. They had had only one private conversation, a few moments snatched under the pretext of discussing Peter's studies. Hugo and Clare had let Barstead, he told her, but the current tenants would be leaving in a fortnight or so, and it should then be possible to arrange a visit. Meanwhile there was nothing to do but wait.

The infrequency of their meetings should have been a relief, but Fiona found herself strangely restless. It was her anxiety about the will, of course—that and the fact that, short of traveling to Castleton, she was unsure where she could next seek for information about her mother.

Fiona moved to the dressing table and ran a brush through her hair, then coiled it into her customary chignon and clasped a garnet pendant about her neck. It had been a gift from her father on her eighteenth birthday, and it was the only real piece of jewelry she still possessed. She'd been forced to sell her pearls during those frightening days before Mr. Camford had come to her assistance in London.

Still the garnets had always been her favorite, and if less valuable than the pearls, they were certainly more dramatic. The blue silk was cut soberly, but the fabric was good and the modest V-shaped neckline, discreetly edged with lace, was low enough to set off the pendant to advantage. The sleeves were unadorned, but they were slightly gathered and ended just above the elbow. Fiona drew on her long white gloves, also a gift from the princess, draped the gray silk shawl—impulsively purchased, at much too dear a price, while shopping with Alessa—over her arm, picked up her reticule, and told herself lingering would do nothing to allay her fears.

123

"I say." Simon was waiting for her on the second floor landing, perched on a gold damask settee which was more ornamental than comfortable. "Best watch out," he cautioned as she smiled at him. "If you put Alessa in the shade, she'll be in the dev—the deuce of a temper."

Fiona laughed. "That's the least of my worries." But she was in rather better spirits as she entered the small saloon where Alessa was pirouetting to show off the vandyked lace border on her new pale pink sarcenet to her mother. "Very pretty," the princess said. "Ah, Miss Alastair. I've been telling Alessa that you are likely to return before we do. These embassy functions do tend to drag on."

"But you have to admit the new ambassadress has livened things up a bit," her husband observed, following Fiona into the room.

"You are trying to tease me into making an unbecoming remark," the princess said playfully. "I have never denied that Madame de Lieven is clever, and if I ever said she put on airs, I spoke only in the privacy of our home. And," she continued, "whatever you may think, Michael, it has nothing to do with that fact that she is ten years my junior and has half London at her feet."

"How could it," Langley returned, crossing to her side and raising her hand to his lips, "when the other half remains securely at your own?"

Princess Sofia threw her husband a look of mingled amusement and affection, then rose with a glitter of spangled satin and diamonds and rang for the carriages. Langley turned to smile impartially at his stepdaughter and her companion. A younger son from an untitled family and a man of liberal principles, he had from the first treated Fiona as more a guest than a servant. He and the princess had been married less than eight months, but their romance had begun nearly twenty years ago, when Sofia was barely eighteen and Langley was a young attaché at the British Embassy in St. Petersburg. The princess's parents had made haste to separate the lovers and find their daughter a husband of more exalted position. Sofia had been a dutiful wife to the Prince di Tassio, but his death had left her free to follow the promptings of her heart. When she met Langley in England the romance flared, made stronger by the years of denial.

The princess was now blissfully happy and, Fiona considered, far gentler in her handling of both her children. She was also less likely to thwart her daughter's first attachment. Though the marquis had not yet spoken to Alessa, tonight's dinner indicated that his intentions were more than serious. Fiona was surprised that the marchioness had not chosen to delay the entertainment until the princess could attend, but perhaps Lady Parminter felt it would be easier to inspect Alessa without her mother present. Once she'd given her tacit consent, nothing would stand in the way of a betrothal, save perhaps the matter of the couple's religious differences. But this was not an insurmountable difficulty. Aristocratic marriages between Anglicans and Catholics, though rare, were certainly not unheard of, and Alessa's mother, Russian Orthodox by birth, Catholic by her first marriage, had recently married a Protestant.

The significance of the dinner had not been lost on Alessa. Despite the youthful pink frock, there was something very mature about her manner this evening, and her eyes were bright with expectancy, like those of a nervous actress who knows that all will be well when she steps before her audience. She was uncharacteristically quiet as they settled themselves in the carriage, but then she spoke suddenly, as if she was picking up in the middle of a conversation. "Lady Parminter is very particular about the family, you know. Lady Lydia had the greatest difficulty persuading her to agree to the match with Mr. Barrington-Forbes . . . not that Adrian would not marry without her permission, of course, but it would be

125

so much more comfortable if he did not have to do so."

"No," Alessa continued, in response to a look of inquiry from her governess, "he has not offered for me. Not in so many words. And I only use his given name when we are private." Her voice was calm, but she reached up to adjust one of her combs, a nervous gesture to which she rarely succumbed. "I must say, I'm glad you're with me, Fiona. I don't know if *Maman* would understand, for she never seems to be afraid of anything, but I do rather feel I can use all the support I can get."

Not knowing the marchioness, Fiona was unsure whether she should try to calm Alessa's fears or bolster her courage. Nothing more was said until they reached Bloomsbury Square and passed through a pedimented stone gateway into the spacious forecourt of Parminter House. The coachman reined the horses to a slow walk and, though the windows were closed, Fiona was conscious of the sound of rushing water. As they moved toward the house itself, she found herself staring at an enormous circular fountain that sported some ill-defined water deities in the Italian mode.

"How pretty," Alessa exclaimed.

"Yes," Fiona said, as the carriage came to a standstill. "I wonder what they do when the horses want to drink out of it."

Alessa giggled. "Lady Lydia says her grandmother is inordinately proud of the house. They say it's the handsomest in London."

Fiona knew that Parminter House was one of the oldest of the great London houses, but though she'd long since lost her countrified awe at the opulent scale on which the Tassios lived, she was unprepared for the sight which met her eyes when she stepped out of the carriage. Were it not for the muffled sounds of traffic from the street, she would have thought she stood before a country estate, not a house in the middle of a bustling city. Fiona knew little about architecture, but history was her passion, and the red brick building, linked to flanking wings by a pair of graceful colonnades, immediately spoke of the late seventeenth century.

As a footman relieved them of their wraps in the vast entrance hall Alessa glanced at the plaster ceiling showing what must be the Melchett coat of arms, three griffins rampant. Her nervousness returned, but she quickly masked it. Not even bothering to glance in the silver-framed mirror which hung between two pedestals supporting classical busts, Alessa lifted her head and followed the footman up the cedar staircase with an assurance very nearly equal to her mother's.

On the first floor the footman opened a pair of tall beveled doors and announced Lady Alessandra di Tassio and Miss Alastair. Fiona had a brief impression of dark wainscotted walls, a number of ornately framed pictures, and a ceiling painted in rich, glowing colors which were echoed in the carpet at her feet. Her eyes went immediately to George, who was standing with one hand placed negligently on the back of Lady Lydia's chair, but she forced her gaze to move on to the rest of the company: Lord Parminter; a young man of about twenty who must be his brother, Lord Robert; and Hermione Melchett, Marchioness of Parminter.

Lady Parminter was seated in a simple walnut armchair which she managed to endow with the attributes of a throne. Though she had four grown grandchildren and a great-granddaughter, her hair was as much blond as gray, her complexion was soft and supple, with the delicate color of a much younger woman, and her gown, cut conservatively but without complete disregard for current fashion, showed a still slender figure. Fiona could see where Lord Parminter and Lady Lydia got their looks as well as their assurance, but there was a strength in the marchioness's face which her grandchildren lacked. Strength and, about her mouth, a faint cast of disappointment as if, though she would never admit it, life had not given her everything she wanted.

"Lady Alessandra." Lord Parminter stepped forward with a confident smile which did him no good in Fiona's eyes. If Alessa was as essential to his happiness as he was to hers, surely he would feel some trepidation at presenting her to his formidable grandmother. With a belated nod in Fiona's direction, Parminter took Alessa's arm and led her to the marchioness's chair. "Grandmama, allow me to present Lady Alessandra di Tassio. And her companion, Miss Alastair."

"My dear." The marchioness rose with a smile which was probably as warm as her smiles ever became. "I'm so pleased to meet you at last."

Alessa dropped a very pretty curtsy and offered her mother's compliments in a well-modulated voice. The marchioness greeted Fiona—at once making it clear that Miss Alastair was not quite an equal and that she must not allow it to make her feel out of place in the company this evening—and then turned to introduce her grandson Lord Robert and her granddaughter's husband, George Barrington-Forbes.

What followed was almost anticlimactic. A smile, a nod, a murmured greeting, and it was over. Lady Parminter gestured for Alessa to sit beside her on a small sofa, upholstered, like most of the furniture in the room, in a pale rose velvet which set off the Melchett coloring to advantage. Lady Lydia drew Fiona to a group of chairs near the fireplace, Lord Robert picked up the book he had been reading when the guests arrived, and Parminter and George moved farther down the room. George had not shown the smallest sign of surprise nor indicated that he had any prior acquaintance with Miss Alastair. Clare must have warned him. For the first time in years, Fiona had cause to be grateful to her sister.

While she made desultory conversation with Lydia, Fiona had ample opportunity to observe the family. The five years which had been so harsh to Gideon had been

128

kind to George. Though his sandy hair, always rather thin, was perhaps a trifle more sparse, his face, well favored and enlivened by a perpetual air of sardonic amusement, seemed unchanged. Once Fiona had felt flattered to have captured the attentions of such a man. Once she had been impressed by his understanding and had admired his wit. Once Gideon had been merely a shadowy presence in her life.

Both George and Parminter wore black coats and cream-colored kneebreeches—a concession to the marchioness, no doubt—and oddly enough the comparison did not work to the handsome marquis's advantage. There were ten years between the men, Parminter was a trifle shorter and slighter than his brother-in-law, and beside George he looked rather callow. He was laughing now at something George had said, apparently indifferent to his grandmother's inquisition of the girl he hoped to marry.

Like her brother, Lady Lydia had thick fair hair, clear skin, and finely drawn features. Her face was rather thin and her chin a trifle too pointed for classical perfection, but a pair of large, wide gray-green eyes more than compensated for these defects. Her eyes were presently fixed on George with all the intensity lacking when her brother looked at Alessa. Fiona was startled. She had not expected Lydia, a pattern card of fashion from her *à la grecque* coiffure to her azure silk Italian slippers, to appear so unfashionably in love with her husband. It helped to ease Fiona's conscience, for had she been George's wife, she would never have been able to look at him so.

Whether or not George's feelings for Lydia were equally strong was debatable. But then, though he was adept at practiced compliments, George's declarations of love had always had a false ring. Even during their brief betrothal, Fiona had sensed that he was less in love with her than proud of having won her. And if he had been proud of winning an illegitimate young woman with no more than a modest dowry, how much more must it mean to him to have secured the only daughter of the Marquis of Parminter. George's income was comfortable, but it could not support his tastes. He would be in his element in Parminter House. Fiona studied a pair of exquisite pink-and-white porcelain vases set on a marble-topped table beneath a small oil which, unless she was very much mistaken, was a Van Dyke, and wondered how George ever could have dreamed of offering for James Woodbourn's bastard.

As time wore on and none of the other dinner guests made an appearance, Fiona began to suspect that their early arrival was no accident. Her suspicions were confirmed a quarter hour later with the arrival of Sir Phillip Addison, a handsome white-haired gentleman of the marchioness's generation, closely followed by the equally handsome but much younger Lord Granville Leveson-Gower and his even younger wife Harriet. Fiona was pleased to see the Leveson-Gowers, who were frequent guests in Bolton Street. Granville and Michael Langley had been at Oxford together, and both had been stationed in Russia in the course of their diplomatic careers.

"How lovely to see you, Miss Alastair. I was so sorry you were out when I last called in Bolton Street," Harriet said warmly. Inclined to plumpness and very conscious that she'd not inherited her mother's fabled beauty, she always seemed more at ease with Fiona than with the stylish princess. Granville greeted Fiona with a smile which was as practiced as George's but seemed a good deal more genuine, and Harriet sat beside her and asked after Simon until the next arrivals claimed everyone's attention.

It was a family party this time, a stout gentleman of middle years, a handsome dark-haired woman, and a vivid girl of about Alessa's age with a riot of titian hair. Even before the introductions, Fiona recognized the gentleman as Earl Buckleigh. She was startled, for she would not have expected a staunch Tory like Buckleigh to be on such close terms with the Whig Parminters. "I know," said an amused voice at her side some minutes later when Harriet had been drawn off by Lady Buckleigh. "Buckleigh's as Tory as they come, and we've been Whigs since the exclusion crisis—I say, do you like history?"

It was Lord Robert Melchett. Slightly built, with hair of a middling brown, he was not as handsome as his brother and sister, but Fiona suspected he might be their superior in understanding and wit. "Very much," she said. "In fact I must confess that the first Lord Parminter I heard of was not your brother but your ancestor, the friend of Shaftesbury and Monmouth."

"Oh, yes, the fourth marquis. Crafty devil. I trust you note that he managed to avoid sharing in either of his friends' falls from grace. Self-preservation has always been one of our strongest family traits. That's his wife," Lord Robert added, settling himself in Harriet's vacated chair and gesturing toward the portrait which hung over the lofty gray marble fireplace. "Penelope Quentin. Her father was a London merchant who contrived to keep both sides happy during the Civil War and Interregnum and made a fortune in the process. He wanted a title for his daughter and the fourth marquis wanted money—the family'd gone into a bit of a decline after Elizabeth, you see. It was Penelope's money that built Parminter House and Sundon, our place in Bedfordshire. Before that, the Melchetts were living on a drafty estate in the wilds of Cumberland."

Fiona craned her neck to look up at the picture. The features which marked the current marchioness and her grandchildren could easily be traced in Penelope Quentin. She must have been in her early twenties when the portrait was taken, a slender, elegant young woman in a shimmering ice-blue gown with the low neck and full sleeves popular during the Restoration. Her pale blond hair, dressed in loose ringlets and threaded with pearls, framed a delicate face which showed unexpected strength, and her calm gray eyes reflected an absolute certainty that she could order the world precisely as she wished.

"I'm not surprised her husband managed to avoid being caught in his friend's misfortunes," Fiona said. "She looks equal to any crisis."

"Yes, I've always liked her, though judging by her houses she was a bit of a show-off. I say, it *is* nice to find a kindred spirit," Lord Robert added, turning from the picture to Fiona. "I'm reading history at Cambridge and the rest of the family haven't the faintest idea what I'm talking about. Oh, I was explaining about Buckleigh, wasn't I? He's my cousin."

"Cousin?" Fiona asked.

"My mother's cousin, to be more precise. His father was Grandmama's brother, and—"

"Don't you know it's bad manners to leave your guests hopelessly muddled on their first visit, Robin?" Lord Buckleigh's daughter, the vivid redhead, drew up a chair on Fiona's other side. "Hullo," she said, extending her hand, "I hope you haven't let Robin give you a headache."

"She likes history," Robin protested, as Fiona shook hands with Lady Demetra. His tone was defensive but his eyes still glinted with amusement. "Besides, it's all perfectly straightforward. Isn't it, Miss Alastair?"

"I think so." Fiona was smiling. She had never expected to feel so much at ease in the Parminter drawing room, but then, neither had she expected to encounter anyone like Lord Robert or Lady Demetra there. "The two of you must be second cousins."

"Precisely," said Robin with great satisfaction. He directed a look of triumph at Demetra, who appeared unimpressed.

"That's only the beginning," Demetra warned Fiona, even as the double doors opened once again and the footman announced the Honorable Mr. and Mrs. Kittredge. They proved to be a handsomely dressed couple, somewhat older than the Buckleighs, but considerably younger than the marchioness. The introductions did not make clear their relationships to the Parminters, but Fiona thought she heard Mrs. Kittredge address Lady Parminter as "Aunt." She looked at Robin. "Another cousin?"

"Quite. Buckleigh's father was Grandmama's brother," he explained, while Demetra put her head in her gloved hands, "and their sister is Mrs. Kittredge's mother."

"You see what I mean?" Demetra demanded, emerging from behind her hands. "And this is only the English branch of the family. Remember the last time we all visited Castleton?" she said, grinning at her cousin.

Fiona didn't hear Robin's reply. Ever since her talk with Tom Constable, she'd been pondering a way to learn more about the area where her father had been staying when she was conceived. To hear it mentioned so casually was not only startling, it was an opportunity she could not afford to miss. "Castleton?" she repeated, looking from one cousin to the other.

"Yes, do you know it?" Robin seemed surprised. "It's confoundedly remote. Nothing to do but talk to one's relations." He pulled a face at Demetra.

"Mrs. Kittredge's mother is married to Lord Selkirk, who has a house near Castleton," Demetra explained, ignoring her cousin, "and we all visit them from time to time. Robin's exaggerating, but it is rather isolated. Have you ever been—oh, of course, Alastair. You must be Scottish."

"Several generations back," Fiona said truthfully, for before she'd left for Sardinia she'd adopted the name of one of her father's maternal ancestors. "I've never been to Scotland but an acquaintance of mine recently mentioned a family who lives near Castleton. Bowder, I think the name was."

To her surprise, Demetra nodded as if she knew the Bowders well. "They have the only other large house for some ten miles, so there's much visiting between the two families."

Fiona's heart quickened. Clenching the folds of her gown, she looked to the sofa where Mrs. Kittredge was seated beside Lady Buckleigh. Could this plump, rather vacuous matron possibly be—it was so absurd that she stifled an hysterical desire to laugh. And yet . . . Mrs. Kittredge was the right age, and her elaborate turban of silver frosted crêpe revealed pale gold hair and a face which, though it had coarsened with the years, still showed the remnants of girlish beauty.

"Does Mrs. Kittredge have a large family in Castleton?" Fiona asked, groping for the self-control which had served her so well through the years.

"Her parents are living, and both her sisters married Scotsmen." Demetra looked an intelligent young woman, but she seemed to have no inkling that Miss Alastair was more than casually interested in the particulars of the family. Perhaps her self-control hadn't deserted her after all.

"And then, of course, there are their children," Robin added. "Don't look daggers at me, Demetra, you're the one who brought up Castleton."

For some minutes Fiona struggled to assimilate this new information and still take part in the conversation with reasonable coherence. There were three Selkirk sisters of the right generation and Mr. Constable had said Jack Bowder came from a large family. If Lord Robert and Lady Demetra were to be believed, and if Constable had remembered correctly, her mother had almost certainly been one of the Bowders or one of the Selkirks. And it was very likely that she was still alive.

Fiona was relieved when the drawing room doors

opened, for she assumed the butler had come to announce dinner, and the removal to the dining room would give her a few moments' respite. But she had not realized that the numbers were not yet even. It was not the butler but the footman who entered the room, and he had come to announce not dinner but the last of the guests, Viscount Carne.

For all her worries about the evening, it had never occurred to Fiona that she might encounter Gideon at Parminter House. The marquis was some ten years his junior, and though they were both partners in Woodbourn-Prebble, Gideon had spoken of the younger man with something close to contempt. Now, as she watched Gideon shake hands with the marquis and bow to the marchioness, Fiona realized that, whatever his opinion of the Parminter family, they were far from strangers to him.

"I always said war was stupid," Robin murmured softly, his eyes fixed on Gideon.

"Yes," Demetra agreed, "but it *is* good to see him back in one piece."

For the sake of simple self-preservation, Fiona decided she'd best learn as much as possible. "I know Lord Carne slightly," she said, "for his son does lessons with Lady Alessandra's brother. I hadn't realized he and Lord Parminter were friends."

Robin turned back to Fiona. "They aren't," he said bluntly, as if determined to set the record straight. "Carne used to be my father's secretary. He lived with us for three years."

This explained Gideon's connection to the Parminters, but it was strangely disconcerting to find she knew nothing of a three-year interval in the life of a man who'd once meant so much to her. That was absurd, of course; physical intimacy had little to do with knowing a person. There had been a time when she'd thought she understood Gideon as well as he seemed to understand her, but he'd proved her wrong to devastating effect.

Across the room, Gideon was shaking George's hand with at least a veneer of cordiality. He said something to Lydia which, to judge by her response, was probably a compliment, exchanged a few words with Harriet and Granville, then made his way toward the cluster of chairs where Fiona, Robin, and Demetra were seated.

"Lady Demetra. It would be stating the obvious to say you've grown up. Are you still fond of unsuitable reading matter?"

Demetra giggled. "When I was twelve, Lord Carne found me in the Parminter House library looking for Paine's *Common Sense*. He was very nice about helping me locate it. I really did read it, you know," she told him.

"I make no doubt of it." Gideon turned to Fiona. "Peter most specifically asked to be remembered to you, Miss Alastair." His gaze moved on and his expression changed. "I'm sorry about your father, Robin."

Robin swallowed. "So am I." For a moment, the young man seemed to be struggling for self-mastery. "He . . . he would have been glad you're back, sir."

Gideon smiled, a wry smile, Fiona thought, but he made no reply. From a distance he had seemed to be as faultlessly dressed as George or Parminter, but as he drew up a chair she realized that his coat was not cut in the current style.

"I think you knew an acquaintance of mine on the Peninsula, Lord Carne," Demetra said into the somewhat awkward silence. "Captain Hawksley."

"Frank Hawksley?" Gideon seemed relieved at the change of subject. "Yes, I met him at Torres Vedras, shortly before he was invalided out. He had the most damnable talent for asking questions his superiors couldn't answer. I'm glad he's gone into politics. We could use more like him."

Demetra laughed, but when Robin said, "This

Hawksley sounds a capital fellow, 'Metra, I'd like to meet him," she became uncharacteristically subdued. "He's only an acquaintance," she murmured, smoothing the pleated ivory crêpe of her skirt. Robin raised his brows, but Gideon, his eyes showing shrewd amusement, tactfully steered the conversation into a discussion in which they could all participate. Fiona began to enjoy herself until Lady Parminter summoned a grimacing Robin to her side only moments after Lydia had taken Demetra away, and she suddenly found herself alone with Gideon.

"Peter would have sent his respects," Gideon said softly, shifting his chair so that his back was to the room, "had he known you would be here, which he did not. Nor did I. I trust there have been no difficulties."

When Gideon looked at her with such obviously genuine concern, Fiona knew she was at her most vulnerable. "In truth, I am enjoying myself more than I expected," she told him. "Lord Robert and Lady Demetra are very entertaining."

Gideon smiled. "How Lord and Lady Buckleigh managed to produce an imp like Demetra baffles me. As for Robin, he's the only one of the current crop of Melchetts to take after his father."

"I understand you were his secretary," Fiona said, curiosity getting the better of her.

"Until I came into the title. Robert Melchett was a good man." He paused, as if he would have ended there, then added, "He was the closest I came to having a real father."

Once again Fiona was thrown off balance, filled with sympathy for the sense of loss in his voice, irrationally hurt that she knew nothing of someone who'd played such an important role in his life. She was not sure how to respond and was saved by an interruption, though not one she welcomed.

"Well, well," said George, approaching with Lady Lydia at his side, "this is turning out to be quite a reunion, isn't it? I refer, of course," he continued, after a pause which was a fraction of a second too long, "to your return to Parminter House, Carne. Do you find it much changed?"

With a careful show of deliberation, Gideon surveyed the room. "I fancy the drapes are new," he said at last. "And unless my memory's at fault, that landscape near the door used to hang in the blue saloon. Am I correct, Lady Lydia?"

Lydia, who usually cultivated a look of languid boredom, gave an unaffected smile. "Papa always said you were observant, Gideon." She hesitated, glanced at her husband, and then, almost as if she was responding to a stage cue, added, "He wanted you to have some of his books—his favorites, the ones he kept in his study. I've laid them out." She gestured toward a pier table which stood between the windows at the far end of the room. "Perhaps you would care to look at them."

Gideon hesitated—which was singularly foolish for it only risked stirring suspicions—but in the end he inclined his head and offered Lady Lydia his arm. Now that their initial meeting was over, Fiona found that she felt tolerably composed in George's presence. Gideon had warned her against him, but then, he and Gideon had never been friends. Whatever George's faults, it had never occurred to Fiona to be afraid of him. She folded her hands in her lap and waited, governess-like, for George to speak.

He regarded her for a long moment. "I did not realize you and Carne were such great friends, Miss Alastair."

The words surprised her, as did the edge to his voice. "You are mistaken, Mr. Barrington-Forbes. It is Lord Carne's son Peter and the Prince di Tassio who are great friends. Since they both left school, I have been giving Peter lessons along with the prince."

"And you have therefore come to know Lord Carne. Of course. I knew there must be some explanation."

The irony in his tone could not be ignored. Perhaps she should have expected a scene of this sort, for George had never been able to resist the urge to be clever, but she'd forgotten how much his wit was tinged with malice. Or was George the one who'd changed?

"I must make you my compliments," he continued when she did not respond. "I confess I would not have thought you had the nerve to carry it off."

However malicious or angry he might be, Fiona had not thought George would refer openly to the past while his wife was in the same room. "I do not quite understand you, Mr. Barrington-Forbes," she said pleasantly, "but perhaps I should remind you that you do not know me at all. Now, if you will forgive me, I should return to Lady Alessandra."

"Don't be hasty, Fiona." The lazy voice with its razorsharp undercurrent stopped her as she made to rise. "I'm playing along with your charade. The least you can do is grant me a few moments of your time."

Fiona settled back into her chair, subduing an uneasy sensation in the pit of her stomach. This was not the George she remembered. As much as she hated to admit it, it was beginning to appear that Gideon was right. "You have something you wish to say to me, Mr. Barrington-Forbes?"

George laughed, though the sound was not pleasant. "Come, Fiona, surely you don't need an explanation when a man wishes to spend time in your company." He surveyed her dispassionately, his gaze lingering on her demure *décolletage*. He had looked at her so more than once in the past, though to be fair, he'd never tried to seduce her, even after she'd agreed to be his wife. "Clare said you were faded," he remarked, with an air of detached interest, "but then, Clare's never been impartial where you were concerned. No, I'd say if anything, you're even more beautiful. You didn't have such style five years ago."

For all his sangfroid, George was angry, angrier than she'd ever seen him, and he wanted to hurt her. "You'd best be careful, Mr. Barrington-Forbes," Fiona said, reminding herself that George could do nothing to her without exposing himself to ridicule. "I don't think your wife cares to see you having a tête-à-tête with another woman, even a governess."

George followed Fiona's gaze to the other end of the room. Lady Lydia was dutifully showing Gideon her father's books, but every few moments she glanced back at her husband, a look of mingled anxiety and petulance on her lovely face. "Ah, yes, dear Lydia. The child adores me. Mind you, it has its advantages, but there are times when it becomes a bit wearying. You and I would have dealt together better."

"I doubt it."

"We'll never know, of course. But you'd best resign yourself to my company, Fiona," he said, looking toward the low couch where Alessa and Parminter were laughing together over a private joke. "I imagine we'll see a good deal of you at Parminter House while they plan the wedding."

"You are somewhat premature, Mr. Barrington-Forbes," Fiona returned, though she knew George was only too right. "There is no betrothal yet."

"Concerned for your charge, Fiona?" George inquired with a show of sympathy. "Most people would call it an unexceptionable match. Parminter's quite a catch. And though I'll grant you he's young, he'll make the girl an experienced husband."

Fiona would not give him the satisfaction of responding to this crudeness. At twenty-seven, Parminter could not be blamed for having women in his past, though if he was presently keeping a mistress it would be another indication that his feelings for Alessa were shallower than she'd have wished. Fiona wondered if he was, and if George would tell her, and if such information would carry any weight with the princess. At this date she could think of little else that would delay the betrothal.

Something of this must have shown in her face. "You didn't know?" George asked, looking immensely pleased about it. "Your young charge, my dear Fiona, is about to become betrothed to your sister's lover."

Chapter Eight

Gideon would have given his soul to know what was now passing between Fiona and George. He picked up a volume at random and ran his hands over the smooth, worn calf skin. He knew it at once, an early copy of Locke he had once admired. For a moment he had an acute sense of Robert Melchett's presence and then, with an unbearable sadness, of his loss.

"I'd like very much to have this one." He turned to Lydia and saw that her attention was engaged by the couple at the end of the room. Since it was now safe to do so, he followed the direction of her gaze. George was leaning over Fiona, his stance filled with assurance and malice. Or so Gideon read it. Lydia did not, and a fine line appeared between her pale brows. "I see that George is being gallant," he said, wanting to divert her attention. "It's kind of him. Companions tend to be ignored."

"She used to be Lady Alessandra's governess, did you know that? Not that I've any objection, but it seems odd for the princess to send her daughter into company with a woman—" She broke off, as though aware she might be committing an indelicacy.

He finished the thought for her. "With a woman who has the audacity to be well under forty and uncommonly handsome? You're a goose, Lydy." It was the name he'd used when she was five years old and he'd carried her about on his shoulders.

This reference to the past seemed to put her in good humor. Do you admire her, Lord Carne?"

"Not nearly so much as I admire you." He watched her glow with the compliment and wondered that a woman's beauty could so depend on the image reflected in a man's eyes.

"Ah. Well, then." She toyed with a small ivory fan with a border of painted flowers. "I would not have you think I have cause for jealousy. George is the most devoted of husbands."

Gideon knew he should leave it at that. Lydia had been a vain and demanding little girl, and she did not seem much different as a woman. But there had always been a streak of wistfulness in her manner that came, he suspected, from growing up in the shadow of two much-cherished elder brothers, and he wanted to armor her against disappointment. "George," he said, "likes to preen himself in the company of personable women." He lowered his voice as though to impart a secret. "It is, I fear, a weakness of our sex. Be wise, Lydia. It's an idle amusement and means nothing."

"I never said it did," she retorted, closing her fan with a snap. She did not want his advice, and the moment of intimacy between them was gone. She dropped her eyes and caught sight of the book he was still holding in his hands. "Would you like that one?"

"If I may, I'd be most grateful."

"Oh, take the lot," she said with a petulant shrug. "Adrian will never miss them. I'll have them boxed and sent to you."

"Thank you, Lydia. You're very kind."

"I'm not kind at all. Grandmama told me to see to it. And what Grandmama wants. . . . As a result," she continued after a moment, "I'm being sent down to dinner with Lord Buckleigh. Cousin or no, he's quite dreadful. I do think if a man insists on being gallant, he should have the decency to be more than passably good-looking."

"Careful, Lydia. I shall think you an incorrigible flirt."

She gave him an arch smile. "Then you're forewarned. You're placed on my other side, Lord Carne, and I have no intention of letting Grandmama monopolize you through the entire meal." With that she turned and walked away, swaying slightly with a gait she'd perfected at fifteen.

Gideon watched her, an appreciative smile on his face. Of the four Parminter children, it was Lydia he knew best. Adrian had been at Harrow when Gideon first came to live in Parminter House, and in the years after, when he visited Robert, William and Robin were at school as well. But his acquaintance with Lydia would hardly account for his invitation to dine with the family tonight.

His speculations were cut short by the butler who entered the room to announce dinner. Gideon put down the book he was holding and went to join the others, where he learned that he was to take the marchioness down to dinner. He had a moment of surprise until it occurred to him that he was so honored only because he outranked all the other men present, save Adrian, her grandson, and Lord Buckleigh, her nephew. Lady Parminter, he remembered, took these matters seriously.

They had never been close, but Gideon could not help but admire her. She was a woman of strong—and in Gideon's eyes, thoroughly wrongheaded—principles, but she was honorable in her way, and if she lacked charity toward the weaknesses of others, she tolerated none in herself. Her passion was her family, or rather, the family line. She was the great-granddaughter of the Fourth Marquis of Parminter, and she had married her cousin, who became the Sixth. The marriage was not blessed with sons, and she'd prudently married her daughter to Robert Melchett, the nearest male heir.

Adrian now had the title. He had the house too,

144

though Gideon had no doubt that Hermione Melchett was still its core. As he helped her into her chair, he saw her eyes go briefly to her grandson, who was performing the same office for the young Tassio girl at the other end of the table, and knew what she was thinking. Adrian was twenty-seven. It was time he had a son.

The marchioness had always treated Gideon with the faint disapproval that she reserved for those who made political life their passion, but there was no sign of disapproval in her demeanor tonight. She touched on his war experiences with delicacy, acknowledging that they were not a fit subject for the dinner table and that she knew men did not like to be reminded of them, she expressed her condolences on the untimely death of his wife, she asked after his children. And then she turned and spoke to Sir Phillip, leaving Gideon to the ministrations of her granddaughter.

Gideon would have preferred to be left alone. It was the first time he'd dined in London company in over five years, and he had the ridiculous sense that he was in a foreign land. At the same time he was assailed by memories he would as soon forget. It was at this table that he had watched a young Adrian become captivated by Aline, had seen Aline become aware of her conquest, had glimpsed the calculation in her eyes. It was here that he had known, with dreadful finality, that his marriage was destroyed. It was here too, on a later night, that he had made the decision to confront Aline, a decision that led to his flight to Hartwood and his fateful affair with Fiona.

He heard a bark of laughter from Lord Buckleigh. Now that Lydia was occupied, the earl was free to devote himself to Fiona, who was seated on his left. She'd been brought into dinner by Robin who, as the youngest son, was expected to take care of women of socially awkward position. Fiona seemed on easy terms with the young man, and she seemed equally at ease with the earl who was surveying her with frank appreciation. She's in fine looks, Gideon thought, remembering not to let his eyes linger on her too long. She's learned to be charming, and she's learned to keep her place. She gives nothing away.

He smiled at Lydia, to indicate that his attention was on her alone, and let his mind dredge up images of a younger Fiona, fair hair streaming free, eyes shining, mouth eager. Nothing like the cool stranger sitting half-way down the table, the stranger his own folly had made. Gideon suppressed a groan. She had not been his first piece of folly, but God willing, she would be his last.

It was a relief when the ladies finally left the room. Gideon pushed back his chair and eased his right leg which was still painful if he remained too long in one position.

"You were wounded, I believe." Lord Buckleigh shook his head. "Nasty business."

Robin leaned forward. "What was it like?"

It was an impossible question. Gideon made a great show of filling his glass and returned an evasive answer. Then, because he feared he had rebuffed Robin, he asked him about his brother William. The conversation turned naturally to India and soon involved the entire table. Leveson-Gower had a friend who was teaching Oriental languages at Fort William College in Calcutta. Sir Philip suggested that the Hindus might be better employed in learning English. He was warmly seconded by Buckleigh, who added that any dozen books in a good British library were worth more than everything that had ever been written in the Sanskrit tongue. Kittredge, who was on the Board of Control which oversaw the East India Company, assured the group that the future of the inhabitants of that benighted continent rested in a decent English education. Roused to anger by this remark, Robin said that with all respect, an English education left much to be desired, and had any of them actually read the *Bhagavad Gita?*

Gideon listened and kept his own counsel. He'd learned little for his efforts, but the evening had not been uninstructive. When the men went upstairs to rejoin the ladies, he thought to plead the press of business and take his leave, but he was forestalled by a footman who informed him that Lady Parminter wished him to attend her in her sitting room. Gideon said he would find his own way and strode rapidly down the hall. A summons. At last he was to be told the reason for tonight's invitation.

The door of the sitting room was opened by a dark, dour-faced woman who carried a tray with a small bottle, a spoon, and a glass bearing traces of a sticky liquid. "You are not to tire her, do you hear?" she said, dropping him a belated curtsy.

"You may leave, Jenkins." The marchioness's soft voice carried clearly across the room. "Lord Carne will escort me back to the drawing room when we are through."

The maid might have said more, but at a gesture from her mistress she confined herself to a loud sniff and left the room.

"You must not mind Jenkins," Lady Parminter said. "She has been with me over forty years and is convinced I am as fragile as an autumn leaf."

"I find you in remarkably good health."

"There is nothing remarkable about my health. I am an old woman, and you may congratulate me, I suppose, on being alive at all. Sit down, Carne. No, over here, near me. My eyes are not what they used to be."

The blue of her eyes might have faded, but the irises were clear and her skin retained a youthful trace of pink. She had been well past sixty when Gideon had first come to Parminter House, and accounted handsome even then. To his eye she was little changed. The fine wrinkles around her mouth and eyes were scarcely visible in the candlelight, and the arrogant tilt of her head tightened the soft folds of skin under her chin.

"I do not go out as much as I used to," she continued. A faint smile crossed her face. "Judging by the look of you, you do not either. You have grown rusty, Carne. But then, you never cared for the drawing room, did you?"

He returned her smile but said nothing.

"We are not likely to meet in the ordinary course of things. I wanted to talk with you."

"I am at your service."

She made a small gesture of impatience. "You need not be polite, not with me. You are wondering why. If I tell you it is for Robert's sake, that is as near the truth as I am able to come."

Gideon waited. She wanted something. Lady Parminter never did anything without reason. But she was silent and her eyes seemed to turn inward, as though she were searching her memories. He wondered if he had misjudged her, if she was merely lonely, as people get when they contemplate their death, or if she was bent on re-writing the past to make it more palatable to her present understanding. Her next words surprised him.

"I was thinking of your wife." Her eyes now held his own. "You were unfortunate in your choice, Carne. No, Robert said nothing to me, but any fool could see the dance she led you. I did not like her, I confess that, and you may hold it against me, but such women are dangerous. They want too much from life. They promise too much. They are never satisfied."

It was, he supposed, a good description of Aline, but he did not want to hear it from Lady Parminter. "My wife is dead, madam."

"And left you in a sorry pass. Don't get on the high ropes, Carne. I hear things, you know. Whatever happened between you, you did not deserve this."

"What I did or did not deserve—" He broke off, aware that he was about to say something impolitic.

148

"Is no concern of mine. Yes, you have cause to be offended, but I do not speak of these things out of a vulgar love of gossip. I speak of them because they are true and because I would like to help you."

He didn't believe her, not for a moment. When he spoke he kept his voice light, to indicate that he was willing to play her game, at least for the length of this interview. "For Robert's sake."

"For my own. Come, Carne. I am not a sentimental woman, and I am not a fool. You were a man of uncommon understanding, and I believed you to be honest, but you encouraged Robert in the worst excesses of his republican ideas, you persuaded him to turn his back on his duty to the family name, and I deplored your influence. Now I am not so sure. Robert was not as weak as I feared, and the influence, I suspect, was his as well as yours. If I offer you help now, it is because I would think better of myself."

"This is unnecessary. I have never had cause to think you unfair to me."

She ignored this. "And it is, I will be frank with you, because of Adrian. My grandson. That is why I spoke, perhaps unfeelingly, of your wife. I understand she placed you in partnership with her brother, and the venture is not doing well. This is not what George tells me, but he has a reckless streak and he is in any case a friend of Prebble's. Now Adrian is involved. I do not know how much money he has committed to it, but he has committed his name, and that is infinitely more dangerous."

Gideon smiled. The Parminter name, he knew very well, was Hugo's hope for a new infusion of capital. "Do you think his name will be tarnished? Let me assure you, it is done every day and no one will think the worse of the Parminters."

"Yes, yes, I know that this is true, though I do not understand it." She struck the arms of her chair. "Land,

Carne. I understand land. Land is real. Land is to be cared for, it is to be preserved, it is to be increased. Robert, God rest his soul, would not take land seriously. But this passion for making money out of money, nothing but evil will come from it."

"I am inclined to agree with you, but with all respect, Lady Parminter, the Woodbourn-Prebble partners hope to make money from the sale of goods."

"Trade."

"Trade. The word is not evil in itself. It is an old profession and the lifeblood of the country."

"A gentleman has other things to do."

"A gentleman is often forced to improbable expedients to keep his land intact. But I take it that is not the case with your grandson. He is perhaps amusing himself."

"He is a spendthrift. But he is young and he will change. In the meantime, there must be no breath of scandal."

Gideon raised his brows. "Scandal?"

"Do not play with me, Carne. There has been a fire. A man is dead and there has been an inquest. There have been questions enough already."

"You fear Adrian will be touched. I think it unlikely, but if you are concerned, why not persuade him to withdraw his interest?"

"He would not. He is obsessed with India and the thought of making a fortune—a fortune, I need hardly tell you, of which he has no need. I fear the matter may get out of hand, and what I know of Sir Hugo does not make me confident that he can see this through. I must rely on you, Carne. You are clever and you will do what is right."

"I do what is in my own interest."

She regarded him intently. "I would expect nothing else. But you are hampered by debts not of your own making. If I am wrong, you will forgive my impertinence. If it is true, if three or four thousand pounds would help you out of your immediate difficulties. . . . There. I know you are a proud man. You may consider it a loan if you like, but it is not necessary. You would be looking after the interests of my grandson."

Gideon remained quite still while he returned the marchioness's gaze. It was an extraordinary offer. There was nothing, absolutely nothing that would justify it. Lady Parminter's concern seemed to be solely for Adrian. She must know that Jimson's death had been ruled an accident and that the marquis had nothing to fear from police questions. Nor could Gideon's own inquiries about George's groom be seen as a threat to Adrian. What was it she feared he had done? What was it she feared he might do?

Lady Parminter had respect for money and would not spend it lightly. Yet she was prepared to bribe him, and bribe him generously, to see that he asked no more questions that touched the name of Parminter. There was something here that he did not understand. "I daresay your grandson's interests coincide with my own." Gideon smiled to indicate he had taken no offense and intended to give none. "I appreciate your offer, Lady Parminter, but I am not yet in desperate straits."

She studied his face, as though seeking confirmation of his words. She must have found an answer, for she nodded and said, "As you wish. Help me up, Carne. It is time we returned to the others."

She moved slowly, but the pressure of her hand on his arm was light. "I have hopes of the Tassio girl," she told him. "She has pride. It is a rare commodity." She said no more until they reached the door, where she turned and looked up at him. "My grandson is not always wise. If there is a problem, you will come to me."

By which Gideon understood that he was to stand surety for Lord Parminter's good behavior and he could command any price he chose.

* * *

Fiona sat in a straight-backed armchair, close to but not quite part of the group gathered around the tea table. It was a skill she'd perfected in the months since she'd been companioning Alessa. She did not want to appear to be encroaching, a real danger for a woman in her position, nor did she want to arouse unwelcome curiosity. Now, seated within earshot of Countess Buckleigh, she was at least protected from the importunities of the earl, who had asked more questions of her at dinner than she was quite prepared to answer.

George, thank heaven, showed no inclination to renew their conversation, and no one else had approached her after dinner save Robin Melchett and his cousin Demetra. But the two young people were now gathered around the piano where George's wife was playing, and Fiona was free to watch Alessa and think about what George had told her and wonder why neither the marchioness nor Gideon was in the room.

She supposed they were together. It was only natural that Lady Parminter might wish to renew what had apparently been a long acquaintance. Still, a tête-à-tête could have been arranged easily enough in the cavernous drawing room. Fiona told herself sternly that it was none of her affair. Another voice reminded her that she was responsible for Alessa and anything that concerned the Parminters concerned her as well. A third admitted that she was enormously curious about Gideon Carne.

She knew so little about him. He had, she gathered, been a lonely child, but he would never discuss his parents. He was a man of liberal principles, but he scoffed at efforts to put them into practice. He was kind to his children, but he kept them at a distance. He was disappointed in his wife.

What on earth had they talked about, in those brief days before their intimacy had put an end to any need to talk at all? Books, yes; they had quickly discovered that they had similar tastes. He had drawn her out and had seemed genuinely interested in her opinions. It had been a heady sort of flattery, quite unlike George's appreciative references to her person, and she had seen the possibility of a new kind of relationship between a man and a woman. Before they became lovers, she thought they had become friends. Even now she could not reconcile the sting of his rejection with the man he had first appeared to be, nor understand his callous taking of Jamie's life.

Fiona was made aware that Lady Parminter had returned only by a slight disturbance in the arrangement of the room. George hurried forward, Lady Buckleigh's voice was distinctly moderated, and Lydia took her hands from the piano. The marchioness indicated that the music should continue and allowed George to hand her into her chair. Fiona watched carefully but could see nothing in the meeting, beyond George's desire to stand well with the matriarch of Parminter House. It was, she thought, unlike him. As she remembered her onetime fiancé, he stood quite high in his own estimation and needed no one else's approval, a bit of arrogance she'd once found oddly attractive. His arrogance certainly had not diminished. He must have his reasons for his attentions to the marchioness. It was, she supposed, a question of money.

Fiona felt suddenly oppressed by the opulence of the Parminter drawing room, but she knew Alessa would never agree to leave at such an early hour. Cards were mentioned and she was pressed into service at a table that included Lady Parminter, Sir Phillip, and Mr. Kittredge. It was nearly two hours later before Lady Parminter, who was a bold and skillful player and had a passion for cards, rose at last and brought the entertainment to an end.

If Fiona had found the evening a trial, the same could not be said of Alessa. "It was most satisfactory," she said as their carriage drove out of the forecourt. Her voice, the set of her head, and the smile that played about her lips disclosed a confidence that had not been evident when they left Bolton Street. "It is so very English, and I do like English ways. I am sure *Maman* means to stay here, at least until Bonaparte stops making life at home so insupportable. I know I could be quite happy here myself."

"You found the company to your taste as well?"

"But naturally. Lady Lydia is my dearest friend, and Lady Harriet is clever and kind, and Lady Demetra is clever and amusing. I like Robin Melchett. He reminds me of Simon. And Lord Parminter is the most agreeable man in the world. Don't you think so?"

"In the whole world? I could hardly judge."

"You're mocking me, Fiona. That is unkind."

"I did not mean to be unkind. I meant only to say that you have not made the acquaintance of very many men. You will certainly meet others who are equally agreeable."

"You are so unfeeling, Fiona. I have no desire to meet anyone else at all. Indeed, I have no need to. Lady Parminter approves of me, Lord Parminter told me so himself."

Fiona was silent. It was not her place to interfere, and yet she longed to urge caution on her charge.

Alessa must have sensed what Fiona could not bring herself to say, for her next words were accusing. "You do not like Adrian, I can tell it by your face. What right have you to judge him so? He is the most amiable of men, and his family is nearly as old as my father's. Not that you would understand such things, but they are important. Why shouldn't I marry an Englishman? *Maman* did, and she is blissfully happy. I think you are utterly without passion."

To this there was no possible reply, and they completed the journey in silence. When they found that the princess and her husband had already returned home, Alessa hurried up the stairs and it was left to Fiona to discover

154

from the footman that the princess was gravely overset as Mr. Langley was being sent off to Sweden on some mission or other and no one knew when they would see him again.

It was not the best of times to lay her concerns about Alessa's future before the princess. Fiona spent a restless night, rose early, and occupied herself in reading Cicero with Simon until an hour when she might properly ask for an interview with her mistress. But it was the princess who summoned her, shortly before ten o'clock.

She was in the very pretty dressing room which adjoined her bedchamber. The *Morning Chronicle* and a breakfast tray lay neglected on the table at which she was seated. Her hair was unbound and her face was tinged with melancholy, but she was courteous enough as she greeted Fiona and asked her to join her in a cup of chocolate. "Alessa has complained much of you," the princess said. "Does she have cause?"

Fiona smiled. "By her lights, perhaps. She has an impatient heart, and I was urging caution."

"You do not like the young man?"

"Alessa is very young, and I am concerned for her happiness."

"I am her mother, Miss Alastair, and I am concerned for her happiness."

Fiona accepted the rebuke but did not lower her eyes.

"You believe he does not care for her?"

"I do not know that. I was told last night that he has a mistress."

"Men do these things. They mean nothing."

"A married lady. A woman of his own class."

The princess looked at her sharply. "Her name?" Fiona was silent and the princess frowned. "No, perhaps you are right. It is of no moment. I will speak to him. It must be broken off before he proceeds."

Fiona felt a moment of foreboding. "It is decided then?"

"It will be. The young people are agreed, and neither family has any objection. I wish my daughter happy, Miss Alastair. I will not keep her from a man she truly loves. Not," she added, "when he is as supremely eligible as the Marquis of Parminter."

The interview was at an end. "Then I wish her every happiness." Fiona rose and left the room, determined to bury her misgivings. Who knew what would make a woman happy? She should not judge Alessa's chance of felicity by her own unfortunate experience.

Fiona had hoped to delay the betrothal, but the next day she learned that her interference might have inadvertently hastened the event. The princess summoned the marquis to Bolton Street at an hour when she knew Alessa would be out. He gave her, the princess later informed Fiona, the most fervent assurances that the affair in question had ended the moment he'd set eyes on her daughter. The princess had her doubts about this, but she was convinced that Parminter now meant to give his mistress her congé.

That evening Alessa returned from Mrs. Davenport's soiree and raced into the sitting room where Fiona was reading. "Congratulate me," she said, her annoyance with her governess quite forgot. "I'm going to become the Marchioness of Parminter."

Chapter Nine

Simon cast a sapient eye over the stack of cards on the hall table. "I should think," he remarked as he and Fiona descended the front steps, "that it will be a great relief to the servants when Alessa gets married." He paused on the last step, his expression suddenly serious. "I can't believe she's really accepted Parminter. I don't much like him, Fiona."

"Nor do I," Fiona admitted, "but Alessa feels differently."

"Do you honestly think she'll be happy with him?" When Fiona did not answer at once, Simon took it as confirmation of his own feelings. "Exactly. It's not just that he tries to talk to me at my own level—whatever that is. The thing is, he doesn't look at Alessa the way Michael looks at *Maman*." Simon frowned. "I am the head of the family. Do you suppose it would be any help if I forbade the match?"

"None at all."

"Yes, that's what I was afraid of. Mind you, I think girls ought to be able to decide these things for themselves. But you can't expect me just to stand by while my sister acts like a prize idiot." He kicked at a loose paving stone with the toe of his boot. "If I say anything to *Maman* she'll tell me I'm too young to understand these things. Perhaps you should talk to her, Fiona. She listens to you. Unless," he amended, looking up at his governess, "you've talked to her already."

Fiona smiled. "Have I ever told you that you are an abominably perceptive boy, Simon?"

"Several times," he said cheerfully. "What did *Maman* say?"

"She doesn't want anyone interfering in Alessa's life the way her parents interfered in hers."

Simon groaned. "But it's not the same thing at all. *Maman* was in love with Michael and Alessa's in love with Parminter."

"Some people might find the distinction less than clear cut."

"Not if they had any sense." Simon fell silent as they passed a tired nursemaid and three young children returning home from an early morning outing. *"Maman* would listen to Michael," he continued. "And Michael would listen to you."

"Yes," Fiona agreed, "I think he might. I mean to speak to him as soon as he returns." She did not add that she feared it would do little good, and Simon, who placed an unwarranted faith in her ability to right matters, seemed much cheered. They had reached Berkley Square, and perhaps it was the proximity of their destination which turned his thoughts to their luncheon engagement.

"I suppose I'll have to tell Verity about the betrothal, though Alessa really should have done it herself." A look of sudden horror crossed his face. "Fiona, you don't suppose Verity will be like Alessa in ten years or so, do you?"

"I shouldn't worry," Fiona told him, "sisters can turn out remarkably different." She might have added that Verity Drake resembled Alessa about as much as she herself resembled Clare. The comparison was unfair to Alessa, but the circumstances were not dissimilar. Like Fiona, Verity was a bastard, the product of an indiscretion committed by Simon's father on a trip to England nearly nine years ago. The relationship was not generally known, but the princess and Langley were on good terms with Verity's guardians, Lord and Lady Windham, and they saw to it that the children had frequent opportunities to meet. Alessa, wrapped up in herself, showed only sporadic interest in the child, but Simon had been delighted to discover the existence of a little sister. By the time they reached the Windham house in Hill Street he was grinning almost like the boy he was, his concerns about his elder sister eclipsed by the delight of seeing the younger.

Fiona's feelings were rather more mixed. In the two days since the Parminter dinner, she had realized that if she were to pursue the question of her mother's identity, she would require an ally. She had, of course, already accepted Gideon's help, however grudgingly. Because of today's luncheon engagement, Peter had come to Bolton Street in the morning, and when Gideon called for him, they had arranged to meet in Hyde Park the following day. But the very fact that she found herself looking forward to the meeting made Fiona more determined than ever to ask nothing further from Gideon. Besides, the search for her mother required someone who moved through the best drawing rooms in London, someone very much like Lady Windham. But if she were to ask for Lady Windham's help she would have to confess at least some of what she had been at such pains to conceal for the past five years.

When the footman showed them into the back garden, they found Lady Windham standing on a white-painted settee, attempting to retrieve something from the branches of an oak tree, while Verity and a half-grown brown-and-white puppy looked on with interest. Verity caught sight of her half-brother out of the corner of her eye and hurried over to greet him, long brown hair bouncing on her shoulders. The footman, aware that this

159

was no time to stand on ceremony, quietly withdrew. The puppy continued to look anxiously at Lady Windham. Lady Windham pulled a battered stick from the branches and tossed it to the puppy, who caught it in midair and retired beneath the table, clutching her toy possessively.

"Miss Alastair, Simon, I'm so glad to see you." Calmly brushing the dirt from her hands, Lady Windham gathered up the skirt of a Parisian wrapping dress, every bit as smart as anything Princess Sofia possessed, and jumped to the ground. "I'm afraid Perdita's stick ended up in the tree again and whenever that happens she acts as though we've stolen her last shilling."

"I'm the one who threw it into the tree," Verity confessed, "but I couldn't reach up far enough to get it down. You've got something in your hair, Mummy."

Grinning, Lady Windham pulled a twig from her short red-gold curls and gestured for her guests to be seated. "It's such a nice day we thought we'd have a luncheon alfresco," she explained, indicating the wrought-iron table which had been laid for four. "Charles is sorry he couldn't be here. He had to go to the House."

"It's about the India charter," Verity told Simon. "Daddy says he's not at all sure we have the right to decide these matters for the Indians," she continued in careful tones, as if quoting her foster father's exact words, "but if we insist on doing so, the least we owe them is proper consideration."

Simon frowned. He'd been a small boy when the Tassios and the rest of the Savoyard Court fled to Sardinia and from an early age he had been aware of the anger many Sardinians felt toward their Savoyard rulers. "I thought the charter had to do with commerce, not government," he said at last.

"I sometimes wonder if the two can ever be separated," Lady Windham said, absently righting Verity's cloth doll, which had been knocked over during the contretemps with the stick.

Still frowning, Simon nodded; he was roused from his abstraction only when Verity asked after Alessa. His frown deepened. "She's going to marry—that is, she's betrothed to Lord Parminter," he said bluntly.

"Oh." Verity stared at her half-brother for a long moment.

"I thought they looked rather secretive at the Davenports' last night," Lady Windham said into the silence. "You must give her our congratulations, Simon."

Simon nodded, and Verity tactfully began to tell him about *La Dama Soldata,* an opera which her parents had taken her to see two days previously. Simon was diverted and luncheon passed pleasantly, but Fiona continued to mull over whether or not to seek Lady Windham's help. For all their friendly conversations about the children, Fiona did not really know her very well. They had met the previous September when Simon and Verity were both in danger, and in that crisis the social distinction between a governess and a baron's daughter had seemed unimportant. Lady Windham, with her cheerful disregard for convention, would probably claim that it still was, but Fiona knew better. As they finished an assortment of fresh fruit from the Windham estate in Devon, Fiona finally made her decision and asked her hostess if she could speak to her for a few minutes.

Lady Windham was somewhat unconventional, but in some ways she was more well bred than many of her peers. "Perhaps we'd best go inside," she said, with no hint of surprise or curiosity. "Perdita wants to play, and that makes the garden a rather precarious place."

Perdita had emerged from hiding, the stick still in her mouth, and was regarding everyone expectantly. When the footman returned to clear away the luncheon things, Lady Windham left the children to entertain the dog and each other and led Fiona through a pair of French windows into a small room with pale gray walls, a lovingly polished pianoforte, and a great deal of clutter.

"Charles said if I was going to spend so much time at the piano I might as well try composing," she explained, shifting a stack of loose paper covered with musical notations from a work table to the pianoforte itself. "I tried a bit when I was younger, but then I discovered men and got distracted. Please excuse the mess. If you hand me that enormous folio, you'll find there's quite a comfortable chair underneath."

She was doing her best to put her visitor at ease. Fiona studied the other woman for a moment. "I've no right, but I must ask for your help, Lady Windham," she said, still wondering whether she was being sensible or completely mad.

"I should say you've every right, considering what a help you were to us last September. Is it about Simon? I've already told Charles we'll have to think twice before we send any son of ours into the purgatory of public school."

Fiona smiled. "No, the difficulty is my own." She hesitated, acutely conscious that she'd left her gloves and reticule outside and had nothing with which to occupy her hands. "My parents were not married, you see," Fiona said steadily. "I was raised by my father, who led me to believe that my mother had been a shopgirl who'd died when I was born. Since my return to England, I have learned that he may have been less than candid with me."

Fiona was not sure what sort of reaction she expected, but it was certainly not the one she got. "Parents can be dreadful, can't they?" Lady Windham said with feeling. "I wouldn't dream of saying so in front of Simon, but I think his father was shockingly negligent where Verity was concerned. You suspect your mother is not dead? Or that she was well born? If the second is true, it would explain why your father lied about the first."

"Exactly." Until that moment Fiona had doubted the wisdom of her decision. Now her fears vanished. Omitting any mention of Gideon Carne or Woodbourn-Prebble or the fact that her name was not Alastair, she told Lady Windham the story of her birth as she had pieced it together thus far.

Lady Windham listened carefully, her hazel eyes intent but free of censure or surprise. "Then it remains only to determine which of the Bowder or Selkirk girls made a trip abroad with her mother in the spring of 1784," she said when Fiona stopped speaking. "Or no, I suppose the older lady could have been an aunt or companion. I'm not well acquainted with either family, but it shouldn't be too difficult to make inquiries. Do you know what became of the daughters?"

"Maria Selkirk married a Mr. Kittredge. I believe he is connected with the Board of Control."

"Of course, I know their daughter slightly. I'll call on her as soon as possible. And I'll write to Charles's mother. She lives near Edinburgh and will likely know something of the families. I daresay my own mother will be able to help as well. She's an endless font of information on just about everything."

Her expression more pensive, Lady Windham looked out into the garden where Simon and Verity were attempting to persuade Perdita to shake hands with Verity's doll. "Verity must take after her mother, she doesn't look a bit like a Tassio. It's odd, she never asks about her parents. I suppose it's because she has us as substitutes, but if I were she, I think I'd have turned my unknown mother into someone out of a fairytale."

"It's remarkably easy to do," Fiona said, forcing a smile. Throughout the years of Uncle James's casual neglect and her stepmother's veiled disapproval, she had told herself that if only her mother had lived, her life would have been different. The illusion faded as she grew older, but it had taken her discoveries of the past fortnight for it to shatter completely. She could not, of course, know the circumstances which had forced her

163

mother to give her up. But after her glimpse of Mrs. Kittredge, she knew she must be prepared to find that her mother was not a very interesting woman and perhaps not even a particularly nice one. It was silly that it mattered so much, but she could not deny that it did.

"I know I may not like what I find out," she assured Lady Windham. "You needn't worry that I'm not prepared to face reality."

Lady Windham smiled. "I find it hard to imagine anything you wouldn't be prepared to face, Miss Alastair. I'll do my best to help you discover the truth. And I hope you realize that whatever happens, you may count me your friend."

Gideon was frowning as he followed his children and their nursemaid through the Chesterfield Gate. In the quarter-hour since they'd left Dover Street, his conversational gambits had been treated with polite indifference by everyone but Barbara, who seemed torn between disapproval of her employer and sympathy for the obvious difficulty he was having with the children. He had run out of ideas when they drewn back to let a lone horseman on a handsome sorrel canter past. The sight stirred a chord of memory. Gideon glanced at Peter, hesitated, then decided he had nothing to lose. "I used to take you up on Benjamin when I went out for a morning ride. Do you remember?"

Involuntarily Peter turned to his father, his face lit by the same memory. Then, in the split second it takes for instinct to give way to reason, his eyes hardened. "I was Teddy's age when you left. I remember a lot of things."

. In silence they turned onto the footpath which led to the Serpentine. Beth, as usual, walked a little apart. Teddy was frowning in what appeared to be an effort of concentration. "Was Benjamin a black horse?" he asked suddenly.

164

Gideon smiled. "Black as coal," he said, warning himself not to push too far. "I took you up on him as well, but I'd have thought you were too young to remember." In those days he had made an effort not to favor Peter, who he never doubted was his son, over Teddy, who he suspected was not.

Teddy was still frowning. "I'm not sure whether I remember or not. Maybe it's just that I've heard Peter talk . . ." He stopped as if he was not sure he ought to repeat his brother's words. "What happened to Benjamin?" he asked with concern.

"I asked a friend of mine, Mr. Camford, to look after him while I was away. Perhaps we could get him back now. Would you like that?"

Teddy's face brightened, but anything he might have said was cut off by his elder brother. "You asked someone to take care of your *horse?*" Peter, who had walked on ahead, stopped and looked back at Gideon. He did not finish the thought, but the implication was clear enough. Gideon had shown more concern for his horse than for his children. Strictly speaking, it was not true. He had left the children to Aline, who for all her faults had not been without affection for her offspring. But he could with justice be accused of letting his self-disgust blind him to the needs of others.

If Teddy did not entirely comprehend the exchange between his father and brother, he understood the sentiment behind it. For a moment he looked from one to the other in puzzlement, but when Peter turned away and began walking on, Teddy hurried forward and ranged himself at his side.

Gideon was watching the two boys with their identical straight-backed posture when he felt a small tug at his fingers. Beth had fallen into step beside him and taken hold of his hand. As Gideon looked down, she raised her dark gray eyes and gave a shy, but utterly trusting smile. Gideon smiled back, though he had the unnerving sense that he had just been asked for something he did not have to give.

Unlike their earlier meeting in the park, Fiona and Simon were the first to arrive. Peter saw them sitting on a bench in the trees along the bank of the Serpentine and hurried forward, followed closely by Teddy. Beth, normally as active as her brothers, remained at Gideon's side. By the time they reached the bench, Teddy, armed with a packet of stale rolls Fiona had brought, had run to a small outcropping of rock, followed at a more dignified pace by Peter and Simon. Ducks were already swimming toward them from every direction: brightly plumed males, soft, brown females, and downy young ones who darted about in enthusiastic imitation of their elders, though they did not seem to have grasped the point of the exercise.

"Come on, Beth." Barbara cast a veiled glance from her employer to Miss Alastair, then held out her hand to the little girl. "Let's make sure the boys stay out of trouble."

Beth took the nursemaid's hand without objection, but as they left she turned to look back at Gideon for a long moment. "It seems you've acquired an admirer," Fiona remarked.

"She's too young to know any better." Gideon grinned, though in truth he was not sure what to make of Beth's behavior. He paused, partly to allow Beth and Barbara to move off, partly because there was something oddly seductive about sitting here beside Fiona in what might almost be called a companionable silence.

The children's shouts drifted back to them, mingled with the insistent guttural honking and softer clacking noises made by the ducks. The water was dappled dark and light by the shadows of the trees which were in turn reflected back, shimmering. It was impossible not to recall the less ornamental stream which ran along the boundary between Digby Hall and Hartwood, and the scenes which had transpired along its banks five years before.

"You've learned something?" Fiona's voice, crisper and less musical than usual, broke the silence.

Gideon reluctantly returned to the present. "I think it's safe to say that. Exactly what I've learned is a matter of debate." In the dispassionate tone he'd found the best antidote to unwanted feeling, he told her how Adam had traced Jimson to George's groom and then described his own confrontations with Hugo and George.

Fiona listened closely but without visible change of emotion. "Do you believe what Hugo told you?"

"I believe George has bamboozled Hugo—not exactly a Herculean labor."

Her mouth curved in a smile which held a touch of mischief, and for a moment he thought the old Fiona had broken through, but when he returned the smile she looked away at once. "Why didn't you tell me about George earlier?"

"I meant to, but our private conversation has been limited. I'm sorry, if I'd known you were to dine at Parminter House I'd have warned you."

Fiona shrugged, a reminder that she could take care of herself. Then her brows knit together. "Gideon, when did George become a partner in Woodbourn-Prebble?"

"Early in the new year, I believe," Gideon said, schooling his voice not to betray surprise.

Fiona seemed quite unaware that she'd used his given name. Her gaze was fixed on a lone duck trailing smooth glassy eddies of water in its wake as it hurried to join its fellows. "By then George must have known Woodbourn-Prebble was all you had left."

"A vendetta? Surely that's a bit melodramatic for Barrington-Forbes."

"A week ago I would have agreed." Fiona turned back to him, her eyes free of anything but the need to communicate her anxiety. "A week ago I thought you were foolish to see him as a threat. But after the dinner party . . . he's angry, Gideon, far angrier than I expected. I think he'd like nothing better than to hurt both of us."

Recalling the scene in the Parminter drawing room, Gideon again felt the helpless rage which had gripped him when he realized he had been outmaneuvered by George and now had no choice but to leave Fiona alone in the other man's company. "What did Barrington-Forbes say to you?" he demanded, more roughly than he intended.

"It was quite tiresome," she said, adjusting the gray folds of her skirt. "He made some rather vague threats about the precarious nature of my position, which was ridiculous, considering that if the truth ever came out, it would deal an enormous blow to his *amour-propre—* "

"Damnation." Gideon was not deceived by her light tone. "What else?"

"Very little. Except that he assured me Lord Parminter will make Lady Alessandra an experienced husband, for he's been Clare's lover these past eight months." She paused and looked at him. "Did you know?"

"I suspected," Gideon said, shifting his position on the hard bench as casually as possible. "Interesting, but it hardly provides a motive for the fire."

"No. Is your leg bothering you? Perhaps we should walk for a bit."

Gideon grinned. "So much for stoicism," he said, getting to his feet. He started to extend his hand to her but checked himself before the gesture became too obvious.

Fiona moved toward the water to see how Barbara and the children were faring. The rolls were long since gone, and Simon and the young Carnes were now staring in fascination at a duck with brilliant black and green markings who had seized a smaller brown duck by the neck and was making vigorous attempts to climb on top of her. The breeze had quickened and it carried back an anxious cry from Beth. "He's hurting her!" Barbara's reply was not quite audible, but it produced nervous laughs from all four children. Fiona started to laugh herself and then, suddenly conscious of Gideon beside her, felt her face grow warm. She raised one hand to tuck a strand of hair, loosened by the breeze, back beneath her bonnet, thus blocking her expression from his view.

As they turned and began walking in the opposite direction, Gideon once again carefully clasped his hands behind his back. "I haven't yet told you the reason I asked you to meet me today. I had an interview with the marchioness before I left Parminter House on Thursday."

"Let me guess," Fiona said, feeling more at ease. "She tried to persuade you, with the greatest possible tact, to stop your inquiries into the fire?"

"More or less. Rather a lot of money was mentioned."

"And?" Fiona said, after a moment.

"If I mention the word honor, you'll probably laugh in my face, so let's just say I don't like to feel I'm being manipulated. The important thing is that the marchioness must realize the risk she ran in offering me a bribe. I'll lay you odds she knows more about the fire than either of us."

Fiona nodded slowly even as a quite incredible thought began to take shape in her head. The Marchioness of Parminter was aunt to the three Selkirk sisters, and one of them might have had an illicit affair with James Woodbourn. The box Jimson had been investigating when the fire started contained James's papers. Could the marchioness have hired Jimson to break into the warehouse because she feared those papers contained some reference to her niece's indiscretion?

It seemed completely mad and yet had its own curious logic. If it was true, where did George fit in? The thought that he might be privy to the secrets of her birth brought a bitter taste to Fiona's mouth. Suddenly her desire to talk was stronger than any scruples about involving Gideon in her personal affairs. Except for that brief, rather ridiculous moment with the ducks, she had been feeling quite comfortable in his presence today. Besides, if there was even a remote chance it involved the fire, in all fairness she should tell Gideon the whole. But when she spoke his name and he swung round to face her, the words died on her lips.

Sitting at opposite ends of the bench, walking some inches apart, she had found it possible to forget the complex web of emotions which lay between them. Only now, standing so close that she could see that the fine line which ran from his temple into his hair was actually the remnant of a scar, forced to look into the dark eyes which held too many memories, did she realize how easily those emotions could overwhelm her. Throughout the past weeks the anger that was her only defense against him had slowly worn away, leaving only a thin veneer.

"What is it?" Gideon's voice had softened. It was almost caressing, like rough velvet.

Fiona drew a ragged breath. Jamie, she must think of Jamie, she must think of something to keep herself from becoming wholly vulnerable. "Nothing," she said, drawing her tattered reserve about her as best she could. "That is, I thought it was important, but it really isn't. I'm sorry."

Suddenly brusque, he nodded, then turned, as if to indicate that their tête-à-tête was at an end, and started walking rapidly toward the children. Against every caution of her better judgment, Fiona hurried after him. "Gideon."

He stopped again and looked at her in inquiry, but if he was surprised he gave no sign of it. Fiona was suddenly breathless, no doubt because she'd had to run to catch up with him. "Watch out for George. You were right. He's a dangerous man."

Now she did see surprise in his face, followed by a smile that was rueful and entirely unforced. "You'd do better to save your concern for a worthier object, Fiona."

"You're forgetting our agreement," she reminded him. "Until we resolve the matter of the will, I have a stake in what becomes of you."

"In that case, I can only say what you have so often said to me. I can take care of myself. In fact I'm damnably good at it, as I learned in the Peninsula, rather to my disappointment."

By the time she grasped the meaning of his last words, he had started forward once more and was calling to the children. Fiona stared after him. He was being ironic, of course; he must be. If Gideon had really wanted to get himself killed he'd have had plenty of opportunity. Fiona joined the others and said abruptly that it was nearing twelve o'clock and time they were leaving.

It was only natural for the two parties to walk together. Simon, who had taken an unaccountable liking to Gideon, asked if he'd heard any of the debates on the East India Company's charter and proceeded to pose several difficult questions. Beth clung to her father's side, but Peter and Teddy fell behind with Fiona and Barbara. Following his brother's example, Teddy treated Fiona as an old friend, but Barbara regarded her with a wariness which bordered on disapproval.

They separated at Bolton Street. Peter was to accompany Simon home for luncheon and lessons, and Fiona had just realized that she should give some thought to the afternoon's instruction when they reached the Langley house and were greeted by an unhappy Christopher. He smiled at the boys but addressed Fiona. "The princess wants to see you, Miss Alastair—immediately. She's in her dressing room."

The footman's concern was touching and rather amusing. Fiona had long since grown accustomed to Princess Sofia's mercurial moods. With Langley's departure, her temper had worsened noticeably, and Fiona had known it was only a matter of time until something set her off.

She sent the boys on to her sitting room, decided she'd better not take time to remove her bonnet, and proceeded to the princess's suite, wondering what had happened to annoy Simon's mother this time. Most likely it involved Alessa. Fiona was constantly being called upon to moderate between the strong-willed mother and daughter.

She found the princess seated on a silk daybed, her hands clenched, her back straight, her eyes glittering like her famous emeralds. "You'd best sit down, Miss Alastair."

Fiona sank into a small lyre-back chair near the daybed. The princess regarded her in silence for what seemed an exceptionally long interval. Her eyes, normally so full of life, were colder than Fiona had ever seen them, and her generous mouth was drawn into an uncompromising line. "There are a number of things we must discuss," she said at last, her tone, if possible, even colder than her expression. "Perhaps you had best start by telling me why you willfully lied to us from the very beginning."

Chapter Ten

It would not help matters to be sick all over the Savonnerie carpet, and she was not going to be sick, no matter how horribly her insides churned. "I needed a job, Princess. Quite desperately."

Sometimes such blunt honesty broke through the princess's anger. This was not one of those occasions. *"Juste ciel,* have you no shame?" she demanded.

Another woman might have flung herself at the princess's knees and begged forgiveness, but Fiona could not bring herself to plead or offer up excuses. "Would it make any difference if I had?" she asked quietly.

The princess regarded her in disbelief for a moment, then rose and paced to the window where she stood in silence for a long moment, staring out at the garden below. "Lady Prebble called on me this morning. Though we've never been introduced, she felt it her duty to tell me the truth about the woman who has charge of my children."

Fiona had scarcely had time to wonder who had betrayed her secret, but she was conscious of surprise. After their interview last October, she had felt confident that Clare had nothing to gain from spreading the story. What had changed her mind? "Lady Prebble," Fiona returned, "has been aware of my position in your household since last October. Did she explain why it took her nine months to act upon her sense of duty?"

The princess turned and her eyes flickered, acknowledging that Fiona had made a point. "I have heard Lady Prebble's version of events, Miss Alastair," she said in a more moderate tone, returning to the daybed. "I would like to hear your own. I think you will agree that it is long overdue."

Fiona could not deny the justice of this claim, but it was the first time she had told the story to anyone and it was difficult for her to know how or where to begin. "I was born Fiona Martin," she said at last. "My father, James Woodbourn, and his wife brought me up along with their legitimate children, Clare—now Lady Prebble—and Jamie. After my stepmother died six years ago, I went to stay with my sister and help look after her children. The following spring I became betrothed to Mr. Barrington-Forbes, a friend of Sir Hugo's."

Put like that, it sounded as if Clare had done her utmost to find her sister a husband, as she'd promised Uncle James when she'd persuaded him to leave Fiona at Digby Hall. In fact, Clare had been as surprised as Fiona when her husband's friend offered for her sister. They had met on a number of occasions, for George was a frequent visitor at Digby Hall when Hugo and Clare were in residence, but beyond the usual practiced gallantries he had not distinguished Fiona with any particular attentions. Then, during a brief visit in June, he had offered her his hand. She was still not sure why he had done so.

"And Mr. Barrington-Forbes subsequently married Lydia Melchett," the princess said. "Go on . . . how did you become acquainted with Lord Carne? Lady Prebble said there was a family connection."

"Lord Carne's wife was Sir Hugo's sister, and the Carnes are the Prebbles' nearest neighbors in Hertfordshire. But though I frequently took the Prebble children to see their Carne cousins, I seldom saw Lord Carne, who spent most of his time in London. Then, soon after our betrothal, Mr. Barrington-Forbes returned to London along with Sir Hugo and Lady Prebble. I was alone with the children when Lord Carne arrived in the country unexpectedly. Suddenly we found ourselves thrown together and . . . I think you know what transpired after that."

Even as she spoke, an unbidden mosaic of images formed behind Fiona's eyes: the accidental meeting at the boundary of the Prebble and Carne properties, the daily meetings thereafter, the moment she'd known irrevocably that she'd give her heart to this angry, wounded man, the delirium of surrender. "I was very much in love and was foolish enough to believe the feeling was returned," she said, surprised to find her voice so steady. "I scarcely gave a thought to the future, but when Mr. Barrington-Forbes and the others returned to Hertfordshire I knew I could not go through with my wedding. We had an informal dinner party that night—my brother and a friend of his had come up from London with the Prebbles—and I contrived a few moments alone with Lord Carne and offered—practically insisted—that he set me up as his mistress."

"I see." Princess Sofia's face and voice were devoid of any expression. "And then?"

"Lord Carne told me I was a fool, that I should marry Mr. Barrington-Forbes and take my lovers where I could." Even now, Fiona could not repeat the words without bitterness. "I was hurt as only the very naive can be. I had already broken my engagement to Mr. Barrington-Forbes, but even had I not, I knew the marriage was impossible. I went upstairs and began to pack my things, intending to return to my father's home in Kent. The whole sorry matter might have ended there had my brother not got wind of it. When I woke the next morning I learned that he and Lord Carne had fought and Jamie was dead."

"And so Lord Carne left the country?"

"No. Not because of the law, at any rate. Sir Hugo saw to it that word of the duel was hushed up. Jamie's death had been accidental—Lord Carne wasn't shooting to kill, and he was badly wounded himself." But that Gideon had accepted the challenge of an untried boy at all was sheer lunacy. And if, with perverse male logic, he had felt impelled to fight, why hadn't he deloped?

"The Prebbles took Jamie's body back to Kent for burial," Fiona continued steadily. "I accompanied them, but when we arrived, my father refused to speak to me, so the day after the funeral I took the stage to London. I visited all the registry offices but it was quite impossible to find a job without references and my money soon began to run out. That was when I heard you were looking for a governess to go out to Sardinia. And yes, I did forge my references. As I said, I was desperate."

The princess was watching her closely. One could not precisely say that her face had softened, but she certainly looked more thoughtful than she had at the start of the interview. "I am not a stranger to passion, Miss Alastair," she said at last. "And I am aware that the world is not always kind to women, especially those so unfortunate as to lack the protection of family and fortune. I make no judgment on your actions before you came to us. But," she continued, her voice regaining the edge it had lost, "when you lied to us about those actions, you risked tainting my children with your scandal. That I can never forgive."

Fiona started to protest, but the princess raised a hand to silence her. "I said I am aware that the world is not always kind, but it is the world we must live in. It is the world in which Alessa must make her way. *Mon Dieu.*" The reversion to French was a sure sign of the princess's returning anger. "I entrusted Alessa to your care. Did you not consider what the effect would be on her should the scandal ever become public?"

The charge that she'd been negligent in her duties was not something Fiona could let pass. "If I had suspected that Alessa or Simon could be hurt—"

"If you did not suspect it, you are either more foolish or more naive than I credited. Scandal has always been the most contagious of diseases. It was you who introduced Lord Carne into our household." This recollection seemed to stir the princess's temper. "Is he your lover still?"

"No," Fiona said, rather too sharply. "And if you will recollect, it was Simon's friendship with Peter Carne which led Lord Carne to call on you. I was not pleased that they had become acquainted, but I did not want my personal concerns to prevent Simon from seeing his friend."

"Very well. I will not accuse you of mendacity on that account. But if your past became known, people could be pardoned for drawing the worst inference from Lord Carne's visits to our house, and it could not but reflect on all of us. Mr. Barrington-Forbes's involvement in the story makes it doubly dangerous, for it could damage Alessa's relations with the Parminter family. I need hardly add that the talk would do no good for my husband's career either.

"You have dined at our table," the princess continued, as if this was the most unforgivable of Fiona's crimes. "Dear God, I had even thought of finding you a husband."

This last was news to Fiona, and she was not pleased by the air of *noblesse oblige.* In five years she had not

177

managed to learn deference. "Thank you, Princess, but I have no desire to marry." She rose. "If you have nothing more to say to me, perhaps I should pack my things."

The princess regarded her for a moment, baffled by her betrayal. Then with a brisk nod she rose as well and moved to a delicate *bonheur-de-jour* writing desk. "Your wages to the end of the quarter," she said, lifting a packet from the desk top. She hesitated, something almost like sympathy creeping into her eyes. "I have added a little more, but you understand, I'm sure, that under the circumstances I cannot possibly furnish you with a reference. Christopher will summon you a hackney."

Fiona took the packet, keeping her head high and her face expressionless, but before she could speak the sitting room door opened. *"Maman*—oh, Fiona, I didn't know you were back."

Alessa's color was high and she wore a new riding habit, trimmed *à la militaire,* which reminded Fiona that her charge had gone riding with her betrothed and Lady Lydia that very morning. "I'm sorry," Alessa said, an unaccustomed note of uncertainty creeping into her voice as she looked from her mother to her governess, "I didn't mean to interrupt."

"It's all right." Fiona smiled at Alessa and told herself not to do anything as morbid as wonder when she would see her again. "I was just going." Without a backward glance she left the room and went straight to her sitting room, where she found Peter and Simon flopped in a patch of sun by the windows with Simon's chess set laid out between them.

Simon greeted his governess with a grin. "We were beginning to think we'd get off lessons for the whole afternoon. Was *Maman* in a dreadful temper? I suppose it would be too much to hope she and Alessa had a row about Parminter."

Fiona closed the door, unsure how to conduct the scene ahead. "As it happens," she said, dropping down beside the boys in an informal pose she had adopted hundreds of times in the past, "we aren't going to have any lessons this afternoon. I'm going away."

"Away?" Simon scrambled to his knees. "Where? Was I right about Parminter? Is *Maman* sending you off with Alessa? Why can't someone else go with her?"

"No, I'm going alone. Your mother and I have agreed that it will be best."

"Best? Best for whom?" The implications were so incredible that it took a moment for Simon to comprehend what lay behind her words. *"Maman* asked you to leave? She can't." The words were flat and succinct, but Simon's straight dark brows had drawn together in what, twenty years hence, would be a ferocious scowl. "I won't let her."

Fiona summoned a smile. "Haven't I told you never to make categorical statements before you know all the facts? As it happens your mother has every right to ask me to leave. No, Simon," she continued, forestalling his protest, "hear me out. When I came to work for your family, I was not entirely honest about my background."

Fiona was relieved to see no anger or disgust in Simon's expression. "Then you must have had your reasons," he said, the stubborn set of his face unaltered.

"I did. But it doesn't excuse the fact that I lied."

Simon made a rude noise. "Father lied to all of us about Verity," he pointed out, then glanced involuntarily at Peter, for he wasn't supposed to speak of his half-sister to anyone outside the family.

"Are you saying he was right to do so?" Fiona asked.

"No, of course not, but—you know what *Maman* is

179

like when she's angry, she says things she doesn't mean. I daresay she'll have forgotten all about it by tonight."

Fiona shook her head. "This is different. Believe me, I know." She turned to Simon's friend. "I'm sorry you were caught in the middle of this, Peter."

Peter gave an awkward smile. Simon was by no means ready to let the scene end, but before he could speak his sister burst into the room. "Fiona, thank goodness you're still here." Alessa hurried across the room and knelt beside them, quite as if she were still a child of seventeen. "There's no reasoning with *Maman,* but Michael should be back within a fortnight, and I know he'll be able to make her see sense."

Fiona suspected that Langley, kindly and reasonable though he was, would take the same position as his wife, but she was touched by Alessa's concern. Simon seconded his sister's suggestion. Fiona must tell them her direction. Well, if she did not yet know, she must send them word as soon as she was settled. It was only with some difficulty that she was able to prevent Simon from pressing his pocket money on her, and even Alessa insisted that Fiona contact them if she found herself in straitened circumstances.

Fiona made an evasive response and escaped into her bedchamber, her eyes beginning to smart. Sternly reminding herself that she could not afford the luxury of tears, she threw her night things, a change of linen, and her garnet pendant into a worn valise. Alessa and the boys trooped beside her to the entrance hall where Christopher was waiting, his face showing mingled shock and outrage. "Miss Alastair, if there's anything I can do—"

"Thank you, Christopher. Could you tell the princess I'll send for the rest of my things when I'm settled?"

"Of course . . . anything." He would no doubt have said more, but Fiona forestalled him by moving to the door and he got there barely in time to open it for her.

She was out of the house but she still had to take leave of the children, who had followed her onto the front steps. Alessa flung her arms around her governess and repeated that everything was sure to come right. Simon's hug was even fiercer than his sister's, but his voice was carefully matter-of-fact: "I think it would be best if you left word for us with the Windhams'. *They'll* be on our side."

When Fiona and Simon broke apart, Peter moved forward and held out his hand. "Good-bye, Miss Alastair. I *know* I'll see you again."

The hackney driver watched the protracted farewells with evident impatience. "Where to, miss?" he asked, when Fiona had at last descended the steps.

Fiona hesitated. She could look for lodgings, but though the princess had been generous, the longer she could make her money last, the better. She suspected the Windhams would give her shelter for as long as she needed, but to ask it of them would be to jeopardize their friendship with the Langleys and possibly cause a breach between Simon and Verity. Tom Constable would help her, but it would cause talk if she stayed under his roof in his wife's absence. That left only one option. She could not impose on Margaret for long, but it would be a temporary haven.

"Aylesbury Street, Clerkenwell," Fiona told the driver, and allowed him to hand her into the carriage.

"She'll be all right for a fortnight or so, Simon," Alessa said, regarding her brother across the Pembroke table in Fiona's sitting room. "*Maman* won't have turned her off penniless."

"*Maman* turned her off without a reference, Alessa." Simon repeated the words slowly, as if his sister's wits had gone begging. "You know what Michael says about what happens to people who can't find work."

Alessa could not but recall some of their stepfather's stories about the evils of poverty, but she held her ground. "Michael will be back long before Fiona is in such desperate straits."

"How on earth do you know?" Simon demanded, giving the table leg a vicious kick. "You've never had to get by on your own for so much as an hour, have you?"

A retort sprang to Alessa's lips, but she suppressed it. Simon's anger was only a sign of how upset he was, and his young friend Peter looked every bit as concerned. In Fiona's absence, Alessa was very conscious of her duties as elder sister. "I'm sorry, Simon. If it would make you feel better I suppose I could ask Lord Parminter—"

"No." Simon gripped the tabletop. "Thank you," he added. "But I don't think Fiona would want a lot of strangers to know about this."

"Lord Parminter is hardly a stranger, he's—oh, very well." Alessa frowned. For reasons she could not quite explain, she agreed with Simon. Adrian was a paragon among men, but he was not the man for this particular problem. "I must go and change," she said, pushing back her chair, as if by doing so she could push aside the disconcerting thought. "I promised *Maman* I'd join her for luncheon." She got to her feet and gathered up the trailing skirt of her riding habit but hesitated, her eyes on her brother. "It will be all right, Simon. You'll see."

"Of course it will be all right." Simon's chin was set with determination, making his delicate face appear surprisingly square. "I'm going to see to it."

Alessa smiled and said good-bye to Peter. Simon

snorted as the door closed behind her. "Ask Parminter for help. Of all the idiot notions—"

Peter stared fixedly at the tabletop. Though Lord Parminter had never shown much interest in the Carne children, he'd been a shadowy but constant presence in their lives for over four years. Peter had seen the way his mother and Parminter smiled at each other and he'd been aware of the servants' whispers. Eager to avoid talking about the marquis, he sought to change the subject. "Miss Alastair gave an address to the hackney driver. We could visit her and make sure she's all right."

Simon shook his head. "If Fiona's in trouble she'll never admit it to us, and even if we could find out, she'd never take our money." He fixed his friend with a level gaze. "There's no other alternative, Peter. You'll have to tell your father."

"My father?" Peter sat back in his chair, recoiling instinctively from the suggestion.

"Say that Fiona's gone to Margaret's," Simon continued, ignoring Peter's objection. "Your father will understand, he's been there before."

"He's what? How do you know?"

"Because I was there too. With Fiona. Margaret used to work for her family, you see—"

"No, I don't see." Whatever his feelings for his father, Peter did not care for the idea that Simon knew more about Gideon than he did. "Why did my father visit Miss Alastair's family's servant? And why didn't you tell me about it?"

"I don't know why he went to visit her. Not exactly. And I would have told you, but you rather tend to fly into the boughs whenever I mention him."

Recognizing the justice of this accusation, Peter was silent. Simon pressed his advantage. "I'm not saying you don't have reason to be angry with your father, Peter, but please don't let it get in the way now. He's the only person who can help us. Help Fiona, I mean."

Recalling his talk with his father on the night of the fire, Peter realized Simon was right. Whatever his faults, Gideon would know how to help Miss Alastair. He reluctantly acquiesced and Simon slumped back in his chair with an unprincely sigh of relief.

They learned no more about the reasons behind Miss Alastair's departure before Peter left Davies Street. Thomas, the most junior of the footmen, brought in their luncheon and then returned to see Peter home. It was only when they reached Dover Street that Peter discovered that Thomas had a letter from the princess for his father. Adam, who greeted them at the door, took the letter without comment. His face remained impassive until five seconds after the door closed behind Thomas. Then he looked at Peter in friendly inquiry.

It was difficult not to like Adam, and Peter had long since given up the attempt. "I'm not sure what's in the note," he said truthfully, "but I need to talk to my father. Is he at home?"

"In the library. Here," Adam added casually, holding out the note, "you'd best take him this." He grinned as he spoke, almost as if he was trying to bolster Peter's spirits for the interview ahead. Heartened, Peter grinned back, took the sealed note, and started down the hall. Since the night of the fire, he'd spent little time in the library and had never ventured into the adjoining study, but he could vividly remember a time when these apartments had been his favorite in the London house. As he opened the double doors, the familiar smells of ink and leather stirred a host of memories. Once he'd known he could count on a warm welcome here, no matter how busy his father was. Now he wasn't so sure.

Gideon was seated by the windows at the far end of

the room, the desk before him strewn haphazardly with papers and ledgers, his discarded coat tossed over the back of the chair. As the door opened he looked up, surprised, but not angry or even displeased. "I'm sorry to bother you, sir." Peter closed the door and moved hesitantly down the long room. "I need to talk to you, but perhaps you'd better read this first. It's from Simon's mother."

Peter gave his father the letter, then retreated to a chair several feet from the desk while Gideon slit the missive open. There was only a single sheet and the contents were brief for he read it through quickly. Then, to Peter's astonishment, he swore softly but distinctly, and with quite as much violence as Simon had displayed when he'd kicked the table leg. Gideon started to push back his chair but thought better of it. "How much do you know about this?" His voice was calm, but the look in his eyes matched the oath of a few moments before.

"I'm not sure," Peter said cautiously. "Is it about Miss Alastair?"

"It says she is no longer in the princess's employ and that it would be best if you did not come to Bolton Street for the present."

Peter was shocked by this unexpected blow. "I know Miss Alastair won't be there to give me lessons, but can't I still visit Simon? Sir?" he pressed, when Gideon did not answer immediately. "Have I done something wrong?"

"You?" To Peter's relief, Gideon smiled. He had forgotten how comforting he'd once found his father's smile. "No, Peter, you've done nothing worse than to have the misfortune to be caught up in the folly of others." Gideon balanced the letter in his hand and Peter knew that he was weighing a decision. His hand clenched suddenly, crushing the paper. "Do you remem-

ber Miss Martin?"

Preoccupied with his banishment from Simon's house, Peter looked at his father blankly. "She was a connection of Aunt Clare's," Gideon prompted. "She used to look after Sallie and Hugh."

Peter had always seen a good deal of his Prebble cousins. Their governess, a thin woman with spectacles who always looked as if she had the headache, was called Howard, not Martin, and Peter had never heard that she was any relation of Aunt Clare's. But Gideon was talking about the past, probably the time before he'd left England, and suddenly Peter remembered, for Miss Martin's departure had coincided with Gideon's own. Though he hadn't thought about her in years, Peter recalled her quite clearly now, with her fair hair and friendly smile and warm voice.

Her voice. Peter frowned. And her smile. And, come to think of it, her hair, though she'd worn it differently. Sallie and Hugh had called her Fanny . . . for Frances, he'd thought, if he'd thought about it at all. But could it have been a childish corruption of—? No, it made no sense. It was impossible, wasn't it? Peter looked up and met Gideon's gaze. "She's Miss Alastair, isn't she?" Incredibly, he knew it had to be the truth. "Is that why the princess sent her away? Because she found out?"

"I'm afraid so."

There was anger and disgust in Gideon's voice, but it did not seem to be directed at Peter or even at the princess. No, Peter realized with surprise, his father was angry at himself. He had a sudden impulse to reach out, as he might to Teddy or Beth, and tell him that whatever had happened, it could not possibly be his fault. He did not do so, but when he spoke it was softly and without hostility. "Why did Miss Martin leave Aunt Clare's? No one ever told me."

With obvious effort, Gideon relaxed his fingers and let the crumpled letter fall to the desk top. "How much do you know about what happened?"

"Hardly anything." The pain and confusion of losing his father had prevented Peter from taking any great interest in Miss Martin's departure, but he had realized that the two events might be connected. His father had liked Miss Martin. In those last weeks, when he'd become so inexplicably withdrawn, he would still join the nursery party when she brought Sallie and Hugh to visit. "I knew you and Miss Martin were friends. Then Mama came back from London and the next morning she told us you were sick and Teddy and I were to go to the cottage in Dorset. When we got back, you'd left for the Peninsula." He did not add that Gideon had not so much as written them a farewell note. "Sallie said Miss Martin had gone away and they didn't know why and they weren't supposed to talk about her anymore." Peter hesitated. With his additional five years' experience, he could guess what might have driven Miss Martin away. "Were you in love with her?"

Gideon thought he'd regained his self-command, but this question momentarily shattered his defenses. Or if not the question itself, the fact that for a moment he was unsure of the answer. For a moment only. Fiona had stirred him as few other women had, arousing feelings that went far beyond simple desire. Those feelings remained, no less strong for five years' separation or the weight of guilt he carried, but he was not such a fool as to call them love.

It was clear what Peter had meant. Gideon could dimly recall a time when he too had believed that an affair was synonymous with love. He'd thought he was in love with Aline, but that illusion died when he realized she was far more shallow than the woman he imagined her to be. No, the only woman he'd really

187

loved, in a quite unromantic way, was Amy Higgins, who'd been his nursemaid from the time he was two until a night shortly after his eighth birthday when she woke him to say she was leaving to care for her sick sister and would be back soon. It was six years before he saw her again, driving a very smart phaeton in Hyde Park. He followed her to a suite of rooms near Portman Square where she received him with a nervousness which was explained a quarter-hour later by the arrival of his father, obviously a frequent visitor.

Gideon smiled bitterly at the memory. He had been scarcely older than Peter, who was still staring at him, self-conscious but unwavering. "I was very fond of Miss Martin," Gideon told him. "And I feel responsible for what happens to her."

"Then you have to go after her," Peter said with sudden urgency. "Simon and his sister are going to talk to Mr. Langley when he gets back from Sweden, but that won't be for weeks."

"I have every intention of going after her. Do you have any idea where she is?"

"Simon said to tell you she's gone to Margaret's. He said you'd know what that meant."

Gideon, already pulling on his coat, did not miss the undercurrent in his son's voice. "You deserve an explanation, Peter, but I have to find Miss Alastair first."

"Of course." Peter was silent until Gideon had buttoned the coat and crossed to the door. "Sir."

Gideon turned back to see Peter regarding him with the air of one about to make a confession. "Simon said I should tell you about Miss Alastair. I didn't want to at first. But I—I'm glad I did."

As he looked at his son, it occurred to Gideon that in the past quarter-hour, without trying, he'd broken through Peter's hostility as he'd not been able to since his return to England. He smiled. "So am I."

Fiona arrived at Margaret's in time for the midday meal, and by its end she knew her stay would have to be of very limited duration. Margaret could not have been more welcoming, but her brother clearly resented the imposition. His son Albert, a lanky young man of some twenty years, was all too openly admiring of the visitor, and Albert's fiancée Susan, who worked in the shop below, was pardonably jealous.

Fiona was helping Margaret with the washing up, calculating how long she could get by on her last wages and how much longer if she pawned the garnets as well, when Susan unexpectedly returned to the tiny kitchen. "You've a visitor, Miss Alastair," she said, regarding Fiona with eyes that were at once hostile and curious. "A gentleman. He's waiting in the parlor."

"Well, isn't that nice," Margaret said brightly. Fiona was not sure she agreed. It had to be Gideon. Who else would have traced her to the Slaters'? But she did not want Gideon to see her in these circumstances, even after their scene this morning. Especially after it. Fiona removed the apron Margaret had loaned her, adjusted a hairpin, and, ignoring Susan's curious gaze, opened the door to the parlor.

Her visitor was standing by the fireplace, studying the earthenware dog which Margaret had set in pride of place on the mantel. As she entered the room the man turned toward her. "Your friend's home is quite a revelation. One hears, of course, that such places exist, but I don't think I truly believed it until now," said George Barrington-Forbes.

Chapter Eleven

Fiona had armed herself against Gideon. She had no defense against George, whose improbable presence in the cramped Slater parlor robbed her of speech.

Predictably, George was amused. "Aren't you going to ask me to sit down? You'd better, you know," he added when she failed to respond. "You're hardly in a position to turn down an offer of help."

Fiona forced herself to answer in the same tone. "Is that why you're here, to help me? I must be grateful for your concern, but I assure you, I'm quite able to help myself."

"Don't be hasty, Fiona." He came closer and she was suddenly aware of his physical presence. This was the first man whose arms she had known, the man who had singled her out as his life's companion. It had been a heady triumph, securing George. It had meant escape from the dreariness of playing housekeeper to her father or nursemaid to her sister's children. It had meant the safety of a name she could acknowledge, and initiation into a world of the senses she'd hardly dared hope would be open to her.

Even then George had never pretended to be a friend. He was no friend to her now, though his eyes told her he desired her still. Fiona sat down abruptly, wishing she had done so at once, and motioned him to a chair as far away from her as the small room would allow. "It was Clare, wasn't it? She told you she'd been to see the princess."

He crossed one long leg over the other and leaned back in his chair. "Dear Clare. She was quite livid when she learned of Parminter's defection. That was your doing, wasn't it? Protecting your little charge. You'd have done better to hold your tongue."

Fiona remembered that she would have done so had George not made a point of telling her about the liaison. "How did you find me?"

"I had you followed. I knew it was only a matter of time before the princess turned you off. Dear God," he said, looking around the shabby room, "I never dreamed you'd come to this. What will you do, Fiona? Help in the shop?"

"I'll earn my keep, as I've done these five years. My future need not concern you."

He uncrossed his legs and leaned forward. "Ah, but it does. I do not like to think a woman I once hoped to make my wife will be reduced to selling loaves and buns. It wasn't kind, Fiona, to leave without a word."

No, she had not been kind to him, and the memory of it kept her irresolute in her chair. "I do not excuse my behavior. I did not mean to cause you pain. Please, George. You have a lovely young wife and a child and, I am sure, more fortune than I could ever have brought you. Let it suffice. Forget that I exist."

He shook his head slowly. "I would have wed you still."

Fiona stared at him. It was not possible; no man would have taken another man's leavings, not without a love that went far beyond desire, not without a compassion George could never have felt. Oh, George was clever. Clever enough to put her in the wrong, to keep her anger at bay, to distract her from the knowledge that he had set the whole sorry breach with the princess in motion by the secret he had disclosed to her at Parminter House.

She saw the pattern now. George's disclosures had been deliberate. He knew she would take them to the princess, just as he knew the princess would confront Lord Parminter. Clare's fury had been carefully fanned. She would go to George, her husband's friend and Lord Parminter's brother-in-law, to learn how it was possible that Lord Parminter had been persuaded to give her up, and George would tell her, with willful malice, just who was responsible for her loss.

Fiona's anger returned in full force and she stood up as abruptly as she'd sat down. "I wish you to leave, Mr. Barrington-Forbes. I have nothing further to say to you."

He got to his feet and looked down at her. He was tall, taller than she remembered, and she fought an impulse to step back. "You haven't heard me out," he said.

"I've heard all I wish to hear."

"You're not a fool." His voice was suddenly harsh. Fiona was relieved, for what would follow would at least be honest. "Where will you go? What will you do? You were dismissed without a character, am I right? Yes, of course, I can see it in your face. Who will employ you now, Fiona? Will you change your name once more, and—yes, that must be how you did it—forge references from a mythical family? It won't be so easy in England, not while *I* remain here. Make sure of that, wherever you go I will find you."

Fiona drew a sharp breath. "Do you hate me so much?"

"Hate you? Oh, no—my feelings are far from hate. I wanted you from the day I saw you, Fiona Martin. And strangely enough, I want you still." His eyes explored her face, as though he would commit her features to memory. "I cannot offer you marriage now, but I can offer you protection. You shall want for nothing it is in my power to give."

She drew back and saw her recoil reflected in the sudden hardness in his eyes.

"Take care, Fiona. What other choice do you have, save what I offer you? You accepted my hands once, do you remember? You accepted my kisses and did not turn away." He reached out and clasped the back of her neck. The shock of his touch brought an instant physical response, followed by a revulsion so strong that she broke away and retreated behind a chair.

"You did not used to be so nice." The anger came through the quietness of his words. "You cannot afford it now."

She laughed. "I am hardly in such desperate straits."

He watched her for a while. "Think of the alternatives, Fiona. Will you hire yourself out as a shop assistant? I will find you. Will you become one of those creatures who eke out a living doing needlework and go early to the grave? No, you're a sensible woman and will seek protection where you can. Where will you find a lover who does not disgust you? Don't let your guilt blind you to your own self-interest. Don't let it make you forget what was once between us."

For answer she walked to the door and stood there, hand on the knob.

"I see." George picked up his hat and gloves. "You think to go to Carne, is that it?"

She would not give him the satisfaction of a reply.

He smiled. "Wise girl. Carne is ruined, he can barely keep himself."

Fiona opened the door. "Good-bye, George," she said, at once acknowledging the relationship that had stood between them and affirming that it was over.

He stepped through the door and looked back at her. A smile played about his lips, but she could tell that he was angry. "Remember that you may call on me at any time. We are not finished, you and I." And with these words he turned and ran quickly down the narrow stairs.

Fiona shut the door and walked back into the parlor, trembling with the effort to keep herself under control. There was tightness in her chest, in her throat, in her temples. Nothing but a scream of fury and despair would bring her release, but she could not allow herself such indulgence, not in Margaret's house. Indeed, she'd learned early not to give voice to her feelings, and it was many years since she'd been able to cry.

But she could not sit still, and she paced about the room, taking the measure of her cage. She'd let George use her. In that brief exchange at Parminter House she'd walked into his trap. And then, merciful God, she'd warned Gideon that he was dangerous. Why hadn't she had the sense to warn herself?

Very well . . . it was done; and there was nothing to be gained by dwelling on her own stupidity. She must think of the future. George at least had made clear what lay ahead.

She was not entirely without resources. Lady Windham would help her, but she would not take that path unless she were truly desperate, and she was not desperate yet. No, she would wait for Mr. Langley to come back from Sweden and appeal to him to intercede with the princess. Perhaps, if she promised to tell her new employer the whole, he would be willing to provide her with a reference.

Fiona was dimly aware of Margaret's voice and knew that she would not be alone for long. There were so many ifs. If she could find a place to stay . . . if she could find a way to make her money last . . . if Mr. Langley proved more understanding than his wife . . . if the princess could be brought to change her mind . . . if another family could be persuaded to hire a woman who had been unchaste . . . .

She heard the parlor door open and hastily composed her features. But it was not Margaret who entered the room. "Peter told me what happened,"

194

Gideon said, striding toward her. "Are you all right?"

"Yes, quite all right," she said, wrapping the remnants of her pride about her. After her scene with George, the sight of Gideon, his eyes filled with concern, brought her dangerously close to tears. "There was no need for you to come."

"I have my own needs," he said impatiently. "I would know how you are situated and what you intend to do."

"Why, as to that, I do not know myself. I left Bolton Street scarcely two hours ago." She thought of Simon and Peter standing on the sidewalk, bewildered and distressed. "Peter told you."

"He brought me a letter from the princess."

"She spoke of him?"

"He is not to visit young Tassio again."

"Oh no, I am so sorry. I would not for the world have the boys pay for my folly. Surely if you spoke to the princess—" She broke off, realizing that in the princess's eyes Gideon was as tainted as she.

"How did she learn of it, Fiona?"

It would be a relief to share the story. Fiona took a breath, feeling some of the tension leave her body, and told him what Clare had done. "I think it was her revenge for the loss of her lover."

"I rather think the revenge was George's."

Fiona had looked away, but at these words she raised her startled eyes to his. "How did you know?"

"I saw him leaving here. It reeks of his hand. He told Clare, didn't he? He wanted to make sure she knew where the blame lay."

Fiona felt suddenly weary. She could not cope with Gideon's anger or Gideon's compassion, and at this moment she wished nothing so much as that he would take his eyes and his person out of the room and the house and her life. "I expect that's how it happened," she said carefully. "It doesn't matter now. The story was bound to come out."

"You must let me help you."

"I seem to have a surfeit of offers of help. It almost restores my faith in the generosity of man. No, Lord Carne—I told George and now I'll tell you. I need no help from anyone."

The color surged in his face. "For the love of God, Fiona, think what you're about. You were turned off, weren't you? How much money do you have? How long will it last? What will you do when it is gone?"

It was so much what George had said that she had to stifle an hysterical desire to laugh. "Oh, I am not without resources. If all else fails, I can turn to George. He has offered me a *carte blanche*." She saw Gideon's anger and disbelief and felt an insane desire to wound both him and herself. "Why not? Is it so unthinkable? Am I unfit for the game? Or perhaps I'm too old, is that it?" She made an abrupt gesture of dismissal. "Oh, go away, Gideon, go away. I have no intention of going to George. I'll go to no man. I'll find a way out, but don't ask me now, I can't think and I want to be left alone."

He did not answer and the silence grew between them. Fiona waited for the sound of the door to signal his departure but heard nothing. When she looked up she found his eyes still upon her and she was forced to look away, unwilling to read their expression. "I won't offer you a *carte blanche*, Fiona. I will offer you marriage."

Fiona stared at him. Gideon's offer shocked her as much as George's proposal to set her up as his mistress. "No," she told him, "you owe me nothing."

"I am not paying a debt. I am offering you a way out. It is an honorable one."

"Oh, honor," she said, dismissing the thought as though it were a luxury she could not afford. "I want only to survive."

"Then it is a way you can do so. I am not trying to take advantage of you," he added, uncharacteristically awkward. "You can have marriage on any terms you please. My affairs are in ruinous condition and I can give you little now in the way of creature comforts, but I hope to come about. In the meantime you can have the protection of my home and my name, and nothing George can do or say will ever touch you again."

It was a generous offer. Fiona turned away, to shut out the image of his face, and busied herself with straightening a chair George had dislodged in passing. It was tempting, more tempting than she'd have thought possible. Reminding herself that Gideon was the man who'd used her, who'd held her love cheap, who'd wantonly taken her brother's life, she grasped the back of the chair to stop the trembling of her hands and forced herself to meet his eyes. "There's no way I would consider becoming your wife."

A shadow of pain crossed his face and she almost regretted the harshness of her words. "As you wish," he said with a rueful smile. "I won't press you further. But you must allow me to help you—consider it a loan, if you like—at least until you are settled. I would not like to see you on the streets."

"Oh, it will hardly come to that. If I must sell myself, I will not do it cheaply." Then, because she regretted the flippancy of her words, she spoke more seriously. "Thank you, but I have no need of your money, Lord Carne."

Gideon was a soft-spoken man, but his fine-toned voice now rose to a roar that filled the small room. "Good God, woman, you've made that plain enough. You'll take neither my person nor my purse. But think, Fiona. Think for a moment with your head, not with your bruised and sentimental heart. You must have help if you're to survive. Shall I kill George to make you safe? I've had my fill of death, but if that's what it will take . . ."

His anger had done what his compassion could not. Her trembling ceased, her head was clear, and she was in control once more. "Don't be absurd. I will depend on no one but myself. I will use my wits and such skills as I have acquired and I will earn my keep."

"I doubt neither your wit nor skill, nor do I doubt the force of your resolve, though you may find it hard to bend the world to it. If your father's will can be found, perhaps there will be a way out of your dilemma. In the meantime, let me offer you the chance to work for which you seem so eager."

He had surprised her. She waited for him to continue.

"I have three children and no one to look after them but the young woman you met in the park. Peter should have a tutor, but I cannot afford one now. Teddy is of an age for regular lessons. I cannot pay you what you are worth, but I will hire you as a governess for as long as you care to remain."

She burst into laughter. "I believe you are the one person in all of England who would accept me without a reference."

"Then you must accept the one offer of employment you are likely to receive."

She turned sober. If it had come from anyone else, she'd have embraced the offer eagerly. But not from Gideon, whose very presence stirred feelings she'd as soon forget. Not from Gideon, whose obvious concern for her well-being confounded her memories of the man he had been. "I don't think it would be wise for me to do so."

"In the ordinary way of things, perhaps not. But your situation is not ordinary. You have to act. You have to take the chances that are offered.

Fiona felt her resolution weakening. "People will talk. It will not be pleasant for the children."

"People will talk in any event. And the children's lives will hardly be less pleasant than they've already been. Come with me, Miss Alastair. I have need of you, and no one else will put up with such a ramshackle and black-tempered employer."

His good humor undid her. Telling herself that it was the only sensible thing to do, she went in search of Margaret to inform her that she would no longer impose on the Slater household. Margaret's relief was so palpable that any doubts Fiona felt about the wisdom of her action were driven away.

Margaret came outside to see her off, as did Susan, who bade her farewell with considerably more warmth than she'd heretofore shown. Gideon tossed a coin to the boy who'd been watching the horses, then crossed the road to speak to a man in brown livery who was lounging in the doorway of a bootmaker's shop. "George left him on watch," he said when he returned to the carriage. He started the grays at a brisk pace down Aylesbury Street.

Fiona's fingers tightened on the strings of her reticule. "I suppose it was bound to happen." Somehow, illogically, she'd thought she'd put George behind her. "What did you tell him?"

"That I was putting you on a coach for Bath and I'd wring the neck of any man who dared follow you."

She forced herself to smile. "Do you think that will put George off the scent?"

"Not for long. But it will tell him that one way or another you are under my protection."

Gideon was right. There was nothing George could do to make her situation worse. It might be better if the story did come out. At least then there would be no further need to hide. Sitting beside Gideon in the curricle, careful not to touch his arm or thigh, Fiona realized what a strain the past five years had been. She thought of herself now as Miss Alastair, but Miss Alastair was a careful woman who had secrets to keep. She wondered if she should take back the name of Martin and decided she had no desire to do so. Martin was no more her name than Alastair, and she could not go back to the woman she'd been.

Gideon, thank heaven, showed no disposition for further talk. She was free to dip into the book of the past, to call up images of her family and her younger self. She had not, she supposed, been actively unhappy. Her father would hear nothing against her, though in those days he was absent from home as often as not and she was left to the grudging toleration of her stepmother and Clare's bouts of jealousy. Jamie had been her only friend and she had loved him fiercely. She sat with him during his lessons and acquired a wide if haphazard education, she walked with him and rode with him and talked to him without reservation. When she was fourteen and Jamie went off to school, she lived for the days when he returned to Barstead, bringing friends and noise and laughter to their home.

She remembered the way he had teased her at Clare's wedding. Her turn would be next, he said, and it hadn't seemed so unlikely. She had always known that she could not aim high, a London season was out of the question; but she was more than presentable, and her father had promised her a small dowry. But her stepmother, to her surprise, was in no hurry to let her go. She was a fretful woman, frequently ailing, and Fiona was needed for companionship, for nursing, for seeing to her father's comfort and the running of the house. There were no men in the neighborhood to tempt her, and somehow the years slipped by until she met George and knew that a different life was possible.

Gideon drew sharply on the reins to avoid a collision with a heavy coach-and-four and Fiona grasped the seat to keep her balance. She forced her thoughts away from the past and considered what had happened to her today. It was hard to believe that this morning she'd awakened in the Langley house. It was even harder to believe that she was to spend the night in the house of Gideon Carne.

When they reached Dover Street, the door was opened

by a small dark man who regarded her with frank curiosity. "This is Adam," Gideon said cheerfully. "He's my conscience and my keeper, and he runs the house. Adam, this is Miss Alastair. She's been governess to the Prince di Tassio, and now she's going to be Peter's governess. Peter's and Teddy's. Find Barbara and tell her to turn out one of the bedrooms, then see to the horses. You can fetch Miss Alastair's boxes tomorrow."

Adam gave her an appraising stare. It was clear he did not approve of her presence, but that could not be helped.

Nor did Barbara seem at all pleased by her arrival. "Which room should I make ready, Lord Carne?" Her manner indicated that she'd quite enough on her hands as it was.

Gideon hesitated. "The south bedroom, I think. The last on the right." He turned to Fiona. "It's small, but it gets the morning sun. Barbara is in the room next to the children, and I think it best to make no change."

Seemingly mollified by her employer's unwillingness to displace her, Barbara turned to go back up the stairs.

"You must allow me to help you," Fiona said, untying her bonnet and laying it on a nearby table "I am not at all a helpless creature and I do not expect to be waited on. If you'll show me where things are, I'm sure I can attend to the bedroom myself. I expect you're shorthanded."

Fiona could see that she'd won a small but important victory. She would have to come to terms with Barbara if her life in the Carne household was to be tolerable. "I scarcely know the children," she added as she followed the other woman up the stairs. "Perhaps you could tell me about them so I'll know how to get on."

Barbara turned and looked back at Gideon, who was watching them from below. "They're in the kitchen."

"I'll bring them up," Gideon said.

When they arrived some ten minutes later, Fiona was

in her room, folding the holland sheets which had covered the furniture. The windows were open to receive the afternoon breeze and the bedclothes were stripped away to air the mattress.

"I say, Miss Alastair," Peter said, "I'm awfully glad—I mean, I'm awfully sorry, about Simon, but I'm glad you're going to be here. Teddy is too, aren't you, Teddy?" He looked at his younger brother, who was standing close beside him. Teddy nodded but didn't say a word.

Beth came forward and studied Fiona with solemn eyes. "I think I'm glad too."

Fiona suppressed an impulse to hug the girl. She mustn't go too fast. "I'm very happy to be here," she said carefully. "I'll be through with the room in a few minutes, and then, perhaps, if you're not too busy, you can show me the house and garden." For the first time since she'd agreed to Gideon's proposal, Fiona felt she was not making a monumental mistake.

The children, bless them, must have expected to be set to lessons at once, for their faces broke into smiles and they ran from the room. "I hope you'll be comfortable," Gideon said. "Barbara is two doors down the hall, and the children's rooms are beyond that. Adam's in a room off the kitchen, and I have a bed in my study, on the ground floor. If there's anything you need, ask Barbara or Adam."

"I'm sure I'll do very well."

"The children like you, you know." He turned to leave the room, but at the door he stopped and looked back at her. "Thank you for coming."

"She's a lady," Barbara said, "but she's not afraid of work. I'll grant her that." She was in the kitchen, helping Adam with the dinner.

Adam grunted. He was not ready to grant Miss Alastair anything at all.

Barbara picked up a basin of shelled peas and dumped them in a pot. "She lived in Sardinia with a prince and princess, but they weren't royal. Peter explained it to me, but I'm not sure I understand. His friend Simon is the prince now. Hand me that knife, will you? Peter thinks there's something havey-cavey about why she left."

"Who?"

"Who've we been talking about? Miss Alastair. This morning she was working for the princess, and tonight she's working for Lord Carne. Simon thinks a lot of her," Barbara went on. "That's what Peter says. Peter likes her too. I suppose she'll be all right," she added with obvious reluctance. Adam made no reply and they worked in silence for a while. But Barbara could not leave the subject alone. "She's Scottish, did you know? She has some strange name. Fiona, that's it, Fiona Alastair."

Adam had been tasting the soup simmering on the stove, but at these words he dropped the spoon and swore.

"Burn yourself?"

"No," he returned angrily, unwilling to tell Barbara what he knew. Fiona Carne couldn't be that foolish. Now they were in the suds.

Chapter Twelve

"*Marriage?*" Adam stared at Barbara as though she'd just suggested a frontal assault against impossible odds. "It was a wife that got Carne into this mess. The last thing he needs is another."

"It was Lady Carne who got him into this mess. Anyone with two eyes in his head could see Miss Alastair isn't a bit like her." Barbara calmly pulled a wooden pin from her apron pocket and fastened one of Teddy's shirts to the worsted line Adam had rigged up in the back garden.

"I never knew Lady Carne. But it is obvious Carne's been in a worse state than ever since he brought Miss Alastair into the house." Adam bent down and absently pulled the next article of clothing from the laundry basket at their feet. It proved to be a lady's undergarment. He scowled at the fine linen even as he deftly smoothed the muslin frill at the neck.

"Of course he has," Barbara said cheerfully, replenishing her store of pins from a box on the ground. "All the more reason why he should marry her."

Adam grinned dryly. Though he found women capital company in bed and out of it, he saw little to be gained from a permanent arrangement. He was tempted to say that Gideon had best bed Miss Alastair and be done with it, but he feared his employer's relationship with Miss

Alastair could not be resolved by such a simple expedient.

Barbara thought the acquaintance between Gideon and Miss Alastair was only of a few weeks' standing and to imply differently would be to betray both of them. Adam had no desire to see Miss Alastair hurt. Quite the reverse, in fact, which was why the sooner she got out of the house, the better. "My word, Bab," Adam said, more lightly than he felt. "Who would have thought you were a romantic?"

Feeling herself color, Barbara moved further down the line and began pinning up linen with ferocious determination. Just because a girl was plain, it didn't stop her from thinking, but she could hardly expect Adam to understand. Besides, she knew a thing or two more than he did about Lord Carne and Miss Alastair. Barbara straightened one of Beth's small dresses. In the ten days since Miss Alastair's arrival, Barbara's resentment of the governess had quite vanished. It had begun to crumble that first day, when Miss Alastair told Barbara to call her Fiona and showed herself willing to help with the washing up or polishing or sweeping or any of the myriad other tasks which always needed doing in this ramshackle household. And then she had set to work altering the children's clothes, with the result that the young Carnes now had garments that fit them properly for the first time in months.

Four days after her arrival Fiona had won Barbara's loyalty completely. Adam was right about Lord Carne's temper growing worse since Fiona's arrival, but it was he who'd suggested an expedition to see the illuminations in honor of Wellington's latest victory at a place called Vittoria. For Barbara, less than a month in London, it had been a magical night, and she had vivid memories of the dazzling white and colored lamps strung up all over the city. Lord Carne had seemed in an unusually easy mood, cheerfully pointing out the different buildings and hold-

205

ing up Beth and Teddy so they could see over the heads of the taller spectators. And if he and Adam couldn't resist occasional gibes about the army, the Government, and war in general, Barbara, who'd lost a brother at Salamanca, decided it was all to the good for the children to hear such talk.

Then, when they were standing before the Spanish Embassy, Barbara glanced away from a transparency of Lord Wellington with the flags of England, Spain, and Portugal over his head, and saw Lord Carne looking at Fiona with a naked intensity of which she would never have thought him capable. It was later that same evening, when they were having a cup of tea in the makeshift schoolroom, that Fiona made a confession which was as astounding as, on reflection, it was logical.

Barbara had seen Miss Martin only from a distance, but like everyone else within ten miles of Hartwood and Digby Hall, she'd engaged in her share of speculation about what had transpired between Miss Martin and Lord Carne in the summer of 1808. Her father and the other Carne tenants had not looked kindly on the woman who'd driven away their caring and concerned landlord, but Barbara had been inclined to take Miss Martin's side even then. Now, hearing the story from Fiona herself, there could be no doubt where her sympathies lay.

She could not, of course, mention any of this to Adam without betraying Fiona's trust, but she was not about to concede the argument. "Lord Carne needs a wife," she said, searching for the mate to a stocking which had somehow got lost in the basket. "I've thought so from the first. Goodness knows the children need a mother—"

"Oh, well, that's different." Adam was disentangling a nightshirt from a petticoat which, Barbara realized with a twinge of embarrassment, was her own. "But they've got you. You make a capital mother."

"It's not the same thing." Barbara felt a flush of pride

at the compliment, though motherhood was not exactly the role in which she wanted Adam to see her. "Besides, I'm not thinking just of the children. People need other people—and I don't mean only in that way," she added, as Adam grinned, "though of course that's part of it. Don't look at me like that. I grew up on a farm, you know."

"If it comes to that, so did I, leastways until my mother married my stepfather and we moved to Bristol." Barbara's cheeks were flushed with color, and her cap had slipped back, allowing the fitful afternoon sun to pick out strands of gold in her brown hair. Though she was plainly more than a bit embarrassed, she held her ground defiantly. "The thing is, Bab," Adam said seriously, "marriage can do the damnedest things to the nicest people. My mum and my stepfather were the mildest sorts imaginable till they'd been wed a year or so."

No one else called her Bab. She was coming to quite like it, but his last words made her frown. "Was that why you left home?"

Adam grinned again. "That and a few other things. There wasn't much money, so they sent me out to work for my keep. I lasted a fortnight before I ran away."

"And joined the army?"

"Yes, well, I was a bit deluded in those days. I thought the army would be easier. Still, it had its compensations. For instance, if I hadn't spent all those years sweating or freezing on the Peninsula, I might not be here now, talking to you."

"Oh, there you are, Adam." Lord Carne looked out the door from the back hall before the startled Barbara could think of an answer. "I'll need you to hire a carriage for tomorrow. Miss Alastair and I are taking the children to Kent." He nodded to Barbara and returned to whatever business he had in the house.

Barbara grinned.

Adam groaned.

The smoky green of the Kentish countryside was a vivid contrast to the brilliant white stone and bright blue water of Sardinia, but it was the ruined walls of Denton Chapel, just out of Gravesend, which were Fiona's first unmistakable sign of home. She was surprised at the wellspring of emotion the sight stirred in her, and she sternly reminded herself that this trip had nothing to do with sentiment. But it was seductively easy to imagine — as the ostlers at the inn in Dartford had evidently assumed — that the man sitting across from her was her husband, that the three children peering out the windows were her own, and that she was taking them to see her childhood home.

Fiona pushed these fantasies aside. They were making this journey because Barstead was at last empty of its tenants. Hugo had traveled down yesterday to confer with the estate agent, so it now seemed safe to search for the will which her father might or might not have concealed in the house. Gideon had suggested bringing the children. They would enjoy the drive, he said, and if they came across anyone at Barstead, they could say they'd been on a family outing and Fiona had wanted to revisit her old home. Fiona suspected that he had another, unspoken reason. Since the day she came into his house, Gideon had been careful to avoid being alone with her. If they had to spend the day together, the children would serve as a buffer between them.

To his credit, Gideon had not allowed Fiona's presence to keep him from the children. Though they no longer needed an excuse to meet, the outings to the park continued and Gideon had taken to joining them for dinner in the kitchen. He and Peter seemed on remarkably improved terms, and Beth clearly adored her father with the single-minded worship of the very young. It was Teddy who was in danger of being lost, as middle children so often are. Fiona had mentioned this to Gideon in one of their few private conversations, and the next day Gideon had returned home with Benjamin. The horse went to the park with them that afternoon and Teddy was given the first ride.

A few days after her removal to Dover Street, Fiona received a letter from Lady Windham, inviting her and her new charges to lunch the following Sunday, by which time Lady Windham believed she'd have completed Miss Alastair's commission. She also enclosed letters from Simon, one addressed to Fiona, the other to Peter. It was, Simon told his former governess, deadly dull without her, and the only good thing he had to report was that his mother had not yet engaged a tutor.

The carriage lurched as Adam negotiated the turn off the Dover Road, and Beth spilled some of the lemonade Fiona had just poured from the flask in the picnic basket. Sunday was tomorrow, but as she wiped up the lemonade Fiona tried not to dwell on the visit. Lady Windham must have learned something, but it was highly unlikely that she'd discovered the identity of Fiona's mother.

Teddy and Peter, who had slumped in their respective corners of the carriage, tired of the journey, tired even of the nonsense games their father and governess had devised to pass the time, perked up and peered out the windows with renewed interest. Beth, who was sitting on the other side of the carriage, wanted to see what they found so interesting, which resulted in another accident with the lemonade.

"I say," Teddy was kneeling on the seat, his face pressed to the glass, "Is *that* the house, Fiona?"

Fiona looked over his shoulder in time to see the vine-covered lodge gates of Shorton Place, home of the Otford family. Gerald Otford, a rather dull young man who'd paid Fiona considerable attention until his parents gently but firmly put a stop to it, would be well past thirty now. Bella Otford, Fiona's closest friend among

209

the neighboring children, had married and gone to live in Northumberland some years before Fiona had left England. And Ralph, the youngest Otford . . . but perhaps it would be best not to think about Ralph; he had been Jamie's best friend and Jamie's second in the duel that had taken his young life.

"No," Fiona told Teddy. "Barstead is a bit further on. We have to pass Little Shorham first."

But the tiny village was soon left behind, and rather before Fiona was ready for it Adam turned down the oak-lined drive and pulled up before the house. Eager to be moving about, the children tumbled to the ground. Fiona allowed Adam to hand her down, told him where to take the horses, and only then forced her eyes to roam over the steep tiled roof, the brick facing, mellowed to a warm rose and broken by orderly sashed windows, and the white pillared entranceway of which her stepmother had been so proud.

"I take it the door you mentioned is around the back?" Gideon's dispassionate voice was a welcome reminder of the present. The children, who'd already been told they wouldn't be allowed inside the house but had been promised a picnic afterward, were quite willing to accompany Adam to the stable yard. Fiona and Gideon walked part of the way with them, then continued on through the vegetable garden, already showing signs of neglect, to the kitchen door. Here Gideon produced a short length of wire and in little more than a minute pushed the door open.

"They do teach you useful things in the army, don't they?" Fiona observed, stepping into her father's house for the first time in five years.

"Actually, Adam taught me. I thought it best not to ask where he'd learned it. Maddox said he witnessed the will in your father's bedchamber. Since he was sick, I doubt he'd have hidden it anywhere else. Upstairs?"

As she led the way up the service stairs, Fiona realized

that Gideon's brisk air was deliberate. He was trying to make this as easy for her as possible. Uncle James's room was near the stairhead, but before they reached it, the door to the adjoining chamber — once Aunt Charlotte's — flew open. A young man who wore neither coat nor waistcoat and was even now attempting to do up the buttons on his breeches stepped into the corridor. "What the devil?" he demanded, quite as startled by their appearance as they were by his. And then, in different accents, "Good God, *Fiona?*"

"Hullo, Ralph," Fiona said, her voice composed. "What a lovely surprise. I do hope your mother is well."

Ralph Otford gulped and lifted a hand to adjust his crumpled cravat. "Oh — ah — Mother's fine. Father too, for that matter. I say, Fiona, I had no idea — " He broke off again, looking past her into the shadows of the stairwell. "Lord Carne?" he asked, surprised, and uncertain, but not revolted or enraged, as Fiona had expected.

"Your servant, Otford." Gideon came to stand beside Fiona, seeming quite at ease. "Sorry we took you by surprise. Miss Martin wanted to see the house again."

"Yes, of course . . . very understandable." Ralph raked his fingers through his already disarranged hair. "Look, this is rather awkward. You see — "

"Ralph!" The name was uttered in tones of great distress by a petite young woman with large, pleading brown eyes who stood in the doorway of Charlotte's room. She wore a habit shirt and the skirt of a riding dress, but there was no sign of a jacket, and her honey-brown hair had been only partially pinned up. The delicate hand, presently clutching the doorknob for support, clearly displayed a wedding ring.

Ralph spun round with an agility that reminded Fiona he'd been quite splendid at cricket, but he seemed unsure what to do next. The young woman had no such difficulty. "I have lost a comb," she informed him in tragic accents.

"Oh, Lord, Celia, I'm sorry." Ralph drew a breath.

Celia glanced down the corridor and frowned, seeing the visitors. "I thought you told me the tenants had left."

"You must allow me to apologize for the intrusion," Gideon said, stepping forward. "My name is Carne, and this is Miss Martin. She once lived in the house and as we were passing by we decided to pay an impromptu visit."

"I see." Celia's face cleared. Then she frowned again and turned back to Ralph. "Weren't the people who used to live here called Woodbourn? Well, never mind," she continued, as Ralph stared dumbly at her. "I don't think you heard me properly, Ralph. I have lost one of my combs." She looked back at Gideon and Fiona. "I can't possibly leave until it is found, which is excessively awkward as the Allingtons are dining with us tonight and I quite forgot to tell Cook that Mr. Allington can't abide lobster salad."

"I understand completely," Fiona said, moving forward to stand beside Gideon. "Were you wearing a hat with a veil? I've found that combs have the most tiresome habit of becoming entangled in them."

"How very clever of you," Celia exclaimed. "I'm so glad you happened to be here, Ralph is never helpful about these things." She gave a sunny smile and returned to the bedroom, assuring Ralph that she could manage quite well without him. With an heroic effort, Ralph looked Gideon and Fiona in the eye. "I'm sorry, I'd give anything for . . . Sir Hugo left a spare set of keys with Father, you see, so it was easy enough . . . but you mustn't think I do this as a rule."

"On the contrary," Gideon returned cheerfully, "I'd say it's a perfectly normal activity for a healthy young man. You must allow me to compliment you on your taste."

Ralph's eyes brightened with enthusiasm. "Celia's a smasher, isn't she? Oh, I say, Fiona, I'm sorry—forgot myself."

"Very understandable, under the circumstances," Fiona assured him.

A few minutes later Celia returned to the hall, wearing the jacket to her riding habit, her hair pinned into place beneath a jaunty hat which boasted a billowy veil. She thanked Fiona warmly for the helpful suggestion and said she hoped they'd forgive her but she really must hurry home.

"My children are playing in the stable yard," Gideon said, with one of his more practiced smiles. "They're a mannerly enough brood, but they can be a bit overwhelming. Perhaps you'll allow me to escort you to your horse?"

Celia was only too delighted, and Ralph appeared relieved to have her off his hands. He returned to the bedroom to don his coat and waistcoat, leaving Fiona to realize it would be prudent to ensure that her presence at Barstead was kept secret. When Ralph came back into the hall, Fiona led him downstairs. The drawing room had always been Charlotte's domain, so Fiona took him to the morning room, a sitting room-cum-breakfast parlor in which she'd always felt more at ease. The furniture was under holland covers, but the back wall was still lined with the cushioned windowseats on which she'd so often curled up to read.

"It's good to see you, Fiona," Ralph said seriously, looking several years older than he had upstairs. Though he'd always been cast into the shade by Jamie, he was a well set-up young man, and in the past five years he'd lost the spots which had once plagued him so. "I've often wondered . . . well, at all events, it's a relief to find you looking so well. Carne seems in fine shape too," he added after a moment.

Fiona regarded him levelly. "I am governess to Lord Carne's children, Ralph. And difficult as it may be to believe, I am nothing more."

"Lord, Fiona, that's none of my business. Especially

after . . ." He made a vague gesture toward the upper reaches of the house. "I heard Carne had gone to the Peninsula. I'm glad to see he still has a whole skin."

"Your concern does you credit." Once again Fiona was puzzled by Ralph's lack of animosity toward Gideon, and it occurred to her that he could tell her a great deal about the past. She moved to the windowseat and gestured for Ralph to sit beside her. "I'd think you'd every right to feel the exact opposite."

"Good God, Fiona," Ralph exclaimed, "I may not always think things through very well, but I'd never let friendship blind me to honor. You should know that."

"Honor?" Fiona repeated, even more puzzled.

Ralph's gaze was fixed on the windowseat cushions, which had been recovered in an inferior-looking chintz. "It was dishonorable, Fiona. I know how much you loved Jamie, but you can't deny . . ." He let the thought trail off and looked at her, appalled. "You don't know, do you?"

"About the duel? I only know that Jamie's death was some sort of accident. I'd like to hear what happened," she added, when her brother's friend made no reply.

"Hell, Fiona." Ralph was on his feet, running a hand through his hair. He made no apology for his language. "It's not a pretty story. I don't know that I'd have wanted Jamie to tell Bella had the situations been reversed."

"Yes, but Bella was always a bit squeamish. I never have been."

"It's not that." The tension in the set of Ralph's shoulders was echoed by the strain in his voice. "I should have stopped him."

In trying to confront her own demons, Fiona had neglected to consider whether her brother's friend might feel guilty as well. Poor Ralph, invited by Jamie to stay at Clare's grand estate, caught up in events he'd barely understood. "That's foolish," she told him. "We both know how pigheaded Jamie could be."

"I'd never seen him as determined as he was that night." Ralph gave a wry smile. "Perhaps if I'd been able to talk to him before he issued the challenge—but I didn't even know he'd gone to Hartwood.

"I'd retired to my room, you see," he explained, moving back to the windowseat. "Then Jamie came banging on my door and asked me to be his second. Actually, it was more of a demand. Carne's estate agent—Linton, his name was—came over and we had a talk. He was a decent enough chap and really tried to patch things up. Of course, Carne hadn't wanted to fight in the first place—"

"What do you mean?" Fiona demanded.

He hesitated. "Just that. Carne didn't want to accept Jamie's challenge. In fact, he refused it."

"Then why did he fight?"

Ralph's eyes strayed to the expanse of lawn beyond the window, then moved back to her face. "Look, Fiona, if you were Bella—"

"If I was Bella none of this would have happened. Why did Lord Carne accept the challenge?"

"Jamie . . . Jamie threatened him."

"With what?" Fiona spoke with more urgency than she'd intended, but perhaps it was that urgency which convinced Ralph to respond.

"He threatened to make it public," Ralph said in a rush, "—everything, including your name."

It took a moment for Fiona to comprehend what this meant. Jamie had been willing to sacrifice her happiness and reputation to his ridiculous notions of honor. And Gideon . . . "So the meeting was arranged for dawn?" she said, her voice expressionless.

"Yes, Jamie insisted on it. Linton managed to locate a surgeon. I tried to talk to Jamie again in the morning but there was no reasoning with him. He wanted Carne dead. He said he owed it to you."

Fiona felt a surge of anger toward her dead brother. "Of all the idiotic—I'm sorry, Ralph. Please go on."

215

"Well, Carne had a set of dueling pistols and Jamie—ah—borrowed Sir Hugo's pistols. They agreed to use Carne's pistols, but Sir Hugo's were loaded in case there was a further exchange of shots. Linton gave the signal—I didn't trust myself to do it—and Jamie—I'm afraid Jamie fired early."

Dear God. So Jamie, who'd put honor before his sister's happiness, had not behaved honorably himself. "And Lord Carne?" Fiona asked, braced for an account of her brother's death.

"Oh, Carne would have deloped, there's no question about that."

"Would have? You mean he didn't fire at all?"

"I told you, Jamie jumped the count. Carne fell to his knees and Linton and I ran over to him—it was obvious he'd been badly wounded."

"And Jamie?" Fiona's voice was tight.

Ralph had gone very pale, revealing that, though his spots were gone, he still had a generous smattering of freckles. "I was running over to Carne when the surgeon called out a warning. I looked back and—Jamie wasn't himself, Fiona, you have to remember that."

"What happened, Ralph?"

"He'd picked up one of Sir Hugo's pistols and he was taking aim again."

Fiona stared at him. "After Lord Carne fell?"

Ralph nodded miserably. "When Carne heard the warning, he looked up and fired his own pistol. I think he was trying to hit Jamie in the arm to deflect the shot, but he'd already been wounded himself and Jamie was moving—" Ralph drew a breath. "So you see, I can't hate Carne, Fiona. Jamie very nearly murdered him."

Chapter Thirteen

Fiona found Gideon in her father's room, standing on a chair in his stocking feet and unscrewing one of the finials from the bedframe. "Good, I could use some help," he said without looking up. "Otford gone?"

"With solemn promises not to mention the encounter to anyone." Fiona shut the door. "Why didn't you tell me what happened when you and Jamie fought?"

For a moment Gideon stood absolutely still. Then he examined the finial, rather longer than was required to ascertain whether or not it contained any papers. "One does not, in general, discuss such details with the sisters of men one has murdered."

"If Ralph is to be believed, it was self-defense."

Gideon fitted the finial back on top of the bedpost with great care. "I'm sorry," he said, in a different tone. "Otford shouldn't have told you."

"On the contrary. I only wish I'd known sooner. Dear God, for five years I thought—"

"For five years you thought I killed your brother, which happens to be the truth. Let's leave it at that, shall we? Do you know of any hiding places I might have overlooked?" he continued, jumping down from the chair with surprising grace for a man with a bad leg. "No? Then perhaps you'll have a look around and tell me if everything is as you remember it."

Fiona remained where she was standing. Her eyes hadn't left him since she'd entered the room. He'd yet to look at her directly. "I'm serious, Gideon."

"So am I. It's possible that Woodbourn left the will in another room, but it's more likely he put it in a piece of furniture which was later shifted to another part of the house. If you could remember the original disposition of the furniture it would simplify our task enormously."

He spoke rather more rapidly than usual, but otherwise one could almost believe he was only interested in locating the will. "All right," Fiona said with great cordiality. "But first I owe you an apology."

At that Gideon did look her full in the face and she had the satisfaction of knowing she had indeed taken him by surprise. "You made me no promises," she explained. "And yet because of an affair I entered into willingly you were blackmailed into fighting a duel and were nearly shot down in cold blood for your pains. I think that warrants an apology, don't you?"

"Christ, Fiona," Gideon said with a violence she hadn't heard since their scene in Margaret's parlor, "aren't things bad enough without your playing martyr?"

"An interesting remark, coming from a man so determined to shoulder the blame himself. I don't see Uncle James's writing table anywhere."

Gideon gave a twisted smile. "Anything else?"

Though by no means ready to admit that the matter of the duel was settled, Fiona gave the room an honest appraisal: the Queen Anne wing chair by the fireplace where Uncle James had read the paper, the handsome Sheraton dressing table by the windows—Uncle James had liked his luxuries—and the small watercolor by the door, one of her own early efforts. That he had not taken it down was a great comfort. Fiona's eyes moved on to the washstand and she frowned. It looked different. Gideon, who'd taken paper and pencil from a pocket, calmly made a note of it.

They examined the adjoining dressing room, then, armed with the list Gideon had made, they moved through the rest of the house and began a methodical search for the missing bits of furniture. Fiona's only comments concerned the furnishings and other accoutrements until they'd climbed the worn stairs to the attic.

"You must believe that I had no notion Jamie intended to challenge you," she said suddenly. "It was criminal to tell the story of what lay between us to such an impulsive boy."

Gideon was on his knees, examining the drawers of the washstand they'd finally located, badly in want of polishing and with a scratched finish. "You were hardly in a state to be responsible for your actions," he said briskly, trying to cut through her attack of conscience. Fiona's anger was the most effective barrier between them, but it had started to dim even before she removed to Dover Street. If it faded altogether, he wasn't sure how they could continue to live under the same roof.

When she made no response, Gideon turned, fearing he'd deepened her hurt, and saw Fiona staring at him in disbelief. "You think *I* told Jamie the story?"

For five years Gideon hadn't doubted that she'd done just that. "Jamie told me you had," he said, getting slowly to his feet. "He said—" Gideon broke off, the angry words young Woodbourn had hurled at him echoing vividly in his mind. "He said his sister had told him the whole," Gideon concluded flatly. He paused, studying Fiona. "It was Clare, wasn't it?"

"Of course it was Clare. How could you possibly think I'd behave so irresponsibly? I may have been foolish enough to fling myself at your head, but I was not lost to all sense of honor."

Gideon was silent. Why had he been so ready to think badly of Fiona? Not to ease his own guilt, nothing so paltry could do that. But perhaps he'd been tempted to believe anything which might tarnish Fiona and weaken his feelings for her, feelings which had grown far stronger than he'd ever intended. He could not, of course, say this to her, so he skirted the issue. "It seems I've wronged you in more ways than one. I'm sorry."

Fiona gave a rueful, entirely too charming smile. "And I, please note, am quite capable of accepting an apology. I didn't mean to sound so angry. But I would like to believe you thought better of me. I take it there's nothing in the washstand?"

"Only a mildewed handtowel." Relieved, Gideon transferred his gaze from Fiona's face to the innocuous list of missing pieces of furniture. The only thing still unaccounted for was the writing table, but a thorough search of the rest of the attic failed to bring it to light.

"Things are gone from other rooms too," Fiona said, sinking into a battered armchair which had lost most of its stuffing. "I haven't seen the dining room sideboard anywhere. Or the Chinese firescreen of which Aunt Charlotte was so proud."

Gideon leaned against a table stacked haphazardly with miscellaneous smaller pieces. "Clare has a very handsome Chinese firescreen in her drawing room. Pale green with mountains."

"That's it exactly." Fiona leaned toward him. "Clare must have gone through the house and taken anything she thought halfway decent."

"And the writing table?"

"It was rosewood with ebony inlay, even finer than the dressing table. It must be in Davies Street or at Digby Hall. But more likely Davies Street. Clare never cared much for the country. The only remaining problem is how I can make an excuse to call on her and search her house."

Gideon grinned. How like Fiona to be so utterly practical. "Surely such a task is better left to me. Clare can hardly show me the door."

"No."

Gideon's grin changed abruptly to a scowl. "For the hundredth time, you stubborn woman, I know you despise my help, but if you insist on doing everything alone—"

"It's not that," Fiona said quickly. "Don't you see, if Clare finds out the truth, I must seem to be acting alone. You can't afford to turn Clare and Hugo against you."

Gideon felt the tension leave his body. "A sobering estimate of my talents. I assure you, I'm quite capable of dealing with both your sister and her husband."

"Yes, but I see no need for you to jeopardize your children's future proving it. You must think me a selfish creature indeed if you imagine I'd put my interests before theirs."

Fiona was beautiful in all moods—angry, reserved, cool, ironic—but perhaps never more so than now, when her eyes shone with sincerity. "I'd have to be a fool to think that," he told her. "Fiona, I haven't properly thanked you . . ."

"I've done nothing but be there when I was needed," Fiona said, getting to her feet. "And speaking of the children, if we don't join them soon, I can't answer for their patience."

This was incontrovertible, so they left the house without having properly settled the question of who was to call on Clare in search of the missing writing table. They found the boys and Beth slumped on a bench in the stable yard, exhausted and disheveled. The games Adam had learned in the streets of Bristol tended to be vigorous. At the sight of Gideon and Fiona, all three children roused themselves and demanded food, a definite sign of improvement. Ten days before, they'd have held their tongues and looked wistful.

Fiona led them away from the formal gardens and into open park land. Teddy and Beth danced along beside her, Teddy chattering in a way Gideon had once thought impossible. Beth was still quiet, but she smiled more.

221

She'd taken to Fiona at once, though she continued to seek out Gideon, reaching for his hand or climbing on his lap at unexpected moments. The reasons for such devotion still baffled him, but he was beginning to enjoy it.

Peter walked beside his father and Adam, matching his stride to Gideon's own. The better relations between them continued to develop through the most commonplace sort of activities, such as cleaning the stable or grooming the horses. Gideon frowned. Bringing Benjamin back had been a great success, but Peter should have his own horse and Teddy should have a pony. Beth would soon be wanting one as well. Perhaps if Woodbourn-Prebble's next voyage paid a healthy dividend . . .

Fiona stopped beside an alder tree which provided ample shade and she and Adam began unpacking the hamper. The children fell on the food ravenously, but Beth, who objected to anything with a very strong flavor, stared dubiously at the Cheshire cheese. "I don't like that."

"I know," Fiona said cheerfully, "I packed some double Gloucester for you." She reached across the picnic cloth for the cheese, managing to upset the open lemonade flask in the process. When she lunged after it she lost her balance, and Gideon automatically grasped her shoulder to steady her.

It was far less intimate than the dozens of socially sanctioned ways in which a man and woman might touch. But at their first meeting in the park, Fiona had made it clear that she did not wish to take his arm, and when they left Margaret's she'd climbed in and out of the curricle before he could assist her. Knowing she'd chosen the sensible course, he refrained from offering to help her with her wraps, and when he held out a chair for her, he was careful not to allow his hands to brush her shoulders. They'd managed to avoid any physical contact . . . until now.

It was bound to have happened sooner or later. It was

probably just as well that it had occurred in a setting which made it impossible to act impulsively. But though he checked any number of stronger impulses, Gideon could not help turning to look at Fiona and in that same moment her eyes flew to his face. It was only a matter of seconds before she looked away, but that moment assured him that she'd been quite as affected as he.

Beth tugged at her governess's sleeve. "Could I have some of the cheese, Fiona?" Fiona complied with great industry. Gideon leaned back on his elbows and began to tell an amusing, highly edited version of one of his exploits on the Peninsula. Adam paid rather closer attention to the story than might have been expected but gave no other sign that he'd noticed anything out of the ordinary. The children's attention seemed wholly taken up by luncheon and their father's adventures in Spain. Not that it made a great deal of difference. Whatever the others thought, he and Fiona could not possibly pretend that nothing had happened.

The only good thing about that unsettling moment at the picnic, Fiona decided—apart from the wholly inappropriate tremor of delight she'd felt—was that it took her mind off her visit to Lady Windham. In the face of something as tangible and alive as what had passed between her and Gideon, the identity of the mother she'd never met no longer seemed of all-consuming importance. It was not until she and the children were walking to Hill Street that she began to consider what lay ahead and to feel corresponding anticipation and dread.

Lady Windham and Verity were once again in the garden playing with Perdita, but this time they were accompanied by Lord Windham and Simon di Tassio. "Verity reminded me that Simon and Master Carne were friends, so I thought it would be nice to have you all over at once," Lady Windham explained, with a look which assured Fiona that she knew precisely what she was doing.

223

Peter's grinning face did away with any qualms Fiona felt at acting behind the princess's back.

Lord Windham—a fair-haired, deceptively soft-spoken man who seemed an unlikely match for the lively Lady Windham until one observed them together for an hour or so—greeted Fiona with the warmth and informality of an old friend and told the young Carnes that he was very pleased to make their acquaintance. "I was speaking to your father about the India bill only a few days ago, and it appears we're much of a mind on the subject."

"Did you know him?" Peter asked with evident curiosity. "Before, I mean?"

"Before he left for the Peninsula?" Windham smiled. "Slightly. I'd just taken my seat in the House, and Carne was one of my heroes. And I saw him again in Lisbon in ought-nine. I'm glad he's back in England."

"So am I," said Peter, and Fiona realized that both he and Lord Windham meant it.

Beth and Teddy were inclined to cling to Fiona's skirts until Verity brought Perdita over to meet them. Soon Teddy was talking happily about the dogs at Hartwood, and Fiona was free to sit with Simon and Peter. "We had a betrothal dinner last week," Simon told her with a grimace. "All Parminter's family, including the Buck- leighs. *Maman* said I could dine at table, and it wasn't as bad as I expected. Lady Demetra and Robin Melchett both asked after you, Fiona. We had a capital talk. De- metra's a very decent sort. I don't know why Alessa couldn't have turned out more like her. And it's hard to believe that Robin is Parminter's brother."

"When will the wedding take place?" Fiona asked.

"Not until after *Maman's* confinement, thank good- ness. When Michael comes home we're all to go to Par- minter's country house—Sundon, it's called. I bet Robin a shilling that *Maman* and the marchioness will come to blows before we've been there a week." Simon looked up at Fiona with a more sober expression. "Alessa and I

224

MORE PASSION AND ADVENTURE AWAIT... YOUR TRIP TO A BIG ADVENTUROUS WORLD BEGINS WHEN YOU ACCEPT YOUR FIRST 4 NOVELS ABSOLUTELY *FREE*
(AN $18.00 VALUE)

Accept your Free gift and start to experience more of the passion and adventure you like in a historical romance novel. Each Zebra novel is filled with proud men, spirited women and tempestuous love that you'll remember long after you turn the last page.

Zebra Historical Romances are the finest novels of their kind. They are written by authors who really know how to weave tales of romance and adventure in the historical settings you love. You'll feel like you've actually gone back in time with the thrilling stories that each Zebra novel offers.

GET YOUR FREE GIFT WITH THE START OF YOUR HOME SUBSCRIPTION

Our readers tell us that these books sell out very fast in book stores and often they miss the newest titles. So Zebra has made arrangements for you to receive the four newest novels published each month.

You'll be guaranteed that you'll never miss a title, and home delivery is so convenient. And to show you just how easy it is to get Zebra Historical Romances, we'll send you your first 4 books absolutely FREE! Our gift to you just for trying our home subscription service.

BIG SAVINGS AND FREE HOME DELIVERY

Each month, you'll receive the four newest titles as soon as they are published. You'll probably receive them even before the bookstores do. What's more, you may preview these exciting novels free for 10 days. If you like them as much as we think you will, just pay the low preferred subscriber's price of just $3.75 each. *You'll save $3.00 each month off the publisher's price.* AND, your savings are even greater because there are never any shipping, handling or other hidden charges—FREE Home Delivery. Of course you can return any shipment within 10 days for full credit, no questions asked. There is no minimum number of books you must buy.

GET
FOUR
FREE
BOOKS

(AN $18.00 VALUE)

ZEBRA HOME SUBSCRIPTION
SERVICE, INC.
P.O. Box 5214
120 BRIGHTON ROAD
CLIFTON, NEW JERSEY 07015-5214

haven't been agreeing about very much lately, but we're definitely going to talk to Michael before we leave for the country."

Fiona smiled but said nothing. Peter's gaze was fixed on the gravel at his feet, and Fiona realized he wasn't at all happy with the thought of her returning to Bolton Street. She was unlikely to do so, but sooner or later she would have to leave the Carne house. For the first time she considered what a wrench this would be.

Because the party was such a large one, luncheon was served inside, but the meal was quite as lively as it might have been in the garden. By the time Beth had consumed her second lemon cream the last of her shyness had quite evaporated, and she was not in the least disturbed when Lady Windham took Fiona off at the end of the meal. The same could not be said of Fiona, who found herself wondering if Mr. Constable had been right to question whether she really wanted to learn the truth.

"What delightful children," Lady Windham said, ushering her guest into the music room, which appeared slightly more tidy than it had on Fiona's previous visit. "Forgive me," she continued when the door was shut, "but we've been so worried since we got Simon's note. Are you quite all right?"

"Quite," Fiona assured her, glad to put off talking about her mother. She hesitated. "Alastair is not the name I was born with."

"I didn't think it was," Lady Windham said cheerfully.

Fiona was relieved but felt impelled to add, "The princess would not be pleased to hear you've received me, especially with Simon present."

"That," said Lady Windham, a distinctly martial light in her eye, "is a matter for the princess and me to settle. Assuming she finds out, which I do not consider at all likely. Charles feels the same way, I assure you. There is no need for you to tell us more."

None, Fiona thought, except the debt of friendship.

"How much do you know?" she asked.

"Very little. Simon sent word that you'd left Bolton Street. The princess has said nothing at all."

"But you've heard talk?"

Unaccustomedly embarrassed, Lady Windham began to tidy the papers on the pianoforte. "When a single man hires a beautiful woman to look after his children, there is always talk."

Fiona knew what inference the princess would draw when she sent for her things to be delivered to Gideon's house, but if there had been gossip it was not Princess Sofia's doing. Fiona should have guessed that George would seek to do her and Gideon mischief. "But this talk, I suspect, hints that the relationship between us is of longer standing. It's quite true. I was briefly Lord Carne's mistress five years ago. When the princess dismissed me, he offered me a post as his children's governess, but the rumors are false if they suggest there is anything between us now."

Lady Windham's hands stilled on the papers. Her expression was wholly without levity. "You needn't have told me that," she said quietly.

"I know." Fiona smiled. "I think perhaps that's why I did."

Lady Windham grinned, then said seriously, "I hope you know that if circumstances ever force you to leave Lord Carne's roof, you may always come to us."

Though her concern for Simon and Verity would prevent her from accepting such an invitation in all but the most dire circumstances, Fiona thanked Lady Windham warmly. Then, as Lady Windham unlocked a rolltop desk against the back wall, she steeled herself to face whatever her friend had discovered.

"The first thing I did was call on Lucy Harrington—Lucy Kittredge, that was—whose mother is a Selkirk," Lady Windham said, taking a sheet of paper from the desk and moving to a chair. "I'm afraid I didn't meet

226

with great success. Lucy always was a widgeon, and of course I had to be careful not to reveal what I was about. But I did learn that her mother has both an older sister and a younger one, and that all three girls would have been about the right age. Katherine, the eldest, was married in 1781, which doesn't necessarily prove anything, but her eldest son was born in August 1784, so I don't see how she could possibly have given birth to you in September of the same year."

Fiona nodded, grateful for Lady Windham's matter-of-fact tone. It was the only possible way to conduct such a conversation. "Fortunately all the Selkirk girls spent at least a season in London," Lady Windham continued, "and I was sure my mother would know something of them, but she's been visiting my brother—his wife was just confined—so I had to wait until she returned to town. Meanwhile, I wrote to Charles's mother in Scotland, and most fortunately, her husband—her second husband, that is—has relatives who are acquainted with the Bowders. Your father's friend, Jack Bowder, has two sisters, Mary and Janet. Mary, the elder, made quite a respectable match to a gentleman from Edinburgh in April of 1784. The wedding was very public, and given the fashions of the time I do not see how she could have been increasing. Her younger sister Janet did not marry until some years later. My mother-in-law could not ascertain the exact date, but she did say that Janet, like most of the Bowders, is distinguished by her dark hair." Lady Windham paused and looked up from the paper. "Your father—?"

"His hair was chestnut. His parents died before I was born, but judging by their portraits, they were both dark as well."

"As were Mr. and Mrs. Bowder," Lady Windham said cheerfully. "One can't be certain, of course—no one knows why I turned out with hair like copper—but one wouldn't expect two such parents to produce a child with

227

your coloring. As for the Selkirks," she continued, lowering her eyes to the paper in her lap, "Mama returned to town two days ago. She'd another engagement this afternoon, but she asked to be remembered to you. I'm afraid I had to tell her something of your story."

"That's very understandable." Fiona knew Lady Crawford could be relied upon.

Lady Windham looked relieved. "I asked Mama to bring her letters for the period in question when she returned to London—she carries on a voluminous correspondence and she saves everything. My father was posted to Brussels in 1784, and Mama received a great many letters from friends at home describing the events of the Season. Apparently Henrietta Selkirk's coming-out ball in May was one of the highlights. I'm sure someone would have noticed if Henrietta had been eight months pregnant."

"Was Maria at the ball?"

"That's where the story becomes interesting. Maria, who had made her début two years before, was expected to accompany her mother and sister to town, but instead she remained in Scotland, suffering from an attack of measles. It caused some talk."

Fiona drew a steadying breath and told herself it was too soon for her to be sure of anything. "My mother was accompanied to France by a woman who was supposed to be her own mother."

"Yes, and Lady Selkirk was certainly in London with Henrietta. But Lady Selkirk's sister, the Marchioness of Parminter, was traveling on the Continent for the whole of the spring. Her own daughter accompanied her."

"And perhaps instead of languishing in Scotland with the measles, Maria was in France with them, giving birth to me."

"Perhaps." Frowning slightly, Lady Windham adjusted one of the pale green ribbons which confined the sleeves of her jaconet gown. "It occurred to Mama and me that either the Bowders or the Selkirks could have had other guests besides your father that summer."

"You're saying that I can never be sure, that my mother could be almost anyone?"

"That's always possible, of course. But Mama was remembering that Lady Parminter's daughter, Penelope, often visited her Selkirk cousins. We don't know if she stayed with them in August of 1783, but we do know that she and her mother went abroad the following spring."

Fiona stared at Lady Windham with what she feared was a rather stupid expression. "But that would mean — that would mean Lady Parminter is my grandmother."

"If Maria is your mother, Lady Parminter is your great-aunt. I think it likely that she is one or the other."

Fiona made an effort to collect herself. "Was Penelope the Parminters' only daughter?"

"Their only child. She married her cousin Robert, who was her father's heir, but she died before he came into the title. The present Lord Parminter is her son." Lady Windham studied her friend. "You have the Melchett coloring, and you obviously didn't get it from your father."

"Maria Kittredge looks much the same," Fiona said quickly. The facts were all on the side of Maria. They did not know that Penelope had been in Scotland at the requisite time, and Lady Windham said there had been gossip about Maria's attack of measles. And, Fiona acknowledged as she and Lady Windham rejoined the others, somehow it was easier for her to believe herself the child of Maria Kittredge, who stood at the edge of the Parminter world, than the child of Penelope Melchett, who was at its very heart.

The sudden glow on Beth's face told Fiona that Gideon had appeared in the nursery doorway. Lately he'd been making a habit of coming up to say goodnight to the children.

"Don't stop on my account," Gideon said, for Fiona had broken off in the midst of a bedtime story.

"Fiona's telling us about Richard III and Anne Neville," Teddy volunteered. "Only he wasn't Richard III then, just Duke of Gloucester."

"He didn't have a crooked back," Beth added, her eyes trained on Gideon.

"He'd known Lady Anne since they were children, but her family made her marry someone else." Teddy's dark eyes showed genuine indignation.

"And even after her husband died, people kept trying to keep them apart." Peter was as caught up in the story as his younger siblings. "Because of the inheritance."

"Then by all means we must find out what happened." Gideon moved to a chair, but the boys made room for him on Teddy's bed and after a moment's hesitation he joined them.

"Go on," said Beth, curled up on her own bed beside Fiona. "What happened after Lady Anne ran away and dressed up like a kitchen maid?"

By concluding with Richard and Anne's marriage, before less pleasant events overtook them, Fiona was able to bring the story to a most satisfactory conclusion. Gideon listened with what appeared to be genuine interest, and when she was done he helped her tuck Teddy and Beth into bed, which earned him a look of approbation from his elder son. Then Peter took himself off to his own room and Fiona and Gideon found themselves walking downstairs together, alone for the first time since their trip to Barstead the previous day.

"You're an excellent teacher," Gideon said after an awkward pause. "I wish I'd been tutored by someone half so entertaining."

Fiona laughed, a release of nervous tension. "In all seriousness, Richard is an excellent example of the ambigu-

230

ities in history and the need to examine the evidence and form one's own opinion. And Anne perfectly illustrates the plight of women at the time."

"So you're teaching my children about the plight of women?" Gideon asked with a grin as they reached the first floor landing.

"Do you object?"

"Not in the least. But I trust you tell them that in that area, not to mention others, time has brought about little improvement."

"Of course. Lessons about the past should always be used to illuminate the present." She paused, for Anne Neville, a pawn in her father's political maneuvering, had more than a little in common with her own mother.

Gideon too was silent until they reached the ground-floor hall, but when Fiona started for the kitchen he stayed her. "I don't know what happened this afternoon, but it's clear something has upset you. If you don't wish to talk about it, say so, but if I can be of service—"

Even as she turned back to him, intending to say politely but firmly that it was her own affair, it occurred to Fiona that Gideon might be precisely the person to tell her more about the Melchett and Selkirk families. After yesterday, she should be doubly determined to hold him at arm's length, but in Gideon's company she had a disconcerting tendency to act on instinct rather than logic. Without realizing quite how it had happened, she found herself sitting on the library sofa, recounting the story with surprising ease to an impassive Gideon, a considerable stretch of Persian carpet between them. "And so," she concluded as prosaically as possible, "it seems most likely that Maria Kittredge is my mother."

"Who named you?" Gideon asked abruptly.

Fiona was taken aback. "My father, I presume . . . or perhaps my mother. Why?"

"Just a thought." Gideon crossed his legs. "Fiona is an unusual name. Do you know where it comes from?"

231

"Only that it's Gaelic. My father's maternal grandmother was Scottish, and now I know that Scotland is where my parents met. Perhaps there was a Fiona on the Bowder estate."

"Perhaps. I suspect your father or mother meant to name you Fionnguala and quite sensibly decided to shorten it." Gideon rested his head against the chair back. "I once accompanied Robert Melchett on a visit to the Parminter estates in Ireland. The tenants all have the most fascinating names which the English typically proceed to anglicize. Eithne becomes Anna; Ian, John; and Fionnguala," Gideon said, fixing his gaze on Fiona, "is translated as Penelope."

Chapter Fourteen

Penelope. Penelope Melchett. Fiona felt an hysterical desire to laugh. "It's impossible. Because if it's true—but it can't be true—then Lord Parminter is my brother."

She looked at Gideon, willing him to say that the names meant nothing, that it had all been a joke, but his face was serious and there was no trace of amusement in his eyes. Indeed, he seemed as shocked by the idea as she. "And Lady Lydia is your sister. And George—"

"No."

"George is also your brother."

The idea sobered Fiona at once. "No," she said again, thankful that she had regained her wits, "you're letting your imagination run riot. My father had no particular learning. If he named me, it was for some Scottish forebear or because the name pleased him. And if my mother named me, it was for the same reason. It must be Maria Selkirk." The thought depressed her.

"Penelope Melchett had your coloring as well," Gideon reminded her.

"Penelope Melchett came from one of the proudest families in England. Can you imagine the daughter of Lady Parminter looking seriously at a young man with neither prospects nor name to recommend him?"

"She had her share of pride," Gideon admitted. "But she was willful and stubborn and in constant search of distraction. And your father was a well-favored man."

It was hard to think of a parent in such a light, but Uncle James had, Fiona supposed, been considered handsome in his youth. "Why are you so determined that it be Penelope Melchett?"

"Why are you so determined that it not?"

"I don't know." She smiled wryly. "Neither my feelings nor yours will make it so. I'm at an impasse. I shall never know, shall I, unless I ask."

"Mrs. Kittredge?"

"No, Lady Parminter."

It was a decision that gave Fiona a sleepless night. Maria Kittredge would be easier to approach, but the lady would be quite capable of calling for her vinaigrette and having Fiona thrown out of the house. Lady Parminter might show her the door as well, but first she would hear her out. And Lady Parminter would know whether her father's young love was the giddy Maria Selkirk or the improbable Penelope Melchett. Lady Parminter was unlikely to tell Alessa's discredited governess what she wanted to know, but Fiona had to make the attempt. She debated writing a letter to request an interview, then decided against it. Her only hope lay in taking the marchioness unawares. She might then produce a look of guilt or complicity that would tell her the name of the woman who was her mother.

It was the most she could hope for. She could not expect public recognition. Even her father had not acknowledged her openly, and a woman's reputation was far more fragile than a man's. The marchioness could not be expected to expose her niece's shame. Or, if Gideon was right, her daughter's.

But Fiona knew she wanted more, and for this reason she hoped Gideon was wrong. Penelope Melchett was dead and beyond her reach, but Maria Selkirk—Maria Kittredge—was very much alive, and with Lady Parminter's help she might be brought to confess privately to the bond between them. Silly and shallow she might be, but she had not seemed an unkind woman. Surely she would have some feeling for the child she'd given up. A moment of recognition, that was all Fiona asked, and a hint of the love that should have been hers and for which she had longed all her life.

Fiona was a realist and she chided herself for these thoughts as she saw to the beds, helped with the washing up, and set the children their morning lessons. She told herself more than once to give it up, but by the time the clock struck eleven she'd draped the gray silk shawl over her best morning dress, a blue-green lutestring with a modest lace collar, and left the house in search of a hackney that would take her to Bloomsbury Square.

The journey seemed interminable. By the time the hackney pulled into the forecourt of Parminter House, she'd acquired an unaccustomed headache. The sight of the fountain made her realize that her mouth had gone quite dry, and she found that she was shivering, though the day was warm. She descended from the hackney, paid the driver off, and moved resolutely toward the broad steps that led to the front door.

The house seemed even more imposing by day, a structure solid rather than graceful, though the central dome and the pavilions projecting at each end of the main block gave variety to the symmetry of the whole. Two wings, set at right angles to the house proper, enclosed the sides of the forecourt, one of which, from its wide, high doors and the carriage waiting outside, seemed to house the stables. The other must be devoted to more domestic offices, for Fiona glimpsed several servants and two or three people who appeared to be tradesmen entering and leaving.

It could hardly be called a house. It was rather a small, self-contained village, a description that was not inapt, for it was home to two families. The Barrington-Forbeses, Robin Melchett had told her, now occupied the apartments that once housed his own parents, while his grandmother ruled the whole from the quarters that had been hers from the day she'd married the sixth marquis. It was here that Lord Parminter would bring Alessa to establish her own domain. Alessa had enough confidence to essay the role, but she seemed very young to take Lady Parminter's place.

The footman who opened the door studied Fiona a moment, as though debating whether or not she should be sent round to the housekeeper. "I am Miss Alastair," Fiona said, summoning all the authority at her command, "and I wish to see Lady Parminter." She held out the carefully sealed note she'd penned that morning. "I will wait for a reply."

To Fiona's relief, the footman directed her to a small anteroom off the hall where she could be assured of relative privacy. It was not yet noon, and the marchioness was sure to be at home. Robin had told her his grandmother never went out in the morning, but she had no wish to face the curiosity of other members of the family. Fiona glanced at her watch. It was a large house. Three minutes for the footman to climb the stairs and find the marchioness's door, three more to hand her the letter and wait for her instructions, three to return to the anteroom. It seemed far longer to Fiona, but she'd been well schooled in deferring to the whims of others. She sat quietly, betraying none of the fear and pride that warred within her.

When the summons came she felt a moment of panic, but she rose without haste and followed the footman up one of the twin staircases, down a long hall and then another, stopping finally before a double pedimented door. The footman threw open the doors, told her to wait, and withdrew.

It must be one of the smaller parlors, but it would have dwarfed the drawing room at Barstead. The cedar walls rose to a white plaster ceiling elaborately carved with designs of acanthus leaves and a central medallion which bore a painting of Danäe under a shower of gold. The furniture was of more recent design, chosen for both elegance and comfort. Drapes of blue and white damask hung at the windows and the blue was repeated in the upholstery of the chairs and in the handsome Persian carpet, which covered a third of the polished floor, defining an area where one might reasonably expect to talk without having to raise one's voice.

It was not more than two or three minutes before a sound caused Fiona to turn around. The door to an adjoining room had opened and the marchioness stood framed in the doorway. Fiona rose and made a slight curtsy. "Thank you for seeing me, Lady Parminter."

The marchioness inclined her head, closed the door behind her, and came slowly into the room, leaning on her walking stick. She waved her visitor to a chair and eased herself into another that must have been reserved for her use, for it had an extra cushion at the back and heavy carved arms that could be used to support her when she sat or stood. "Now, Miss Alastair," the marchioness said when she was settled. "You have something to say to me."

Dear Mother of God, how was she to begin? There was no precedent for an inquiry of this sort. Fiona looked into the woman's faded blue eyes and knew she'd be allowed no time for pleasantries, no time to prepare the way for what would be a monstrous accusation. "It is this, Lady Parminter," she began, forcing herself to speak before she decided it would be better not to speak at all. "I am looking for my mother, and I believe you can tell me who she is."

Had she imagined it, the slight intake of breath, that faint tightening of the knuckles about her stick? Probably. The marchioness made no response, but regarded her with thoughtful eyes. So might she look at anyone who came to her with such a cock-and-bull request. "You had best explain yourself, Miss Alastair."

It was easier now. "I was born of an irregular union," Fiona said without hesitation. "I was raised as my father's ward and have never known my mother's identity."

"An unfortunate story," the marchioness said, her tone indicating that she'd little sympathy for the speaker. "But I do not see how I can help you."

"I am sure you can, Lady Parminter. For I believe—indeed, I am almost certain—that you are my great-aunt. Or my grandmother."

The marchioness's lips tightened. "I am not to be trifled with, Miss Alastair. Explain yourself."

"My father's name was James Woodbourn. In September of 1783, the month in which I was conceived, he was paying a visit to some friends by the name of Bowder who live in Scotland near Castleton. Your sister's home is nearby, and I believe the families are close." She looked for some reaction from the other woman, but Lady Parminter's face betrayed nothing. "It must have been one of the young women he met there," Fiona went on, "one of the Bowder girls or one of the Selkirks, or someone who was visiting them at the time."

"Nonsense. If it happened as you say it was most likely one of the servants. Or a girl from the village."

"Who was taken to France to deliver her child? Taken by an older woman who must have been either her mother or a close relative? My father went to France to claim me, Lady Parminter. My mother was English, and a lady."

There was a moment of silence while they took each other's measure. "Very well," Lady Parminter said. "Go on."

"The important thing, of course, is what happened the following spring. I learned what I could of the movements of each of the young women with whom my father might have established a liaison."

"You are enterprising, Miss Alastair."

238

Fiona ignored the jibe. "I narrowed the possibilities to three: Janet Bowder, Maria Selkirk, and Penelope Melchett. Miss Bowder, I'm told, was dark, as was my father. It does not seem likely they would produce a child with my coloring. Your daughter was abroad that spring; you took her to France. Perhaps you took Miss Selkirk as well. She was reported to have measles and did not come to London for the Season." Fiona paused. "Now you see, Lady Parminter, why I've come to you for information."

The marchioness said nothing, but she pursed her lips as though considering the implications of what she'd been told. Fiona held her breath. The story held water, just, but there were other explanations: a liaison formed before her father went to Castleton, or after he left, though the time of her birth made this unlikely; or a visitor to the Bowders whose name she'd not yet heard. Fiona knew, with a certainty she could not have explained, that none of these was true, but Lady Parminter could easily fasten on one of them, could deny everything and send her on her way. "I hope you can help me," Fiona said, aware that the marchioness would not yield to persuasion but might yield to threat, "for if you cannot, I have no choice but to go to Mrs. Kittredge. And if she too cannot help me, then I must go to Scotland to continue my inquiries."

The marchioness stirred in her chair, but gave no other indication that she was discomposed. "May I ask, Miss Alastair, the reason for this determination? Why are you so eager to find a mother who in—what is it, nearly thirty years?—has given no sign that she is aware of your existence? Who would hardly welcome a reminder of a youthful indiscretion?"

"If you cannot understand it, Lady Parminter, then I doubt I could explain it to you." Fiona could scarce explain it to herself, but she knew, in a way that was beyond reason, that she had to learn the truth.

"I see. You are quite resolved, then?"

Fiona met the passionless blue eyes that seemed to will her to submission, but her gaze did not falter. For the first time since the beginning of this extraordinary interview, she felt she and the marchioness were equals. "I am resolved."

The marchioness sighed and lowered her gaze to the floor. With grave deliberation she traced the pattern in the rug with her stick. Fiona, watching the silent struggle, forced herself to remain quite still.

Lady Parminter looked up suddenly. "What are you called, Miss Alastair? What is your given name?"

"Fiona," she said, surprised that it mattered.

"Fiona . . . then he kept the name." The marchioness seemed to be speaking to herself, but now she put both hands on her stick and regarded her visitor with resolution. "You are quite right, Miss Alastair. I know the name of your mother. It is not a happy memory and I would rather not speak of it, but you leave me no choice. You are the daughter of my own daughter, Penelope Melchett."

Fiona had not expected this bald admission. "Then you are—"

"I am your grandmother. Do not presume on the relationship. It is not one that can be acknowledged."

"I do not expect to be recognized publicly, Lady Parminter. I only—" She broke off, not sure how to give form to the tumult of feelings within her.

"I know what you want, Miss Alastair. You cannot have it. My daughter is dead and can give you nothing. I am not given to sentiment, and I will not embrace you as a beloved grandchild. There will be no return of the prodigal here."

"I am not asking for that," Fiona said, furious that there were tears in her eyes. "I want only to know how it happened."

The marchioness sighed. "Very well. It is a simple

240

enough story, and I am sure you have worked out its outlines for yourself. In 1783 my daughter went, as she did most summers, to pay a visit to her Selkirk cousins. She formed an attachment there to a young man who was visiting the Bowders. Your father's behavior was shameful, but I must say that he was not wholly to blame. Penelope was eighteen and imprudent, and the consequences were disastrous. At Christmas time she told us she was with child. In February I took her to France for an extended visit. Maria did not come with us. She knew *nothing* of what had happened and spent the spring in Castleton recovering from a virulent bout of the measles."

"And my mother?"

"There was no question of keeping you, you will understand. Penelope was agreed on that point. She knew she could never have married a man of—you will forgive me—of indifferent birth and no prospects, and she could never acknowledge James Woodbourn's child. She was bored and restless during our stay in Picardy, but fortunately you were a small baby and the birth was easy. You were given almost immediately to a wet nurse, but yes, Miss Alastair, your mother did hold you in her arms, and she chose your name herself."

It was, Fiona supposed, as close as the marchioness could come to kindness. "When did my father—"

"He came when you were two weeks old. He'd been told there would be a child, and he agreed to have the care of you."

Her father at least had wanted her. It was something to cling to. "Did my mother know—did she ever ask about me?"

"You are being mawkish," Lady Parminter said dryly. "My daughter could not afford to be interested in you, and to my knowledge she never spoke or thought of you at all. We had done our duty. Your father took full responsibility for you and was paid handsomely for his trouble."

"Paid?" In the midst of this personal drama, the thought of money was incongruous.

"He made it a condition of his taking you."

So *that* was why he agreed to bring her up. Fiona shivered. The money he received must be the legacy that had enabled him to become Silas Woodbourn's partner, the legacy that had made his fortune. Oh, he owed her a lot.

There was nothing more to be said. Feeling more depressed than she had in many months, Fiona picked up her reticule and gloves. "Thank you, Lady Parminter."

"You have no need to thank me. I would prefer not to have spoken, but since you have forced me to it, I will confess that I do not regret the conversation. Perhaps now you will satisfy my own curiosity and tell me how it is that you took employment as a companion and, if I have heard rightly, a governess. Was your father then unsuccessful? Did he leave you nothing?"

It was a reasonable exchange and, as denoting some interest in her person, not one to which Fiona could object, but she was reluctant to share any of herself with this smug woman who was her grandmother. "My father provided for me while he lived," she said cautiously, "but he had legitimate children to consider as well. I have chosen the path of independence."

"An admirable choice, Miss Alastair, but a difficult one for a woman to achieve. I understand you are no longer in the Princess Sofia's employ."

The statement should not have surprised her. The marchioness would have heard it from Alessa, if not from George. "That is true," Fiona replied, wondering how much else the marchioness knew.

"I will not pry, Miss Alastair, but you should know that I have some concern in the matter. It was always intended that you be provided for. I do not care to see someone of my own blood reduced to poverty."

"I will make my way, Lady Parminter."

"You have found other employment?"

"I am governess to Lord Carne's children."

"Ah." Lady Parminter's expression grew thoughtful. "The arrangement is not likely to last. You hope, of course, that his recommendation will count with a future employer. For your sake, I hope that it will, though you must know that you have lost the confidence of the Princess Sofia." The marchioness studied her a moment, as though trying to reach a decision. "I fear for your future, Miss Alastair. I would like to make some provision for you. Let me give you the name of my solicitor and he can work out the details."

She should have seen where the discussion of her employment was leading, but Fiona was shocked by the proposal nonetheless. Lady Parminter was offering her money, perhaps even the independence for which she longed, but it made no sense. This woman was by her own account free of sentiment. Why should she care what happened to her daughter's bastard.

Or was it a bribe, such as she'd offered Gideon? Miss Alastair had asked too many inconvenient questions, and she would be paid to ensure that she asked no more. Fiona rose quickly, conscious only of an intense desire to be free of the oppressive opulence of this house. "No, Lady Parminter, you have given me what I came for. I want nothing more from you."

The marchioness pursed her lips. "You have pride, girl. Do not let it make you foolish."

Fiona shook her head, not trusting herself to speak.

"As you wish." The marchioness got to her feet and walked to the bell-rope, leaning heavily on her stick as though suddenly conscious of her years. But when she turned back to Fiona, she stood erect and her eyes were bright. "You are a woman of spirit and quality, Miss Alastair. It is more than I'd have expected."

On that same afternoon Gideon left the House after several dreary hours. He had forgot how tedious the business of government could be. Necessary, yes, but good God, Irish distillers? Ireland had occupied a good deal of the peers' attention that day, what with bills on licenses and Catholic officers and court houses and insolvent debtors. Gideon had a strong feeling that they'd all be much better off if they simply left that troubled island alone.

Since the partners' meeting he had taken to spending a portion of each day at the House, not for the sake of the debates, with which he'd little patience, but to renew old acquaintances and learn what he could of India and the matter of trade. When he was not in the House he was down by the docks or in coffeehouses or taverns, seeking out ships' captains and merchants and men who'd made their fortune on the subcontinent and brought it home to England.

What he learned left him with distinctly mixed feelings. There was iron in India, abundant and of exceptional purity, and wages, God knew, were low enough. Only five years before, the East India Company had sent out a Mr. Duncan to look into the possibility of working the ore, but the factory he had established at Kasimbazar had not shown much promise. Coal was available too, but there was no way to transport it save by boat, and the rivers were often navigable only during the rainy season.

Gold did not present them problems, and gold there certainly was. Even Herodotus spoke of it. The hill streams, Gideon was told, were commonly washed for gold, and there had once been extensive workings in Mysore, but no one in the native population was getting rich from his efforts. It seemed unlikely there would be enough to provide the endless source of wealth that Adrian claimed was there for the taking — damn William for filling his brother's head with such nonsense — even assuming a severe exploitation of the native workers. Gideon had heard enough stories of the foreign planters' treatment of the native growers of indigo to make him wary on this account alone.

He called again on Magnus Melchett to discuss what he'd learned, but the banker brushed his reservations aside. A good factor was all that was needed, and he knew of several men with experience in India who'd know how to get the most out of the natives. Cheap labor was what made it all possible. As for the question of gold, he'd never taken it seriously, but gold was a useful lure and the partnership was expanding rapidly, offering them needed capital. Parminter had brought in his cousin Kittredge and the Earl of Berresford, and three or four other men had expressed interest in investing in Woodbourn-Prebble. When the expected shipment of iron arrived from Riga, there would be a handsome profit to distribute among the original partners.

Melchett had taken control of the company. He had paid the delinquent accounts, thus increasing his own investment. He had also installed his own clerk to keep the books and hired his own agent to replace the stores lost in the fire. Hugo should have protested this loss of control, but he did little more than fret and complain. In the face of Melchett's energy and efficiency there was little else he could do. As for Gideon, he dared not quarrel with the promise of payment from the *Apollo's* cargo. The roof at Hartwood required immediate attention and the mortgage would soon come due. Melchett did not allude to this, but Gideon knew it would be well to keep the matter straight between them.

But on this day, as he left the House and made for Dover Street, Gideon's thoughts were not on India and Woodbourn-Prebble. It had been two days since he'd taken Fiona and the children into Kent, and the memory of the journey was still vivid before him. They were, God be praised, easier together, and for this he had to thank the dalliance of that engaging young man they had surprised *in flagrante delicto*. Fiona now knew the truth of the duel, and he knew—how, knowing what she was, could he have ever thought otherwise?—that she was innocent of bringing it about.

But he knew now something more. This woman, with whom he'd once taken his pleasure, could ignite his senses with the lightest, most casual touch. Surely it had not been that way before. He could hardly recall the brief weeks of their liaison. He had entered it deliberately, out of needs that had little to do with her, and his feelings had not been engaged. Not till the end, when it was over, when he realized that what had been between them was more intense and more fragile than anything he'd heretofore known, and by then he was able to feel nothing but anger and guilt.

He turned into Margaret Street, glad he'd decided to walk and leave the horses at home. Fiona was an uncommon woman and he desired her now as he'd never desired her before, but he was not about to repeat his earlier mistake. On the contrary, he'd do everything in his power to make her independent of him and the appetites of men, free to choose, freer than she'd have been had he never intruded on her life.

This ennobling fantasy was interrupted by the sound of a voice calling his name. He turned and saw Charles Windham approaching. Gideon welcomed him with relief. He did not much fancy the saintly role, and his ruminations were becoming a burden.

The two men fell in together and proceeded along Parliament Street. Windham had not been in the House that day, and Gideon reported the proceedings in full, unburdening himself on the inanity of politics and the futility of reasoned debate. The outburst left him feeling quite cheerful, a circumstance that caused him some surprise. He'd complained in this fashion many times before and had always finished the argument in a fit of black depression.

Perhaps he was losing his sense that the future was irremediably dark. Or perhaps it was simply the effect of Windham's company. He'd nodded several times during Gideon's tirade, but did not try, as others did, to argue him out of his position—or worse, to outdo his indignation. Gideon liked Windham, who was a man of sanguine temperament and infinite patience, but blessed with wit and an eye for folly. Four years ago they'd both been guests of Lord Lyndale, a British diplomat in Lisbon, and the House had been full of giddy young officers paying court to Lyndale's daughter. It had been a relief, Gideon told Windham, to have someone sensible to talk to.

A shadow crossed Windham's face. "She married one of those giddy young officers. He was my wife's cousin. We've just learned that he was killed at Vittoria."

Gideon grimaced and offered his condolences, knowing words were never adequate. He'd seen the names of more than one of his former comrades on that casualty list. It was ironic that it was the men who had something to live for who'd fallen in battle. And then it occurred to him that he was very glad he'd survived.

Gideon was readily persuaded to bear Windham company at dinner, and some hours later they found themselves at Brook's, where they were joined by Frank Hawksley, who'd just escaped the debate in the Commons.

"I have tried," Hawksley said, running a hand through his already unruly hair, "the devil knows I've tried to give the argument the attention it deserves, but I cannot stomach the sanctimonious self-righteousness of some of my fellow members." He threw himself into a chair beside the others, then immediately leaned forward to give emphasis to his point. "I have nothing against the Church attending to the welfare of its own people, but when I am told that it is our duty to take pity on the poor, miserable Hindus, that we are bound to correct their bad qualities and that this can be achieved only by bringing them the Christian faith—" He threw up his hands. "Egod!"

There was a moment of silent accord, and then Hawksley was off again. "Not that everyone is on the side of the saints. Forbes read several letters from men who'd lived in India, each professing concern about efforts to convert the natives. One of them claimed the saints won't retreat from their position until there's a massacre of all the British in India. Another said that the business of putting missionaries in India must be due to—now, what were his words?—yes, to some underhanded influence of Bonaparte. To which Stephen said it was the first time he'd heard Bonaparte accused of saintship."

This was met by a roar of laughter and the conversation turned to other elements of the charter and the probable effects on the economies of both India and England. "I'd like to improve my own economy," Hawksley said. "I hear you're going to make a fortune, Carne."

"I have no objection to a fortune," Gideon said dryly, "but I see scant hope of one. I'll be happy enough to come out of this with a whole skin. It's the question of gold, isn't it? What addle cove is spreading the story this time?"

"Hillman. He may or may not be unfurnished in the upper story, but he's becoming a partner in Woodbourn-Prebble. Didn't you know?"

Gideon groaned and shook his head. Hillman was a youngish man with little to distinguish him save a large fortune and a passion for gaming.

"He said Melchett and Prebble had agreed," Hawksley went on, "but it was Parminter's doing. Hillman had the devil of a time persuading Parminter to cut him in. Why would he want to? Parminter, I mean. They aren't particular friends."

"Parminter owes him money," Windham said quietly. "The word is that it's a matter of six or seven thousand pounds."

Gideon went cold. He knew Parminter was impetuous and careless with his tongue. Was it possible he was selling favors as well? It was several minutes before he again attended to the conversation, which had turned to other matters, and then he quickly made his excuses and left the club.

He walked briskly toward Dover Street, mulling over what he'd heard. The pleasures of the evening had quite dissipated, and he reached home in a dissatisfied frame of mind, cursing the Eighth Marquis of Parminter. It was past midnight and the house was dark. Gideon let himself in and went through the library to his study. There was nothing for it but to sleep away his ill humor and deal with the problem in the morning. He considered ringing for Adam but decided speech was the last thing he wanted. He would manage his boots by himself.

Five minutes later he was divested of coat, cravat, and boots and found he'd absolutely no desire to sleep. A book, that was what he needed. One of Robert's books that Lydia had sent round. He went back into the library, set his candle down on the table, and picked up a volume at random, opening it for the pleasure of seeing the inscription in Robert's hand. It was Pascal, and he thumbed through the pages, stopping when he came across a paper once apparently inserted as a page marker. He unfolded the sheet and found it was a note from William urging his father to buy the absolutely splendid hunter he'd just seen at Tattarsall's. Gideon smiled: it was the plea of a very young man. He read the note again, wondering how long it would be before he received such messages from Peter. Not too many years, but unless his fortunes mended, Peter would have scant hope of having his appeals answered.

Gideon looked at the scrawled note once more and frowned. It must be William's hand, yet it did not look very like the hand that had penned the letter he'd seen at Hugo's house. A monstrous suspicion made its way into Gideon's head. No, there were many years between the letters, and he could not trust his own memory of the more recent one. He would have to make sure. In a thoughtful mood, Gideon folded the letter and put it back in the book. It had lain hidden there for several years and would be safe enough for a few days more.

He found he had lost all desire to read and was about to return to the study when he heard a scratching at the door. He opened it to see a slender figure bearing a candle . . . Fiona.

"I thought I heard you come in," she said. Her voice was curiously tentative. "I know it's late, but would you mind if we talked?"

Chapter Fifteen

She'd been waiting for him all afternoon. All evening, too. Ever since she'd returned from Parminter House, stunned and angry and depressed, all through the hours of hearing Peter's translation and setting sums for Teddy and teaching Beth her letters and helping Barbara change the sheets, through the daily walk to the park so the children would get some exercise, and the simple dinner in the cavernous kitchen, and the nighttime story, she'd longed for Gideon to come home. She had no one else to talk to.

Once the children were settled, she retired to her room, where she sat by the window in the dark, watching the street below for Gideon's return. She felt adrift and curiously weightless. She'd found the truth of her birth, as she'd intended, but she did not know how to make use of this truth, how to incorporate it into some coherent image of her self. Her mother was no more than a name, an insubstantial image, a story that might have come from a book, or a dream that, dreaming, one knows will not bear the light of day. Had she lived, would she have turned her back on the claims of her firstborn child? Would she have denied Fiona's right to exist?

It was past twelve when, by the dim light of the streetlamp, she saw a man approach the house. She knew it was Gideon by his carriage and the set of his shoulders and the slight dragging of his right leg when he walked. Fiona forced herself to wait. Gideon usually called for Adam on his return to the house, and she did not want Adam to know she was seeking a midnight interview with her employer. When she judged the moment was right, she lit a candle and made her way to the door and thence down the two flights of stairs to the library. No light showed from beneath the door, but he must be in. She scratched on the door and after a moment heard the faint sounds that indicated someone was approaching. Then the door opened and he was there. A single candle burned in the room behind him. By the light of her own candle she saw that he was in shirtsleeves, without a cravat; his shirt, partially unbuttoned, gave a glimpse of the dark hair that grew in a remembered pattern on his chest. The unexpected intimacy unnerved her and she felt her face grow warm. "I thought I heard you come in," she said. "I know it's late, but would you mind if we talked?"

"Of course," Gideon said, masking his surprise. He flung the door wide and she entered, holding her candle up to light the way. He indicated a chair and took the candle from her, placing it on a table near his own, then sat down himself. Not too close. The width of the table lay between them, the candles making flickering pools of light on its polished surface. How dark his eyes were. She could scarcely see his face, but his eyes, perhaps through some trick of the candle flame, seemed luminous. She held his gaze, unable to look away, and for a moment had the absurd feeling that they had been transported to an unknown land in which nothing existed save themselves, and the dark, and the light of the two candles.

The moment passed. Objects took shape—the pile of books on the table at which they sat, the desk against the wall, the large portrait of a Carne ancestor over the mantel. Gideon was waiting for her to speak, and she did not know how to begin. *I know who my mother is, Lord Carne, and I wish to God I did not?*

"I called on the Marchioness of Parminter today," Fiona said at last, thankful that her voice betrayed no hint of what the visit had cost her.

"A formidable lady." Was it another trick of the light, or did his body tense, coiling as though for a spring? "Did she receive you?"

"She did, with very little delay. You were right," she added. "About her daughter . . . Lady Parminter is my grandmother."

Gideon's breath escaped in a wordless sigh. "She admitted it then."

"Not at first. Not till I had convinced her that I intended to pursue the matter, that I was prepared to go to Mrs. Kittredge or even to Castleton." She closed her eyes for a moment, trying to recall the marchioness's words, the exact shades of expression on her face. "I told her I was looking for my mother and I thought she could tell me who she is.

Gideon laughed. "You do have effrontery."

It was suddenly easy to talk, and Fiona told him the whole of the extraordinary interview. "There seems to have been no question of a marriage. My mother was quite ready to give me up, and my father was generously paid for rearing me. He had all the pleasure of standing well with the angels and being able to buy into the Woodbourn company to boot. You have me to thank for your present predicament, Lord Carne."

"The sins of the fathers?"

"My mother's, rather."

"Or the folly of both." There was a brief silence, and then he said, "She will not acknowledge you."

"That is true. But she offered me money."

"Good God." He stood up abruptly and looked down

253

at her. "She's frightened, isn't she? Not a breath of scandal must touch the name of Parminter. That's why she told you, lest your questions raise speculation elsewhere." He turned away and walked to his desk, where he riffled idly through some papers. "So she has tried to buy us both."

"I think she is a woman who will buy anything. Safety, reputation, a daughter's future."

"She can afford to buy anything."

"She did not buy you."

"I cannot afford to be bought. Once down that road . . . I would retain some measure of control over my life."

"And I over mine. Though my pride is likely to have cost me dearly. I have probably been a fool. She called me as much."

"My dear girl," he said, his voice very gentle, "you need not defend yourself to me. I would not have censured you for taking what you could. You are owed far more than she can ever give you. No more will I censure you for giving it up. You wanted to know the truth of your birth and you have found it. That should be enough."

"The truth," Fiona said, meeting his eyes, "has not made me very happy."

"The truth rarely does. But we must seek it all the same."

He was still standing by the desk and she rose and walked toward him. "Tell me about my mother."

Gideon studied her face as though seeking to learn what her question really meant. "She was a beautiful woman, though not, I think, as beautiful as you. You have her coloring, but her face was rounder, her features . . . softer, I would say, and her figure fuller. She did not have quite your height. But she was much admired."

"Yes, but besides that?"

He thought a moment. "She must have had a fair understanding—she could not be Lady Parminter's daughter otherwise. But she was restless and impatient with anything that required sustained thought. Her feelings I would judge were shallow, but she craved sensation. She was entirely wrong for Robert Melchett."

"Were they unhappy?"

"He was very patient with her, and she—she relied on him. I suppose they were no more unhappy than most couples."

"And her children? How did she feel about her children?"

A wry smile crossed his face. "She doted on Adrian, though no more than his grandparents did. He was the heir. As for the others, she was conscientious enough, but children were not her chief interest."

It was not much of a heritage. Gideon must have read her disappointment in her face, for he said, "You might have had far worse. You were not wholly abandoned."

"I would to God I had been." Fiona's voice was suffused with sudden passion. "Then I would belong only to myself. I feel tainted."

He said nothing while she struggled to bring her feelings under control. Then, "None of them is worth this distress. Save Robin," he added. "I have hope of him."

"Yes, I like Robin."

"And there is Beth."

"Beth?" She stared at him in astonishment.

"She is your niece."

Fiona tried to put it together. Lady Carne's youngest child, but not by Gideon. Lord Parminter? Or the absent William? She raised her eyes to his face. "Which?"

"Adrian." She saw a shadow of pain cross his face as he spoke the name. "Does he know?"

"I think he must. He cared for Aline as much as he is capable of caring for anyone, but he doesn't seem to have the least interest in their daughter."

"How long have you known?"

"Since just before I left the country. Aline was with child, and I knew it could not be mine. We quarreled. It was a . . . it was not a very edifying scene. She told me he'd been her lover for months, the child was his, and I could have the pleasure of raising it."

Fiona made a wordless sound of dismay.

"It doesn't matter now."

She knew he was lying. "But it did then."

"Oh, yes. It seemed the final humiliation. I left the house and rode for Hertfordshire with the devil on my tail. And the next day I tried to walk off my anger and came across you."

And poured his burden of misery into her heart and her body. Was that how it had been? Was his wooing not love but desperation? And was his final cruelty only the shock of a man awakening to a world he was trying to forget?

He had turned away, and in the dim light of the candles she studied his expression, trying to discover him anew. The lines in his face did not measure the passage of years but the memory of pain. She could see that he lived with it still. Fiona felt a welling of sympathy, not for the man but for his suffering.

She laid a hand on his arm, a gesture of friendship, no more, an effort to suck the poison from his blood. He seized it and brought her palm to his lips. The shock of the contact ran the whole length of her body. His eyes, those luminous dark eyes, sought and held her own and she was trapped, caught in the web of her own desire, remembering, remembering, dear God, how long it had been since he'd first opened that door.

The years vanished and they were back in the

meadow at Hartwood. The scent of hawthorn was heavy in the air, and when he said her name, a faint breath of sound that spoke of endless longing, she walked straight into his arms.

Meadow and library were one. She was lost in an infinite space measured by the circle of his arms and of her own. And all the while she was very conscious of the present, the feel of his body—surely harder and leaner than it had been before—the roughness of his cheek and chin, the taste of wine in his mouth.

A current of physical longing swept through her, too sharp to be denied. In another moment she'd be past all rational thought. She struggled to remember who Gideon was and what he had done to her, to remember what she'd been and what she'd become, but it was futile. She could no longer separate herself from him, or his desire from her own.

After an eternity of time he released her. She stood before him, feeling quite giddy and unsteady on her feet, while he raised his hands and with the greatest gentleness removed the pins from her hair. It tumbled about her shoulders and she felt an intoxicating sense of freedom. She laughed in joy and he buried his hands in the heavy strands and pulled her close to him again. Then he groaned and picked her up and carried her across the room and through a door—she could see the lintel as they passed beneath—to what she fervently hoped would be a bed.

She pulled him down and felt the welcome weight of his body while his lips found her throat and eyes and hair. Drunk with his touch, she prayed he would never stop. Then he drew away and began to fumble with her clothing. She tried to help, but it was hard because she couldn't bear to let him go. His hands, rough and callused, found her bare skin and sent a shiver coursing through her body, but when they touched the soft inner flesh of her thighs she was conscious of nothing but heat. "It's absurd," he murmured, his face buried in her hair, "it's absurd, but I can't wait." His movements were growing frantic and she arched up to meet him because she knew she couldn't wait either. And then suddenly she was invaded and filled and her soul spilled out and she was hurled spinning into a night lit with myriad unseen stars.

She came back to bedclothes rumpled and damp with their lovemaking. Gideon lay heavy across her. She listened to his breathing, regular and deep, and watched the faint glow of the candles that illuminated the doorway through which he'd carried her. She ought to think about what had happened, but thought eluded her. She ought to get up and take her candle and return to her room, but her limbs felt heavy and she was reluctant to move.

She must have slept for she opened her eyes to find that Gideon was no longer beside her. It was lighter than it had been, but surely it was not yet day. She turned her head and saw that a lamp was now burning on a nearby table. Gideon was seated at the edge of the bed, looking down at her with an unaccustomed smile on his face.

In the flickering light of the lamp it seemed a gentle face, incapable of the cruelty he'd once shown her. Strange, when she looked at him she no longer felt anger, only tenderness and pity and gratitude. He'd used her tonight, as he'd used her before, but no more than she'd used him. For a short while he'd banished her loneliness and given her intense pleasure and brought her bodily peace. That was probably akin to love, at least as close as she would dare let herself go. She would never give herself wholly to any man again.

She smiled back and pushed herself to a sitting position, tangling the coverlet he'd thrown over her legs.

Her dress was twisted round her hips. She shifted her body to free it, conscious of the dampness between her legs, and threw back the hair which half covered her face. She looked at him again and laughed. "There is no etiquette pertaining to such a moment. Shall I thank you?"

The lamplight danced in his eyes. "I believe it is customary," Gideon said with mock gravity, "for the gentleman to thank the lady."

"A foolish custom when the pleasure is mutually taken."

"Then let us thank each other." He seized her hand and would have brought it to his lips, but she pulled away, unwilling to make the moment more than it was.

"I hadn't expected—" she began, then broke off, leaving the thought in the air between them.

"Nor had I."

"Lady Parminter upset me more than I knew. But that was not the only reason I came to you tonight," she continued rapidly, as though words would deny what had just passed between them. "I have had an idea. It seemed fantastic at first, but after today I am no longer sure. Gideon, suppose Lady Parminter was responsible for the fire."

"Lady Parminter?"

"Yes, it fits," Fiona said, relieved that she'd finally decided to tell him. "It's never made any sense that George's groom should hire a man to break into the Woodbourn warehouse. There was nothing there that George could not have seen for the asking, save the boxes of my father's papers, and George would have no interest in those. But Lady Parminter would. She's tried so long to keep the secret of my birth. Suppose she thought my father had some letters that might disclose it? She could hardly go look for them herself, but she could ask George to arrange it. She wouldn't

259

have needed to tell him her reasons. He's eager to please her."

Gideon flung himself back on the bed and lay staring at the ceiling. "Assuming you're right, there's still a problem. Why should Lady Parminter do it now? Why, after all these years, should she suddenly be worried about some papers that might be in your father's possession?"

"Because she learned the identity of Alessa's companion."

"Through George? I thought he hadn't seen you before the night of the dinner."

"No, but he learned of my return from Clare. He could have told Lady Parminter that her grandson's intended had a companion—masquerading under an assumed name—who was James Woodbourn's disinherited ward. He could even have told her of—of our past relationship. Then she learned that you were back in England as well . . . and both of us in want of money. She must have known who I was the night of the dinner. I always thought it odd that she invited Alessa on a night when the princess had a previous engagement, but now I think she did so deliberately. She wanted to observe you and me together. It must have occurred to her that we might join forces."

Gideon looked at her with appreciation. "A well-reasoned argument. You almost convince me."

"What do we do?"

"My dear girl, we do nothing. We cannot touch Lady Parminter."

"But there's George. He's clever, and he'd wonder about her interest in the Woodbourns. He might even guess the truth!"

"It doesn't matter if he does. George is no danger to you now. You're quite safe, Fiona."

He was right; there was nothing to be done and

260

nothing to fear. There was also nothing more to say. She ought to leave now, but she was reluctant to break the rapport between them. She turned and looked down at him. His eyes, as always, were disconcerting. So was the smile which was beginning to change the contours of his mouth. He raised his hand and lifted her hair from her shoulder, then drew his fingers down her neck until they met the collar of her dress. She shivered with the heat of his touch. "I have a great longing," he said, "to remove your clothes . . . all of them. If I do it very slowly and very carefully, do you think . . ." He did not finish the sentence because slowly and carefully she was lowering her lips to his.

He was quite right, Fiona thought a few minutes later; it was much better without clothes, especially without her shoes, which had remained firmly on her feet throughout their earlier lovemaking. She watched the play of shadow on his skin, dark and light, hollow and down, which transformed him into a figure of bronze. He was, she saw now, scarred—those were new, those chronicles of injury that marred the perfection of his body, that bitter cicatrix running down his thigh. She touched them lightly, acquainting herself with this new Gideon who'd gone to war and come back not quite whole.

And all this time his hands were busy, and his eyes and his mouth forcing her attention back to the familiar demon that was driving out her reason. But this time there was no urgency in his touch. Indeed, he was so gentle and so patient that she grew quite frantic, and by the time he took her—or she him, there was no telling which—she thought she would die.

After that they slept. When at last she woke she saw a faint glimmer of light from the far window on which the drapes were not quite closed. She was aware of an unfamiliar sense of well-being. Then she realized it was morning. She slipped out of bed and hurriedly searched for her clothes, stepping into drawers, petticoat, the blue-green dress that took an eternity to fasten. It wouldn't do to be seen disheveled by anyone else in the household, least of all the children. She retrieved her shoes and stockings—which, unaccountably, had found their way beneath the bed—then moved to the library to search for her comb and pins. Praying she had left no telltale pin on the floor, she hastily wrapped her hair into a knot, jammed the pins into place, and returned to the study for one last look at Gideon. He lay on his back, one arm flung over his face, the other stretched out on the pillow from which she'd just risen. She watched the slow rise and fall of his chest and knew his sleep was deep. Suppressing a desire to move closer and touch his face, she turned quickly and left the room.

It must have been earlier than she thought, for there was no sound anywhere in the house. Fiona made her way noiselessly up the two flights of stairs to her room, closed the door quietly behind her, and stripped off her clothes. Her dress would have to be sponged and her undergarments washed. Those were tasks she'd reserve for herself. For the rest, she would have to make do with cold water. She poured a generous amount in the basin and squeezed out a sponge. As she lifted it she caught sight of herself in the mirror and stared wondering at her reflection. Five years ago her body had betrayed her, and since that time she'd taken to ignoring it, beyond the need to make sure that it was neatly and soberly clad. But this morning, with the betrayal of the night behind her, she found nothing but pleasure in the image of the woman in the mirror. She raised the sponge to her neck—Gideon had touched her there—and shivered at its cold wetness against her skin. Then slowly, deliberately, she washed her entire body, following the memory of his hands and mouth. How strange that she could feel heat and cold at once.

It was, Fiona decided as she released her hair once more and began to brush it, an estimable body. Not as ample as some might like, but firm and supple and reasonably rounded at breast and hip. Gideon had taught her that, to take pleasure in the sight and scent and touch of her skin. It was a lesson she was glad to relearn. Perhaps, if he wanted, she would become his mistress after all. Not as she'd once proposed, because she was wiser now and knew the difference between love and passion, but with full awareness of what they could and could not give each other.

By the time she had dressed and made her way to the kitchen, it was nearly seven and Adam was stoking the fire. He was usually rather taciturn in the morning, but he returned her greeting as she set about making tea. A kind of wary camaraderie had grown up among the three of them, Adam, Barbara, and herself, and Fiona had learned to treasure it. In the Tassio household, she'd been considered too grand for the servants and not nearly grand enough for anyone else.

"You're uncommon cheerful," Adam remarked.

"I slept well," she said and could have bit her tongue. If she was to enjoy any other such nights with Gideon, she'd have to be very careful or her position in the household would be in jeopardy. It would be in any case, she realized as she poured boiling water into the teapot, careful or not. Secrets like that are never kept. Barbara, who'd grown quite friendly, would resent the change in her status, and Adam, who was so fiercely protective of Gideon, would swear she was bringing him nothing but ruin.

Adam left to take Gideon his shaving water. Fiona continued to set the table for breakfast, but her joyous mood had vanished. She did not regret last night, not one moment of it, but she could not repeat the act. It was madness to think that she could care for the children by day and bed their father by night, here in the house that had belonged to their mother. Her own position would be unpleasant enough. It would be intolerable for them.

She was at the stove, stirring the children's porridge, when Adam returned to the kitchen and gave her a speculative look. "You're wanted upstairs," he said, "and he's not in a mood to wait."

Fiona left the room quickly to avoid the questions in Adam's eyes and climbed the stairs that led to the entrance hall, wishing desperately that Gideon had not done this to her. The trouble with a night of passion was that it was inevitably followed by a morning of soiled clothes and second thoughts and warming the pot to make tea. Wondering where she'd dredged up this particular bit of wisdom, Fiona crossed the hall to the library. The door was ajar and she pushed it open, closing it behind her with a firm click that immediately brought him to the doorway of the study.

As the night before, Gideon was in his shirtsleeves. He seemed to have been shaving, for he was holding a towel in his hands and his skin was shiny and moist. But it was the sight of a disregarded bit of lather just below his left ear that almost undid her resolution. Then he spoke and shattered the spell. "What the devil do you mean by leaving me without a word?"

It was an absurd question, but she tried to grant it the dignity of a reply. "I saw nothing to be gained by proclaiming my indiscretion to the entire household."

"Our indiscretion, if I remember." He smiled and all the harshness left his face. "And I'd proclaim it to the world."

"Oh, the world." Gideon was being remarkably slow

witted. "I was thinking of Peter and Teddy and Beth. And Barbara. I was even thinking of Adam."

"Yes, Adam is a bit of a problem, isn't he?" He dabbed at his face, removing the remaining bit of lather, and threw the towel on a chair. "Fiona, we have to talk."

"No, there's nothing to say. It's done. I don't regret it — I hope you don't, either — but it must end here. And you must not call me Fiona. If I'm to remain in this house, I can be no one but Miss Alastair."

Her words were was meant to fend him off, but she knew as she said them what a feeble attempt they constituted. On Gideon they had no effect whatsoever. "Good God, woman," he said, striding toward her, "I don't want you to be Miss Alastair. I want to make you Lady Carne."

Fiona had not anticipated this, and because she was taken by surprise she said the first words that came into her head, regretting them almost before they were uttered. "Why? It wasn't necessary before."

"It wasn't possible before."

But it was possible now. What had she expected from him? That he would ignore what had happened till his need drove him to her again, confident that he could take her when he would? No, he was not so devoid of honor. That he would set her up in her own establishment? She had proposed it once, but he could hardly afford to take her up on it now. She could not live with him openly as his mistress, not in this house, not before his children. Nor would he want her to. Perhaps marriage had seemed the only alternative, marriage or abstinence, and his eyes were telling her that abstinence was the furthest thing from his mind.

Abstinence was the only solution, but his nearness made it hard to contemplate. After last night one would think she'd be sated, not filled with images of lying beneath him on his bed. Even now, at arm's-length, she was aware of the heat of his body. She stepped back to escape him, telling herself over and over that marriage to Gideon was beyond the bounds of reason.

He must have sensed her struggle, for he came no nearer; and when he spoke again his voice was unexpectedly gentle. "Marry me, Fiona. My fortune's gone, but you will have my name. I owe you that, at least."

"You owe me nothing."

"You've told me you'll take nothing. But you must, you know. You're a generous woman, but you must learn to take from other people. Take what I can give. It's little enough, but you've no other choice."

"I can leave."

"Oh? And go where?"

Where indeed? Her options were few, and irremediably bleak. "Oh, why must it change?" she cried, feeling like an animal caught in a net. "Why can't it be like it was before?"

"Because of what passed between us last night. Can you go back? I can't."

No more could she; she knew that now. She looked away and he pressed his advantage. "I need you, Fiona. The children need you."

It was unfair of him to mention the children. She laughed to cover her disquiet. "I see . . . a marriage of convenience."

"If you like. But for your convenience as well as mine."

Once Fiona had dreamed of being Gideon's wife, knowing it could never come to pass. And now, in a perverse way, he was offering to make her dream reality—wife to a man she could not allow herself to love, mistress of a ruined house, mother to children of doubtful children of doubtful birth, one of whom was her niece. It would be a bitter victory. But on the other hand . . . On the other hand, she would no longer need to lie or pretend to be anything other than herself. George's malice could not touch her, nor Clare's. And there would be endless nights of forgetting.

"I'll be your lover," Gideon said softly, "and your protector and your friend. Isn't that enough?" He studied her face as though he would read her soul. "I don't want to lie to you, Fiona. I won't insult you by pretending to talk of love. Aline made the word a mockery, and I can't travel that road again."

She knew that he could not, and it was futile to ask for more. He was honest, she would give him that. And if she was fated to depend on someone for her survival, at least it would not be as servant to an uncertain master. She could meet Gideon as an equal. If he disturbed her, he also brought her release. She would not be free, but she would be infinitely more alive. It was not a bad bargain. "Very well," she said and held out her hand.

He bent over it in a curiously formal gesture, barely brushing it with his lips . . . and that was all. He must have read in her face what her admission had cost her, for he did not try to kiss or otherwise embrace her. But their eyes met, and she knew with a traitorous joy that she would go to him again that night.

Chapter Sixteen

The children's reaction to the news that their father was to take a new wife was more subdued than Gideon had expected. He should not have been surprised. It was less than a year since Aline's death, and though she'd been an indifferent mother, for five years she was the only parent they'd had. Peter, who'd known her best, was very quiet, and Teddy followed his lead. Beth's disappointment was evident. Her approachable governess was to become an unapproachable mother, and the change was not to her liking. It took all of Fiona's assurances and the warmth of her embrace before Beth was induced to smile once more. Adam said nothing at all, which boded ill for Gideon's future comfort. Only Barbara showed any sign of approval.

But it didn't matter. They'd come round, all of them, and in the meantime there was the promise he had read in Fiona's eyes. He would not allow her to regret her decision. There might not be love between them, but there was passion, on her side as well as his. He could give her that at least, and friendship, and the protection of his home and name. It would go some way toward making up for the five years he'd cost her.

Nor would he lose by the transaction. Not since his first days with Aline had he known a woman in whom he could lose himself as he could in Fiona. And Fiona was an infinitely finer woman, honest and direct, without a trace of coquetry. They would deal well together, and he would be proud to call her his own.

He left the children in Fiona's care and returned to the library in a remarkably cheerful mood. The future was no longer bleak, and even the precarious state of the company's affairs could not depress his spirits. It was the thought of Woodbourn-Prebble that reminded Gideon of his discovery of the previous night. When he reached the library he picked up the volume of Pascal, extracted William's youthful letter, and studied it thoughtfully. He thought to compare it with the letter Adrian had produced at the partners' meeting two weeks ago, but even that might not be conclusive. The passage of years alone could account for discrepancies in the hand. Besides, Adrian's letter was now in Magnus's hands, and Gideon was reluctant to voice suspicions which might prove unfounded. But if he could obtain a more recent sample of William's handwriting. . . . Gideon went to his desk and penned a letter to Robin Melchett, then rang for Adam and requested he deliver it at once to Parminter House. He intended to lay the problem squarely in Robin's lap.

A short time later, Gideon left the house to obtain a license for his marriage. He wanted the ceremony to take place as soon as possible, lest Fiona change her mind, and for her sake he wanted no public reading of the banns. By the time he'd made the arrangements for the ceremony (at the parish church a week hence, with only the members of their own small household in attendance) it was nearly the hour he'd appointed for his meeting with Robin. Wondering again about the wisdom of approaching Adrian's young brother, Gideon made his way to George's Coffee House, where he found Robin waiting for him. "I thought it better not to go to Parminter House," Gideon said when they were settled in an obscure corner. "When you hear what I have to say, you'll know why."

"Fire away, Carne," Robin said cheerfully.

Gideon did not answer right away. He stretched out his legs, carefully positioning the one that gave him trouble, and stared at the table. "When did you last hear from William?"

"Oh, years." Robin seemed surprised that Gideon was asking about his family, but he was willing to follow his lead. "William's not one for writing much. No, wait . . . Grandmama had a letter around the New Year."

Gideon nodded. "Do you know where he's stationed?"

"In Madras, I think. But he's been everywhere. He's restless, you know. He travels whenever he has leave, and he manages to get sent out as a courier—he's clever that way. When he wrote to Grandmama, he said he'd been a guest of the Sultan of Mysore. Leave it to William to look after himself." Robin frowned. "I say, Carne, what's this all about?"

"Probably nothing at all," Gideon said, wishing he'd not begun the inquiry. "Got a bee in my head."

Robin's eager face turned serious and suddenly he looked far older than his nineteen years. "This isn't about William, is it? It's about India. Adrian said that company you're all in would benefit if the charter were to go your way."

"Yes, it's about India," Gideon admitted. "But it's about William too."

Robin's face was still clouded. "Adrian could tell you more than I can. He's closer to William than any of us. William may have written to him."

Gideon met the candid gray eyes and wondered for a fleeting moment if he could trace some resemblance to Fiona. "He did. Parminter had a letter from your

270

brother some two weeks ago. He read it to us at a partners' meeting."

Robin looked disconcerted. "You'd think he'd have told us. What did William say?"

"That he'd been in Mysore—"

"That's right."

"—and that he'd found riches beyond imagining, ready for anyone bold enough to take them."

"That doesn't sound like William."

Gideon smiled. "I may have embroidered a bit. He was talking about gold. That's why Adrian read us the letter. He was enthusiastic about the opportunity, and he managed to raise some interest among the other partners."

"Is that what worries you, that you can't trust William's judgment?"

"No, it's Adrian's judgment that concerns me. On the strength of William's story, Adrian has been soliciting investments in the company, promising untold wealth. Injudicious, to say the least—but there are flats all over London, and if their greed betrays them, they must take their chances. There's certainly some gold to be found in India, though according to everyone I've talked to, not in any significant quantity. Still, the matter is worth exploration."

Robin considered this. "Adrian's in debt. His income's enough to feed half of London, but he lives well beyond it. He'd want it to be true about the gold." Then he was struck by a new idea. "You're worried that William was telling a cock-and-bull story."

"Would he?"

"No, he doesn't have that much imagination." Robin stared at Gideon and a look of horror passed over his face. "You think that Adrian—"

Gideon sighed. "I don't know. I saw the letter, you see. I had no reason to question that it was in William's hand, but last night I came across another letter of William's, inside one of the books your father left me. It wasn't dated, but it must be eight or ten years old. It doesn't look like the same hand as the letter Adrian showed us, but the passage of time might account for that. Robin, you don't have to go on with this. I don't have to know."

"Of course you have to know," Robin said with great dignity. "We both do. I won't say that I believe Adrian forged a letter from William, not unless he did it as a lark. But if he did forge it because he thought he could make something out of it, that's despicable. He should be stopped before it goes any further."

Gideon studied the boy, wondering if he knew what was at stake. "If my suspicions are correct, it may be awkward for the family."

"I know what you're thinking, Carne. Adrian's my brother and I've got some feeling for him, but I know his faults. Grandmama has excused a lot, but she won't condone this. She'd want it stopped too."

"At the price of Adrian's reputation?"

It was a moment before Robin replied. "Even that. Very well," he went on, his voice suddenly brisk, "we have to know if William wrote the letter Adrian read to you. What happened to it?"

"Magnus Melchett has it."

"That's a problem. Still, if I bring you the last letter Grandmama received from William, you could find a way of comparing the two."

Gideon nodded. "If I'm wrong, we'll let the matter drop."

"But if you aren't . . ."

Gideon did not answer immediately. At the moment he was not sure what he would do, though he was conscious of the beginning of a plan. "Let's not cross that bridge now."

They ordered more coffee and sat a while in silence. After a time Robin asked about India and what the Woodbourn partners hoped to achieve there. Gideon grimaced. "Profit. Prebble lives beyond his means, and you tell me your brother does too. I'm deeply dipped myself. I don't know about Barrington-Forbes. As for Melchett, profit is his reason for existence. There will be money made in India, Robin, but God knows at what cost. We're all pirates, and India is a ship ready for plunder."

When they were about to leave, Robin said with unaccustomed diffidence, "I've been wondering about Miss Alastair. Young Simon said she'd gone to work for you. I know it's none of my affair, but I liked her, you see, and I wondered if she was all right."

"She's governess to my children—"

"Oh, of course. I didn't mean to imply—"

"And will shortly be my wife." Gideon had not meant to reveal this, but Robin had earned the right to know. "In a week's time. I'd rather you didn't say anything for the moment."

Robin's pleasure was evident. "No, not a word. Tell her I asked about her and that I wish her every happiness."

They left the table and proceeded out of the coffee house. Outside Gideon turned to Robin and held out his hand. "I'm in your debt."

Robin clasped it firmly. "It's all right. And Carne, thank you for trusting me." He did not say whether he referred to the letter or to the news of Gideon's marriage. Perhaps he meant both.

On this day that had changed her life forever, Fiona felt very much as she had when she'd embarked for Sardinia. Burning bridges came into it, and an intoxicating exhilaration, and a distressing sense that she was

273

merely exchanging one prison for another. Save that in this case, she knew very well what her new prison would be like and exactly what she would find most exhilarating in it.

She decreed there'd be no lessons for today and took the children for a long and vigorous walk up and down the length of the Serpentine, trusting that the air and exercise would do away with some of the diffidence they were now showing in her presence. While Teddy and Beth were intent on some joyous exploration near the bank of the stream, and Peter, with all the dignity of twelve, was trying to conceal his own interest in their game, Fiona was free to think of how she would manage her role as Gideon's wife.

But it was hard to think of anything beyond the night that had just passed. And the one that was to come. A sudden breeze blew a tendril of hair across her cheek, and as she tucked it back in place she recalled the feel of Gideon's hands releasing her hair from its pins. And that led her to remember other intimacies and to imagine new ones that made her face grow hot. It was absurd. She was acting like an impressionable schoolgirl, not the responsible woman she would have to be.

There was, she thought as she strolled down the path, keeping an eye on the children all the while, the matter of consequences. Gideon had shown her years ago how to avoid them. She had given no thought to the matter last night, but a hasty calculation this morning told her she was probably safe. She would have to be more careful in the future. She would be Gideon's wife, but she did not want to have his child. That kind of intimacy would be too much to bear. Whatever became of this convenient marriage, it must leave some part of herself free.

She was brought back to the present by Beth, who

ran up to her cradling some treasure in her hands. It proved to be a small bird, its dull brown plumage made duller still by death. "It's hurt," Beth said. "Can you make it well?"

"Of course she can't. It's dead." Teddy had followed close behind his sister.

Peter walked up to the group and stared down at the stiff little body with its sunken eyes. "Things don't come back, even if you want them to."

Beth stared at the bird, her face showing curiosity rather than sorrow. "Was it old, like Mr. Talbot? Or sick, like Mama?"

At the mention of their mother, Teddy scowled. "Throw it away. It's no good to anyone now."

"*No . . .* no," Fiona repeated more quietly, sensing that something more than a dead creature was at stake. "The bird is dead. We don't know why death comes to animals, or to people either, but sooner or later we must all return to the earth." There was a moment of silence, and then Fiona said briskly, "So. What do you think we should do with it?"

Beth looked at her with solemn eyes. "Put it in the ground?"

"We'll dig a grave." Teddy seemed eager for activity.

"We'll have a funeral," Peter said. "A proper one."

Fired with enthusiasm, the children set about the preparations. The selection of a resting place for the small bird took a long time, but they settled at last on a spot beneath a tree at some distance from the path. "So people won't step on it," Beth said. They dug the grave with their hands, to the great detriment of their clothes and nails, and Fiona contributed a handkerchief for a shroud. Peter said a prayer, followed by fragments of phrases from the burial service, that Fiona found quite moving.

When it was over, the children seemed more cheerful

and not at all disposed to avoid her company. I've passed some test, Fiona thought, and then realized that the test had been their own.

"Do birds have souls?" Teddy asked his brother as they walked home.

Peter scowled. "I don't know. Do they, Fiona?"

"I believe they do," she said, "as much as any other living thing."

"Where did the bird's soul go?" Beth asked.

That, as Simon would say, was a facer. "Everywhere, I imagine. Or nowhere. Somewhere happy."

"Oh. That's all right, then." Beth let go of Fiona's hand and ran ahead. Teddy gave a shout and ran after her. Peter stayed by Fiona's side and she took the opportunity to compliment him on his handling of the incident of the dead bird.

He seemed embarrassed by her praise. "It's just that they didn't understand it before," he explained. "You know, Mama dying, and the funeral, and putting her in the ground. I thought if they could do it for themselves—so it wasn't something happening to them, but something they made happen—it would be easier. The other, I mean."

Fiona looked at him with renewed respect. Like Simon, Peter was a surprisingly perceptive boy. She set herself to draw him out and succeeded so well that by the time they reached the house they were chattering like old friends and were in perfect charity with one another.

The younger children had caught their mood. When they entered they created such a clamor that Adam pushed through the baize door at the back of the hall to see what all the noise was about. "We had a funeral," Teddy announced, and then proceeded to tell Adam the entire story, with frequent interruptions from his sister.

"We're going upstairs," Fiona told them when she could make herself heard, "and you're going to wash your hands—"

"No!" Teddy protested.

"—and put on clean clothes. And," she added, fearing their welcome high spirits were getting out of hand, "do you think you could manage to be just a little more quiet until it's time for dinner?"

Beth looked puzzled. "Does that mean we can be noisy at dinner?"

"No."

"Then you misspoke," Teddy said triumphantly. "We have to be quiet at dinner too." He moved toward the stairs with the others, stamping his feet and chanting, "Quiet, quiet, quiet. Forever and forever and forever after that."

Fiona hurried after them, leaving Adam behind in the hall, shaking his head. Adam had the gravest misgivings about this marriage, and the peculiar behavior of the children made him no more sanguine about its prospects of success. Feeling in need of conversation, he made his way to the kitchen, where he found Barbara making a cake for supper. Adam was happy enough to share the culinary chores, for though he had a way with meat, his skills did not extend to baking. Besides, he liked having Barbara around. There was something soothing in her neat, economical movements, in her pleasant face bent seriously over her task. He propped himself against a cupboard and told her about the scene in the hall upstairs. "They're certainly in a strange mood," he concluded.

Barbara added more flour to the bowl and began to beat the mixture vigorously.

"They weren't this morning," he went on when she made no comment. "Nor when they left the house this afternoon."

"Then something happened before they came back." She brushed back a wayward lock of hair and left a streak of flour on her cheek.

"A dead bird, that's what happened. Explain that to me if you can. And a proper burial, with a shroud and prayers said over the grave before they shoveled back the earth. Is a funeral something to make you happy?"

She had resumed her beating, but at this she set down the bowl and faced him. "It's clear enough if you'd only use your head. The young ones saw their mother put under the earth and they were trying to . . . well, to work out how it was; and when they did, they no doubt felt better. They've a right to kick up a bit of a lark after what they've been through, and Master Peter almost finding a dead body and nearly getting himself burned to a cinder." She picked up the bowl again. "And they've a right to be happy they're going to have a proper mother again."

"Hah!"

She looked up, her eyes fierce. "Don't you say *one word* against her."

"I'll tell you this," he said, leaning forward and resting his hands on the table, "those two were together last night. You know what I mean? I can tell when he's had it, and there's no one else in the house except —"

Barbara blushed. Adam knew he should not have embarrassed her, but he was too annoyed to care. "And I don't think it was you."

"I should hope not," she said hotly. She began to add currants and citron and bits of orange peel to the batter. "No more should you think it was Fiona Alastair. It could be any woman in London."

"He isn't marrying any woman in London. He's marrying *her.*"

"So?"

Adam stepped back and folded his arms. He'd known the Alastair woman was wrong when he saw Carne's face the day he brought her to the house. But he could not explain how he knew this, so he said merely, "I don't like it."

"What you like or don't has nothing to say to it, Adam Rutledge."

Her use of his surname made him uneasy. His mother had given it to him in defiance of the man who'd abandoned her and her inconvenient child, and he used it as little as possible. Where had Bab learned it? Most people knew him simply as Adam. "I know Carne," he said shortly. "You don't."

There was no answer to this, and to his relief Barbara did not try to make one. She spooned the batter into a greased and floured pan, then opened the door to judge the heat of the oven. Satisfied, she set the cake inside and began to clean up the baking things strewn about the table. Adam checked the stew that was bubbling quietly on the back of the stove. After a moment Barbara said, "Don't judge everyone by yourself."

Would the woman never have done? He tasted the stew, added a pinch of salt, tasted it again, then replaced the cover. "I won't ask what you mean," he said, laying down the spoon, "because I know you're going to tell me." He glanced over his shoulder and saw her glaring at him. He thought, incongruously, that she was almost pretty so, with her color heightened and her fine brown eyes showing glittering points of light.

Barbara's color intensified under his gaze, but she held her ground. "I know what you think of marriage, but not everyone's to your way of thinking. Carne's a steadfast man, and he needs a steadfast woman like Miss Alastair. It's not him I'm worried about, it's her.

279

She needs to have a family to belong to and a name she won't be ashamed to call her own, and—" She broke off, as though conscious that she'd said more than she intended.

"Here, what are you saying?" But the information she'd inadvertently conveyed was perfectly plain from the expression on Bab's worried face. The elegant Miss Alastair had been born on the wrong side of the blanket.

"It's been known to happen." Barbara resumed scrubbing an already spotless table. Then she stopped and faced him again. "But it's nothing you need talk about. The poor lady's suffered enough from it already."

He threw up his hands in a gesture of reproach. "I? Talk? I've no one to tell it to but Carne, and it's not a thing as would bother him anyway. I wish the lady well, whatever she does." This last sentiment was quite genuine. He didn't know how it was, but a flawed Miss Alastair seemed far safer than the woman he'd thought her to be. Maybe the marriage wouldn't be so inauspicious as he'd feared. "Peace, woman. I'll say no more about it." He grinned and was rewarded with a grudging smile. "They'll do what they like, whatever we think about it, and all we can do is look to ourselves."

For some unaccountable reason, this made Barbara blush.

The cake provided a festive end to the evening meal. Teddy was so moved that he left his seat and ran around the table to give Barbara a hug and a promise that he'd marry her as soon as he was old enough to be allowed to. Barbara said that she would be pleased and proud to wait for him, as she'd met no other man who could tempt her to that fate. This exchange provoked delighted laughter from the others, but Fiona noted that Adam drew his brows together in a thoughtful frown.

It was not the first time Fiona had suspected there might be something brewing between them. Barbara, she was certain, harbored tender sentiments toward Gideon's man which she carefully hid for fear they would never be returned. She'd been less sure about Adam's feelings until now. Had Teddy not been seven years old, she'd have sworn that Adam's scowl was a clear expression of jealousy.

These thoughts were driven from her mind a few minutes later when Gideon told the children that he'd seen their Aunt Clare driving in the park with her friend Lady Trousdale and that she'd asked to be remembered to them. Peter wanted to know if his father had told Aunt Clare about his marriage and seemed relieved when Gideon said that he had not. Better to wait till after the ceremony, and in any case their aunt was extremely busy with the social engagements that crowded everyone's calendar toward the end of the Season. She was going to the theater and a supper party tonight, a reception and two routs tomorrow, and the day after was driving to Richmond for a breakfast given by Lord and Lady Elton, which of course would last well into the evening. He did not know her schedule beyond Thursday, but he was sure it was equally full.

Gideon made the children laugh with his recital, but Fiona grew thoughtful. Since their trip to Barstead she'd vainly sought some excuse that would allow her to call on Clare and search for the writing table that had been in her father's bedroom. The mention of Richmond caught her attention. Clare would be out of London and Hugo was never at home in the afternoon. If she could convince the footman to admit her and then persuade him to leave her alone in the house. . . .

No, it seemed too unlikely. Her perplexity must have shown in her face, for she caught Peter's eyes upon her. She forced herself to smile and rejoin the conversation. She would think about it after the children were in bed.

But when she had them settled for the night and had retired to her room, she was surprised by Peter, who came to her door and wanted to talk. He seemed uncomfortable with what he had to say and sat for a few minutes twisting his hands and staring at the floor. Then he looked up and blurted out a question. "The house we visited, the house where you were born, was that Aunt Clare's house too?"

Fiona tried to mask her shock. How in the name of heaven had he learned that? "Yes," she said as calmly as she could, "your Aunt Clare lived there before her marriage."

He stared at her, puzzled. She could almost guess his thoughts. She and Clare were of an age, therefore she could not have been Clare's governess. For the same reason she could not have been a servant in the house. "Are you sisters?" he asked at last.

She could lie, but what would be the point? He would learn it someday and she would then forfeit his trust. "Not exactly. We had the same father, but different mothers." She let him think about that for a moment. "You see, Peter—"

But Peter did see. He grew suddenly red. "It doesn't matter, Fiona, really it doesn't. I heard Aunt Clare talk about Barstead once, and so I wondered . . . but that isn't the only reason I came to see you tonight. You were looking for something at Barstead, weren't you? And you didn't find it."

Fiona nodded, not trusting herself to speak.

"I wasn't sure, but I thought it was something like that. Then when Father talked about Aunt Clare going to Richmond I thought you were wondering if it could be in her house in London." He took a breath. "You don't have to tell me what it is, because if it was in your house it's probably something that belongs to you. But if you want to look for it at the Prebbles' house, I thought I might be able to help. I know a way we could do it."

Peter left soon after, having extracted a reluctant promise from Fiona that she would not go to Davies Street without him. She did not want to involve the boy but saw no better course of action. It was her only chance to discover her father's will, if one existed. However little he'd left her, she would not then go empty-handed into her marriage.

Fiona sat in her room, as she had the night before, listening to the house fall asleep. Gideon was waiting for her. He'd said nothing, but she'd seen it in his eyes when he'd come up to say goodnight to the children, and she knew then she could not deny him. No more could she deny herself, and this knowledge told her how profoundly she'd become trapped by her desire. Fiona picked up her candle and moved to the door. If this was a trap, she'd entered it with knowledge and joy.

Gideon had lit the lamp in the study and was sitting with a book in hand, though his eyes were not focused on the page. He rose at her entrance and regarded her for a long speaking moment. "I wasn't sure you would come."

Fiona smiled. "Liar." She closed the door behind her and walked straight into his arms.

Chapter Seventeen

Though Peter had assured her he knew precisely who was on hall duty in the Prebble house on Thursday afternoons, Fiona breathed a tiny sigh of relief when the door was opened not by the arrogant footman who'd greeted her the previous October but by a lanky young man whose freckled face broke into a grin when he saw the visitors. "Master Peter!"

"Hullo, Alfred, it's good to see you again." Peter peered into the hall, then lowered his voice to a conspiratorial whisper. "Are my aunt and uncle in?"

"No, Lady Prebble's gone to a breakfast at Richmond and Sir Hugo's at his club. Did you need to see them about something in particular?"

"Actually," Peter confided, "it's probably better that they aren't here. I can't find my Latin grammar anywhere, you see, and Miss Alastair wants it for Teddy—oh, this is Miss Alastair, my new governess." He indicated her with a casual wave of his hand. "I think I must have left the book here when I stopped in London on my way to Digby Hall for the Easter holidays. I hate to bother Aunt Clare and Uncle Hugo, but if I could have a look around before they get back . . . ?"

Alfred merely grinned again and stepped aside to allow them to enter the house. It was encouraging to see that someone could retain his good nature after so many months in Hugo's and Clare's service. Peter led the way down the hall with an assurance almost equal to Simon's. They were nearly at the library door when Fiona saw that a young girl—an upstairs maid, to judge by her dress and the polishing cloth in her hand—stood staring at them with surprise and curiosity over the railing of the first floor gallery.

"It's all right, Meg," Alfred told her, "Master Peter's just come by with his governess to look for a book he left here."

Meg raised her brows, then shrugged. "Have it your own way. But it's on your head if Lady Prebble finds out and kicks up a fuss."

"Get along," Alfred said amiably.

Peter hesitated, his surface bravado gone. "I don't want to get you in trouble, Alfred."

"No fear of that," Alfred assured him. "Meg's a bit of a busybody, but she won't tattle. Besides, Lady Prebble could hardly object to your looking for your Latin grammar."

"No," Peter agreed, "she could hardly object to that." He said nothing more until he and Fiona were in the library, but then he asked, with some anxiety, "You don't think Alfred will get in trouble, do you?"

Fiona, keenly aware of the perils of having to depend upon the favor of one's employer, had suffered qualms herself on this score. "I shouldn't think so," she said. "Even if she learns the truth—which isn't at all likely—Clare never wastes enough energy on servants to get really angry at them."

Relieved, Peter began to look around the library. Fiona did likewise, though she did not expect to find the writing table here, for Gideon hadn't noticed it on his previous visit. The apartment had a more formal aspect than the library in Dover Street. There were fewer books, and the volumes seemed to have been arranged more for appearance than convenience. But as at Dover Street, a

285

door at the end of the room led to an adjoining chamber which with luck would prove to be Hugo's study. Fiona suspected the table was in Hugo's possession, as Clare preferred more delicate furnishings. If it was not in the study, they would have to slip upstairs to Hugo's apartments.

Accustomed to planning for the worst, Fiona had already begun to consider how they would set about this task when Peter called to her. He was standing in the open doorway of the drab room that was indeed Hugo's study. A handsome mahogany desk stood squarely in the center of the floor. But a little to one side, in front of a tall window, was the ebony-inlaid writing table which had once graced her father's bedchamber.

It all seemed so ridiculously easy that Fiona stared at the table for a long moment, certain her memory was playing tricks, that this was not really the table in question. She crossed the room quickly, then stopped and stared at it again. "Fiona?" Peter's voice came from just behind her. "Is it the right one?"

"I think so. It certainly looks very like." Impatient with her own hesitation, Fiona tugged open the single long drawer. Not surprisingly, it proved empty. With his desk so near, Hugo didn't really need the table, but he liked fine things. Fiona lifted the drawer out and placed it on the table's tooled-leather top, then stripped off her gloves and knelt to examine the interior of the frame. Peter crouched beside her, eager to share in the excitement, though in truth there was little enough to do. It was only when she straightened up, certain that no papers had been tucked into the grooves or wedged behind the drawer, that Fiona realized this was the end of her search. If the will was not here, Clare must have already destroyed it . . . or there had never been a will.

"It looks as if it isn't here," she told Peter on a false note of brightness. "I'm sorry I put you to so much trouble."

"But we can't just give up! Couldn't there be a secret drawer or something?"

Fiona reached for her gloves. She was about to say that if there'd been such a drawer in her father's writing table she certainly would have known of it, but she checked herself before the words left her lips. Uncle James had had a great many serious secrets of which she'd known nothing. Why should this be any different?

She studied the empty drawer which now reposed on the table top. The two knobs were set far apart, and the panel between them was slightly raised in order to display the intricate ebony work to best advantage . . . or so it seemed. Could there be another reason for that extra half inch of wood?

"There's a desk with a secret compartment at Hartwood," Peter volunteered. "When you press the right part of the carving at the front it springs open, but the panel's come loose, so it's not much of a secret anymore."

Fiona nodded. She'd never seen a secret compartment, but she knew they were common enough. "You take one end, I'll take the other," she said, beginning to run her fingers over the inlaid wood. Peter nodded, his face alight with a sense of adventure. The pattern was complicated, so it was painstaking work and probably futile. After all, Fiona thought, running her fingers over yet another acanthus leaf, it would be a bit too convenient . . .

With the groan of a hinge in want of oiling, the entire front panel fell away from the drawer, revealing a shallow compartment. Peter gave a whoop of delight and Fiona laughed in relief and amazement as a yellowed paper, released from its long imprisonment, tumbled to the carpet between them.

Fiona heard Peter say something, but she scarcely made sense of the words. Aware that her fingers were trembling, she dropped to her knees, lifted the fragile paper, and unfolded it with great care. She saw the words "Last Will and Testament" in her father's familiar though somewhat shaky hand and for the first time truly believed in the existence of a second will.

The contents were brief. James Woodbourn had left two-thirds of his estate and other possessions to his daughter, Clare Prebble, and one-third to his ward, Fiona Martin. It was more than Fiona had expected. She might have cried had she not remembered that her father had built his fortune with the money her grandparents had paid him to keep quiet about her birth. God knew what the will would mean. One third of the rents from Barstead and a share in Woodbourn-Prebble hardly constituted a fortune, but it was something. She did not want to be wholly dependent on Gideon.

Peter's sharp intake of breath cut in on her thoughts, but before she could respond, an outraged cry ripped across the small room. "What the devil are you doing here?"

Though more shrill than usual, the voice was unmistakable. Fiona twisted round to look at the doorway, where she knew her sister would be standing. Clare was as impeccably dressed as ever, but the face so artfully framed by a high-standing ruff was mottled with anger, one hand clenched her fragile jaconet skirt, and the other gripped the door frame so tightly that her knuckles showed through her white gloves.

"Hullo, Aunt Clare," Peter said. "I'm looking for my Latin grammar."

Clare ignored him and kept her gaze fixed on Fiona. As she got to her feet, Fiona realized that her sister's blotched complexion was the result of something more serious than anger. Clare had been crying, and her mantle was crumpled, as if she hadn't taken the time to settle the jonquil satin properly when she got into the carriage. Fiona suspected that Parminter and Alessa had been at the breakfast. "I told you never to come near my house again," Clare said, in a voice stripped of its well-mannered veneer. "If you imagine I'll tolerate your presence simply because you're sleeping with Gideon—"

"Aunt Clare!"

Even Clare could not ignore Peter's outraged exclamation, but if she regretted speaking so in front of him, she gave no sign of it. Fiona cut in before Peter could say more. "The house may be yours, Clare, but the writing table belonged to Uncle James."

"Did it?" Clare moved into the room, making an obvious effort to compose herself. Fiona and Peter blocked her view of the table and she seemed uninterested in the paper in Fiona's hand. "It makes no difference. Everything that was his is now mine. I thought you understood that bastards have no right of inheritance."

Fiona clapped a hand on Peter's shoulder to prevent him from speaking. "True enough," she agreed. "Unless, of course, they are remembered in a parent's will."

A spasm of fear crossed Clare's face. Had Fiona not already discovered the will, that look would have told her that Clare had not done so either. Yet even now Clare did not seem to realize that the document might be, quite literally, in her sister's possession. "Papa tore up his will," Clare said. "You can thank your own wanton behavior for that."

Though she'd certainly not wanted Clare to discover her in the house, Fiona could not deny that she relished the scene. Not because Clare had betrayed her to the princess, not even because Clare had told Jamie of her affair with Gideon. It was the oldest jealousies, those formed before they'd left the nursery and nourished through all the years of their growing up, which died the hardest. "Uncle James tore up his first will. But he made another. I can scarcely blame you for not finding it. Apparently he didn't tell either of us that his writing table has a secret compartment."

Clare's eyes went to the paper in Fiona's hand. As she

realized what it must contain, her last shred of control snapped. "Let me see that."

"I think not." Fiona folded the paper carefully. "This is a matter for our solicitors. Do you still use Mr. Bridges, or have you found someone more fashionable?"

"Damn you, Fiona." Clare's eyes were wild with anger and fear. It seemed she would try to wrest the paper from Fiona's hand, but instead she turned abruptly and crossed to Hugo's desk. "The deluded impulse of a sick man," she said, jerking open a desk drawer. "It will never hold up."

"Perhaps. Perhaps not. As I said, this is a matter for our solicitors. And our barristers, if it comes to that."

"It will not come to that, you may be sure of it. Give me the paper, Fiona. Now." Clare raised her hands from the drawer and leveled a silver-mounted gun at her sister and nephew.

In the suddenly still room, Peter's soft gasp sounded unnaturally loud. Dear God, he was all of twelve years old, and thanks to the woman who to all intents and purposes was his stepmother, he was facing a loaded gun. Fiona cursed herself, but she was determined not to betray her alarm. "Don't be a fool, Clare," she said, pushing Peter behind her.

"Fool?" Clare gave a brittle laugh. Her hands were shaking, and it seemed not unlikely that the gun would go off. "It's you who's been the fool, Fiona. How dare you speak to me with such insolence!"

"If I've been insolent, then I apologize," Fiona said in the soothing voice she'd perfected with the temperamental Alessa. "Perhaps I should say that Uncle James left two-thirds of everything to you."

"Then it seems only fair that I keep the will." Clare steadied her hands and voice. "Don't trifle with me, Fiona. I'm prepared to take desperate measures to protect my children's inheritance."

This last was too much for Peter. "Sallie and Hugh

wouldn't care," he said indignantly, emerging from behind Fiona.

"For heaven's sake, Clare," Fiona admonished, "we're only talking about—"

"I know exactly what we're talking about," Clare said, and Fiona realized that for both of them this went far beyond a simple question of money and property. "Gideon has given you the trust of his children, Fiona. If you value that trust you will do as I ask."

Fiona dared not take her eyes away from the gun. She could feel Peter's rapid breathing through the cloth of his coat and she sensed his stillness. Had she been alone, she might have turned her back on her sister and walked from the room, might even have enjoyed doing it. But Clare was right: she could not take such a risk with Peter. Fiona walked forward and tossed the precious piece of paper onto her brother-in-law's desk. She had no hope of ever seeing it again.

Declining to accompany Charles Windham to Brooks's after the House rose, Gideon returned home and was conscious of keen disappointment when Adam informed him that Fiona was out. Surprisingly she'd taken Peter with her but not the younger children. But it was probably good for Peter not to always have to play elder brother. The boy took his responsibilities too seriously, which was understandable, considering that both his parents—in their different ways—had been wantonly neglectful.

"Bab's in the garden with the little ones," Adam volunteered.

Gideon grinned. He was in no mood these days to dwell on the mistakes of the past. Recalling with wonder that time not so long ago when visits to the nursery had been an effort, he made his way to the garden and told Barbara to take a well-deserved break. Teddy and Beth were playing with a set of lead knights, though not the ones Gideon had given Peter for his fifth birthday. Aline must have bought Teddy his own. Even before he left she'd been extravagant in her gifts to the children, as if to compensate for her long bouts of inattention.

Beth had mixed feelings about the game. "There aren't any ladies," she said as Gideon settled beside them. "We were going to play the story Fiona told us about King Richard and Lady Anne, but there's no one to be Anne."

She looked up at her father, certain he could hit upon a solution. One of these days she was going to be disappointed, but this was a problem Gideon thought he could solve. He went into the library, returned with paper, pencil, and sissors, and contrived to sketch a lady in the flowing robes of the fifteenth century. Beth clapped her hands in delight. Teddy peered at the drawing as Gideon cut it out. "That looks like Fiona."

Gideon stared ruefully at the tiny figure. Teddy was right. He'd drawn Lady Anne with long, flowing blond hair, a long, elegant neck, and a graceful pose which unmistakably suggested the woman he was about to marry. She must be even more prominent in his thoughts than he'd realized.

"That's just what I thought she looked like," Beth said happily.

One of the garden's stone benches proved to be a very effective castle and they were all three happily absorbed in the game when Adam came out half an hour later to tell Gideon that Lord Robert Melchett had called and was waiting in the library.

Gideon found Robin in a chair by the fireplace, hunched over a large, well-worn volume. "I say, Carne, this is a first-rate edition of Ludlow. Mind if I borrow it?"

"Not in the least."

"Thanks." Robin's face was lit with enthusiasm. "He does shed a different light on the Restoration than

Clarendon, doesn't he? I like the part about the major saying this is the time to be against things rather than for them."

Gideon grinned. "Sounds like the sort of thing you might hear at Brooks's today."

"Rather, though if you ask me, things were a lot worse in Ludlow's time. And no, I haven't forgot why I came," Robin continued, extracting two sheets of paper from a coat pocket. "I got the January letter from Grandmama easily enough but then it occurred to me that if Adrian did write the letter about gold, he'd have had to hold back any actual letters he received from William at the same time. I had a look around and found this"—he indicated the second piece of paper—"in one of his dressing table drawers."

Gideon took the letters without comment and moved to a nearby chair. Each was covered with a half-legible scrawl little different from that in the note he'd found in Robert's book. The more recent letter contained considerable detail about a new mistress and even greater detail about a new horse, but lacked even the smallest mention of gold. He was, William wrote, glad to be gone from Mysore, which had been a plaguey sort of place, interesting in its way, but little good to a proper sort of Englishman. The letter was sent from Madras on December 12, the same day he had supposedly written to Adrian from Mysore about the wondrous promise of gold.

"Adrian's really put his foot in it this time, hasn't he?" Robin remarked.

"Yes, it looks as if he has." Gideon surveyed the younger man. Despite Robin's assurance that he had no compunctions about exposing Adrian's wrongdoing, Gideon could not ignore the fact that they were brothers. For that matter, Adrian was Fiona's brother too. Someday Robin should know the truth about his secret sister, but that was for Fiona to decide. The problem now was what to do with the paper in his hand and how Robin would

293

feel about giving him the power to use it. "It's not going to be pleasant for Adrian if the truth comes out," he said.

"Adrian always was a bit of a dunderhead," Robin said cheerfully. "The sooner he's exposed the better, especially for Lady Alessandra's sake. She deserves better than Adrian. Do you think the letter might change her mind?"

"It's possible." Gideon never committed himself to an uncertainty. "She should know of it."

"Then you'd best act soon. We're all to go up to Sundon as soon as Mr. Langley returns from abroad. Grandmama and Lydia are leaving tomorrow to make things ready. They were supposed to go this morning, but with all the kick-up Grandmama decided to stay in town a day longer."

"Kick-up?" Gideon asked.

"Oh, Lord, you don't know, do you? Demetra's run off to Scotland with that Hawksley fellow," Robin said with great satisfaction.

"Good God." Demetra's question about Hawksley at the Parminter dinner had stirred Gideon's suspicions, but he hadn't expected it to go this far. By birth, fortune, and political beliefs Hawksley would be completely unacceptable to Lord and Lady Buckleigh. Gideon grinned. "Then more power to them."

"My sentiments exactly. I haven't met Hawksley, but if Demetra chose him he must be all right. Buckleigh's gone after them, but I doubt he'll catch them in time, and even if he does I wouldn't bet on his chances of bringing Demetra back."

After discussing the elopement for a few minutes more, Robin got to his feet and gathered up the volumes of Ludlow. But when they reached the front door he spoke impulsively. "Listen, Carne, if you're wondering what Father would have said, you must know he'd have told you to do whatever you think best."

That sounded so exactly like Robert Melchett that Gideon grinned. He returned to the library and stowed William's letter from Madras in a cabinet with a sturdy lock. He should act on it without delay, before Adrian brought any more partners into Woodbourn-Prebble with false promises of riches. There were going to be enough people angry with them as it was. Influential people who might, among other things, prevent Woodbourn-Prebble from gaining access to India even after the new charter passed. After listening to Magnus these past weeks, Gideon was not sure this would be such a bad thing, but without a good return from Woodbourn-Prebble's ventures he could lose any hope of redeeming Hartwood.

Damn Adrian. His lies would reflect on all of them. The best they could do was try to soften the blow. Little as he liked Magnus Melchett, Gideon knew it would be wise to take the letter to him first—perhaps even tonight.

"Gideon." Facing the cabinet, he hadn't heard the door open, but Fiona's quietly urgent voice hit him like a volley of shots. She and Peter were standing side by side, their pallor exaggerated by the dark wood of the door behind them. Though Fiona appeared composed, Gideon could tell exactly how much effort that composure had cost her. The look on Peter's face reminded him of young soldiers hours after their first battle, just beginning to realize how truly hellish war was. Meeting Fiona's eyes, Gideon checked the impulse to simultaneously take her in his arms and hug his son. His years in Spain had taught him that restraint was best in times of crisis, but it was difficult to remember that now, when Peter and Fiona were the objects of concern.

"What happened?" he said quietly.

"Aunt Clare." The dazed look was gone from Peter's eyes and he almost quivered with indignation. "She took it. Right in front of us."

Of course. He should have guessed that was where they'd gone. "You found the will."

"Peter hit upon a way to get into the house." At another time, Fiona might have felt awkward telling Gideon they had acted behind his back, but now it seemed of scant importance. She told him what had happened, briefly and matter-of-factly, but Gideon's eyes darkened with anger at the mention of the pistol. Had Clare been in the room, Fiona was not sure what he would have done. As it was, he merely expressed an intention of going directly to Davies Street.

"No, don't." Fiona sank into a chair. "She'll have burned it long since."

Never one to deny reality, Gideon crossed to her side and laid a hand on her shoulder, at once a source of comfort and of strength. "I'm sorry. I know how much this meant to you."

"Yes." Fiona did not feel able to say more, but she reached up to clasp his hand.

Perched on a cushioned bench, Peter was staring at the plaster medallions on the fireplace with a scowl which rivaled Gideon's own. "I'm sorry you had to witness such a scene," Gideon said, sitting beside him. "Your Aunt Clare has a quick temper. Anger can make people do unexpected things."

"It wasn't *fair*. I know," Peter amended, looking up at his father, "lots of things in life aren't fair, but—"

"But it's hard to witness them, especially when one is powerless to stop the injustice. Weapons have a funny way of changing the odds."

"Perhaps if I'd yelled when I first saw the gun—"

"I doubt it. Second-guessing is never wise. The important thing is that you've both returned in one piece."

Peter did not look entirely convinced. Then he suddenly sat bolt upright, fumbled in his jacket pocket, and produced a creased sheet of paper. "I know nothing can make it up to you, Fiona, but maybe this will be some help. It was in the secret compartment," he explained, as she and Gideon regarded him with astonishment, "but it didn't fall out when the will did. I'm sorry it got so crumpled. I picked it up while you were reading the will, and when Aunt Clare came into the room I stuffed it in my pocket."

"Thank you, Peter." Fiona fingered the brittle paper, refusing to let herself hope. It had been in the secret compartment, but it did not necessarily follow that it had anything to do with the will. Indeed, it was far more likely that it did not. Curiously reluctant to face the truth, she smoothed out the paper in her lap.

It appeared to be a document of some sort, with a scrolled border and tall capitals at the top that proclaimed *"KINGDOM OF SCOTLAND."* Below this were several lines of printing with blank spaces filled in by hand and signatures at the bottom. Fiona's eyes skimmed over the page. Then, her heart hammering in her throat, she read it through again, certain there must be some mistake. Its import was so incredible that she had to read it three times before she let herself believe what it plainly said. James Woodbourn and Penelope Melchett had been married according to the Laws of Scotland on the seventeenth day of September 1783.

Chapter Eighteen

When Fiona raised her eyes and smiled at Peter, Gideon knew she was searching for a way to thank the boy without telling him what the paper contained. "This means a great deal to me, Peter. I'm not sure what use it will be, but I'm very grateful to have it."

Peter had already got to his feet. "You want me to leave."

"I know it seems dreadfully unfair when you were the one to find the paper—"

"It's all right. I'm glad you didn't lie and tell me it wasn't important."

Recalling that he'd done just that when Simon di Tassio had given him the papers from the warehouse, Gideon felt a twinge of guilt. "Teddy and Beth are acting out the domestic side of the Wars of the Roses," he told his son. "I think they're in the kitchen with Adam. Tell them we'll be down in a bit."

Peter nodded and left the room without further question. Fiona's eyes returned to the paper in her hands. She said nothing and did not even look at him. It occurred to Gideon that she might want him to leave as well, a thought which he found disturbing for far more complex reasons than simple curiosity. Finally, in the most disinterested voice he could manage, Gideon asked if she would like to be left alone.

In answer, Fiona handed him the paper, a simple gesture which spoke of trust more eloquently than any words. Gideon felt himself relax and realized he'd been braced for rejection. Then he read the document and froze, taken completely by surprise.

He looked up to find Fiona watching him, her eyes smudges of near black in a face even paler than it had been when she'd entered the room. "Perhaps I should have guessed," Gideon said. "I thought it odd that a woman as hardheaded and practical as the marchioness would stoop to theft and bribery merely to conceal her daughter's thirty-year-old indiscretion."

"There could have been an annulment." Like Peter, Fiona seemed to be in shock.

"With Penelope three months pregnant? I doubt it. And even if it weren't for the pregnancy, they couldn't risk the possibility of gossip."

"There was no risk of gossip when my mother bore a secret child?"

"She wasn't the first woman to do so. And gossip about a secret child is not the same as gossip about a secret marriage."

Fiona laughed, a harsh, brittle sound on the edge of hysteria. "Better it be said that my mother bore a child out of wedlock than that she made a *mésalliance*."

"Infinitely better from your grandparents' point of view."

Now that she had accepted the reality of her parents' marriage, Fiona was forced to consider how that marriage had begun and ended. Though the picture was still cloudy, she already knew it was not pretty. "So they simply pretended the marriage had never taken place? How could they? What about the minister? The witnesses? The parish register, for heaven's sake?"

"The minister of a small country church? And two witnesses"—Gideon glanced down at the certificate—"who appear to have been related to him? If Melchett money couldn't buy them, the Melchett name could probably intimidate them. The page in the register was almost certainly burned."

"Dear God." Fiona had thought she had no illusions about her parents and grandparents, but she felt a chill run the length of her body, despite the fact that she had not removed her shawl and gloves.

"Lord Berkeley did much the same thing, at much the same time, though he later repented and regularized the marriage. It caused endless problems with the succession. Your parents and grandparents were more thorough." Gideon subdued any urge to soften the story. Penelope and James Woodbourn and the Parminters had treated Fiona abominably and it would be a cold day in hell before he served as their apologist.

"But why run the risk? My father may not have been considered the Melchetts' equal, but he was not wholly ineligible. Surely it would have been safer to accept the match."

"Perhaps. But Penelope was to marry her cousin Robert. That had been decided long before." Gideon cast his mind back to his years in Parminter House, to fragments of family history he had largely ignored, snatches of conversation he had inadvertently overheard, and rare times when Robert Melchett, unusually tired or angry or drunk, had discussed his personal life. "You remember the painting over the mantel in the drawing room at Parminter House?"

Fiona nodded, conjuring up an image of the blonde woman in the full-sleeved blue dress who must be—what? Her great-great-grandmother?

"Penelope Quentin," Gideon said. "She married the fourth marquis and rejuvenated the Melchett fortunes. Their son, your great-grandfather, was born late in life. He had a sister who was some twenty years his senior. Her granddaughter is the present marchioness. She was raised with the expectation that she would marry the sixth marquis and unite the two branches of the family.

300

It was a great disappointment to everyone when the only surviving child she produced was a somewhat sickly girl."

"My mother." The words sounded strangely alien to Fiona's ears.

"Your mother. Penelope Melchett. If Penelope married Robert, her father's heir, the Parminters could ensure that their grandson would carry the title one day."

At Gideon's last words, anger and disgust welled up in Fiona's throat and for a moment she thought she was going to vomit. She wasn't sure which was worse, that her grandparents had treated her parents and herself as dynastic chess pieces or that her parents had allowed them to do so. "My parents didn't have to give in," she said, with a bitterness she'd never before heard in her voice. "The law would have been on their side."

"Your father was penniless and I'm sure the Parminters threatened to leave Penelope in a similar state. They'd have had to live on love alone."

"And love, presumably, was beginning to wear rather thin. My mother could become a marchioness and my father could have a comfortable income if only they agreed to give each other up."

"And bastardize their child," Gideon said quietly.

This had been clear from the beginning, of course, but it took Gideon's words to bring home how cheaply her parents had held her. One hand going to her mouth, Fiona rose, as if she could physically distance herself from the ugliness she had discovered. She reached the fireplace in a few unsteady strides and gripped the cold marble of the mantel. There was a stir of movement behind her and then Gideon's hands touched her shoulders and he turned her around and drew her into his arms.

It was the first time he had embraced her in comfort rather than passion and Fiona clung to him as she had to the mantel, for simple support. "What they did to you was despicable," he said after a moment, into her hair,

301

"don't try to deny it. Talk if you want. Scream if you must. Cry if you can."

"I can't," Fiona said, with a desperate little laugh, her voice muffled by his shoulder. "I'm too angry."

She heard Gideon laugh as well, a rich, warm, hearteningly human sound. With a sigh which released some of the tension from her body, she turned her head so that it was easier to speak. "And yet for all that, my father kept the marriage certificate. I suppose he couldn't bring himself to destroy it. You'd think my grandparents would have insisted on seeing it burned."

"It was certainly an oversight," Gideon agreed, adjusting his hands to a more comfortable hold and caressing her disordered hair. "But once he had married again, they must have felt they were safe. He couldn't do anything without branding himself a bigamist."

"Poor Aunt Charlotte. She'd have been dreadfully shocked to learn she was living in sin all those years. Gideon," Fiona said suddenly, "the will. I'm sure Clare destroyed it, because in the absence of a will everything would go to her as Uncle James's only surviving legitimate child. But if his marriage to Aunt Charlotte wasn't valid—"

"Then you are his heir. Nice to know there's some justice in the world after all. The will would have given Clare two-thirds of the inheritance. Without a will she can make no claim on your father's estate."

Fiona thought of the scene in Hugo's study, of her interview with Clare the previous October, of a thousand past slights. She bit her lip, then choked on a gurgle of genuine mirth. "She'll be"—Fiona choked again—"she'll be very angry."

"Not half as angry as Adrian when he learns he is no longer Marquis of Parminter."

Fiona stiffened. In her anger at learning how expendable she'd been to her family, she had barely considered how her discovery would affect her own future, let alone anyone else's. Gideon's hand stilled on her hair. "What do you want to do about this, Fiona?" he asked gently.

"I don't know." At once appalled and exhilarated, Fiona realized the number of lives she could affect with that crumpled piece of paper. When Alessa had first pointed out Parminter to her in the Duchess of Waterford's ballroom she had never dreamed . . .

Alessa. Fiona raised her head, almost relieved that events had made a decision for her. "I must go to the princess. It would be criminal to let Alessa marry Parminter without knowing the truth."

"It would indeed. But the princess will almost certainly demand an explanation from the marchioness. You'd best decide how you mean to proceed before you let the secret out."

"Would the marriage certificate hold up? Legally, I mean."

"It certainly appears valid," Gideon said, in the same voice he'd used the day before when they were discussing whether or not to buy Peter a horse. "But I'm no expert, and I know Scottish marriages can be questionable under English law. I think we'd best pay Camford a visit this evening."

Fiona nodded. Her first rush of anger had faded and soon she would have to face myriad decisions . . . but not just yet. It was comfortable in Gideon's arms and she was reluctant to leave, reluctant to break the tranquility between them. Gideon seemed to feel the same, for he gathered her closer and let his chin rest on her hair.

"This must be a day for revelations about Scottish marriages," he remarked. "I saw Robin Melchett this afternoon and he told me Demetra has eloped with Frank Hawksley."

"The man she was asking about at the Parminter dinner?" Fiona asked in surprise. "He's a friend of yours?"

"We were together on the Peninsula. Hawksley's a good man, even if he does rather remind me of myself

303

eons ago. I wish them well, though they won't have an easy time of it. Demetra's parents are almost sure to cut her off without a shilling and Hawksley has pockets to let."

Want of money was not to be taken lightly, as Fiona had cause to know, but she would have liked to believe Demetra's love would prove more durable than her mother's. This reminded her of the certificate and what would happen if it became public, and soon her thoughts drifted in a direction that compelled her to speak. "Gideon, did Robert Melchett have a brother? Who would be marquis if his marriage to Penelope wasn't valid?"

It took so long for Gideon to answer that Fiona again drew back to look at him. He was frowning, as if he'd just realized something and was considering its implications. "No, Robert didn't have any brothers," he said at last, "and his father and Penelope's father were the fifth marquis's only sons."

"So if Robert's children are bastardized—"

"If Robert's children are bastardized," Gideon said thoughtfully, "the title goes to Magnus Melchett."

"I've read about contested peerages, but I've never actually been involved with one first hand." Richard Camford's normally mild brown eyes glowed with enthusiasm. "Forgive me, Miss Alastair, I forget that we are speaking of your family."

Fiona assured the solicitor that she had taken no offense. Her prior acquaintance with Mr. Camford had been brief, but she'd formed a very favorable opinion of him. Though he'd come in search of her at Gideon's request, he had been genuinely concerned for her well-being and, however much he had denied it, she knew he'd put himself at some risk in arranging for her position with the Tassios.

"Cut the line, Richard," Gideon said, leaning back in his chair. "Where do we stand?"

Camford's open features drew into frowning concentration as he lowered his eyes to the certificate on the desk before him. An hour ago in the Carne kitchen, as she'd listened to the children's chatter, and complimented Adam on the onion sauce, and cut up Beth's mutton, Fiona had found it hard to believe the events of the afternoon had the remotest connection to the real world. Now in Camford's study, a moderate-sized chamber cramped by the vast number of books it contained, their reality could not be denied.

"Scottish marriages are certainly valid," Camford said at last. "Lord and Lady Jersey were married at Gretna Green. But there are sometimes questions—couples frequently choose to have a second marriage in an English church, just to be safe." He tented his ink-stained hands and rested his chin upon them. "I need hardly say that Lord Parminter would almost certainly contest the validity of his mother's first marriage."

"And then?" Fiona asked.

Camford hesitated again, still wearing the cautious frown Fiona remembered so well. This was a man used to dealing in subtleties and nuances. "If I were advising the Parminter family, I would encourage them to offer you a financial settlement in exchange for the marriage certificate."

"And if I refused such an offer?" Fiona inquired, deliberately settling back into her chair, which was upholstered in a shabby dark red damask and seemed, like everything else in the room, to have been selected more for comfort than effect..

"I would do my utmost to make the case drag on as long as possible. It could well last years." Camford's enthusiasm had been replaced by a cool calculation which made him seem at once older and more hardened. "The Melchetts can afford such a battle. You cannot. On the other hand . . ." He looked at Gideon. "Who is the next heir if the current line is invalidated?"

"Magnus Melchett." Though he'd said little, Gideon was following the conversation intently.

"So I suspected." Camford turned back to Fiona with a smile that was almost boyish. "This improves your position no end. Melchett is a wealthy man and presumably would be as interested as you in proving the validity of your parents' marriage."

Ever since Gideon had told her the identity of the next heir, Fiona had known it would come to this. "And if you were advising the Parminters, knowing they'd have to face Mr. Melchett as well as me?"

"First, I would have to learn more about Melchett. You know him, Carne. Can he be bought off?"

Gideon grinned. "I doubt it. He may have his price, but I don't think the Parminters can afford it."

"Then their only recourse would be to fight it out before the law and the House of Lords." This time there was genuine concern beneath Camford's professional mask. "Make no mistake about it, Miss Alastair, this will be a long and unpleasant battle." He fidgeted with a pen which lay loose on the desk top. "Your past relationship with Lord Carne would almost certainly be brought up, if not in open court then as common gossip."

"Why?" Gideon's voice cut through the room, resonant with anger.

Camford regarded him with sympathy. They had been at school together and were clearly still on terms of friendship. "In order to turn public opinion and the House of Lords against Miss Alastair. And in order to cast doubt on the marriage certificate."

Gideon ran a hand through his already disordered hair, a gesture Fiona recognized as an attempt to recover his temper. "Forgive me, Richard, we don't all have legal minds. How would it cast doubt on the marriage certificate?"

This time Camford looked Gideon directly in the eye. "The Parminter lawyers will say that you and Miss Alastair concocted this scheme together in an effort to raise money. Your financial circumstances will almost certainly be discussed."

"And my late wife's indiscretions, financial and otherwise?" Gideon's voice was level, but his eyes were hard.

"Very probably." Camford was all professional detachment once again. "It's possible, of course, that such tactics would only create sympathy for Miss Alastair. On the other hand, the fact that she is living under your roof would lend credence to the stories."

"By the time any of these stories could circulate, Miss Alastair will be my wife," Gideon informed him.

Camford's face relaxed into a smile. "Then you must allow me to wish you both every happiness. It won't stop the Parminters from bringing up the past, however. Ultimately it will come down to a vote in the House of Lords. Miss Alastair's plight might arouse their chivalrous instincts. On the other hand, though Parminter may be a bit feckless, he is one of their own, while Magnus Melchett has made it a point not to be. And at last report you had your own share of enemies within its ranks, Gideon."

Gideon grinned again but sobered abruptly. "Are you saying Miss Alastair would be better off without me?"

"I doubt it, for any number of reasons," Camford said dispassionately. "I didn't mean to paint so black a picture. But you should know what you may be in for before you decide how to proceed."

"I'm most grateful for your candor," Fiona assured him. "Until I do make a decision, I think it would be best if you kept the marriage certificate."

Camford said he would be happy to do so and happy to render whatever other services should prove necessary. Fiona and Gideon declined an offer to take tea with the Camford family, but as Camford was seeing them to the front door, a sturdy little boy of about Teddy's age burst into the hall and announced that his father had been an age and Mama wouldn't let them bring in the tea tray until he came back.

"Harry, our eldest," Camford said by way of introduction, catching his son by the shoulders before the boy could run full-tilt into the visitors. "Miss Alastair and Lord Carne, Harry, and you can tell your mother I'll be along as soon as I've seen them out."

Harry studied the visitors with curiosity. "You're my godfather," he informed Gideon.

If Gideon had forgotten this fact, he gave no sign of it. "So I am," he agreed. "I'm afraid I can't say I'd have recognized you."

"That's all right," Harry assured him. "I don't remember you at all."

As she watched Gideon bend down to speak to the young boy, Fiona found herself blurting out the time and place of their marriage and inviting the Camford family to attend. Surprised but pleased, Camford said they would be very happy to do so. "Do you mind?" Fiona asked Gideon when they were in the curricle. "I can't help but feel that I owe Mr. Camford a great deal. God knows what would have become of me five years ago if it hadn't been for him."

Gideon drew in his breath. "Don't think I ever forget it," he said, in a voice so low that she heard the bitter undertone more than the words.

"That's not what I meant." Fiona was genuinely contrite. "It was your doing as much as his that I managed to survive. Don't think *I* ever forget *that*."

From the horses' slight start, Fiona knew that Gideon's hands had tightened on the reins. "Didn't I tell you acting the martyr doesn't suit you?" he said.

"We'll never contrive to deal together if we pretend the past didn't happen," Fiona pointed out.

"Nor if we pretend the past is other than it was," he returned in a more moderate tone.

Fiona didn't try to answer this, and they covered the

rest of the distance to Dover Street in silence. Even then it was some time before they could talk. Teddy and Beth were in bed but not yet asleep, and when Fiona looked in on them they demanded that Gideon come up to say goodnight. Then Peter intercepted his father and governess in the downstairs hall and said Barbara had made lemon biscuits and did they want some. He seemed eager for their company, and Fiona, feeling she'd neglected him most shabbily after their adventure of the afternoon, could not but comply.

So she spent a pleasant half-hour drinking tea and eating lemon biscuits and pretending all was well, which proved easier than might have been expected, as Adam and Barbara were paying more and more attention to each other these days and less and less to anyone else. Then, following what was now an established pattern, Fiona went up to her bedchamber and changed into her nightdress and dressing gown, leaving her hair for Gideon's ministrations. When she was sure the house was quiet, she slipped downstairs to the study.

Gideon's face was in shadow, but the light from the single lamp on the table beside him glowed richly against the burgundy silk of his dressing gown. Fiona closed the door with care. "Magnus Melchett holds the mortgage on Hartwood."

"What makes you think that?" Gideon's response was a shade too quick.

"Adam told me."

"Adam talks too much."

"On the contrary, Adam is the soul of discretion when it comes to your affairs. I took it as a great sign of trust that he mentioned it." Fiona moved to the only other seat in the room, a shield-back chair near the fireplace. "Mr. Camford assumed Magnus Melchett would want the marquisate. Do you agree? Or would he prefer to show contempt for the Parminters and all they represent?"

Gideon turned up the lamp, so that light spilled across

the intricate pattern of the carpet between them. Their eyes met and Fiona knew that he'd guessed her decision and was determined to oppose it. "Magnus certainly enjoys looking askance at the Parminters," he said at last, "but for that very reason I doubt he'd be able to resist the thought of becoming marquis. It would vindicate every slight his branch of the family has suffered for four generations."

"Then the solution is simple. Magnus can have the marriage certificate in exchange for the mortgage on Hartwood."

"If you imagine," Gideon told her, in a pleasant but quite implacable voice, "that I am going to let you trade your name for Hartwood, you are very much mistaken."

"I knew you'd be tiresome," Fiona said cheerfully. "But the name's hardly worth much, after all. It's not as if the Parminters are one of those enlightened families like the Marlboroughs who let the title pass to daughters. Don't you want Hartwood back? I always thought it quite a pretty house."

"Think, Fiona. I didn't mortgage Hartwood, Aline did. Do you really want to pay her debts?"

"The law," Fiona pointed out, "recognizes no difference between husband and wife. Therefore Aline's debts are yours and as of Tuesday they are mine."

"Doing it much too brown, my girl. Aside from the dubious logic of that statement, you're the last person I'd have thought to find upholding the virtues of our marriage laws."

"I didn't say anything about virtues. But it is the law and at present there's no going around it."

"Hartwood's been run into the ground. Even if we can put it to rights, we won't have the income I had before," Gideon warned her. "Aline went through everything I had in the funds and sold the Leicester estate. Paying off the mortgage won't make us wealthy."

"Wealth is a relative term." Fiona sobered and leaned

toward him, chin cupped in one hand. "Forget about pride for a moment, Gideon. Without the mortgage, you—we—will have the income from Hartwood. That may not make us rich, but we'll be able to live in reasonable comfort. More important, we'll be able to provide for the boys and Beth and any other children we may have."

It was only when she saw Gideon's eyes lighten with unmistakable happiness that Fiona realized what she'd said. When had she changed her mind about having his child? A few days before she had been determined to avoid anything that would tie her so irrevocably to him. Now such fears seemed foolish. Her growing love for Peter and Teddy and Beth already bound her to their father. She found she not only welcomed a child of Gideon's and her own but longed for it.

Gideon had not been able to look ahead to the future enough to think about children, but the thought of a child that was not only unequivocally his but Fiona's as well was a source of unexpected elation . . . and distraction. "You won't be able to wash your hands of the matter so easily," he told her, his voice deliberately harsh. "Magnus will still have to bring suit to win the title. And you'll have Clare to deal with too. If Parminter and his lawyers don't drag in the past, you can be certain Clare will."

Fiona rose with a languorous grace that was wholly deceptive, for by the time he realized what she was about she was standing before him, one leg just brushing his thigh, one hand resting lightly on his shoulder. She seemed not only calm but serene, as if for the first time she looked forward to the future with something more than acceptance. "We'll be married," she said softly. "That will make it easier." And then, before he could protest, she bent down and placed her lips over his own.

Unfair tactics, considering she knew perfectly well that four days had done nothing to dispel his hunger for her.

But then, once they started down that particular road, Fiona was as little in control as he. When Gideon broke away it was only to pull her into his lap and deepen the kiss. And when at length he drew back to look at her, he saw that though she was smiling in amusement as much as triumph, her breathing had quickened and her eyes had turned smoky with need.

"This isn't the end of the discussion," Gideon informed her as firmly as he could, given the state of his own breath, "merely a hiatus."

Fiona's throaty laughter was so infectious that Gideon laughed as well as he began to pull the pins from her hair.

Four days and the prosaic promise of marriage had indeed done nothing to dispel their hunger for each other. Whatever was between them, it was not mere lust for the unattainable. Yet even as he worked at her laces and tangled his fingers in her hair and buried his body in her own, Gideon sensed that something was subtly but unmistakably different tonight. Before, no matter how desperate her desire, no matter how eager her response, Fiona had always held a part of herself aloof. Tonight she was completely and joyfully his, as if their coupling brought her not merely pleasure and release but something far more elusive: happiness.

As their ragged breathing returned to normal, she ran her hands over his back in a gentle caress which stirred memories of a younger Fiona, less skilled in the ways of passion, but with an ardor composed of romantic dreams as much as physical desire, an ardor wasted on a man who . . .

Gideon abruptly rolled to one side, pulling Fiona to rest against him. If he continued that line of thought the weight of guilt would become unendurable. Fiona gave a contented murmur, reached for the hand he had flung across her, and laced her fingers through his own. Turning his face into her hair, Gideon willed his thoughts in another direction. There was a comfort in spending the whole night together that had been lacking from their frantic interludes five years ago. That had been lacking, come to think of it, most of his life. After the first weeks of his marriage, he'd rarely spent more than a few hours with Aline, who complained that he was a restless sleeper. And the pattern he'd established with her he'd later followed with his mistresses—if the word "mistress" could be applied to any of the women with whom he'd formed those transitory liaisons, first in vengeance against a wife who didn't care, then out of boredom and force of habit.

"Personally," Fiona said in an amused voice, "I thought it was quite nice. Why are you groaning?"

Never could it be said that nine years in the House had taught him nothing. An unpleasant question was best answered with another question. "How," Gideon inquired with great interest, "do you manage to keep your hair so sweet smelling?"

"That," Fiona said, turning to face him, but keeping hold of his hand, "is either romantic delusion or an outright lie. My hair has been in want of washing these two days and more, and if it smells like anything it's schoolroom ink."

"Then I never knew how much I liked the smell of ink." Gideon lifted her hand to his lips. "The Parminters owe you more, Fiona."

Fiona sighed. "I might have known I couldn't distract you forever. You aren't being very consistent, Gideon. I thought you agreed with Rousseau that inheritance shouldn't be guaranteed by birth."

"If you mean that I think the world is constituted unfairly," Gideon said, drawing the blankets up over her shoulder and letting his hand rest comfortably on her collar-bone, "I most certainly do. But the world being constituted as it is, you have been treated worse than shabbily."

313

"What do you suggest I do? Sell the certificate to the Parminters?"

"Hardly. But it's conceivable that the marchioness could be persuaded to acknowledge you. Let me talk to her—"

"No." Fiona pulled away from him, her playful humor gone. "I won't humiliate myself by appealing to her again, Gideon. Besides, if you imagine that anything could change her mind, you don't know my grandmother." Fiona pushed herself to a half-sitting position. "That's final. I want to settle this quickly so I can tell the princess and Alessa the truth. Now will you go to Magnus Melchett with my proposition, or do I have to call on him myself?"

Gideon raised himself on one elbow. "I don't know but that you might not strike a better bargain with Melchett than I could. But if you're so set on it, I'll relay your conditions."

As Fiona's thanks took the form of a kiss which rapidly grew more serious than either of them had intended, Gideon was spared from saying more. It was fortunate, because while he had every intention of doing as he'd promised, he hadn't the least intention of letting it go at that. Much later, with a mollified Fiona asleep in his arms and her ink-scented hair spilling over his chest, Gideon stared at the ceiling and began to piece together his plan.

Chapter Nineteen

Gideon woke the next morning with a clarity of mind he had not experienced since the days before his wounds had taken him out of action on the Peninsula. Despite the grosser insanities of war, there had always been something urgent and immediate to be done—fording a river, scouting out the next village, foraging for the day's dinner—small, necessary things that engaged his mind and body and took all the exercise of his wit. His wounds had left him helpless to control his destiny. Once returned to England, he found that Aline, from the grave, had done the same.

But now Fiona had given him a card to play. He would not have chosen to go to Magnus, but it was Fiona's decision and he would respect it. He would not, however, bargain away her birthright for nothing more than the return of his own property. There was much more to be gained and there were other players besides Melchett on the field. Adrian was the key, but ultimately the game would depend upon his grandmother, the marchioness. If he read these two aright, if they could be made to act in ways he could predict, Fiona would be spared the humiliation of being publicly branded a wanton. So he would call on Magnus, but not without first preparing the ground.

He left the house shortly after one o'clock, the memory of his night with Fiona warm within him, and di-

315

rected his horses to Westminster. He had spent the morning going through the seventy-nine folio pages of the East India Company's Charter Bill, which was to be read for a second time that afternoon. At this stage there might be little left to debate, but there were some things Gideon had decided to say.

The House was sparsely filled when he arrived. Gideon nodded at some acquaintances and slipped into a seat beside Charles Windham. "It's the Distillation Prevention Bill," Windham whispered, "the third reading." He showed no more enthusiasm than the other members in the chamber. After a vote was taken which would duly regulate the production of spirits in Ireland, the House moved on to consideration of the Charter Bill. Gideon folded his arms and waited.

Earl Stanhope rose first to present a collection of petitions supporting the diffusion of Christian knowledge in India. Gideon moved restlessly on the hard and uncomfortable bench. A glance at Windham told him that the other man shared his sentiments. The well-meaning people of Yorkshire and Lancashire and Wiltshire and Wales earnestly sought the betterment of a people who had no consciousness that they were of an inferior culture. This was not the first group of petitions that had been laid before the House, and it was not to be the last. Stanhope was followed by Earl Grosvenor, who had his own collection to present.

Then the Earl of Lauderdale rose to speak and a flicker of interest went through the House, accompanied by some audible groans. Lauderdale was a fluent speaker but known for taking unpopular positions. A shrewd, hot-tempered man who'd once been offered the post of governor-general of India (till forced to withdraw by the indignation of the company's directors), his questions and objections to the various clauses of the bill had formed a large part of the debate over the past weeks.

316

He addressed himself now to the subject of the petitions, trusting, he said, that the government would not be tempted to use its power to enforce the adoption of the Christian faith, an action that would be ruinous to the country's burgeoning empire.

The Earl of Buckinghamshire stirred in his seat. Buckinghamshire was also no friend of the company's directors, but as President of the Board of Control which oversaw the company's operations, he was urging the adoption of the bill. Gideon saw him prepare to rise to rebut Lauderdale's accusations and in that instant was on his feet. "My Lords," Gideon said, his voice rising over the babble of voices that served as background to all but the most riveting debates.

There was a moment of silence in the chamber. Gideon glanced around and smiled. He had surprised them. The long-absent, long-silent Viscount Carne had found his voice at last.

"My Lords," he repeated in a lower tone which nonetheless carried throughout the chamber, "I have listened carefully to the debate on the subject of our missionaries which has occupied us these past few weeks, and I am gravely concerned. I do not deny the good intentions of those who would propagate their own faith, but I would remind them that we deny the faith of others at our own peril — peril to our fortunes, our power, our very souls.

"I must therefore support the arguments of the noble earl who has just spoken" — here he nodded at Lauderdale, who was watching him with folded arms, an amused glint in his eye — "and add my voice to his. Wait," he said, holding up his hand. There was a rising hum of voices and he feared he might lose their attention. "This is not all I would say. Some of you know me from years past. I have served the late Marquis of Parminter. I have sat in this chamber with you myself. I have campaigned in the field, and now, for reasons too

317

tedious to go into, I find I have some interest in trade." He paused deliberately and sought their eyes. His association with Woodbourn-Prebble was not unknown, and the hum of voices had subsided. "Trade, gentlemen, is the basis of the prosperity of our country. You may not engage in trade yourselves, but you know this to be true. When trade flourishes, we all gain. When trade is cut off, as the Emperor has tried to do, we all suffer. The war with America has not made it easier. Is it any wonder that our merchants look to Indian markets? Think of what it means, gentlemen. Indian markets. Indian markets for English goods. Customers abroad and prosperity at home. A future to be desired. A future to be pursued."

Gideon pursed his lips and frowned, waiting for the moment when his audience would grow restless. He caught Windham's eye. Windham knew where his argument was going. "There is a flaw, of course," Gideon went on. "There always is. The Indians, benighted souls, show little interest in what we have to sell. It is a problem we did not foresee when we sent the great East India Company there two centuries ago. It is a problem that has plagued them ever since. But we are a resourceful people. Now that we glimpse the possibility of opening up the continent to other traders, we are attacking this problem with all the force and subtlety of which we are capable. Do you know what we're doing with our Indian friends? We're destroying their languages and destroying their gods and destroying their way of life. We're giving them the English tongue and the English god and English tastes, and by God, at last we will give them an appetite for English goods!" On these words Gideon's voice rose to a roar. There was an instant of silence, followed by a noisy murmur. Someone cried, "Blasphemy!" Someone else shouted, "Hear, hear!"

Gideon dropped his voice to little more than a whisper

and the murmurs quieted. "Will our friends in India be better off for becoming English?" He shrugged. "In truth, I do not know." He looked around the room once more, willing their attention. "But I tell you this: if we proceed on the course on which we are embarked, we will create a well of enmity that will one day rise up to destroy us."

Across the room Lauderdale was regarding Gideon with approval. The voices of the others grew in intensity, and then Buckinghamshire, his face suffused with emotion, was on his feet. "If the noble lord is finished—"

Gideon made him a polite bow. "The noble lord is not quite finished." Buckinghamshire sighed and resumed his seat. "If I may be allowed a few more words," Gideon continued, "I have a story to relate, a parable of sorts, though unfortunately it is true. There is here in London a small company that for many years has traded with Hamburg and Riga and other northern ports. Like companies of its kind, it has suffered reversals under the French blockade. It is not surprising that the partners in this company have sought new markets, nor is it surprising that they have given their enthusiastic support to the opening of the India trade. It is perhaps not even surprising that others have sought to buy into the company in the hope of sharing in its future profits."

There was an impatient stir in the chamber. Some of the members were clearly bewildered by the direction he was taking. Others, who knew of Gideon's connection with Woodbourn-Prebble, were showing signs of interest. "Greed is a sorry thing, gentlemen. It clouds the judgment. Throughout the ages, nothing has made men quite as greedy as gold. There is gold in India, to be sure, but throughout the illustrious history of the East India Company no one has claimed that gold exists in quantities worth chasing. On the contrary, we have poured our own gold into the country and have been satisfied to take cotton and indigo and such useful things in return. Prudent men would look warily on rumors of gold."

He had their attention now. Buckinghamshire was scowling, but Lauderdale was regarding him with a sardonic smile. Gideon shook his head in an extravagant gesture of dismay. "I fear there are many imprudent men. One of the partners in this company of which I speak recently came into possession of a letter from a man now resident in India, a letter extolling the abundance and quality of gold to be found in the state of Mysore. As word of this letter got about, he was besieged by offers to provide the capital that would allow the company to exploit these riches."

Gideon paused. "An interesting discovery, if true. But why should I take up your time with what, after all, is a mere commercial matter? I would not do so had it not come to my attention that the letter from India—the purported letter—is a blatant forgery. There may be gold in India, but there is no more and no less than there has ever been." There was a shocked silence, followed by a stir of movement and an outbreak of angry voices. Gideon raised his own. "So I come now to the point of my little digression. Gentlemen, we must beware of our greed. See in this one sorry instance where it has led. We must temper our greed with prudence. We must temper it with humility. Above all, we must be not enter lightly into commerce with a country whose inhabitants have their own interests, their own creeds, and their own sense of honor."

It was doubtful that many of those present heard his last words. Gideon glanced round the chamber. There were angry faces and bewildered ones, raised voices and laughter. Directly ahead, Waterford was regarding him with a disapproving frown, while his neighbor Berresford had gone alarmingly red. "You've kicked up a proper shindy," Windham said as Gideon resumed his seat. "Are you glad to be back in harness?"

Gideon allowed himself the ghost of a smile. "I run when I must." As soon as Lord Buckinghamshire rose to speak and the House quieted, he murmured good-bye to Windham and slipped out of the chamber.

For better or ill, it was done. He had set in motion a scheme that would force the marchioness to recognize her granddaughter. It would give Fiona, a woman he had vowed to help, some recompense for years of slights and casual cruelties. It would do the same for Magnus Melchett, a man he did not want to help at all, but Magnus was part of the game and must be allowed to take his profit.

Feeling an extraordinary elation, Gideon strode quickly to the street where he had left his curricle. To be honest, he had done more than commit himself to changing Fiona's life. He had committed himself to changing his own. The words he had used to bring down Adrian were the words by which he had staked out his right to speak, to have a voice, to make a difference. Futile, yes, unavailing, and probably ineffective, but by God, it had felt good to stand up and have his say. Gideon laughed aloud, lavishly tipped the boy who had held his horses, and set the carriage in motion toward the city. The word would soon be out, though most members of the House would stay for the continuation of the debate and the second reading of the Charter Bill. As for himself, it was time to call on Magnus Melchett.

The banker left Gideon cooling his heels for a good half-hour, but he made him a handsome apology, offered him wine, which Gideon refused, and waved him to a chair which stood at the end of the brass-inlaid mahogany table he used as his desk. "How may I serve you?" Magnus's voice was courteous but held a faint note of impatience.

Gideon came straight to the point. "William Melchett's

321

letter is a forgery."

"Ah." Magnus leaned back in his chair and regarded his visitor with eyes that were at once shrewd and alert. "Your evidence?"

Gideon reached into his pocket and extracted the second of the two letters Robin had brought him. "This came into my hands yesterday."

Magnus took the letter and read it through quickly. Then he laid it on the table, rifled through a pile of papers, and retrieved a letter which he laid beside the first. He glanced several times from one to the other, then read them both through. When he was finished, he leaned back and sighed. "Where did you get this?"

"It was found in Parminter's dressing room," Gideon said carefully.

Magnus regarded him from beneath drawn brows. "But not by you." He turned back to the letters. "They are both from William Melchett. Which is the forgery?"

Gideon smiled. "You're a cautious man." He withdrew another paper. "This is a note I found in one of the late Lord Parminter's books which happened to come into my possession. The note was written much earlier, but the hand matches that of the letter I brought you."

Magnus held out his hand for the note. "Are you playing games with me, Carne?"

Gideon met his eyes and did not smile. "No."

"I thought not." Magnus looked carefully at the note and then at the letters. "So. The forgery is the letter Parminter gave me. It's a clumsy one. Is it his?"

"At a hazard, yes."

Magnus nodded as though in confirmation of a long-held suspicion. "A lack-brained lad."

"Hardly a lad," Gideon reminded him. It was no mere boy that Aline had taken to her bed.

"No. I feared he would do us damage, but he's had his uses. The question of gold is unimportant. There are far

322

greater opportunities in India, and we must convince people that they are there. In the meantime, we must raise capital where we can."

"At the cost of fraudulent misrepresentation?"

Magnus gave him a smile that mixed condescension and pity. "It will hardly be the first time it has been done. This isn't a cricket match, Carne. In the long run it will matter little to investors where their profit is made."

"In the short run, there will be some very angry people."

"If they know. They need not."

"I'm afraid it's too late for that," Gideon said. "By nightfall the story will be all over London."

As the import of Gideon's words sank in, Magnus's face grew red and he half rose from his seat. "You fool! You benighted fool! Do you know what you've drawn down upon our heads?"

"I hope so."

Magnus sat back heavily. His eyes, a changeable gray-green, set deep under shaggy brows, regarded Gideon as though he were some species of dangerous animal. "What exactly have you done?"

Gideon told him, giving an account that left out neither his own words nor the stir they had caused.

"I see. You've managed to ruin Parminter and you're likely to bring down Woodbourn-Prebble as well. Everything we hoped to do in India. Tell me, Carne, is it private vengeance you seek, or is it something more?"

Gideon looked at him sharply. Did Magnus know about Adrian and Aline? As a rule his wife had been discreet. He had assumed her liaisons were not widely known, but obviously he was wrong. To his surprise he found that he no longer cared. "Something more," he said. "I would put some pressure on Parminter."

A crooked smile crossed Magnus's face, making him

appear a good ten years younger. "Now what profit, I wonder, would you find in that?"

"Enough for me," Gideon said carefully, "and enough for you. Melchett, how would you like to be Marquis of Parminter?"

Magnus went very still. "You jest."

"I do not."

The banker said nothing for a long moment while he studied the man in front of him. Suspicion warred with belief in his face. "Your proof?" Magnus's voice was hoarse.

"A piece of paper that will give you the title. Now. At once."

Belief won out. "There was an impediment to the marriage." It was not a question. "Robert Melchett was married before?"

"No. Penelope."

Magnus let out a long sigh. "Extraordinary." There was another silence while he appeared to carry on some internal dialogue. When he looked at Gideon once more, his eyes were calm and alert. "This paper—"

"A certificate of the marriage. It took place in Scotland, near Castleton, in September of '83. The marriage was considered unsuitable."

"Why didn't her parents have it annulled?"

"Penelope was with child—"

"My God."

"—and they were eager for the union with Robert Melchett."

Magnus shook his head. "She's a formidable woman," he said, and Gideon knew he was speaking of the marchioness. "The child is dead?"

"No, she's very much alive. Her name is Fiona Martin," Gideon went on. "Her father was James Woodbourn and she was raised as his ward."

"The devil." Magnus was startled, but in a moment the

crooked smile appeared again. "So Lady Prebble is disinherited and Miss Martin is Woodbourn's heir."

"It would seem so," Gideon said cautiously.

"And what has Miss Martin done about it?"

"Very little so far. The marriage certificate came to light only yesterday. It was in Prebble's house, in a secret compartment of a writing table that had once belonged to Miss Martin's father. You'll want to see the certificate, of course. It's with my solicitor, Richard Camford. I'll direct him to show it to you, but I think it should remain in his hands."

Magnus nodded and sat back in his chair. "So. I'm to be the Marquis of Parminter." A smile that blended vindictiveness with triumph played about his lips. "It won't be easy."

"No," Gideon acknowledged. "Parminter will fight it. It bastardizes him and his brothers and sister. The marchioness will fight it. It destroys everything she has worked for. The Prebbles will fight it too. To fight them all will take time and money and a thick skin. You have them in abundance."

Magnus gave a harsh laugh, then abruptly stood and took a turn or two about the small room, coming to rest at last in front of Gideon. "What is it you want, Carne?"

Gideon rose so that they faced each other on an equal level. Or slightly more than equal, for Gideon was somewhat taller, though it was the consciousness of his superior hand, not his height, that sustained him. "Three things: you will recognize Miss Martin as your legitimate cousin, you will settle an annuity upon her that will give her a reasonable competence for the rest of her life, and"—Gideon permitted himself a small smile—"you will forgive the mortgage which you hold on my property."

Magnus scowled. "You're a bold devil. It may be years before the case is won, and there is no guarantee of

325

success."

"Then you must judge if the prize is worth the gamble."

"And if I refuse?"

"Then I must sell the certificate to someone else."

Their eyes locked as they gauged each other's resolve. It was Magnus who looked away first. Giving a great shout of laughter, he held out his hand. "Done."

"Done." Gideon clasped the other man's hand with a fervor that spoke his relief. Magnus had taken the bait.

The banker sat down at his desk, picked up a pen and scribbled rapidly for a few minutes, then signed his name with a flourish and handed the document to Gideon. "These are the points of our agreement. When I see this certificate of marriage, when I am assured of its authenticity, I will satisfy you on all three."

Gideon perused the paper carefully, then folded it and put it in his pocket. Magnus's terms were generous. The annuity he proposed would give Fiona six hundred pounds a year. "Now," Gideon said, "some words of advice. It will be to your advantage, as well as Miss Martin's, if the thing can be settled without undue contention. Parminter is the weak point. He's in debt—to you, I believe, as well as others—and he's betrothed to Alessandra di Tassio, whose mother knows nothing as yet to his disadvantage. There's leverage there if you care to use it."

"I have reason to see him in any case. I'll ask him to call tonight." Magnus extended his hand once more. Gideon took it without comment and prepared to leave the room. As he reached the door he was arrested by Magnus's voice. "Satisfy my curiosity, Carne. What is your connection to Miss Martin?"

"I intend to marry her."

Magnus looked at him sharply. "Then it *is* all for you. The establishment of her legitimacy, the annuity . . ."

"Perhaps," Gideon said equably. "She is destitute and that may have influenced her decision. I would give her a choice."

"Ah. You're an unexpected man, Carne."

Gideon smiled. "No — only a man concerned for his future comfort." He turned and left the office, well satisfied with what he had done. Magnus had met, nay, had exceeded his expectations. He prayed that Adrian would do the same.

At half-past six, in the saloon at Boodle's, Sir Hugo Prebble learned of Gideon's speech in the House of Lords. He had the news from Poppy Bagshot, a plump, excitable man with whom Hugo had been at school. Bagshot had recently fallen heir to a baronetcy and a snug little fortune and had sought to increase it through an investment in Woodbourn-Prebble. Hugo had put him off, and Bagshot, his small, round eyes gleaming with malice, came up to thank him for it. "In a peck of trouble, old boy," he said. "Glad you steered me clear of it."

Hugo had no idea what he was talking about, but at the word "trouble" he set himself to find out. It took an age, for Bagshot tended to wander at the best of times, and his tale was interrupted at several points by other members who drew round, eager to share their own versions of what had happened.

When he had the whole story, Hugo made his escape. His heart, which was dickey at best, was pounding in his chest, and his face, someone was kind enough to inform him, had grown alarmingly white. He stood for a moment outside the door of the club to catch his breath, then collected his curricle and drove to Parminter House.

At first Hugo had been inclined to think Gideon's accusations pure fabrication, the opening gambit in some game he was playing with them all, but the more he

327

thought about what he knew of the marquis's character and temper, the more likely the entire story became. There was only one thing to be done: he would have to confront Parminter directly.

But Parminter, damn him, was not at home. Nor was George. Hugo left an urgent message for both of them, then returned to his carriage where he sat, indecisive and fuming, gnawing on his glove. The obvious move was to see Carne, but Hugo did not think he would find a sympathetic ear. Acknowledging that he was a little afraid of his brother-in-law, he drove instead to the home of Magnus Melchett.

Melchett agreed that they had a problem. Carne had been to see him, he said, and had shown him the letter. He accepted Carne's word that it was a forgery. Parminter was a clod-pate, and had he not been his own cousin. . . . He let the threat hang in the air. As for the effect of Carne's revelations on Woodbourn-Prebble, surely Sir Hugo understood that they were bound to be severe. Those investors who'd put their money into the company on the strength of Parminter's representations would have to be reimbursed — the company's credit would be irreparably damaged otherwise. They would have to proceed on a more modest scale. Hugo wanted to pursue this last point, but Melchett dismissed him with another spate of words that left Hugo feeling, as he thought about it later, that control of Woodbourn-Prebble was slipping rapidly out of his hands.

Eventually he found George at Brooks's and took him off for a late supper during which he poured out his grievances. George, who had already heard the story, was suitably grim. He was not disturbed by Parminter's deception, but he was furious that Carne had made it public. Hugo continued to feel aggrieved. The immorality of Parminter's action did not concern him, but he felt he should have been told about it in advance.

By the end of the meal Hugo was so disguised that George sent his own groom to see him home. Hugo remembered very little of the journey. Clare was out when he returned to Davies Street and he went straight to bed where, paradoxically, he was unable to sleep. Thinking once more of confronting Parminter, he sat up and swung his legs over the side of the bed, but a wave of nausea forced him to lie down again. He groaned and buried his face in the pillow. No matter, he thought, as sleep at last overtook him, George had promised to talk to the marquis.

"You've been a fool, Adrian. If you want to avoid still worse, you'd best make sure of the Tassio girl while you can." Having delivered himself of this parting shot, George took himself off from his brother-in-law's dressing room. As the door closed, Adrian swore savagely, lurched to the table where he kept a set of decanters at the ready, and splashed a generous amount of brandy into the nearest glass. He barely tasted the expensive liquid as he tossed it down in one draft and it was only with an effort that he refrained from hurling the fine leaded glass into the fireplace.

The day had gone steadily worse from start to finish. He'd spent the afternoon showing his Thames-side villa to his betrothed, her younger brother, and her new companion, a mousy woman who was some connection of Michael Langley's. It had not been the pleasantest of expeditions, as young Simon had a way of asking questions and not being satisfied with the answers. On his return to Parminter House shortly after six, Adrian had found a letter from Magnus Melchett, asking him to call at his earliest convenience. Curious but not concerned, he had stopped by Magnus's rooms in Piccadilly on his way to join a party of friends at Vauxhall.

Magnus had been dining with his sister, Mrs. Ford, a sharp-eyed, sharp-tongued woman, attractive enough in her way, but not a woman with whom a fellow could be comfortable. Adrian had been relieved when Magnus had taken him into the study, but that was before he heard what Magnus had to say. Adrian reached for the decanter again. Grandmama was right, that branch had no sense of what was owed to the family. After all, what Magnus called his grossly stupid deception would never have been discovered had Carne not got hold of William's letter. Adrian scowled, his hand clenching the glass. Carne must have bribed someone to steal the letter for him. A fellow couldn't trust his own servants these days.

And if Magnus's tirade hadn't been bad enough, he had had the audacity to suggest that he could not wait indefinitely for repayment of his loan, for all the world as if Adrian was some stranger and not his own cousin and the head of the family. When Adrian at last made his escape and joined his friends, wanting nothing more than to forget the entire incident, he had been beseiged by questions and some out and out accusations. To crown the evening, for the first time in his twenty-seven years, he'd been given the cut direct. And by Letty Pyne, a nobody who a week ago would have been flattered if he had asked her to stand up with him for a country dance. Why only last Tuesday her brother had offered Adrian a new hunter if he could get him a partnership in Woodbourn-Prebble.

His interview with George had not improved his spirits. As Adrian downed his third glass of brandy, his brother-in-law's parting words echoed in his head. *Best make sure of the Tassio girl while you can.* Fortunately Alessa's mother was away from London for a few days, but this was a mixed blessing, as she had gone to Southampton to meet her husband, who was returning from Sweden. They would both be back in London soon, and if the princess didn't kick up a row about this India business, Langley was sure to do so. Then there was the matter of the debts which Magnus had so unsportingly threatened to call to their attention.

Adrian returned his glass to the table and moved to his writing desk with something approaching a sense of purpose. All was not lost. His fortune might be hemmed in by a lot of archaic restrictions, but he was not a pauper. If Magnus insisted on having the money, there must be some way to raise it. He would call on his solicitor in the morning. And, not being the fool George had called him, he had already considered the need to make sure of Alessa. Pulling open one of the smaller desk drawers, Adrian drew out a special license.

He stared at the document for a long moment. Despite all the congratulations and plans, his marriage had not seemed real until now. He pulled open another drawer, empty save for a miniature lying against a length of black velvet. No one could really capture Aline's elusive quality, but Andrew Robertson had made a fair attempt. The ash brown hair which conjured up visions of moonlight, the blue eyes at once cool and pensive, the full lips curled in a half-smile as vulnerable as it was seductive. Adrian took the miniature in his hand, damned her, not for the first time, for leaving him, then pressed his lips to the picture in apology.

If only Carne had had the decency to get himself killed, Adrian would have married Aline. Alessa could no more fill her place than Clare had done, but marriage to her would certainly improve his situation. He carefully returned Aline's miniature to the drawer, then reached for a sheet of writing paper and penned a brief note to his betrothed. At least Alessa, unlike Aline, could be counted on to comply with his instructions.

* * *

The news of the probable change in her fortune left Fiona with a dizzying sense of freedom. If Magnus Melchett could be trusted, she would be released from the bonds of obligation that had bound her all her life. She could go where she pleased, live as she pleased. She could sleep the morning away, if that was her inclination, and drink chocolate at midnight, and bite her thumb at the censorious, disapproving world. She would do none of these, of course, but the knowledge that she could tore open the armor that had become her second nature, and she laughed so hard that Gideon became concerned and forced some wine upon her to calm her down.

She pushed his hand away, spilling a few drops on the deep red carpet. She dropped to the floor and hastily blotted them with her handkerchief, which turned red as it soaked up the wine. Fiona stared at it and laughed. Red, the color of liberation. Still laughing, she looked up at him. "I have no need of wine. I am dizzy enough."

Gideon helped her up and then released her. He seemed uncommonly serious. "You're free."

"I know," she said, studying his face.

"Of me, if you like."

It was a moment before she understood him. The laughter welling up inside her stilled. Had she once more mistaken his intent? There had been a time when she had thought he loved her, but he had proved her wrong. Now, wiser in the ways of the heart, she thought he came to her out of need, but she was wrong again. He wanted to be free of her, free of responsibility for her future. How clever of Gideon to arrange it so.

But the moment of bitterness quickly passed. Still searching his face, she saw only a mirror of the longing she felt for him, and she knew that what he offered her was the freedom to go or stay. She had no choice. She would not leave him, though she were ten times free.

Holding out her hands, she said, "I am yours, if you want me."

For answer he drew her to him. She could not seek for reassurance in his face, but it was in his arms, and the feel of his lips against her hair, and the heat of his mouth when it sought her own.

That night he was very gentle with her, as though her affirmation had abated the urgency of his need. She woke with a feeling of great joy which carried her through the morning chores and the children's lessons and an hour devoted to darning stockings and mending a great rent in Teddy's best pair of trousers. When Adam came to tell her there was a gentleman waiting in the hall below, she went to meet him feeling nothing but a lively curiosity. Even when she knew the identity of her visitor—she could tell it was George before she was a quarter way down the stairs—her good humor did not desert her. Nothing George could do or say could touch her now.

Still, she had no wish to appear too cordial. She schooled her features to their customary reserve and slowed her pace. "Mr. Barrington-Forbes," she said when she had reached the hall.

He swept her a graceful bow. "Miss Alastair. I trust I find you well."

She nodded but did not give him her hand. Waiting till Adam had disappeared through a door at the back of the hall, she spoke again. "Have you come to call on me or Lord Carne?"

"I came to speak to you, if I may. Please. Forget our last unfortunate encounter. I was quite out of my head with an old jealousy." He gave her a smile that begged forgiveness, causing Fiona to remember that he could be quite charming when he chose. "Is there someplace we can talk? I have had some disturbing news and have been concerned about you."

There was nowhere to take him but the library, which was Gideon's particular preserve. Fiona hesitated. She'd no wish to remain in George's company, but he was probably in Lady Parminter's confidence and she ought to discover what he had to say. She moved to the library door. "In here." The room, Fiona saw with relief, was in order, though the door to Gideon's study was slightly ajar. She resolutely ignored it and motioned George to a seat.

"I called at Prebble's house the night before last," George said. "Hugo was out, but I found Clare. She was in a rare passion. She told me you'd been there, and Carne's son as well. She thought it odd."

"Not at all," Fiona said calmly. "I took Peter to Davies Street to retrieve a book he had left there on his last holiday."

"And did something more, I understand. Did you really find your father's will? Clare said she took it from you at pistol point, but I could hardly credit it. Egad, you might have been hurt."

His concern appeared quite genuine, but Fiona was not deceived. "Clare was overset. When that happens, there is no stopping her. I assure you, I am used to it."

"And she burned the will? You actually saw it, that was what it was?"

There was no reason not to tell him. He had had the whole from Clare, and more perhaps than had actually happened. "Yes, it was a will. I had heard that my father made one shortly before he died. I found it in the drawer of a table that had once stood in his bedroom." Then she added deliberately, "I had hoped he had left a letter as well. We were estranged, you know, and—" She made a small gesture of apology. "I suppose I wanted some sign of forgiveness. But the will was all I found."

There was a barely perceptible relaxation in George's posture, and Fiona knew she had been right. Lady Parminter had told George of her father's marriage to Penelope Melchett when she asked for his help in breaking into the Woodbourn-Prebble warehouse. And when Clare told him of the will, he must have wondered if there were other papers as well. Praying she had persuaded him there were none, Fiona said, "I thank you for your concern, but this is between Clare and me. There is nothing that can be done."

"I would help you if I could." He raised a hand to forestall her protest. "Without conditions. I swear it."

"Thank you, but no."

"Then let me speak to Hugo. Your father must have left you something, and Clare owes it to you."

"Please."

He bowed his head in acquiescence. After a moment he said, "What will you do?"

It would give her great pleasure to tell him, and she did so. "I am going to marry Lord Carne."

Fiona saw with delight that she had surprised him. George sat back and regarded her for a long moment, then slowly shook his head. "I would wish you well, Fiona, if I could. You must not go into this blindly."

"Believe me, I do not."

"I fear you do. There are things about Carne you do not know."

Fiona stiffened. "There is nothing you can tell me about Lord Carne that I wish to hear."

George leaned forward and his voice softened, though every word was distinct. "It pains me to speak of this, but for the sake of your future you must hear it. Carne and I have never been friends, you know that. What you do not know is that there was a time in our acquaintance when he had cause to hate me. He married a woman of great beauty and eager appetites. I would not speak ill of the dead, but you must understand that Aline was—I do not quite know how to put it—she was wanton."

335

"That's enough." Fiona stood up abruptly. "I don't want to hear this."

"Wanton," George repeated, getting lazily to his feet. "I use the word advisedly. Listen to me, Fiona. There is a reason you must know this. I had known Aline for several years, but it was only when I visited Hugo shortly before her wedding that I realized the depths of her corruption. I suppose it was the prospect of marriage that set her burning—I don't exaggerate, she was avid for sensation—and she gave herself to me."

Fiona felt a shock of physical revulsion. How could George speak so of a woman, any woman, but particularly a woman he had used in that way? He must have seen her distaste, for he smiled wryly and said the words calculated to mitigate his fault. "I do not excuse myself. What I did was unforgivable. But I was younger then, and hot-blooded." He shrugged. "It is the way of men. Women learn it to their peril."

But not all men. Fiona was no innocent, but what George had done went beyond the bounds of decency. And Gideon . . . "Did Lord Carne know?"

"Not at the time. I may have been her first lover, my dear, but I was hardly her last, and Carne knew soon enough the kind of woman he had married. Five years ago Aline found herself increasing again, with Parminter's child, I think, and she and Carne had the devil of a row. She told Carne he was her husband and therefore the father of any child she happened to bear. Even Peter—" He stopped, as though some delicacy forbade him to put it into words.

"No." Not Peter. Fiona could believe the rest—many families were casual enough about paternity once a son had been conceived—but not Gideon's firstborn, not his heir. "You can't be sure."

"The lady was quite clear on the point."

Even in her most private moments, Fiona had not

dared censure Lady Carne. But this gratuitous insult went too far. Lady Carne must have known the matter was open to doubt. Gideon must have known it as well, but the uncertainty would be enough to destroy him. It did much to explain the depth of his pain.

George had been watching the play of expression on her face. "You can see now why Carne began to hate me. You can see why he began to dream of revenge. And what better revenge, Fiona, than repeating my own offense."

Fiona held herself quite still, trying to hold the horror at bay.

"He did it carefully, my dear. With deliberation and—if I can judge from the outcome—with consummate skill. Think of the satisfaction he must have taken in returning the compliment. I had soiled the woman he was about to marry. He debauched the woman I intended to make my wife."

Chapter Twenty

When George left, saying he would see himself out, Fiona remained in the library, unable to move or think or feel anything at all. Small things caught her attention: a gap in one of the library shelves, a piece of lint under a nearby table, a corner of the rug that had been disarranged in George's passing. She walked toward the door and straightened the rug with her foot, then looked around the room, his room, Gideon's room, marked with his smell and his presence. It had been Lady Carne's room too, though Fiona doubted that the volatile Aline had spent much time here. The sun, flooding through the windows, made pools of radiance on the rug, its muted colors showing sudden patches of vivid red and lustrous indigo. Strange, with all that sun, that she should feel so cold.

She caught sight of the door into the study, still ajar, and began to tremble. "No," she whispered, and again, "no." Then she ran into the hall and up the stairs, not stopping until she was safely inside her own room with the door shut and locked behind her.

He had not loved her and the knowledge had hurt her bitterly, but through all the long years of her exile she had been sustained by an image of mutual passion and mutual need. He had been in pain, and she had offered him solace. She had been eager to bestow her heart, and he had taken it. But it was a lie, all a lie. Gideon had not wanted her, Fiona Martin, James Woodbourn's bastard daughter. He had wanted the woman who belonged to George Barrington-Forbes, and her face, her figure, her mind, her very soul were a matter of supreme indifference. How plausible he had been—the accidental meetings, the conversations during rambling walks, the delighted discovery of mutual ways of thought and then of eyes and skin and hair, the first tentative touch, and then the bursting of the bonds of restraint. It was all a sham. She felt demeaned and diminished and soiled.

She stripped off her dress, poured water into the basin, and began to wash, her face, her neck, her hands, her arms. Nothing could take away the taint. She began to think about Aline Prebble, a young girl selling her beauty to a man above her station. What was it George had said? Eager for experience? Avid for sensation? Fiona Martin had not been so very different. What a pity she had not married George, as Gideon had advised, and presented him with Gideon's children or those of whichever lover she chose to take. She could have kept her heart and had something to call her own.

Fiona found herself standing with the washcloth in her hand, dripping water onto petticoat and shoes and carpet. She stared at the cloth a moment, then flung it into the basin. She was burning with a feverish heat and shivering uncontrollably with cold. She sank to the floor and began to cry, softly at first, and then with greater and greater abandon, until she thought she would drown in her tears.

When the storm was over she mopped up the carpet, changed her petticoat and gown, and straightened her hair. Then she sat quietly, waiting for the signs of weeping to leave her ravaged face. She was very angry.

After a time the anger subsided, leaving something hard and cold in its place. Fiona left the children to Barbara's care, picked up a basket of mending, and returned to the library to await Gideon's return. She did not know what she would say to him, but she could not continue in his house without speaking of what George had told her.

When he opened the door at last she was letting down the hem of one of Beth's dresses. She took another half-dozen stitches, knotted the thread, and clipped it with her scissors. Only then did she look up. Gideon's smile did not conceal his surprise. Fiona did not usually use the library for domestic offices. As he watched her, his smile faded. "Something's happened."

Fiona folded the dress carefully and placed it in the basket, put scissors, thimble, and needle in her workbox, and stood up to face him. "George was here."

Gideon was immediately alert. Fiona could almost see the muscles in his arms and shoulders tightening, ready to attack. "Did he threaten you?"

"On the contrary. He made me an apology of sorts."

"But he said something," Gideon insisted. "Something to overset you."

Fiona felt an immense weariness. She thought she would gladly be dead. She wished that she could shut away the sight of his face, every line of which her fingers and eyes had traced. "You lied to me, Gideon. Everything was false between us. From the beginning, every word, every look, every touch. You cared nothing for me; you were never conscious of me. You didn't see me, you didn't hear me, you didn't know me. I was nothing but your pawn, a pawn in the monstrous game you were playing with George. Your wife was a pawn too. That was it, wasn't it? An exchange of favors, or was it an eye for an eye? He soiled your bed and you soiled his. How clever, how neat, how fit."

"Fiona! For the love of God!" It was what Gideon had feared from the moment she'd come to him again. It was the nightmare that had haunted him in those fever-wracked months in Spain. It was the core of his self-disgust.

She stood so close in her pride and her pain. He wanted to bury himself in her, to blot out the memory of Aline, to shut out the memory of what he'd done to the woman who, unthinking, had given him her heart. Two steps would have brought him to her, but he could not take them.

"It's true then." Her voice was very quiet.

Gideon knew that she was waiting for a denial, an excuse, an explanation. He could tell her George had distorted what had happened. He could tell her that he had not sought her out, though when they met he welcomed her companionship. And more besides. She was a beautiful woman and it was not to be wondered that he had desired her. But he would not have touched her had she not made it clear that she desired him as well. He could claim that he had recognized her quality even then, that there had indeed been something between them, something caring, though it was not love. But there was a kernel of truth in her accusation. Had she not been George's fiancée, had he not just learned that George had lain with Aline, he might have tempered his desire. "It's true," he said, "but it's not true."

"Don't fence with me, Gideon. Don't batter me with your words."

He knew he had lost her. He would have lost her in any case, no matter how plausible a case he could have made for his actions. "Very well. It's true." It was what she wanted to hear. The seed had been sown, and its bitter fruit was evident in her dead eyes and pale lips. Better now than later, when they were indissolubly tied. Gideon sent up a silent prayer of thanksgiving for the paper that Magnus had signed, the paper that would allow Fiona to leave him with her dignity intact.

All the years of his life he would remember her as she faced him now, the slender, pliant body tensed to withstand the knowledge of his guilt, the wisps of fair hair escaping their confinement to soften the contours of her ravaged face, the finely drawn mouth whose lips would no longer soften beneath his touch, the long gray eyes from which the light had fled. He studied her with a fierce concentration, willing himself to commit every part of her to memory, and he knew, with a sudden blinding certainty, that what he felt for her went beyond passion, beyond pity, beyond guilt. He loved this woman he had ruined so very long ago. He loved her now, he loved her yesterday. He had loved her through all the years of his exile. He had loved her from the very beginning, not as he had loved Aline, not as he had loved any woman before. Fiona held all his hope of happiness, but he had killed her love, her passion, her trust. And for the rest of his life he would have to live with the knowledge of what he had destroyed.

At his last words Gideon heard the faint exhalation of her breath. Her body lost some of its rigidity and she turned and bent to pick up the basket of mending. She had retreated to some distant place where he could not follow. He longed to call her back but did not know what to say. Then the door was unceremoniously opened and Barbara came into the room, bringing a welcome air of ordinary life.

"Oh! I'm sorry, Lord Carne, I didn't know you were at home. Is Peter with you? He seems to have gone missing."

"Nonsense. He's probably in the stable. I'll have a look." Gideon strode to the door, relieved to have a problem with which he could deal.

But Peter was neither in the stable nor in the small garden behind the house. Gideon returned to the hall to find that Fiona had organized a search. They scoured the house from cellar to attic, looking in the rooms they were using and those that were still shut, but Peter was not to be found. Teddy and Beth had not seen him since early afternoon. Nor had anyone else.

"I'll tan his hide," Adam said. "He knows he's not to go off without he tells us."

"Where would he go?" Barbara's voice was sharp with worry.

Gideon frowned. "The question is, why?"

"He's reading." Beth's small, light voice was so soft they did not at first take in her words. "He wanted to read," she insisted as the four adults turned their attention to her. "He went to get a book."

Gideon heard a sound of dismay and turned to see Fiona staring at him, her face white. Comprehension flooded him. Fiona must have taken George to the library. If Peter had been there unseen, if he had heard what George had said . . . Gideon turned abruptly to Adam. "Harness the curricle. I'm going out."

Fiona spoke up. "Please. I'd like to come with you."

He nodded, and they did not speak again until they were seated in the curricle and he had turned the horses toward Piccadilly. "I would swear he was not in the library when I took George there," Fiona said, wrapping her shawl tightly around her, "but he could have gone into the study. The door was ajar."

"He's never gone in there before, at least not since I've been back in London."

"All the more reason to satisfy his curiosity about his father. He went looking for a book and saw that the study door was open. What more natural than to step inside? What more natural than to stay hidden when I brought George into the library? He would wait there, listening till it was safe to come out. He would have heard it all. The question is, where would he go?"

She was trying to be practical, but the look on her

face reminded Gideon of their meeting at Bow Street. Once again he was in no position to comfort her. "He has but one friend in London," Gideon said, concentrating all his attention on the horses, trying to keep his fears at bay. "He'll be with Simon di Tassio."

It took them some time to find that he was not. They stood in the elegant, white-columned circular hall while the footman, who was very glad to see Miss Alastair but not sure that he ought to be, informed them that neither Mr. Langley nor the princess was at home, and there was unfortunately no one else in the house save Miss Moffitt who was serving as companion to Lady Alessandra, but as they were not acquainted with Miss Moffitt he was not certain that she was prepared to receive them. Gideon suppressed an impulse to tell him to go hang Miss Moffitt and asked instead for the Prince di Tassio.

When the footman hesitated, Fiona stepped forward. "I know it's irregular, Christopher, but it's about Simon's friend Peter, and it's most urgent. We won't keep Simon long, and no one else need know we've called."

She gave him her most beguiling smile. Gideon would have done anything for that smile, and Christopher was no more immune than he. The footman directed them into an antechamber and promised to bring the prince to them at once.

"I fear he is not here," Fiona said when they were alone.

Gideon saw nothing but anxious sympathy in her eyes. Their quarrel—no, their rupture—might never have happened. "I know," he said, grateful for this respite. "But perhaps he's managed to send word."

They said nothing more until Simon arrived, somewhat out of breath and with a worried look on his face. "Has something happened to Peter?"

"He seems to have wandered off." Gideon kept his tone light. He did not want to worry young Tassio, and

344

Peter's disappearance might have an innocent explanation. "We thought he might have come to you."

"He didn't." Simon glanced at Fiona, then looked again at Gideon. "I'm not trying to protect him. I would tell you if he had."

"I'm sure you would. I didn't mean to worry you. He'll undoubtedly turn up soon."

It was meant as a signal for their departure, but Simon held his ground. "Sir. It's not something Peter would do. I mean, he wouldn't just wander off. You know that, don't you, Fiona?" She nodded and Simon, reassured, continued. "He must be in some kind of trouble, or he must think he is, and that's just as bad. You don't have to tell me what it is," Simon went on, "but I know you're going to go on looking for him, and I'd like to go with you. I'm sure you'll find him soon, but sometimes a chap needs someone his own age about when he's got a problem."

Gideon hesitated, wondering whether to confide in this serious boy with the face of an angel and a dignity beyond his years. In an odd way, Simon's presence made finding Peter seem much more likely, but there was nothing Simon could actually do and there was no reason to involve him in what was a very private problem. "I daresay you could be a help," Gideon said to ward off Simon's disappointment, "but I can hardly take you off when your mother is not here."

"She needn't know anything about it," Simon said with a flash of youthful impudence. "And I'd be far safer with you than haring off on my own, which is what I'll do if you won't take me."

Fiona had a vivid image of the princess's wrath the previous autumn when Simon had taken it into his head to run off to help Verity find the Windhams. "We had better take him," she told Gideon. "He's quite capable of doing exactly as he's said." They might have need of Simon, too. If Peter had learned that his paternity was in question, he would beat a frightened retreat and Simon might then be the only one who could reach him. "Simon, you will have to leave a letter for your mother."

He grinned. "All right." Then he added in an anxious voice, "You won't leave without me, will you?"

"No," Gideon assured him. "We won't leave." After Simon left the room, he turned to Fiona. "How did you know I'd agree to this mad-brained scheme?"

"You had no choice," she said calmly.

"I did. I need only have asked the footman—"

"To keep him under lock and key? It would do no good. Believe me, I know."

Gideon sighed. "Yes, that's what I thought." Despite his misgivings, he was not entirely unhappy with the idea of Simon's company. His next meeting with Peter would be a difficult one. "You know where he must be, don't you?"

She nodded. "With George. I should have realized it from the beginning. He would want George to tell him directly. That's his way."

"Yes." Gideon paced the room, anxious to be off. He would have wished Peter to be spared the truth about his mother, but the boy was old enough to hear it. Perhaps he was even old enough to forgive.

Simon did not keep them waiting long. Christopher, he said, had been persuaded that there was nothing really irregular in his going out in his former governess's company, and the footman saw them to the door with no evidence of dismay. They were soon crowded together in Gideon's curricle and made the short drive to Parminter House in silence. Simon knew when to hold his tongue. He had achieved his objective and would not jeopardize his position by asking awkward questions.

It was a far grander house than the one in which the young prince now resided, grander even than that belonging to the Duke of Waterford in which he had been a guest when he'd first come to London, and Simon was suitably impressed. "It's much larger than our house in Cagliari," he told Fiona as they waited to be admitted, "but I don't think it's as—" He stopped, not sure how to put his feeling into words.

"As pleasant?"

"Yes, that's it. Fiona, do you think Peter really is here?"

"We'll know soon," she said as the door opened and they were shown into the vast entrance hall. But their search was frustrated by an austere footman in red-and-black livery who informed them that Mr. Barrington-Forbes was not at home and then declined to tell them anything about his whereabouts. The marquis was also away from home, he said in answer to Gideon's question, and then, to forestall any more such demands, he added that the marchioness and Lady Lydia were at Sundon. Perhaps they would care to leave their cards.

Gideon controlled his impatience with difficulty. "I have reason to believe that my son may have called on Mr. Barrington-Forbes this afternoon," he said. "A boy of twelve years. Can you tell me if he's been here?"

The footman raised his brows. His expression said that twelve-year-old boys did not come calling in this house, and if they did, they would certainly not be admitted.

"Were you on duty in the hall this afternoon?" Gideon persisted. "No? Can you tell me who was? Can I see him?"

The footman was growing agitated by this unaccustomed questioning and did not seem sure where the limits of his responsibility lay. Fiona intervened. "Is Lord Robert at home?"

Relieved, the footman said that he was and went off to fetch him. "Why didn't he tell us Robin was at home?" Gideon inquired.

"I daresay it's because Lord Robert is not of age. Servants make these distinctions, and they're careful about whom they allow to give them orders." Fiona smiled at the boy who'd accompanied them. "Simon understands."

Gideon reminded himself that it was a large house and it would take the retainer some time to look in all the places that Robin might be. George's absence was disturbing. Was he in fact at home and had he given orders that his presence be denied? Or had Peter come and been turned away? And if that was the case, where had he gone?

Robin came at last, clattering down the broad staircase with his hand outstretched. "Carne. What's this about your son? Oh, I say," he added as he caught sight of the others. "Miss Alastair, Simon, it's good to see you."

Robin showed no surprise at seeing Lady Alessandra's brother in Gideon and Fiona's company, and Gideon didn't take time to explain the boy's presence. "Robin, my son Peter has disappeared and I have reason to think he may have gone looking for Barrington-Forbes. We were told he's not here, but that doesn't mean Peter didn't come earlier. It could have been any time after three o'clock. Can you help us?"

Robin said he would question the servants at once, but first he led them to a small chamber on the ground floor where they could wait in more comfort. He returned a quarter-hour later with the welcome intelligence that a boy of about Peter's age had indeed called and been received by George and the less welcome news that George had ordered his carriage and taken Peter away.

Gideon made no effort to conceal his dismay. He didn't know what George was about, but by God, he was going to get his son back. "Where did they go? Did anyone in the stable know?"

"They seem to have been bound for Sundon."

"How strange. Lady Parminter is there." Fiona turned

to Gideon. "If George is taking Peter to Sundon, he can mean him no harm."

"Harm?" Robin was shocked. "I should think not. George was going there anyway, though I didn't expect him to leave till tomorrow. Walters said Peter—if it was Peter—was uncommon serious, but he didn't seem at all upset at the prospect of the journey."

Gideon turned to Fiona. "I'm going down at once. I have to get him back tonight."

"We're all going down," Fiona reminded him.

"No, it's getting late, and I can't take you both in the curricle, not that distance. Robin will see you home."

"Of course. Anything I can do to help. Though if it's a matter of a carriage, you can use one of ours. And if it's something to do with George—" Robin broke off, as though embarrassed at intruding on a personal matter. "I mean, I'm not suggesting there's anything havey-cavey about what he's done, but for all he's Lydy's husband, George does have a malicious streak, and you might be glad of some help, and anyway, it will make it easier getting into the grounds and house if one of the family is along."

This time Gideon did not hesitate. "Thank you," he said. "It's a matter of some urgency."

"I'll order the carriage." Robin made for the door, then turned back and looked at Gideon. "I heard about your speech, Carne. It put Adrian atop of the house. Never seen him in such a passion." He grinned. "I'll see that your cattle are sent home. We'll be at Sundon before nine."

Chapter Twenty-one

At five o'clock that afternoon, Sir Hugo Prebble took refuge in a quiet corner of the saloon at Boodle's. He opened his newspaper and held it ostentatiously in front of his face, a discouragement to possible attempts at conversation. The past twenty-four hours had been a disaster, and he needed time to think.

He had wakened late that morning with a vile taste in his mouth and a splitting head, and the day had proved no better than the evening before. Clare had been beside herself with rage at what Gideon had done to Lord Parminter, which became somehow confused with what Fiona had done to her. Hugo eventually made his escape, only to find that the story of Carne's speech, now duly reported in the papers, was on everyone's lips. Lord Mayne, a youngish man who purported to be a friend of Lord Parminter's, was the first to hunt Hugo down. Mayne had put a very sizable legacy that had recently come his way into Woodbourn-Prebble, and he told Hugo, with some choler, that he would never have credited Parminter with such a filthy action and if he were not allowed to withdraw his stake at once he would lay an action against every one of his partners. After a fruitless effort to convince him that gold had never been the company's chief interest and that the investment prospects in iron and coal remained good, Hugo sent Lord Mayne off to see Magnus Melchett.

That was the easiest of his encounters. Parminter, Hugo learned in the course of the afternoon, had pocketed a cool two thousand from one of their new partners (a sum he had not seen fit to share with Hugo) for the privilege of investing his money in the company, while another had been so obliging as to tear up Parminter's vowels (for a gambling debt in four figures) for the same reason. The bloody fool . . . Parminter had more blunt than Hugo would ever see, but there seemed no limit to his greed. Hugo, who considered himself a good judge of men, had been very proud of his friendship with the marquis. These discoveries shook his confidence to the core.

It was for this reason he had taken refuge in his club, Boodle's being a quiet place in which no one would be gauche enough to interrupt his perusal of the *Times* with stories of the Marquis of Parminter. An hour in its peaceful confines did much to restore Hugo's composure and, growing somewhat bored with his own company, he was happy enough to put down his paper when Roy Hillman entered the saloon. Hillman was not a close friend—they had been at school together—but Hugo knew him well enough to accept his offer of a drink.

"Wouldn't have believed it of Parminter," Hillman said some time later with what Hugo considered unnecessary spite. "He must have known it wasn't his brother's hand."

"Not necessarily. William Parminter writes a fearful scrawl. Anyone could have done it. Anyone with cause to harm the company." Hugo leaned forward in a confidential pose. "We have enemies. Bow Street has never been satisfied about the fire."

It was the story Hugo had concocted to make sense of Carne's outrageous accusations, and though he was now less inclined to believe it, the company had to be protected. Hillman did not believe it at all. "Don't be an ass,

Prebble—everyone's saying he wrote it himself."

Hugo felt his face grow warm. "That comes close to slander."

"Here! It's not you I'm accusing." Hillman sank back in his chair and studied the play of light on the amber liquid in his glass. "Though why you would want to defend Parminter, of all people . . ." He let the thought trail off.

Something in his words or manner caught Hugo's attention. "What do you mean, of all people?"

Hillman gave him a look that combined incredulity and disdain. "Good God, Prebble, the man's been covering your wife. It's been going on for months."

The crudeness of the statement was an added blow. Hugo thought inconsequently that Hillman was paying him out for one or two snubs when he had met him in Parminter's company. Better to think of that than of Clare lying down before the handsome golden-haired man with the impeccable lineage who had claimed to be his friend. Hugo stood up, feeling acutely ill.

"I say, Prebble, are you all right?" Hillman's malice showed through the veil of his concern. "Didn't mean to upset you. Thought you knew . . . everybody does."

Everybody. Everybody but the cuckolded husband. Hugo did not know how he got out of the saloon, how he found his way to the street, how he secured his carriage, but by the time he turned his horses into Davies Street the shock had worn off, replaced by a sense of outrage and ill-usage.

It was not sexual pride that aroused Hugo's wrath. A man had his needs and women were necessary to fill them, as well as to do a host of other useful things, yet by and large Hugo preferred the company of men. But he could not bear being made to look the fool, and for that Parminter would pay.

Though not before he had wrung an admission of guilt

352

from Clare. Hugo was a cautious man, and at the back of his mind lurked the thought that Hillman's story could be nothing but a piece of malicious gossip, of the sort that was entertaining enough when it did not involve your own person. So when he reached his house he inquired about his wife's whereabouts, took the stairs two at a time, and strode toward her dressing room, where he flung open the door, dismissed her maid, and prepared to confront the woman who had done him such a grievous wrong.

It was not easy to know how to begin. One could not step forward with an upraised fist and shout, "So, madam! I have found you out at last!" Clare would order him from the room, or worse, she would laugh. So Hugo blurted out the core of his complaint. "Why the hell couldn't you have been more discreet?"

In their normal intercourse, Clare would have returned taunt for taunt, but she said nothing at all, and this, together with her sudden pallor, told him that Hillman was right. He didn't blame his wife. Women were easily led and Clare, with her vanity and her longing to be accepted into a society from which her father's birth and occupation had excluded her, would be easy prey for a marquis. It was Parminter's fault — Parminter, who was ten years his junior and even younger than Clare. Parminter, the man he had made his partner, the man he had given the freedom of his house, the man who had abused his trust and brought his company to ruin.

Hugo had no problem with words now. They came in a torrent: past and present, the affair and the company, the loss of money, and the loss of his own reputation. Clare, recovered from the shock of his accusation, heard him out in silence. He knew she was preparing a counterattack, but he didn't care. Clare could weep and rage all she liked. Nothing would deter him from avenging this insult to his honor.

To his surprise Clare's first words were neither denial nor excuse nor expression of concern for her husband. "What will happen to him? About the letter—no one can prove he wrote it, can they?"

It was incredible. "You admit it, then."

Clare stared at him as though he had raised an irrelevant point. "Don't be a fool, Hugo."

"It's true," he insisted.

"What will happen to him?"

"Tell me it's true."

"It's true," she cried out, "yes, it's true! What if it is? Did you expect me to tell you? I didn't think you'd care."

"You're my wife."

She laughed. "You're ridiculous. Everyone does it. Aline was a wanton and you never said a word."

Hugo was furious. "Aline was never indiscreet."

"Nor was I."

"Everyone knows."

"Not from me."

They stared at each other, breathing hard. He knew now how it had been, and he knew the moment Clare had reached the same conclusion: Parminter. Parminter had boasted of his conquest. He would kill him.

Hugo turned on his heel and left the room.

"Hugo!" Clare was at the door, calling after him. "Where are you going?"

"To find him."

He heard her moan, "Oh, my God!" but by then he was at the stairs and he heard no more.

Fiona's first view of the house in which her mother had been born was across an expanse of water, through a filter of willow trees. Disconcertingly conscious of Gideon's eyes upon her, she had turned to the window more for her own peace of mind than out of any particular curiosity, and she was taken quite by surprise when the carriage lurched around a bend in the winding drive, bringing Sundon into view. Framed by the dark of sky and water, washed almost white by the moonlight, it looked as cool and uncompromising as the family which had shaped her mother's life and her own. And yet there was a certain graceful serenity to the domed building which ran in a long elegant ribbon along the lake. The ghostlike setting lent the illusion that this was more than a mere house, and for a moment Fiona thought she might understand, if not forgive, her grandmother's willingness to sacrifice so much for Sundon and all it represented.

"Considering it's impossibly overdone, it's not half bad," Robin remarked. "I'll say this for Penelope Quentin, she had good taste. A lot of the ideas were hers, though Hawksmoor did the design and supervised the work. Personally I'd prefer something Yorkist or Tudor at the very least, but for a baroque monstrosity, Sundon's better than Blenheim or Castle Howard."

Fiona smiled in gratitude. She doubted if Robin knew how much she welcomed his attempt at distraction. Of course he could not, for he didn't know that by birth Sundon was almost as much a part of her past as it was of his own. He didn't know that she was his sister, though he would know soon enough, just as he would know that he himself was illegitimate. She had given Magnus Melchett the power to prove it. Looking at Robin's friendly, concerned face, Fiona found herself wondering, for the first time since her visit to Mr. Camford, if she had done the right thing. She no longer felt sure of anything. Except the need to find Peter.

Gideon had told them what he'd guessed of the reasons for Peter's disappearance—keeping Fiona out of the story but not sparing himself or George or Aline—then retreated into the carriage's most shadowy corner. But more often than not his eyes were fixed on Fiona and she could sense their burning intensity. Gideon's quietest moments came when his control was about to snap.

They clattered through a gateway and across a bridge, temporarily losing sight of the house, and then suddenly the drive widened and the horses slowed and Sundon loomed before them, less ethereal, and more overpowering. At close range Fiona could see that the stone walls were not white but honey-colored, and that far from being coldly formal, the house was a riot of flourishes and intricate detail.

When the carriage at last drew up in a central courtyard, Robin hurried up the steps which spilled from the entranceway in three widening tiers. By the time the others followed, a footman had opened the double doors. Fiona felt a moment of dizziness as she stared down a seemingly endless expanse of pale gray stone broken by diamonds of black marble. On either side a series of Corinthian columns stretched two stories high only to give way to arches which soared higher still and drew the eye to the iridescent painted dome which crowned the ceiling. More paintings adorned the archways, but it was the golden light from the candle sconces that transformed the hall, so that for all its impossible proportions it seemed warm and almost inviting.

"Barrington-Forbes," Gideon blurted out. "Where is he?"

The footman, a seemingly self-possessed young man, was taken completely by surprise. He glanced at Robin, then cleared his throat. "I believe he is taking the air, sir. But—"

"Thank you. I know the way."

It was the quiet purposefulness of Gideon's voice which alerted Fiona to danger. Acting solely on instinct born of fear, she brushed past the footman and Robin and hurried after him.

Conscious of little beyond the anger which burned in

his chest and throbbed in his temples and propelled him forward like a physical force, Gideon reached the end of the great hall and flung open the doors to the saloon. The long green and gold room was empty, but he could see George through the French windows, leaning against the balustrade of the terrace and staring out over the formal garden which had been Penelope Quentin's crowning achievement.

To cross the room and open the window was but the work of a moment. "What the hell have you done with my son?" Gideon demanded over the rattle of glass as the window fell shut.

George turned round very slowly. He held a cigar in one hand, the only spot of brightness in a landscape drained of color by the moonlight. "Ah, Carne. I was wondering when you'd arrive."

In two strides, Gideon crossed the terrace and grasped the lapels of George's very expensive coat. "Answer me, damn you. Where is my son?"

"An interesting question." George tossed down the cigar and ground it out with his heel. In the blue-tinged light, the angles of his face sharpened by the shadows, he appeared more mocking than ever. "If it's Peter to whom you're referring, I thought the reason he was here was that he isn't your son at all."

A mosaic of images and emotions exploded in Gideon's head: the sting of the caustic comments the undergraduate George had made about anything which smacked of idealism; the bitterness of his disillusionment with Aline; the gut-wrenching pain of learning that Peter was not his; the self-disgust he felt at what that revelation had made him do to Fiona; the agony of knowing he had lost Fiona for good, just when he realized how much she meant to him; the threat of losing Peter as well. They had propelled him down Sundon's lofty hall and across the expanse of saloon and terrace and now they had only one outlet. Gideon, whose primary objective in five years of warfare had been to save as many lives as possible, drew back his fist and attacked.

George gave a highly satisfactory grunt of pain and astonishment. Then he countered with all the skill of a man who spent most of his afternoons in Gentleman Jackson's and all the ferocious force of a man who hated Gideon quite as much as Gideon hated him. Only the agility he had acquired in the back alleys of Spanish towns and the presence of a small table which he lurched into quite by accident saved Gideon from falling.

George had had more practice of late and he had not been wounded. But George had never been forced to fight for his life, and Adam had taught Gideon one or two tricks that were entirely unknown in boxing saloons. He had just got a very advantageous purchase on George's shoulder when his opponent ceased to struggle and said quite calmly, "I hope you realize we aren't alone, Carne."

Though his back was to the house, Gideon knew as certainly as if he were looking at her that Fiona had come onto the terrace—and had the wit to remain quiet and not distract him as George had just done. He did not hesitate for more than a fraction of a second, but it was enough. The next thing he knew, he was sent flying through the air and landed, with a crack of bone which would no doubt be extremely painful, on the hard flagstones. Fortunately he managed to hook one hand around George's ankle just before he went rolling down the terrace steps.

The feel of comparatively soft grass and earth beneath him was a great relief. Head spinning, Gideon staggered to his feet and backed into something cold and hard: marble. Christ, of course, the whole garden was littered with statues. He used a fold of Grecian robe to steady himself and saw a flash of gray above, near the balustrade. Fiona. Yesterday the thought of her would have been enough to stop him, but now it was simply a reminder of everything he had lost. Then she shouted, "Gideon!" not in protest but in warning, and he managed to duck just in time to avoid the blow and let George smash his knuckles into the statue's marble robe.

Gideon fought then with redoubled fury. His leg was beginning to throb, which made some maneuvers impossible, but unlike George, he had experience fighting outdoors, in the half-light, on uncertain ground. He was able to turn the statues, surveying the scene with disinterested dignity, to his advantage, as he had done in the past with trees or scrub or tavern tables or whatever was at hand. But just when he'd managed to corner George against the garden's focal point, a statue of Penelope Quentin garbed as Odysseus's wife, he was once again distracted. "Father!" Peter shouted, running onto the terrace.

Robin understood enough of the rivalry between his brother-in-law and Gideon to know it would be useless to interfere. Instead of following Fiona, he ascertained from the footman that Mr. Barrington-Forbes had indeed brought a young boy down with him and that the boy was presently in the nursery. Without further questions Robin made for the nearest of the two staircases which flanked the hall, gesturing for Simon to follow.

"George and Lydia's little girl is the only one in the nursery," he explained as they climbed the stairs two at a time. "Her nurse is nice enough, but of course she had do whatever George told her." Wasting no more breath on speech, he took a shortcut across the first floor to the whitepainted backstairs, and they ran up two more flights and down a corridor to the nursery apartments.

Robin opened the door to the nursery without knocking and saw his two-year-old niece Hermione watching entranced as a boy who must be Peter Carne added another block to the towering structure on the carpet between them. But the additional block and the gust of air as the door opened were enough to upset the tower's delicate balance. Just as Peter looked up, the blocks cascaded to the floor and Hermione began to scream.

"Here, now, someone's up past her bedtime." Robin lifted Hermione in his arms and nodded to Peter. "You must be young Carne. I'm Robin Melchett, but I suppose we've both grown since we last met. I think your friend Simon wants to have a word with you." Murmuring soothingly to the little girl, Robin moved to the fireplace where the nursemaid was sitting, an expression of utter bewilderment on her face.

Simon advanced slowly into the room and dropped down opposite his friend. Peter obviously wasn't in acute danger, but his face had that pinched look which had been so much in evidence when they'd first met and which had been entirely absent at the Windhams' on Sunday. "Your father brought me down," Simon said quietly. "He's come to take you home."

"It was my father who brought *me* here," Peter said in a voice that was very low and very bitter.

"I mean your real father."

Peter flinched as if the words were a blow. "He's not—"

"He is. Just like Lord Windham is really Verity's father."

Something flickered behind Peter's bleak gaze, but then his face shuttered. "That's because Lord Windham loves Verity. My fath—Lord Carne went away when he found out I wasn't his son. And he came back only because Mama died and he was responsible for us."

"You can't be such a moon-calf as to believe that." Simon sat back on his heels. "I don't think you realize how lucky you are to have a father who cares about you so much."

Peter's gaze wavered, but he did not look convinced. "If he cares about me, why didn't he come up here with you?"

"Because he went looking for Mr. Barrington-Forbes. I expect they're in the middle of a corker of a fight by now."

For a second Peter simply stared at his friend. Then he was on his feet and running out the door. Simon and Robin caught up with him in the corridor and Robin led them down the backstairs, through a baize door, and across the great hall to the saloon. Beyond the French windows they could see Fiona gripping the terrace balustrade and two dim figures on the ground below, overshadowed by an elegantly robed statue. Peter flung open the window and raced onto the terrace, his shout of "Father!" carrying across the garden.

At the sound of his son's voice, Gideon spun round, abruptly releasing George, who sagged against the marble Penelope. "Father," Peter said again, hurrying down the terrace steps. Gideon, striding rapidly toward him, now knew that the name was meant for him and he felt a great wave of relief. "I'm sorry," Peter gasped, "I never meant—" He stopped on the bottom step and Gideon checked his own stride, knowing the next move was not up to him. Peter stared at Gideon for a long moment, then, without another word, ran straight into his father's outstretched arms.

"I hate to interrupt this affecting scene, but there are one or two points I should clarify," George said, getting to his feet. Though he was breathing hard, his voice retained its biting edge. "If anyone knew the truth of the matter it was Aline, and she always maintained that she couldn't be sure which of us had fathered Peter. I don't suppose we'll ever know the truth. Pity, but there it is."

Keeping an arm around Peter's shoulders, Gideon turned to look at the man he had been trying to beat senseless a few moments before. George's pantaloons were begrimed, his coat torn, his cravat spattered by the blood that streamed from his nose, but one could not say that he looked beaten. "On the contrary," Gideon told him. "He's my son. He always has been. Please convey to Lady Parminter my apologies for the intrusion. We must be getting back to London. My younger children will be wondering what's become of us."

Leaning heavily on Peter—his leg had suffered rather more than he'd realized—Gideon climbed the terrace steps. A trio of smiling faces greeted them, but he avoided Fiona's eyes and addressed Robin. "I'm afraid I must trouble you for the carriage."

"Of course. But I think you'd best come inside first. That cut looks as if it wants attention."

Cut? Suddenly aware of a sting in the vicinity of his jawbone, Gideon lifted his hand and felt the familiar damp warmth of blood. It must have happened when he'd fallen down the steps. Or when he'd bumped into Poseidon's trident. Gideon was loath to spend any more time under the Parminter roof, but battlefield experience told him the sooner the cut was attended to, the better. Besides, he wanted to talk to Robin. When they reached the great hall, he gave Peter's shoulder a reassuring squeeze and accepted Robin's help up one of the twin staircases.

When the men had moved out of view, Fiona started for an antechamber to which Robin had directed her. She could hear indistinguishable voices from the west wing of the house and had no desire to encounter any of the Parminter family, but before she and the boys could leave the hall, the saloon doors opened at their back. "Please, you must allow me to apologize for that disgraceful scene you were obliged to witness," George said, closing the doors behind him. "It is very lowering to find one is not as civilized as one has been led to believe."

"There's no need to apologize, Mr. Barrington-Forbes. The scene did nothing to alter my estimate of your character."

"You are too kind, Miss Alastair." The handkerchief George was forced to hold to his nose to staunch the bleeding muffled his voice and impaired his dignity somewhat. "If you will grant me a few moments of your time, there are matters we should discuss."

"I can't imagine what you could have to say to me, Mr. Barrington-Forbes. And I know I have nothing to say to you." Head held high, Fiona turned toward the corridor. The voices from the west wing were still only a garble of sound, but they were accompanied by a laugh which was clear and startlingly familiar. Just as Fiona told herself that her ears must be playing tricks on her, Simon raced past with an outraged cry. "That's my sister!"

Chapter Twenty-two

Without so much as exchanging glances, Fiona and Peter followed Simon into the vaulted corridor which ran along the front of the house at right angles to the great hall. Their feet echoing on the flagstone floor, they ran past ranks of gilded pillars and marble busts, rounded a sharp bend, and stopped only when the corridor widened into a sort of antechamber with a door in the wall to the left. Simon pulled it open without hesitation, and they stepped between columns of black scagliola and found themselves staring down two rows of exquisitely ornate walnut pews at an equally exquisite, equally ornate altar. Before the altar, flanked by branches of glittering, sweet-smelling candles, stood Simon's sister and Fiona's brother, the Marquis of Parminter. Lydia Barrington-Forbes and a simply dressed woman who looked to be some sort of superior servant were standing a little to one side. And, in front of the the altar, half-obscured by Alessa and Adrian, was a balding gentleman who was unmistakably a clergyman.

The clergyman went on speaking in a low, incomprehensible mumble, and no one looked round. Simon moved down the inlaid red-and-gold marble of the aisle and said, in a voice informed by twelve years of training in princely authority and princely responsibilities, "Stop."

The clergyman stopped speaking. The others all

turned, but astonishment kept them momentarily silent. "You can't marry her, Parminter," Simon said, advancing down the aisle with great dignity. "I forbid it."

"Oh, for heaven's sake, Simon, don't be difficult," Alessa exclaimed. "There was no need to come after me, but I'm excessively glad you are here, for now you can give me away."

Fiona suspected that Alessa was more than a little relieved to see her brother. Having learned to judge her former charge's sense of fashion with exactitude, she was sure the elopement had not been Alessa's idea. Lady Lydia was gowned for the evening in buff-colored Portuguese sarcenet with sleeves of scalloped lace, long pearl-and-gold earrings, and a double rope of pearls with a ruby clasp, but Alessa wore a simple white muslin with epaulettes, a blue satin sash, and no jewelry other than her amber cross. It was the sort of ensemble she might have chosen for an afternoon rendezvous with her betrothed, but certainly not for the wedding she had dreamed of for so long.

Simon, who showed cheerful contempt for his sister's preoccupation with fashion at the best of times, did not pause to consider such fine distinctions. "Give you away?" he said furiously. "To *Parminter?* Never."

"Now see here, old chap," the marquis began with a woefully overdone attempt at joviality.

Simon stared at him coldly. The clergyman cleared his throat. "If there is some impediment—"

"My sister is underage," Simon informed him. "And I do not give my consent."

"Really, Simon," Alessa protested.

"May I ask your connection to the bride?" inquired the clergyman, looking as if he very much wished he were elsewhere.

"For the love of God, Tingewick," Adrian exclaimed, "he's a little boy."

"I," Simon declared, enunciating clearly, "am the head of the Tassio family."

"Be that as it may," said a voice from the back of the chapel, "you are not your sister's legal guardian."

Adrian greeted this new arrival with relief. "George, thank heaven. Perhaps you can talk some sense into Tingewick."

"Gladly," said George, brushing past Fiona and Peter as if they were not there. "You have my solemn word, Tingewick, that Lady Alessandra's mother gave her consent to the match more than two weeks since. Surely Lady Parminter wrote you with the news."

"My mother—" Simon began with icy fury.

His words were drowned out by a scream from Lady Lydia as her husband moved out of the shadows. "George! Darling, what happened?" she exclaimed, running down the aisle and nearly colliding with Simon.

"A slight contretemps, nothing more," George assured her, then gave an audible gasp as his wife flung her arms around his bruised ribs.

"But your face," Lydia protested.

"Oh, don't be a watering pot, Lydy," Adrian said impatiently.

"My mother," Simon repeated, moving forward to distance himself from George, "would never countenance Alessandra marrying in such a hugger-mugger manner."

"This," said the goaded marquis, "is a perfectly respectable wedding, in my family chapel, with the local vicar officiating and my sister and her maid to act as witnesses. But now that George is here, he can act instead of Wilton." Adrian gestured toward Lydia's maid. "Thank you, Wilton, we no longer have need of your services."

By tacit agreement everyone remained silent until Wilton—obviously reluctant to be banished from so interesting a scene—had left the chapel. George steered the bewildered Lydia into one of the pews. Adrian left the altar and went to speak to George. Alessa watched them, frowning. Simon held his ground. Fiona took advantage of the silence to slip down a side aisle toward the altar. The wedding had to be stopped and she was not sure Simon would be able to carry it through on his own. "Alessa," she said quietly, "you mustn't. Your mother will be terribly hurt."

Alessa turned, as if her former governess's presence had just registered in her consciousness. She gave a smile of genuine warmth and perhaps relief as well, seemed about to ask a question, then evidently thought better of it. "It's all perfectly respectable, Fiona," she insisted. "We just didn't want to wait. It's already been nearly three weeks and *Maman* and Michael are sure to be so tiresome about the settlements—"

"Only if Parminter doesn't agree to their terms," Simon pointed out, stationing himself at the altar steps.

Alessa, who had begun to look doubtful, rounded on her brother with a flash of fury. "Don't be a beast, Simon, you know it isn't that simple."

"Mr. Tingewick," Fiona said, before the Tassio children could launch into a full scale battle, "you must realize how irregular this is."

"May I ask," inquired the much-tried Mr. Tingewick, "who you might be, ma'am?"

"Certainly. For the last five years I have been Lady Alessandra's governess."

Adrian turned in time to hear this last. "Until," he said with grim satisfaction, "you were dismissed for willfully lying—"

"Adrian!" Alessa said sharply. "You mustn't speak so to Fiona."

While Adrian stared at his betrothed in astonishment, George stepped into the breach. "Miss Alastair's objection is entirely irrelevant. She has no more legal authority over Lady Alessandra than the young prince does. The wedding has already been delayed quite long enough."

"I have more authority over her than anyone else here," Simon retorted, "and as for the wedding—"

"Alessa," Fiona said in an urgent undertone, trusting to the articulate Simon to keep George and Adrian distracted, "you can't go through with this. There are things about Parminter you don't know." It sounded hopelessly melodramatic, but short of blurting out that Alessa's betrothed was a bastard, it was the best she could do.

"If you mean that ridiculous business with the letter, Adrian has already told me. He may have behaved imprudently, but it was too bad of Lord Carne to make such thoughtless accusations, and you must see that it's all the more reason why we should marry now, before *Maman* makes a fuss."

"I don't see anything of the sort," Fiona said, deciding it was useless to try to argue whatever tissue of half-truths Adrian had told his betrothed. "But I wasn't referring to the letter."

For a moment, Alessa's dark eyes were troubled. "What then?"

"I can't explain, love, not now. It's too complicated. In a day or so it will all be clear and if you still feel as you do—"

"No." Alessa shook her head with the vehemence of one attempting to quell her own doubts. "You're only trying to convince me to go home. You've never liked Adrian."

"That's not the point—"

"Isn't it? Even without these horrid secrets you can't divulge you still wouldn't want me to marry him, would you?"

"Alessa—"

"Would you?" Alessa insisted, looking very like her mother. "Tell me the truth, Fiona."

"No, I would not."

"So I thought." Turning her back on her former governess, Alessa stretched out a hand to her betrothed. "Do let us get on with the ceremony, Adrian, it is becoming too ridiculous."

"I know, my darling." Adrian sprang forward and tenderly lifted her hand to his lips, then turned to the clergyman with his most charming smile. "Come, Tingewick, surely you won't be so cruel as to deny us."

Mr. Tingewick hesitated. "I know," Simon said sympathetically, "he's the Marquis of Parminter and you probably owe your living to him, but—"

He broke off as Peter, who was standing behind Fiona, exclaimed, "Oh, Lord," not loudly but with enough emphasis to cause everyone to turn and look at him. Embarrassment flashed across Peter's face, but he held his ground. "I'm sorry," he said, "it's just—" Peter hesitated, taking in the circle of faces turned toward him. "I think," he finished in a rush, "that he may not be the Marquis of Parminter after all."

Such simple words to convey such complexity. Fiona stared at Peter. Peter looked back, part apologetic, part conspiratorial. The secret was out, but it was not greeted as the stunning revelation it in fact was. Mr. Tingewick blinked in surprise. Lydia, whose eyes were fixed on her husband in concern, scarcely seemed to have heard the remark and did not appear to think it of any consequence. Adrian burst out laughing, to the evident relief of Alessa who had turned to him with a look of perplexity.

"You've had a tiring day, Peter," George began, but Simon interrupted him.

"Why wouldn't he be the Marquis of Parminter?" the prince demanded of his friend.

Peter's embarrassment deepened, but then George made to speak again and that seemed to decide him. "Because," he said, "his mother wasn't married to his father."

"What?" Adrian made a rapid transition from amusement to anger. "See here, if you think I'll stand by while you insult my mother's memory—"

"I mean," Peter amended, "she was married to him, but it didn't count." He turned defiant eyes on George. "That's it, isn't it? The reason you brought me down here. Because of what I told you about the paper Fiona and I found."

"What paper?" Simon and Alessa asked simultaneously.

"You brought him down here, George?" Lydia said in bewilderment.

"What the devil do you know about this?" Adrian demanded of his brother-in-law.

Fiona tried to force her brain to work logically. Peter had seen more of the marriage certificate than she had realized. And had told George—how much? And how much of the truth had George already known? Whatever the answers, it was clear that she could no longer count on going quietly back to London and leaving the fight to Magnus Melchett and an army of solicitors. For better or worse, the truth would have to come out tonight.

At least George had the wit to see that any further attempt to hasten the wedding would only force the issue. "We are all a little short of temper," he said with a smile. "Perhaps a brief recess would be in order. Lydia, I'm sure Lady Alessandra and Mr. Tingewick and the young gentlemen would be glad of some refreshment. Adrian—"

"If you imagine," Alessa informed him, "that I have any intention of leaving before someone gives me an explanation, you are very much mistaken."

"I couldn't agree more," said Fiona.

The increasingly annoyed marquis rounded on her. "For God's sake, what do you have to do with this?"

"Quite a lot, as it happens. Mr. Barrington-Forbes could vouch for it, but I imagine he'd prefer that we adjourn to a more suitable location first. Am I correct?" Fiona regarded George with raised brows, very conscious that she had the upper hand. It could not make up for what he had done to her this morning, but in some small way it gave her back her own.

George inclined his head. "I cannot quarrel with your suggestion, Miss Alastair. This is not an appropriate scene for a chapel."

The little cavalcade returned to the corridor in virtual silence. Simon glanced from Peter to Fiona but refrained from voicing the questions he was clearly longing to ask. Both boys knew so much now that there was little sense in trying to shield them from the coming scene, and in recent weeks both had demonstrated that they had the maturity to handle it. As for Alessa, Fiona's only fear was that the revelations about Adrian's birth and morals would only increase her determination to wed him. Love could do strange things to people.

As they left the chapel she was aware of voices up ahead. Robin and Gideon must have returned to the great hall. The thought increased her unease, for she dreaded seeing Robin's face when he learned that she'd betrayed him. As for Gideon, Fiona would not let herself think beyond the fact that her feelings were in a state of utter confusion.

But before she'd taken more than a few steps she realized that the voices were too loud and angry to belong to Gideon or Robin. At least, one of the voices was loud and angry. It sounded vaguely familiar, but Sundon's stone walls were thick and it was not until she'd reached the bend in the corridor and could hear the words that

Fiona recognized it. "Damn it, man, out of my way, I tell you. I have business with the marquis that cannot be postponed!"

"Now, look here, sir, I've told you his lordship isn't—"

Fiona rounded the corner just behind Lydia and Alessa and saw the footman trying to physically restrain a new arrival from rushing into the great hall. It was her brother-in-law, Sir Hugo Prebble.

Lydia took in the scene at a glance and proved that she had more of her grandmother's self-possession than Fiona had credited her. "Sir Hugo," she said, moving down the corridor at a dignified but rapid pace, "this is an unexpected pleasure. It's all right, Jasper, Sir Hugo is a friend of my husband and the marquis. Did Lady Prebble accompany you, Sir Hugo?"

"Ah—no, Lady Lydia." Hugo's face was flushed with exertion and anger, but he did not forget that he was talking to a marquis's daughter. Suddenly aware that he had not yet removed his hat, he made haste to remedy this omission and handed the article to the now wooden footman. But just as it seemed that Hugo's social sense was about to reassert itself, Adrian and George followed the others into the great hall.

"You!" Hugo strode forward, tugging at one of his gloves. Fiona suddenly understood the significance of the oblong box tucked beneath her brother-in-law's arm. She put protective arms about Peter and Simon, who were studying the scene with every evidence of curiosity, and drew them back into a recess between two columns.

"Name your—" Hugo broke off, not because of any lessening of his anger, but because his glove was proving rather difficult to remove. Then, with a vicious tug, it came free and Hugo hurled the York tan to the floor between them. "Name your friends, Parminter, and I will name mine."

Alessa gave an audible gasp. Lydia said something in a

low voice to the footman who vanished up the far staircase. Adrian looked from the glove to his business partner in utter bewilderment. "I say, Hugo, I've already admitted I made a mistake. I meant it for the best, you know."

"You meant it for the—! By God, Parminter—"

"Steady on, old chap." George stepped between them just in time to prevent Hugo from forgetting his challenge and using his fists. "I agree you have a right to be angry, but it's not worth coming to blows."

"Did you know?" Hugo demanded, glaring at the man who'd been his friend since they were at Harrow. "Because so help me, George, if you did—"

"Know? *Of course not*. I never would have let Adrian do anything so foolish. It was bound to become public knowledge sooner or later."

Hugo laughed bitterly. "If Hillman is to be believed, half of London has known about it for months." He turned back to Adrian, the set of his shoulders betraying his fury. "You didn't even have the decency to be discreet."

"I say Hugo, that's a bit much." Adrian sounded genuinely aggrieved. "If it wasn't for Carne, no one would ever have known that William didn't write that blasted letter."

"I fancy Hugo is talking about something different." Gideon and Robin had come down the nearer of the two staircases and emerged into the midst of the scene.

Hugo glanced briefly at them. "Thank you, Carne, I'm glad someone has the wit to see what I'm talking about."

"But if it's not about Woodbourn-Prebble—" Adrian blanched as the truth finally dawned on him.

"Exactly," Hugo said with grim satisfaction. "I suggest we take care of this at once." He waved the box in front of him. "Wasn't sure you kept any of these in the country, so I brought my own. George, I assume you'll act for

373

me. Your brother can act for you, Parminter."

"Hugo." George's voice was low and insistent. "Not before the ladies."

"I couldn't agree with you more. I assume there's a terrace or garden to which we can adjourn."

"For God's sake, Hugo," Adrian protested, finding his voice again, "I haven't seen her in weeks."

"Seen whom?" Alessa, who'd been by turns bewildered and alarmed, now spoke sharply.

"I'm sorry, my sweet, you shouldn't have to be subjected to this." Understanding where the real threat to his interests lay, Adrian slipped an arm around Alessa and guided her toward one of the red velvet benches disposed about the hall, whispering in her ear.

Hugo would have detained him, but Gideon clapped a hand on his shoulder. "Don't be a fool, Hugo, this won't solve anything. For once George and I are in agreement."

"Yes, if anyone's qualified to give advice on the dangers of dueling it's certainly you, Carne," George observed with quiet venom.

It was a more effective hit than any of the blows he had inflicted in the garden and Fiona saw the damage in Gideon's eyes as clearly as she had seen the blood on his cheek. "At least I can claim to have learned something from my folly," Gideon said, his gaze flickering briefly in George's direction. "Hugo, listen—"

"No, by God." Hugo pulled away from his brother-in-law's grasp. Gideon and George moved after him. Adrian turned, then stepped in front of Alessa. Lydia gasped. Mr. Tingewick, hovering by the column which marked the boundary between corridor and hall, mumbled something under his breath that might have been either an invocation or a curse. Peter and Simon watched with a rapt attention that was suspiciously close to glee.

"I say," said Robin, who was looking toward the windows at the front of the house, "someone's coming up

374

the stairs."

Hugo froze, his eyes going to the great double doors. Gideon and George took advantage of the moment to grab him by the arms, just as the doors were flung open and a slender figure in a lavender pelisse ran into the hall, a veil streaming from her bonnet, and flung herself at Adrian.

"You are safe," Clare exclaimed. "Thank God!"

She was completely oblivious of Alessa, who'd risen abruptly and was standing just behind the marquis. Or perhaps, Fiona thought, Clare had carefully calculated her actions to ensure that there was no question of her lover taking a wife in the near future.

"Your concern is understandable, Lady Prebble," George said, as he and Gideon struggled to restrain Hugo, "but I assure you your husband has done the marquis no harm. You need not fear that he will be forced to flee the country."

"Stay out of this, George," Hugo snapped. "You too, Clare. This is a matter between men, and even if Parminter is weak enough to hide behind your skirts, I am not about to let him do so."

"I," said the marquis, putting Clare from him forcibly, "can fight my own battles."

"Pipe down, Adrian," Gideon advised, "if this goes much further it's only going to be a matter between fools, and quite possibly dead fools."

"This is no time to be clever, Gideon," Clare said sharply, managing at the same time to give a tragic moan.

Alessa moved across the hall to stand by her brother and Fiona, speaking with the icy regality that her mother used so well to damp pretensions. "Obviously this is something Lord Parminter and—Sir Hugo, is it? And Lady Prebble, I presume?—obviously this is something

375

they must settle among themselves. And then perhaps Peter will tell us why Lord Parminter may not be the marquis after all."

Aware that Gideon was looking at her in inquiry, Fiona met his gaze, heedless for the moment of their differences. Otherwise, Alessa's announcement did not have quite the effect she intended, for Clare seemed determined to pretend the younger woman did not exist and Hugo was beyond listening to anyone but himself. "I don't care what the blazes he's marquis of," he declared, "I demand—"

He broke off as a seemingly disembodied voice descended on the hall from the upper reaches of the house. "If you insist on fighting with my grandson, I'm afraid I must ask that you do it out of earshot, Sir Hugo. The firing would be sure to upset the servants."

A hush fell over the great hall. Fiona raised her eyes to the gallery which encircled the dome and saw her grandmother looking over the wrought-metal railing at the oddly assembled company in the hall below.

Chapter Twenty-three

The Marchioness of Parminter moved around the gallery and made her way down the stairs. Three of her grandchildren were there—no, four, if one counted Fiona Alastair—and it appeared as though this evening she could not be ignored. As she reached the last step Lady Parminter caught sight of the Tassio girl and then of Mr. Tingewick, and her lips tightened. So that was what Adrian was about. How could he be so witless? She would never forgive him if he had frightened Lady Alessandra off.

"You will go into the small parlor," the marchioness announced. The saloon was closer, but it would be difficult to control the group in a room of that size. The parlor would keep them nicely confined. "I will join you in a moment. Mr. Tingewick, if I might have a word with you." She would have to offer the man some kind of apology. Tingewick had the living of Sundon church and was therefore indebted to her rather than the other way around, but Lady Parminter held strictly to the doctrine of *noblesse oblige*. One did not treat one's retainers shabbily, and one certainly did not rout frail old men out in the middle of the night to perform an office of a clandestine nature.

While the others made their way to the parlor, the marchioness ascertained that Mr. Tingewick had been on

377

the point of retiring for the night when Adrian arrived and insisted that he come at once to the Sundon chapel to perform a ceremony of marriage. It all seemed most irregular, Mr. Tingewick said, but the marquis had a license which bore the signature of the Archbishop of Canterbury and he could not disoblige him; though as it now seemed there was to be no wedding at all . . . would it be possible to procure a torch, for he did not think he could find his way home in the dark.

Lady Parminter assured him that a torch would not be necessary. She summoned a footman and gave orders that Mr. Tingewick was to be escorted to the library, where refreshment would be provided, and that a carriage was to be put at his disposal as quickly as possible. They parted with expressions of mutual respect, and the marchioness, satisfied that a minor skirmish was over, moved on to the scene of the main battle.

Lady Parminter had no doubts about the dangers of the encounter that awaited her. George had arrived unexpectedly with the alarming intelligence that the marriage certificate had come to light—how was that possible? Penelope had always sworn that it had been destroyed—and was in Miss Alastair's possession. Or Carne's, though it made no difference, for he was to marry her. George had had the story from Carne's son, whom he'd brought to Sundon in a prime fit of madness. He hadn't known what to do with the boy, who seemed to think George might be his father, a claim George thought might possibly be true. It had been a startling admission, but at the time the marchioness had scarcely been able to take it in. And then the footman had arrived with a message from Lydia to the effect that Carne was in the house and had apparently made a murderous attack upon George, and that Sir Hugo Prebble has just arrived and seemed bent on doing the same to Adrian. To which stew must be added Adrian's egregious folly, which embraced not only

Lady Alessandra but the woman who appeared to be his mistress.

Lady Parminter took a deep breath and moved to the parlor door. They were in trouble enough if George's story of finding the marriage certificate was true. They did not need stray passions creating a muddle.

Inside the parlor Lady Parminter's entrance was awaited with varying degrees of impatience, or so it seemed to Gideon. Clare, for example, seemed to have no thought for anyone but Adrian. She refused to look at Hugo, and Adrian, hovering near Lady Alessandra, would not look at her. Lady Alessandra had retreated to a far corner of the room, where she sat half hidden by an enormous vase of summer flowers, with a look of tragic dignity on her youthful face. Simon stood protectively behind her. She tolerated his presence but refused to listen to anyone else. She had even rebuffed Fiona, who had sensibly retreated and was now sitting on a small sofa with Peter.

But it was Robin who caused Gideon the most concern. He had told Robin of his mother's marriage to James Woodbourn, and Robin, a young man of quick parts, had not needed to be told the rest: he was a bastard, Miss Alastair was his sister, and Adrian had no claim on the title. He had taken it remarkably well. Bastardy, he said, was no great shame. His father had been innocent of complicity in the deception, and he was still his father's son. He was delighted to welcome Miss Alastair to the family. As for Adrian, he was a disgrace to the Melchetts and did not deserve the title.

That was Robin's public stance. But when the shock of discovery wore off, he would realize what a disclosure of this kind would mean to his family, the pain it would cause, and how his own life would be affected by it. Gideon's resolve had not weakened. He was going to challenge the Parminters and bring them to their proud,

379

inflexible knees, but he prayed that Robin would not be too badly hurt.

The door opened, the voices stilled, and the marchioness entered the room. Gideon watched her appreciatively. She had chosen her setting well. The parlor was large enough to permit a private conversation if one kept one's voice low, but small enough so that a single speaker could command the room. It was an opulently furnished, somewhat oppressive chamber, its walls hung with cream-colored Genoa velvet patterned in a deep red. The red was echoed in the drapes, now closed to shut out the night, and in the damask that covered the two small sofas and the gilt chairs scattered about the room. The carpets, their colors muted through years of use, were thick and served to deaden footfalls. It was not a room for raised voices or hurried steps. Even the pictures, respectable and sober landscapes, served to remind the visitor that the Parminters were a family of taste and substance.

George hurried forward and escorted the marchioness to a chair near the center of the room. She sat down slowly, as though her limbs no longer obeyed her as they should, and surveyed the assembled company. "I did not expect Lord Parminter to bring such a large party with him this weekend. Though perhaps you were not all invited. I do not wish to appear inhospitable, but there are some family matters of moment that are occupying us." She looked pointedly at Hugo, who had left his wife's side and was now standing before the unlit fireplace. "Sir Hugo, whatever your quarrel with my grandson, you will pursue it at another time and in a more suitable manner. There will be no duels fought at Sundon," she added in a tone that would leave no room for doubt. "There has not been a duel fought on these grounds since 1743, and on that occasion both men were in their cups. I trust that is not the case tonight. Civilized people find other ways of settling their differences."

Simon left Alessa's side and approached the marchioness. "I intend to take my sister back to London, Lady Parminter. If you would be kind enough to make a carriage available."

"Ah, yes, the wedding," Lady Parminter said. "Lady Alessandra—come here, child, I cannot see you behind all those flowers—I was under the impression that your mother and I had agreed that it would take place in the autumn, after her confinement. Was there some need for haste?"

"Ma'am!" Simon's eyes glittered with a sense of outrage.

Alessa, as angry as he, came forward and stood beside her brother. "You do not need to defend me, Simon. I have done nothing of which I need be ashamed."

Lady Parminter bowed her head. "I did not mean to imply otherwise. I merely found it odd—"

"It was not Alessa's fault, Grandmama, it was my own." Adrian ranged himself beside his betrothed and gave his grandmother his most winning smile. "I couldn't bear to wait."

"Gammon!" Robin exclaimed. "You wanted to be sure of Lady Alessandra before the princess and her husband heard about your debts and the forged letter."

Adrian rounded on his brother. "For God's sake, Robin!"

"What forged letter?" Lady Parminter's voice was sharp with anxiety. "Tell me at once. No, not you, Adrian. I want to hear it from Robin."

Robin told her, not omitting his own part in establishing the forgery. "Call me a traitor if you will," Robin added hotly after Adrian had done just that, "but it was a despicable act. How many people did you swindle with that story?"

"No more," the marchioness said. "This is a matter for the family alone."

"If you will permit me, Lady Parminter, it concerns me as well." Hugo was still very angry. "That is, it concerns Woodbourn-Prebble."

Lady Parminter stood up, resting her weight heavily on her stick. "I will not have business discussed in this house. Sir Hugo, you will oblige me by taking your wife back to London. Robin, you will take Lady Alessandra and her brother into the saloon. Take Master Carne with you as well."

Alessa would have none of it. She announced that she had no intention of leaving the room until her questions were answered. Adrian, who looked as though he would be pleased to have her go, was now engaged in a fierce argument with Hugo, who refused to yield to his wife's urgent pleas that he leave Sundon at once. George would probably have joined her in urging Hugo to leave, but Lydia was clinging to his arm.

"Quiet, all of you." Lady Parminter struck the floor sharply with her stick, but it was the authority in her voice that stilled the group. "Carne, Miss Alastair—I would like to speak to you in private."

"I think not, Lady Parminter," Gideon said into the sudden silence. There was no better time to force the issue, here, in the isolation of the country, in a room that stood for everything that was at stake. "It concerns all of us. Lady Alessandra too, and Sir Hugo and Lady Prebble."

For a moment no one spoke. Then George left Lydia's side and walked toward Gideon, purpose and contempt in his eyes. "Don't try to play the devil, Carne. This has nothing to do with you."

"Ah, but it does," Gideon said pleasantly, "the lady is to be my wife." That might no longer be true, but he could not afford to have his authority questioned at this juncture. He glanced at Fiona and she nodded her assent.

"Carne, I forbid you to speak." Lady Parminter's voice rang through the room.

It was enough to bring Adrian to her defense. "I don't know what you're doing, Carne, but I don't want to hear any more. Get out of here or I'll finish what George started and throw you out myself."

"You'd better listen to me, Adrian. It concerns your mother." Gideon glanced at Lydia, regretting what he had to say. Penelope and her parents had been grievously at fault, but her children had no share of the blame. "Her marriage wasn't lawful," he continued, "though your father at least did not know that this was the case. Penelope was already married. Her husband was still alive at the time she married Robert Melchett."

"No!" The exclamation was Clare's, but the piercing shriek that followed came from Lydia. Alessa went quite white and sought her brother's hand.

Adrian bounded across the room and grasped Gideon's coat. "That's a despicable lie. How dare you peddle such filth?"

Gideon carefully removed the other man's hands. "There's a certificate of her marriage."

"I don't believe it," Adrian said flatly.

"Nevertheless," Gideon said, "it exists. It's with my solicitor."

Adrian stared at him with uncertain and hate-filled eyes. "It's a forgery. Yes, that's it, a forgery. This is your doing, Carne. It's because of Aline, isn't it? You're trying to ruin me."

"I'm trying to right an old wrong, Parminter, and I don't care a curse whether you're ruined or not. The marriage took place, and the name is written clearly on the certificate. Penelope Melchett. I recognized her hand." Gideon turned to the marchioness. "Lady Parminter?"

The marchioness drew herself erect. "I have nothing to say."

"Grandmama!" Lydia cried out. "You don't mean it's true?"

Lady Parminter turned and began to walk slowly toward the door, but Lydia was before her. "No," she said with unaccustomed firmness. "You cannot leave it like this. If you won't tell us, Gideon will. But you must stay, I insist. We cannot hear it without you."

The marchioness shivered, then raised a hand in a gesture of resignation and allowed Lydia to lead her back to her chair. Lydia sat nearby, as though to forestall any attempts at escape. George would have joined her, but she warned him off with a fierce look. "Tell us, Gideon."

"Very well, Lydia." He glanced at the others to make it clear that the story was for all of them and proceeded to tell them what he had told Robin not an hour since. Lady Parminter, of course, knew it already. George knew or had guessed a part of it. Adrian and Lydia followed the recital with anger and dismay.

"Did Papa know?" Lydia addressed her grandmother.

"He knew that your mother had had an unfortunate entanglement. We did not tell him of the marriage. We assumed it would not be valid in England."

"If it wasn't valid, then there's no need to worry about the certificate." Adrian studied his grandmother, a worried frown on his face. "You weren't sure, were you?"

"We saw no need to put it to the test," the marchioness said dryly.

"But my God, there would be records. The parish register—"

"There is no record." It was close to an admission of a felonious act, but Lady Parminter showed no consciousness of wrong.

"And the marriage certificate?"

"We thought it had been burned."

384

Adrian sat down and turned a ravaged face to his grandmother. "Who was it? Whom did she marry?"

Lady Parminter drew a long breath. "A young man of modest attractions and no particular birth. His name was James Woodbourn."

Adrian's eyes went to Clare. "Woodbourn?"

"Yes, Lady Prebble's father."

"Fiona?" Clare said in a strangled voice. Then, louder, "Fiona? No! No! No!" The last words were no more than incoherent shrieks. Hugo, who'd dealt with his wife's hysteria before, slapped her sharply on the cheek and held her closely in his arms. She fought him fiercely, then collapsed sobbing against his shoulder, her words broken and incoherent.

Lady Parminter watched the display with profound distaste. When she judged the other woman was able to hear her, she said, "Yes, Lady Prebble, Penelope Melchett's child is your sister. If you will think about it, you will realize that we share a common problem."

"The problem, Lady Parminter, is not of my making," Fiona said in a cool voice.

Adrian strode over to Fiona and looked down at her as though he were seeing her for the first time. "If this is true—and I do not admit that it is—what is it you want?"

"My name."

He laughed, a brief harsh sound devoid of mirth. "Woodbourn? You are welcome to it. Or do you want to be known as an offspring of the Melchetts? How can we do that without dishonoring our mother's name?"

"She is my mother too."

"Then more shame to you."

"Adrian." His grandmother's voice warned him not to say any more. "I have spoken to Miss Alastair a few days since. I have acknowledged her as my granddaughter. I have acknowledged our debt to her as a member of our

385

family. Miss Alastair declined my offer of help, and perhaps she was wise to do so. I was not totally honest with her, though at the time I saw no point in speaking of a marriage of which I thought there was no record. But I would repeat my offer now, Miss Alastair. You know all our secrets. You have some claim on our attention. There are ways of arranging matters so that no one will be hurt."

"I have nothing further to say to you, Lady Parminter. The matter is no longer in my hands."

Lady Parminter frowned. "You intend to pursue it, then. That is unwise. We will fight you, of course. It will be expensive"—she glanced meaningfully at Gideon—"and it will take a long time. These matters can drag on for years. Think, my dear. When it is over, what will you have gained?"

"Enough for my needs, Lady Parminter. The marriage certificate will go to a man who has far more to gain than I do myself."

"You fool!" George exclaimed. "You wouldn't dare."

"I already have," Fiona said, "and I am quite satisfied with the arrangement. Magnus Melchett is the rightful Marquis of Parminter."

Adrian groaned. "God help us all."

There was a trace of contempt in the glance that Lady Parminter gave her grandson. "We will provide our own help."

"You'll be sorry, Fiona." George's poise, which seldom deserted him, had vanished. "You think it's Melchett's problem now. But it's your own, yours and your paramour's and his bastard son's. It's all going to come out, your shabby liaison with Carne, your brother's murder, Aline's lovers—"

Hugo sprang forward. "By God, George!"

But George was insensible. "Think about it," he said, leaning over Fiona. "Carne's son, only he's not Carne's son, is he? Perhaps he's mine, or perhaps he's not. She fornicated with half of Hertfordshire."

"Don't you say that!" Peter ran forward and pummeled George with his fists, but Adrian, his eyes glazed with fury, pulled him away and grasped George by the throat. "I'll kill you, do you hear me? I won't hear a word against her. She was an angel, and I've lost her. I've lost her—"

"Enough!" Gideon roared, pushing his way between the two men. Adrian drew back, sobbing, and George mumbled some incoherent words of apology.

"George?" Lydia was at her husband's side, her white face turned up to his. "Is it true, what you said about Lady Carne?"

"Don't be a mooncalf, Lydia. It was long before I'd met you." He turned his back on his wife, denying her the comfort she sought.

"Then it's true," she said in a small, flat voice. "And after Lady Carne there was a woman you were going to marry. It was Mr. Woodbourn's ward, wasn't it?" She glanced at Fiona. "Your name wasn't Alastair then."

"No, it was Martin. I changed it." Knowing what it was like to love a man who wanted you only for what you represented, Fiona felt a moment of intense sympathy for the other woman. She thought again how strange it was that George, who had captured a wealthy woman and the granddaughter of a marquis for his wife, should have once sought out Fiona Martin. And then she knew, with sudden certainty, that it was not strange at all. "Is that why you wanted to marry me, George," she asked, rising to look him in the eye, "because I had some claim on the Parminters?"

George gave her an appraising look. "Don't underrate your charms, my dear."

"And when I gave you your congé," Fiona persisted, "you set your aims higher. How opportune that you were

387

able to attach Lady Lydia. I hope you appreciate your good fortune."

She would not say more, not in front of George's grieving wife, but it was clear now how it had been. If James Woodbourn had been beneath the Parminters' notice, George was not that much better. Lady Parminter would not have granted her granddaughter's whim unless George had persuaded her that it was in her own interest to do so. He knew, he must have known about the marriage. Or, if not the marriage, he knew at least that Lady Parminter's daughter had borne a child. Fiona stifled an impulse to laugh. Gideon had not wanted her for herself, and it seemed that George had not either. It was a lowering reflection, and if she did not laugh she would be tempted to cry.

Then she realized how much they had all been in George's hands. He had used Clare to destroy her and then, when Peter fell into his hands, he had used the boy to destroy Gideon. George was responsible for the fire. Lady Parminter may have agreed to a search of James Woodbourn's papers, but the idea would have come from George. Even now it was George who would lead the fight against them. Lady Lydia, no matter how much George had hurt her, would still jump to her husband's tune, and Lord Parminter, Fiona suspected, would do the same.

But not George alone. Fiona looked at the woman she must now think of as her grandmother and knew that Lady Parminter was a match for them all. When the marchioness spoke, her words commanded immediate attention. "There have been some unpleasant revelations," she said, "and we are all suffering from shock. I suggest we think carefully before doing or saying anything more. Robin, give me your arm."

Robin hastened forward and helped his grandmother to her feet. She turned to Alessa, whose face was desolate with disillusion and grief. "Lady Alessandra, I cannot tell you how much I regret that you should have witnessed this sorry scene."

"No, Lady Parminter," Alessa said with great dignity, "it is I who should apologize for coming here at all. It was unpardonable of me."

Adrian hastened to her side. "I will not let you say such things, Alessa. The blame is mine, only mine." He tried to take her hand, but she pulled it away. He scowled, then forced his face to be pleasant. "I understand that you are angry with me now. But it will all come right, I swear it. It's only an argument about a name. Barrington-Forbes was out of his head. We mean no harm to Miss Alastair, and she has no cause to fight us. I'm sure you can persuade her that that is the case."

Robin regarded his brother with astonishment. "What are you talking about, Adrian? She has every cause."

"Robin." Lady Parminter's voice held a note of warning.

Robin might not have heard her. "Don't you understand? She's the heir."

"Robin," George said sharply.

"She has everything," Robin continued doggedly, "or very nearly so. When it looked as though she wouldn't bear a son, Penelope Quentin insisted that Sundon and Parminter House be entailed so they could pass to the eldest daughter in the event there was no male issue. It's been part of every marriage settlement since."

"You fool," George said furiously.

Fiona was aware of a fleeting satisfaction at seeing George so shaken, but it was drowned by the enormity of what Robin had just said. Robert Melchett had held the title, but the property wasn't his. It had been entailed on his wife. Only she wasn't his wife, she was James Woodbourn's, and the property would go to the child she bore him—to her, Fiona Martin. Magnus Melchett could claim the title, but he would not have Sundon. Fiona wondered if he would care.

She looked at Lady Parminter and felt she could see into her very soul. Robin's claim was true: the marchioness had fought her all the way. When she feared that Fiona might uncover the marriage, she had admitted the birth. And when proof of the marriage became incontrovertible, she withheld knowledge of the inheritance. Did she expect Fiona, unknowing, to sign it away?

It was a moment before Fiona was aware that there was a lot of confused shouting in the room, dominated at last by George's voice. "Adrian," he said with decision. "Lydia. Come with me, we have to talk. You'd better come too, Hugo, you're involved in this as well." They all moved to the door, Clare included, for in matters of money she stood as one with her husband. At the door George turned and looked back at Gideon. "I'll see you in hell, Carne."

Gideon smiled. He seemed in extraordinarily sweet temper. "Of course, George. If that's where you intend to go."

George stormed out, leaving a painful silence in his wake. The marchioness, who had been lost in thought, roused herself and spoke to Alessa. "There is nothing more for you to learn here, child. Don't be hasty in your judgment, there is still much to unfold. But it is late and you have had a trying experience. You and your brother are welcome to stay the night, but if you prefer to return to London I will understand. If you will wait, perhaps Miss Alastair would be willing to accompany you. Robin, I am going to take Miss Alastair and Lord Carne upstairs. See that Lady Alessandra and the boys are offered some refreshment."

Fiona crossed the room and embraced Alessa who clung to her for a moment as though she were still the child she had been when Fiona first became her governess. "I'm all right, Fiona, truly I am," she said as she drew back. Her eyes were dry, but her face bore traces of desolation. "He is still in love with this woman Aline—"

"Alessa, she is dead."

"He loves her still. I can tell it. And he has a liaison with Lady Prebble. He does not love me, I know that now, he is in love with my fortune." She attempted a laugh that ended in a sob. "It seems you were right, Fiona. I'm sorry, I'm so sorry."

Fiona knew that nothing she could say would bring Alessa comfort. "There's nothing to be sorry for. It will pass. You won't believe it, but it will." And with these useless words she turned and followed Gideon and Lady Parminter out of the room.

Chapter Twenty-four

The marchioness led Fiona and Gideon through an archway to a flight of pale stone stairs, their treads worn smooth by two centuries of use. They emerged on the first floor and moved down a long corridor whose floor, of the same stone as the stairs, was interspersed with diamonds of black marble. The walls were broken by pedestals of rose-colored marble, each surmounted by a marble head of a classical figure rendered in the purest white, and a series of closed doors of a dark, polished wood. It seemed endless, like a passage one traverses in a dream. Fiona allowed her fingers to brush against one of the pedestals. This is mine, she thought, not really believing it, this house belongs to me.

At the end of the corridor they turned and entered another. It was narrower than the first, and the stone and marble floor was partly covered by a strip of heavy carpet in a deep patterned red. Halfway down this corridor the marchioness opened the door of a small sitting room whose walls were hung with a pale blue damask figured with gold. Cornice and ceiling were painted white and this, together with the gold-colored drapes and the pale carpet which covered most of the marquetry floor, lightened the room and made it less oppressive than the parlor from which they had come.

Lady Parminter did not ask them to sit but drew them

instead across the room to look at a large portrait that hung over the mantel. A fair-haired woman with soft features and discontented eyes was posed in a sort of ruined grotto. "Penelope," Gideon said quietly.

"Yes, my daughter. Your mother, Miss Alastair."

Fiona's eyes traced the features but saw no resemblance to herself beyond that of coloring. The woman was a stranger. It was the final irony. At the end of her search, she felt no sense of kinship with the woman who'd borne her.

Feeling suddenly oppressed, she turned away. She did not belong to this family, nor did she belong in this house that Robin claimed was rightfully her own. She wanted to leave, to go back to small houses and small rooms and life on a scale she could understand.

It was a moment of cowardice, no more. If this was her inheritance, she would claim it. And she would claim the ties of blood that bound her to the careless, selfish Parminters. Yesterday she had turned everything over to Magnus Melchett, thinking to be free of the Parminters, but now the fight that was looming would be hers as well. She welcomed it. She would fight them if she must, or she would come to some understanding with them, but the terms would be her own.

"We are an old family, Miss Alastair," the marchioness said. She was still staring at the portrait. "We trace our descent back to Sir Robert Melchett, who was knighted by Edward IV in 1478. His grandson was made an earl by Henry VIII, and his great-grandson was created the first marquis by Edward VI, but it was the fourth marquis who made the Parminters a family of consequence." She turned and walked toward a chair, indicating that they should be seated as well. "He was my great-grandfather. Robin was right about the entail. Adrian was not thinking clearly, but he certainly knows of it, for he inherited Sundon and Parminter House on his grandfather's death, though the title went to his father. Still, eventually the title went to Adrian as well. So the entail has never been an issue. Even when I failed to produce a living son." Lady Parminter closed her eyes briefly, as though shutting out some remembered pain. "Only a daughter. Under the terms of my marriage settlement, Penelope would have inherited the bulk of the property on her father's death, while the title would have gone to her cousin Robert, the only son of my husband's younger brother. Robert was a young man of great talent and utter probity, worthy of the name of Parminter, but Sundon and Parminter House would be denied him. They would go to Penelope and her children, who when she married would no longer bear the Melchett name."

The marchioness glanced briefly at the portrait, then turned back to Fiona. "Do you understand me, Miss Alastair? It could not be allowed. It would destroy the greatness of the Parminter line. Robert understood that and so did Penelope. They both wanted the marriage, but Penelope was always ruled by her sensibilities and she developed a fleeting infatuation for James Woodbourn. An infatuation, with all respect to your father, that later horrified her as much as it did her parents."

"Then everything you did . . ." Fiona did not finish the thought.

"Everything I did had one purpose only. Everything I did was to preserve the legacy of the Parminters."

There was a short silence. Lady Parminter had finished her story and Gideon, Fiona guessed, was leaving the next step up to her. "What is it you want, Grandmother?" She used the title deliberately, as a weapon, and was pleased to see that it had found its mark.

"Do you want to be mistress of Sundon, Miss Alastair? No, if I have judged you rightly, you do not. You want recognition and you want independence. I can offer you both."

"Mr. Melchett will do the same, and he will acknowledge my legitimacy. Can you do as much?"

"What Magnus Melchett claims will count for little in the world in which you hope to move. I will acknowledge you as my granddaughter, which you are. Your legitimacy is a matter for the courts, and I do not think the question will be easily resolved. When it is, it may not be to your liking. But that is years away, Miss Alastair, and you are no longer young. Let me give you the life you deserve, a life that is worthy of Penelope's daughter, legitimate or not."

"I am to give up all claim to my mother's property, is that what you are saying? Why should I do that?"

"Because you will receive present benefit in exchange for a doubtful—a very doubtful—future gain."

There was silence in the room. The ticking of the ornate French clock that stood on the mantel seemed unusually loud. Fiona thought she could measure her heartbeats by it.

"I will do for you what I can, Miss Alastair," the marchioness continued. "I owe it to the memory of my daughter. Do not scoff. There is much to admire in you, and were matters other than they are, we might be friends. But I will not cease to fight with every resource left to me to preserve the Parminter legacy intact."

"You will have to fight Mr. Melchett in any case."

"I would prefer not to fight you both, but if necessary I will."

Fiona looked at her grandmother's softened, wrinkled face, saw the determination in her faded blue eyes, and felt some core of stubbornness within herself. She would not bend before this woman. She would not give up her birthright. "I am afraid you must."

Their eyes met in a wordless duel, and the marchioness finally bowed her head. "As you wish, Miss Alastair."

"Lady Parminter," Gideon said. "You are doing this for Adrian?"

"I am doing it for the Parminter name."

"Which Adrian bears, yes—for the moment, at least."

"Understand me, Carne," the marchioness said fiercely, "I will not live to see destroyed what I have given so much to preserve."

"It may be destroyed anyway. Not by Melchett, not by Miss Alastair. By Adrian himself."

"You are saying he is unworthy. Yes, I know of his debts. I know now of the forged letter and his disgraceful behavior with the Tassio girl. He is not the man his father was, but he is young and malleable and Penelope's firstborn son. He is by right of birth Marquis of Parminter and lord of Sundon."

"Which he will sell off piece by piece. By the time this matter has been resolved, the Marquis of Parminter will have nothing with which to support his dignity."

Lady Parminter's face grew pale. "You jest, Carne. It cannot be done."

"Entails can be broken. Adrian is of age and there is no marriage settlement to bind him."

"He would not dare."

"He already has."

"You are lying."

Gideon regarded her levelly. "You know me. I am not."

The marchioness returned his gaze for a long moment, and then made a vague gesture of acquiescence. "What is it you know?"

"Your eldest grandson made inquiries of his solicitor this afternoon. I have had him followed, and I know. They are not the first inquiries he has made. I doubt you know the extent of Adrian's debts or the depths of his desperation."

Lady Parminter clutched the arms of her chair. "He

must be stopped. He *will* be stopped. You are trying to frighten me, Carne, but it will not work. I still have some influence in this family."

"Yes," Gideon acknowledged, "you have some. With Lydia, with Robin, but not with Adrian. He is the marquis, and the property is in his hands."

"To sell off his birthright—it is unconscionable."

Gideon could read her struggle in her face. She could not bear to see Adrian destroy the property, but she could not allow Magnus to get the title. Magnus, that offspring of an inept father and a little French actress who abandoned him and their three young children. But on the other hand, Magnus at least was clever. Magnus had a fierce determination that might serve the Parminter name, and Magnus had the wealth to support it. Magnus was envious and ambitious. If it came to that, if he were given the title, he might be induced to abandon his commercial interests.

As he watched her, Gideon knew that he had won. Lady Parminter would accept Magnus's claim and she would see to it that he had an heir, lest the title pass to his even more disreputable cousin Guy. Gideon grimaced. She might even decide to promote a match between Magnus and Fiona. It would keep everything together.

"What are you proposing, Carne?" Lady Parminter said in a harsh voice.

Gideon looked at Fiona and she nodded. "We would all prefer that this were settled privately. The title is in question in any case, and for that you will have to speak to Melchett. Miss Alastair wants what is her due, but she is prepared to be generous. Her brothers and sister do not need to suffer."

"They will fight it. They have pride and hatred and the strength of possession to support them."

"I thought they would dance to your tune. Perhaps I am mistaken?"

The marchioness smiled. "Don't underestimate me, Carne. They will fight it, but in the end they will do as I say. Give me your arm. I have done here. I can do no more." Gideon helped her to her feet and she turned and looked at her granddaughter. "Fiona. It is a fine, high-bred name. It suits you." And with these words she left the room.

Fiona rubbed her arms, not because she was cold, but because she felt numb to any sensation at all. She looked at the door through which her grandmother had departed and for the first time noticed a small panel over the lintel displaying the Melchett coat of arms . . . her coat of arms. This house, linchpin of the Melchett family and all they represented, would soon be hers.

For the first time in her life she had a family she could claim openly as her own. A grandmother who had accepted her because it was the only way to save the legacy for which she had once abandoned her. A sister who had been sold in marriage to an unscrupulous man to preserve the secret of her own birth. If Lydia did not hate Fiona for making her a bastard, she would hate her for what she had revealed about George.

And then there were her brothers—Adrian, who could probably be persuaded to fall in with his grandmother's wishes, but would no doubt resent Fiona to the end of his days for being the unwitting architect of his downfall; William, as yet unknown, but apt, from all she had heard, to take Adrian's view of the matter; and Robin— well, perhaps there was hope there. Miraculously he seemed to bear her no grudge.

But though Robin offered some small ray of hope, Fiona felt more alone than ever. She had known she'd been a pawn sacrificed for her parents' convenience, but the day she learned of their marriage Gideon had held her in his arms and offered her comfort. No, she must be honest. What she had felt when Gideon held her and when she went to him later that night had gone far beyond comfort or need. It could only be described in words which had vanished from her vocabulary five years ago. And if those words had begun to creep back in recent weeks, this morning George had seen to it that they were permanently erased.

Gideon's voice, quiet and remote, cut in on her thoughts. "What will you do?" He was still standing, staring at the intricate floral pattern on the hearth rug. Fiona looked at him blankly. It seemed that the numbness had extended from her body to her brain, for she could not even begin to think of an answer.

Hell, Gideon thought with an odd detachment, was not a battlefield or a city under sack. It was not even the mockery in Aline's eyes when she told him about Peter, or the sight of Jamie Woodbourn's body oozing blood onto grass still damp with the morning dew. It was here and now, staring at an innocuous blue-and-white hearth rug which was sure to haunt his dreams for years to come. Clasping his hands behind his back so she could not see them trembling, he turned to face her. "I expect you would be welcome to remain at Sundon," he said, fixing his gaze on the tall walnut cabinet just behind Fiona's shoulder. "But Lady Alessandra should have a chaperone on the journey back to London. If you are willing to accompany us, I imagine you could stay the night in Bolton Street."

The cold precision of his words snapped Fiona's last shred of control. "I've never been a real person to any of you, have I?" she demanded harshly, rising from her chair to confront him. "I used to comfort myself with the thought that my father had at least taken me into his home. But now I'll never know if he'd have done so had the Parminters not paid him for it. And George." She laughed. "I was flattered that a man like George would offer for a bastard whose father was in trade. But

George only wanted me because I was the Marquis of Parminter's granddaughter. And you only wanted me because I was betrothed to George."

"Fiona—" Gideon spoke on impulse and went no farther. There was no way to justify his actions, and if he tried to explain his feelings for her, she would only call him a liar and make it worse for both of them.

"If it wasn't for Christopher," Fiona continued in a tight, brittle voice, "I think I'd have quite lost my self-respect. You remember Christopher. The Langleys' footman. He admires me without any ulterior motive at all. At least, I don't think he has an ulterior motive. That would be too lowering."

Gideon could not listen in silence much longer. "You must know that what passed between us these last few days had nothing to do with George and Aline," he told her.

"Didn't it? If it weren't for George and Aline, you wouldn't have acted as you did five years ago, and if you hadn't acted as you did then, you wouldn't have reason to feel guilty about me now. And it's that guilt that's driven everything between us since you came back to England . . . isn't it?" she persisted, determined to force some show of emotion from him.

Gideon had never seen her like this and the knowledge of what he had driven her to was as wrenching as the bullet which had shattered his leg. He drew a breath, trying to make the action appear as natural as possible. "If that's what you believe . . ." he said, and let the thought trail off, hoping it would end the matter. This time he would not let despair blind him to his other responsibilities. Somehow he had to get through this scene, to return the young Tassios home with a minimum of fuss, to make sure he had really mended matters with Peter. He could not think much farther.

"What else can I believe?" Fiona demanded, her voice

trembling with emotions she could not suppress. "Of course, by the time I came to your house I suppose you'd been without a woman so long that anyone would do."

"My resources," Gideon said, his clasped hands now tightly clenched, "were not so strained, I assure you."

"But I was right there under your roof, so much more convenient than seeking out a former mistress, so much less expensive than visiting a brothel. After all, you were economizing on every other household expense. Just how much money did I save you, Lord Carne?"

"Stop it, Fiona."

The quiet voice now had a definite edge, but she wanted a more complete victory. "Why?" she demanded. "Don't I have a right to know what my services were worth?"

It took a supreme effort of will to remain where he was standing and speak at something below a roar. "What do you want, Fiona? Shall I get down on my knees and offer you an apology that can't sound anything but inadequate? Would that satisfy you?"

"I want the truth. It's past time we were honest with each other. Though in all fairness, there's one lie you never told," Fiona said with unleavened bitterness. "I've never heard the word 'love' pass your lips. I should have known you'd be immune to that particular madness. Does some vestige of honor keep you from perjuring yourself? Or do you reserve it for women you can't get on any other terms? Answer me, damn you!"

He moved so suddenly that she was scarcely aware of it until he had crossed the room and seized her, not gently, by the shoulders. "You're right, Fiona . . . it *is* a madness. It's a hell any sane person would try to avoid. Look at me," he insisted fiercely as she turned her head away from the onslaught of his words. "You're the one who wanted the truth. The truth is, it's so bloody terrifying that I spent five years telling myself I was dead to

401

any feeling at all, that it was only my guilty conscience that made you haunt my dreams. Well, I've stopped trying to deny it. I love you, Fiona Martin. In God's name, isn't that punishment enough?"

Gideon flung away from her as he spoke and stood facing the door, both hands pressed to his temples. Fiona began to tremble. These were the words she had once longed for more than anything in the world, words she had long ago given up hope of ever hearing from him. Delivered in passion or apology she would never have believed them, but uttered with the raging anger of a man driven beyond all endurance, they had an undeniable ring of truth. The anger and tension coiled so tightly within her snapped and welled over in dry, wrenching gasps, followed by a deluge of tears.

Gideon turned at the sound and saw Fiona sink to the floor, carried there by the force of the storm. Without hesitation, he dropped down beside her on the carpet, aware as he gathered her to him that it was probably the last time he would hold her. Fiona burrowed her face into his shoulder, her whole body convulsed by sobs.

It was some time before her tears abated and still longer before her breathing returned to normal. She seemed content to remain in his arms, but he could not give in to the temptation to go on holding her. Gently he put her from him, relieved to see that despite the ravages of tears her face was calmer than it had been all day. Though he knew it was a mistake, he smoothed some loosened strands of hair off her face, letting his fingers linger against her cheek for a moment. "Let's not hurt each other any more."

Fiona gave a tremulous smile and reached up a hand to cover his own. "We're bound to quarrel sometimes. I understand it happens in the best of marriages."

For a moment shock held Gideon motionless. Happiness surged through him, then was firmly suppressed. "You don't need me anymore, Fiona," he said quietly.

"Meaning that now I'm a marquis's granddaughter with a substantial fortune, gentlemen won't mind that I'm damaged goods?"

Gideon snatched his hand away. The words were an involuntary reminder of all the reasons he didn't deserve her. "Any gentleman worthy of the name would be proud to win you. With your grandmother to sponsor you, you'll meet many such men."

"I don't doubt it. Though I rather suspect my grandmother will do her utmost to get me to marry Magnus Melchett. I don't know how Mr. Melchett feels, but I have no intention of obliging her." Fiona straightened the twisted sleeves of her gown. Gideon loved her. She could still not quite believe it, but the longing and regret in his eyes told her it must be true. But just as she had begun to see their way clear out of today's nightmare to a happier future than she had dared hoped for, he threw up unexpected obstacles. "I hope you aren't going to be so unhandsome as to retract your offer, Gideon. What about the children? I've already begun to think of myself as their mother."

Gideon hesitated, but he stuck to his course. "You can see them whenever you like."

"It's not at all the same." With sudden desperation Fiona realized that she could still lose him. "You were willing to accept a marriage of convenience," she pointed out. "But now that we have a chance at something more, you want to throw it away. What's the matter? Don't you think you deserve to be happy?"

"It's debatable." He gave a rueful, self-mocking smile. "It won't work, Fiona. The past will always be between us."

"Twenty-nine years," Fiona said softly, holding his eyes with her own. "I was nine-and-twenty last month, and you're the first person ever to say 'I love you' to me. *That* will always be between us."

He gave another smile, a little more amused, a little less derisive. "You make it damnably hard for a man to be noble, my girl."

"There's nothing noble about condemning two people to a wholly unnecessary bleak future," she retorted. Gideon made no response and avoided her gaze. "I love you," she added. "You must know that. I haven't let myself use the words for years, but that couldn't change the way I feel. And if what we feel for each other could endure what's already passed between us, I rather think it could endure anything."

Gideon continued silent a moment longer. Then, with something between a laugh and a groan, he reached out and pulled her tightly against him. Fiona gave a sigh of relief, but when she lifted her face for his kiss, he had one more warning to give. "I have nothing to offer you, Fiona," he cautioned, even as his hand slid behind her neck and his fingers traced the line of her jaw.

"Idiot," Fiona said affectionately, pulling his head down to her own. "You have everything."

Epilogue

August, 1813

"Lady Carne?" Clare turned to the footman standing in the doorway, surprise chasing the look of preoccupation from her face. She made a rapid calculation. "Show her into the drawing room, Daniel. Tell her I'll be with her as soon as I am able. And you'd better send up tea."

The footman bowed impassively and left the room. He was well trained, she'd give him that. Not by the quiver of a brow did he betray the fact that he knew exactly who Lady Carne was and what she meant to the fortunes of this house. It was impossible to keep secrets from the servants, sly things that they were, but at least they had the sense to keep their knowledge to themselves.

Lady Carne . . . how like Fiona to come here flaunting her new position, all cool and appraising and looking as if butter wouldn't melt in her mouth. If only she'd been able to show her strumpet sister the door. But no, Fiona was a viscountess now, whatever she'd been in the past, and she was wealthy, indecently wealthy, wealthy beyond imagining. At the thought, Clare felt a sharp stab of pain in her side and she clasped her hand to her ribs to contain it.

The spasm passed quickly. No, it was not the door for Fiona, it was the drawing room and tea, served in the best china, and pretending none of it had happened.

Hugo said they had to be sensible. Very well, she would be sensible, at least till matters were settled. They'd been at it for the past three weeks, Adrian's solicitor and Gideon's and Magnus Melchett's and Hugo's own man, for George had insisted that they have separate representation. Damn George's eyes, he knew they couldn't afford it.

At the beginning, George had led their fight, but he'd soon realized on which side his bread was buttered. He was ready enough to sacrifice his hatred of Gideon to his own advantage, particularly after Lady Parminter made it clear which way she'd jump. George had weighed Adrian in the balance against the upstart banker who wanted to become the eighth marquis, and George had found Adrian wanting.

Clare shook out the folds of her morning gown and walked to the door, pausing to glance in the pier glass to make certain that her heavy dark hair was as carefully arranged as her maid had left it two hours since. She frowned at her reflection. There was no doubt that the strain of the last few weeks had left its mark on her beauty. She smoothed out the line that had appeared between her brows, but there was nothing to be done about the dark smudges beneath her eyes which even powder could not conceal.

Adrian had been a grave disappointment. She had lost him to the Tassio chit, and when the match was broken off and it looked as though he might wish to resume their relationship, she found she did not want him. It was not just that Hugo had been unspeakably tiresome about the affair. It was not even Adrian's defense of Aline that night at Sundon, though that had been unsettling enough. Dear God, he had actually loved that fornicating little wench. No, it was Adrian himself. He seemed slighter to the eye, his hair less golden, his manner peevish and complaining. He wasn't half the man

George was. Clare watched the ghost of a smile appear on her lips, erasing the signs of strain from her face. George. Why not? It might be amusing, and it would serve Hugo out. The thought cheered her. She turned away from the glass reluctantly, remembering that Fiona was in the house and it would not be politic to keep her waiting.

Clare quickly made her way to the drawing room and pushed open the door. Fiona was standing by the windows, but she turned at Clare's entrance and came toward her, a serious look on her face. "Thank you for seeing me."

"Why shouldn't I see you?" Clare's voice was sharper than she had intended.

"I don't know. That's why I came."

She was uncertain but unafraid, a combination Clare found annoying. "Oh, sit down, Fiona, do. I know you haven't called for the pleasure of my company, but if you have something to say I'm quite prepared to hear you out."

Fiona made no immediate answer, but she took the seat Clare indicated and proceeded to remove her gloves. Clare studied her visitor with care. She had not spent any of her newfound wealth on clothes, for she was wearing a woefully simple high-necked dress with a small lace collar. But her bonnet, a plaited straw with sea-green ribbons that Clare might have bought for herself, was outrageously becoming, her color was good, and she had the kind of glow about her that comes to people whose life is ordered exactly as they wish. Now, here in her presence, Clare realized that it was not Fiona's wealth that galled her most, nor even her newfound legitimacy, but her unmistakable happiness.

"We go to Hartwood tomorrow," Fiona said after the silence had stretched between them. "I take it Sallie and Hugh are still at Digby Hall."

"They are." Clare knew what Fiona was about to say, but she had no wish to make it easier for her.

"They're cousins, Clare. Beth was fathered by Lord Parminter, and Peter and Teddy—that doesn't matter, of course, they're Gideon's children and now they're mine, but Aline bore them and Aline was Hugo's sister. It's been difficult enough for them this past year. I would not want to see them forbidden the company of your children."

Clare had envisioned Fiona as mistress of Sundon. Somehow it had not occurred to her that she would be mistress of Hartwood as well, scarce half a mile from Digby Hall, with the children running back and forth as they had been accustomed to do all their lives. She could stop it, of course. She had no desire to resume the intimacy that had once existed between the two houses, certainly not with Fiona installed in Aline's place. On the other hand, Sallie and Hugh were much attached to their Carne cousins, and Sallie was prone to tantrums when she didn't get her way. And it would be to their advantage to be on good terms with the now wealthy Carnes.

"The children may play together," Clare said grudgingly. "I am not sure that—" She stopped, aware that she was about to say something imprudent.

"That their parents should follow their example? Of course. You have cause to be angry with me, Clare, and I have cause to be angry with you, but we can try to be civil when we meet."

Clare made an impatient gesture. "If we must." She felt her words would choke her. "But to tell the truth, Fiona," she added with sudden anger, "I wish you at the very devil."

"And I wish the same of you," Fiona said cheerfully. "At least we know where we stand."

Her good humor was insufferable, but perversely, Clare felt better. "We go down to Digby Hall later in the week, if Hugo can finish this interminable wrangling with the lawyers. I may go by myself if he can't bring himself to leave. There's absolutely no one left in town."

"Things are more or less agreed, at least as far as you and Hugo are concerned, though it may take the lawyers weeks to put it into properly obscure language. Has Hugo told you what has been decided?"

"Hugo tells me everything, in interminable detail." Clare sighed and looked away. "I suppose I should say that you've been generous."

"Yes, I have," Fiona agreed with a slight smile, "but that does not make it easier to accept. You don't wish to take from me what should be yours by right." She pulled on her gloves and picked up her reticule. "It wasn't your fault, Clare. You've had to pay for our father's imprudence, but in the end you will be no worse off than before."

"No worse off?" Clare looked fiercely at her sister. How could she be no worse off? Nothing would wipe out the stain of illegitimacy, and as for Adrian. . . . Breathing hard, Clare spoke of her last grievance. "Gideon ruined Woodbourn-Prebble."

"Adrian Melchett ruined Woodbourn-Prebble, but his cousin Magnus will put it right."

"His cousin Magnus has withdrawn his interest," Clare said bitterly. "Gideon too, and Adrian, perhaps even George. Hugo is alone."

"Which is where he started. If he's learned to be prudent . . ." Fiona paused, as though recognizing that her advice would be unwelcome. "Don't bother to ring, Clare. I'll see myself out."

When the door closed behind her sister, Clare allowed herself the luxury of a few angry tears. Fiona, damn her, could not be blamed for taking what was hers, and it would have been easier if she had done so. She'd given up all claim to James Woodbourn's estate and had settled money on both Sallie and Hugh. Clare could not fault the arrangement, but it took away her only legitimate grievance.

A scratching at the door announced the arrival of tea. Clare looked impatiently at the footman bearing the tray. "You were long enough about it. Lady Carne has gone, you'd best take it back. No, leave it." Clare indicated a nearby table. When the footman withdrew, she poured herself a cup and sipped it thoughtfully. Tea always had a calming effect, and she needed to think about the advantages to be wrung from her connection to the wealthy Viscountess Carne.

Fiona descended the steps of the Prebble house at a leisurely pace and turned down Davies Street. The day was warm, but there was a slight breeze to freshen the air. She paused for a moment, savoring the day, the clear sky, her own happiness. The past three weeks had been the most joyful she had ever known.

She and Gideon had been married on the Tuesday after that explosive Saturday evening at Sundon, though the wedding had been more elaborate than they had planned. First, Fiona had impulsively asked Robin to give her away. Robin had been delighted. Then she decided to invite the Windham family, and when she called with the invitation, Lady Windham insisted on giving a wedding breakfast. Miss Alastair would be doing her a great favor, she said, for it would be positively her last chance to entertain this season, and impromptu gatherings were just what she liked best.

Fiona smiled at the memory as she continued down Davies Street, suddenly impatient to join Gideon and the children, whom she was to meet at Gunter's. She had talked with Lady Windham on Sunday afternoon. On Monday, she had returned from visiting Mr. Camford and buying a new bonnet for her wedding to find the Princess Sofia waiting for her in Dover Street. She had called, the princess said, to apologize. The reasons for this apology were not entirely clear, but they seemed to be compounded of Fiona's role in rescuing Alessa from a disastrous marriage, her newfound status in the world, and Michael Langley's horror at discovering his wife had summarily dismissed Miss Alastair. Fiona could not but wonder if the princess would speak so warmly to her were she not about to become Lady Carne, but she could not quarrel with the reconciliation which meant that Simon and Peter would be able to visit whenever they wished. Delighted that she would no longer be separated from her former charges, she invited the Langley family to the wedding.

The day of the ceremony had brought still more guests. Magnus Melchett slipped quietly into the church accompanied by a slender auburn-haired woman who Fiona later learned was his sister. As the new head of the family, he wanted to offer his congratulations to his cousin. He smiled as he spoke, but Fiona suspected the words were more serious than even Magnus realized. The banker who'd once laughed at the Parminter preoccupation with the family name was beginning to take his new role to heart.

The wedding and wedding breakfast were everything Fiona could have wished. Even Adam seemed perfectly sincere in offering his congratulations, and when Lady Windham sat down at the piano, he asked Barbara to dance more than once. That relationship was developing nicely, and Fiona suspected that Barbara would soon find herself a married woman.

A week after the wedding, Lady Parminter called in Dover Street. She did not seem entirely pleased with the match—leading Fiona to think her grandmother had indeed hoped she would marry Magnus Melchett—but she was prepared to make the best of matters. She still had powerful friends. She would see to it that Fiona was received everywhere, and she would do the same for Magnus and his sisters. It was apparent that Magnus, who would be the marquis and who was still unmarried, would receive more of her attention than Fiona. Fiona was grateful. By the end of the interview, she thought she and her grandmother could at least say they understood each other.

Two days later, she received a more surprising visit from Lydia, who was still bitterly angry with George and seemed, more than anything, to want someone to talk to. It was an awkward conversation, but it left Fiona feeling that she and Lydia might get on considerably better than she and Clare had ever done.

Strictly speaking, Magnus was not yet Marquis of Parminter and Fiona was not yet mistress of Sundon and Parminter House, though in principle Adrian had agreed not to contest their claims. Fiona did not know precisely what Lady Parminter had said to her eldest grandson, but a few days after the confrontation at Sundon, the Parminter solicitor called on Camford to say that Adrian was willing to discuss terms. Predictably, it was the financial details which were taking the longest to sort out. William and Lydia had already received their portions and there was money set aside for Robin. Adrian remained the problem, and the solicitors were still debating a suitable settlement, as well as the details of the transfer of the property.

It might be months before a formal agreement was reached, but for all practical purposes the matter was settled. Gideon wanted to be back in town when Parliament reconvened, so he and Fiona decided to spend some time in the country while they could. Richard—as she now called Mr. Camford—would keep them informed of the progress of the negotiations. Fiona laughed with sheer delight as she turned into Berkley Square. For a few weeks she would be free of it all. Robin was to join them at Hartwood later in the month, but she would not have to think or worry about the rest of the Parminters.

Gunter's was not crowded, as it often was at the height of the Season, and she saw Gideon and the children at once, sitting at one of the tables in front of the confectioner's. Peter jumped up and offered to procure Fiona an ice, and Teddy and Beth, deciding they wanted a second ice themselves, ran after him.

Gideon held out a chair for Fiona and looked at her in inquiry. "Better than I expected," Fiona told him. "Clare won't stop the children from seeing each other, though she wishes me at the very devil."

"Be grateful," Gideon said, letting his hands rest on her shoulders. "By autumn she'll be angling for an invitation to spend the Christmas holidays at Sundon."

Fiona leaned back to rest her face against his arm. She still could not see herself as mistress of Sundon. "It isn't a house, it's a palace. What on earth are we going to do with it?"

"Living in it won't be a bad start. The children will keep it from seeming too grand." Gideon slipped into the chair beside her own and pulled a letter from his pocket. "This came for you after you left Dover Street."

Fiona stared at the unfamiliar writing, then broke the seal. "It's from Demetra Thane," she said a few moments later, surprised and pleased. "Demetra Hawksley, I should say. Robin wrote to her about—well, about everything—and she's writing to welcome me to the family. She and Captain Hawksley are staying on his father's farm in Durham until Parliament meets again. They haven't a scrap of money and they're blissfully happy." Fiona smiled as she folded the letter. "It's nice to know that love can sometimes be stronger than greed."

Gideon grinned. "It's a pity you're so infernally rich.

We'll never have a chance to put it to the test."

"Here you are, Fiona." Peter set a glistening white currant ice before his stepmother. Teddy sat beside her and began eating his own ice with gusto. Beth set her ice on the table and climbed onto Fiona's lap. She had been sitting on Gideon's lap when Fiona arrived and seemed determined to give them equal treatment.

"Did Aunt Clare say anything about Sallie and Hugh?" Peter asked, his tone studiedly casual.

"Yes, as a matter of fact, she did. They're both still at Digby Hall. You can go and see them as soon as we've settled at Hartwood."

"They won't want to play with me," Beth said, carefully conveying a spoonful of ice to her mouth. "I'm too little."

"They just like games that are more complicated," Peter told her. "It'll be different when you're older."

Beth scowled. "I'm tired of being the baby."

This last managed to distract Teddy. "Lady Windham's going to have one," he said, looking up from his ice. "A baby, I mean. Verity told me," he explained in answer to looks of inquiry from his parents. "At the wedding breakfast."

"That's nice," Peter said.

Beth said nothing at all, but she looked from Fiona to Gideon with an expression of such wistful hope that Fiona was hard pressed to keep her countenance. "It would be nice not to be the baby anymore," Beth said at last, very softly.

"Well," Gideon told her, with perfect equanimity, "perhaps one of these days you won't be."

Beth smiled happily. Peter, a trifle embarrassed, seemed happy as well. Teddy returned to his ice. Fiona smiled at all of them, then reached out a hand to their father. Her husband. Gideon.

Historical Note

Peter's account of life at Eton is based on two actual incidents. A fight similar to the one described in Chapter 3 took place in 1825. It went for sixty rounds and lasted over two hours. During the fight, the boy in question (Ashley-Cooper, a younger brother of Lord Shaftesbury) consumed as much as half a pint of brandy. He collapsed, went into a coma, and (unlike the fictional Norton) died. (Source: Christopher Hollis, *Eton: A History*. London: Hollis & Carter, 1960.)

In 1828, another small boy was scalped, the result of an accident while he was being tossed in a blanket. He recovered and became, later in life, a noted Sanskrit scholar. (Source: Richard Ollard, *An English Education: A Perspective of Eton*. London: Collins, 1982.)

Details of the debates on the East India Company charter and other matters are taken from contemporary issues of *The Morning Chronicle*. The Royal Assent was given to the charter on 21 July, 1813, a few days after the date of Gideon's speech.

THE ROMANCE OF LORDS AND LADIES
IN JANIS LADEN'S REGENCIES

BEWITCHING MINX   (2532, $3.95)

From her first encounter with the Marquis of Penderleigh when he had mistaken her for a common trollop, Penelope had been incensed with the darkly handsome lord. Miss Penelope Larchmont was undoubtedly the most outspoken young lady Penderleigh had ever known, and the most tempting.

A NOBLE MISTRESS   (2169, $3.95)

Moriah Landon had always been a singularly practical young lady. So when her father lost the family estate over a game of picquet, she paid the winner, the notorious Viscount Roane, a visit. And when he suggested the means of payment—that she become Roane's mistress—she agreed without a blink of her eyes.

SAPPHIRE TEMPTATION   (3054, $3.95)

Lady Serena was commonly held to be an unusual young girl—outspoken when she should have been reticent, lively when she should have been demure. But there was one tradition she had not been allowed to break: a Wexley must marry a Gower. Richard Gower intended to teach his wife her duties—in every way.

SCOTTISH ROSE   (2750, $3.95)

The Duke of Milburne returned to Milburne Hall trusting that the new governess, Miss Rose Beacham, had instilled the fear of God into his harum-scarum brood of siblings. But she romped with the children, refused to be cowed by his stern admonitions, and was so pretty that he had the devil of a time keeping his hands off her.

Available wherever paperbacks are sold, or order direct from the Publisher. Send cover price plus 50¢ per copy for mailing and handling to Zebra Books, Dept. 3603, 475 Park Avenue South, New York, N.Y. 10016. Residents of New York, New Jersey and Pennsylvania must include sales tax. DO NOT SEND CASH.